VENGEFUL *Lies*

USA TODAY BESTSELLING AUTHOR
T.L. SMITH
KIA CARRINGTON-RUSSELL

What if I were to say you could have both of us?
But let's keep how you wish he were me to yourself.

Sincerely,
Your book husband.

WARNING

This book contains sexually explicit scenes and adult language and may be considered offensive to some readers. This book is intended for adults ONLY. Please store your books wisely, where they cannot be accessed by under-aged readers.

Dear Kitten,

Marry me and I'll give you the world.

Refuse, and I'll burn yours to the ground.

Sincerely,
Your soon-to-be husband

It started out as a hit. One bullet. One man.

My orders are clear—get close to the mafia heir, Eli Monti, play with his head, and wait for the signal to end it. End him.

I thought he would be my easiest mark yet. But somehow I'm the one being played.

Eli always gets what he wants-and now, he wants me.

His vengeful proposal isn't a request. It's a demand.

When you play games with a man who's been mastering them all his life, you learn some new tricks.

Top of the list: Find the best way to kill my fake fiancé.

ONE
ELI

Another fucking note. What the actual fuck? A tic runs through my jaw as I press the buzzer, and the voice of one of my security team comes over the speaker.

"How can I assist you, Mr. Monti?"

"Who was in my apartment?" I demand, looking toward the bathroom, where the note is pinned to the door by a fucking knife.

I bounce between my apartment in New York City and my mansion just outside of it, staying in whichever suits my needs at the time. Both places have had security breaches recently.

"No one, sir. As instructed, no one is to enter unless they're with you."

Fucking hell. I hang up.

Who's the crafty little motherfucker barking up the

wrong tree? Someone who seems to want a very slow and painful death. I really didn't want to install security cameras within my own home, but it turns out I might have to do exactly that.

I pull the knife from the door, letting the crumpled piece of paper fall to my hand. I unfurl the scrunched-up ball and read the note written in bright red pen.

Why is your underwear so neat and tidy, asshole?

I CLENCH MY JAW. I swear to God, if this is Hawke playing a prank, I'll gut him for it. Then again, the kiss mark at the bottom of the note might indicate a woman. I know better than to underestimate a woman. However, I also know better than to underestimate my less-than-mentally-stable friends.

I fist the note as I walk into my bedroom to find everything in perfect order, as it should be. My left eye twitches at the one drawer wide open... my underwear drawer. I walk over to it and slice a quick glance down, and my teeth grind in irritation. "What the actual fuck?" I say out loud.

Whoever is fucking with me is good, I'll give them that. They know how to break into my apartment without leaving a trace, find my fucking underwear, and leave a dead fucking rat in it.

Maybe it's not Hawke. Maybe it's his twin, Ford? He's a little more silent, but I wouldn't put it past him. They were, after all, adopted at fifteen by Anya Ivanov, head of the underground auctions. Even her husband, River, is known for his creative messages and executions, and I can say, at the very least, the twins are unpredictable. The only person who can keep them in line is their mother because they're shit scared of her. Hell, I'm even a little scared of her.

But even as a prank, I can't see why they'd be so tempted to piss me off, especially with the pressure I'm under from the head of the family—my father. And I adamantly refuse to let him or my mother catch wind of this. I deal with my own shit.

It's infuriating that this has now happened twice, and I still haven't uncovered the person's identity. But I will.

Walking into the kitchen, I find a plastic bag and then head back to my bedroom, where I use the bag to pick the fucking rat from my underwear drawer. Now that I think about it, the whole drawer needs to go. And I need new fucking underwear.

IT DOESN'T TAKE me long to throw out my entire drawer and make a few quick calls for everything to be replaced. I'm adjusting the cuffs of my suit as I step out of my apartment complex. I deal with all manners of filth and torture, but something about a dead rat is just undignified.

"Took your sweet-ass time!" Hawke complains, leaning against my car. His twin, Ford, is flicking through his phone as he waits next to him. Though the two are identical, Hawke has a bulkier build from his extreme love of lifting weights, whereas Ford has a slimmer build, which is better suited for stealth. Both have tattoos, and people actively give a wide berth as they step around them—the two ooze mischief, hell, and death. The jet-black hair and dark brown, almost black eyes do nothing to counter otherwise.

"You said you just had to change your shirt, so what took you so long?" Ford asks, looking up from the phone and pinning me with those dark-brown eyes. I may or may not have just tortured someone, leading me to need to change shirts. I certainly wasn't expecting to find a dead fucking rat before my next meeting.

I ignore them both. They answer to me, not the

other way around. Where my father has only one loyal second, I have two.

"Neither one of you happens to be into wearing lipstick these days, do you?" I ask dryly.

The two share a confused glance. "Only around my cock," Hawke replies as he kicks off my car and comes toward me. As he does, a woman wearing black heels barges between us.

"Whoa there!" Hawke snaps, taking a step back. The woman swings around furiously. She's striking, although black shades cover her eyes, preventing me from getting a look at them. Auburn hair falls past her shoulders, and her bright orange dress is appropriate for the weather but not her ill temperament.

"Asshole," she bites out, and I'm almost shocked by her boldness, considering most people instinctually know not to look our way, let alone speak to us.

"She must be talking to you," Hawke says in shock.

I'm exasperated by his constant antics. "Why must she be talking to me?" I ask, irritated, but for some reason, I'm unable to look away from the woman staring at me with such scorn.

She puts her hands on her hips expectantly. What is she waiting for? An apology?

I can't see her eyes through the dark lenses of her glasses, but I sense she's rolling her eyes as she says with a pout, "You don't even remember me, do you?" I think I would remember if I fucked her.

"Then it's sure as shit not me because I'm trying to be celibate and not fuck anyone," Hawke says as if that's answer enough as to why she's talking about me. I thought she was pissed about barging between us. Wasn't she?

"You literally fucked Tanya last week," Ford reminds him.

"She doesn't count if she's already on the rotation," Hawke says with a casual shrug. "Look, toots, you owe my man here an apology. Don't take it personally that he doesn't remember you."

I realize then we have onlookers, most likely because of what appears to be three men berating one woman. A woman, might I add, who started this shit in the first place.

This time, with a brilliant smile and ignoring Hawke, she points at me and makes it very clear who she's addressing, "Asshole."

Me? I'm the asshole? Not far from the truth, but I still don't remember her.

"See, didn't fuck her," Hawke says proudly like he didn't have any doubts.

"You're either new here or have a screw loose if you think you can speak to me that way," I say with so much ice in my tone even my men beside me straighten. I don't give a fuck who she is; I don't make exceptions for men, women, or their dogs on how they will speak or act around me.

But the woman doesn't flinch; she simply flicks her hair over her shoulder as she starts to walk in the opposite direction. She looks back over her shoulder and adds, "I'm sure I'll be seeing you real soon, sweetheart."

I clench my fists and count to three, as my mother taught me, to reclaim my composure. To be honest, her number was a lot higher, but three seconds seems like enough time to pretend I have the discipline to not immediately break someone's neck.

Before I step forward, she opens the door to a car, a little yellow beetle-looking thing. She doesn't even look back; the most dangerous act she's performed all day, especially with men like us.

Who the fuck is this woman?

She makes a point to wind down the window and flip us off as she drives away.

My jaw tics. As I count to three again, I make a point to memorize her license plate. Outright pulling a woman by her hair in broad daylight in the middle of New York City isn't one of my brightest ideas, which is why I bury the impulse.

Hawke whistles as he casually puts his hands in

the pockets of his torn-up jeans. "She's fiery, that one. I thought you were seeing Michelle?"

"I am *fucking* Michelle," I correct him. She's a means to an end, despite the pressure and stipulation that we should marry to keep our family relationship.

Just then, my phone vibrates, and I pull it out to see a text message from an unknown number.

> Unknown number: Check your pockets, asshole. Thanks for the show.

It's followed by a kiss emoji, and I'm almost certain that my little *I'll leave a dead rat in your drawer* visitor is the same woman in the short orange dress who just flipped me off. It's rather extraordinary she was able to get my number in the first place. That's one thing I do not hand out to women, not even Michelle, who I've known for years and fuck on the regular. The only people who have my number are my family.

I feel the edges of something in my pocket, furious that I hadn't even sensed her featherlight touch as she stepped between Hawke and me.

A cool calm washes over me, hiding the rolling rage within as I pull out a small photo.

"Oh fuck, you keep souvenirs now?" Hawke asks,

looking over my shoulder. I cut a glare in his direction, and he immediately puts his hands up and takes a step back, although the asshole grins me.

It's a picture of me and Michelle, from two weeks ago, outside of her apartment on the balcony as I fucked her against the railing. My hand is over her mouth, smothering her screams. I'm fully clothed as she's bent over, taking my full length, tears streaming down her face.

It was a sufficient night, enough to take the edge off at least. I left shortly after, even with her insistence that I stay.

Scrunching up the image, I dial the number that texted me. It rings and rings with no answer.

So I respond with the calmness of a man who's ready to burn a city down just to find the woman who's stupidly chosen to fuck with me.

I go to slide the picture back into my pocket when I feel another; it's smaller than the first. A wave of cruel delight flushes through me, and I can't help but smile.

"It's always creepy as shit when you smile, man," Hawke says.

The photo is of my underwear drawer...with the fucking rat in it.

A follow-up text message from the same number appears with a single kiss emoji.

I throw Hawke the keys to the car. "You drive. I have some work to do." I don't even look up from my phone as I slip into the back seat, ready to find everything I can from that license plate. I will ruin this woman. She's the perfect distraction, something I can destroy while I manage my fortune and responsibilities as the next head of the mafia in New York.

Someone must have put her up to this, and I'm about to discover who is daring enough to undermine my authority.

It doesn't come as a surprise that the plate comes back as a fake.

The corner of my mouth tilts up, and I reply with a text of my own.

> Me: We can play this cat-and-mouse game, sweetheart. But it will be a deadly game and your body will never be discovered.

I sign off with a kiss emoji.

TWO
JEWEL

But it will be a deadly game, blah, blah, blah.

Men like him make me sick, make me want to vomit all over his pompous, freshly-polished shoes.

I hate men like him the most.

Born into wealth.

Fed on power.

I bet they wouldn't know a day of hard living even if it hit them in the face. And I take slight satisfaction in being the sledgehammer hitting him in the face right now.

"You know you just have to ask, right?" my roommate, Jenny, says as she takes the heels out of my hand.

"I planned to, but you weren't here," I reply with a nonchalant shrug.

"I have a phone, you know." Fair point. "Next time, please just ask."

"I'll do my best," I lie, and I can feel her gaze on my back as I head toward my room.

This apartment and my relationship with her are conveniences. Nothing more, nothing less. Jenny and I have lived together for a year now. And I made it my mission to be exactly what she was gossiping about over the phone with her friend when I first moved in—scary and imposing. She'd only met me that day, but her assessment wasn't far from the truth.

She works some admin job I couldn't care less about. And she thinks I only work at a restaurant; she doesn't know about my "contract" work. I'm very good at what I do, actually. I have very specific and unorthodox ways of making an income... and making people disappear.

In truth, I'm not much of a team player. And I don't need to be.

I throw my phone on the bed and then peel the orange dress off as I mimic the tone of Mr. Asshole. I thought I'd throw in the "You don't remember me, do you?" just to fuck with him.

There's a startling truth to the beautifully unhinged man.

I will certainly be his demise.

Especially when I put a bullet between those ethereal eyes, just like my father taught me. Well, if he were alive now to realize the types of hit jobs I take, he might not be so comfortable with the powerful men I target. But, hey, a girl has to find her own way in life.

I slip into the shower, the scorching heat a comfort as I think about my father. Killing people was the only thing he really left me with the knowledge to do.

He was the one to teach me how to shoot, and when he died when I was fifteen, I never stopped. I took more than a liking to sniper rifles in particular, although I'm well-rounded in close combat, including knives and hand-to-hand. But my biggest thrill is through the scope of a sniper rifle because it challenges my accuracy, even though I never miss the mark.

My mother, who walked out on us when I was six and barely made reappearances in my life, hated my love for weapons. But at least when my father died, she gave me all of his guns. And to be honest, if she hadn't, I would've stolen them anyway. I haven't seen her since his funeral. She has what she once openly told me was her "normal family." Some fluffy white-picket-fence bullshit that I don't entirely understand or care for. I'm good as long as I have my guns.

I lather the shampoo through my hair as I get ready for my day job waitressing because every multi-millionaire with blood money needs a cover story, right? Okay, so this definitely wasn't the direction my father intended for me.

He was one of the best snipers for the Air Force—so a good guy. It was when he told me I was better than him that I knew I wanted to do some type of work around guns—just not the same as what he did. Discipline, rules, and restrictions in the armed forces would be too much for me, considering how much havoc I wreaked for my father, even under his strict guidance.

What can I say? I like to rebel.

The only person who keeps me in check, and I use the phrase "in check" loosely because no one has control over what I do, is my father's friend, Craig. He's a retired contract killer who got me into this game in the first place after someone was looking for the perfect shot. He offered me an opportunity to make the type of money I wasn't familiar with. Turns out I like money—a lot.

I killed my first target at the age of eighteen from two miles away. After that, offers came in from everywhere, and Craig guided me down the bloody path of being one of the best.

When I step out of the shower, I dry my body, my gaze landing on the bright neon bear tattoo with sharp claws and fangs gracing my hip. I roll my eyes every time I look at it, remembering how stupid I'd been when I had some guy ink it on me when I was sixteen.

I stare at myself in the mirror, hating the same light-brown, amber-colored eyes that look just like my mother's. My hair's a tangled mess, and I sigh, exhausted from the recent turn of events surrounding my current target.

I don't often toy with my targets.

Not until I landed in New York City because of another job.

The first hit was easy money. After that, I stayed because I liked New York.

I liked the clothes, the city, and the acceptance to be whoever I wanted to be or pretend to be.

My most recent target: Eli Monti.

Son to the reputedly cruel Crue Monti, who runs the Italian mafia within the city, and Rya Monti, an infamous criminal lawyer. The soon-to-be twenty-six-year-old is intent on taking over the family business. The caveat is, in Monti family tradition, he has to marry before taking ownership of the business. His father was thirty-four when he married and took over, so Eli is certainly an ambitious little prick. Too bad he isn't going to make it to his wedding day.

I'm probably saving him from misery. Marriage only leads to shackles, confinement, and, statistically, divorce. I smirk as I blow dry my hair, thinking of the excessive amount I was once paid to end a powerful businessman so his wife didn't have to go through the motions of a divorce. Instead, she became a widow with a very nice inheritance. That's the only type of divorce I approve of, and at least she kept to her vows of "until death do us part."

Men undermine women far too much, which it gives me great satisfaction being the Grim Reaper.

Had I half a heart, I might feel bad for Eli with the expectation of having to be married before he can take over the business. That's old school, but I guess some traditions don't die. Fuck that. I'm the opposite; happy being single, fucking whoever I want when I want. Commitment is overrated.

I dive onto my bed, the towel loosely wrapped around me as I grab my phone and kick my legs back and forth as I begin whistling a tune. I open up the surveillance app where I can check the cameras and bugs I planted in Eli's penthouse and private home.

I smirk when he comes into view in his mansion. He often switches between the two properties for reasons I don't yet understand. I had my friend Rory help me set up the surveillance equipment. I'm good at sneaking around and killing, but I'm not tech-savvy, and it definitely helps to have eyes and ears on this asshole when I'm playing the long game with him.

Merrily whistling my tune, I take a moment to appreciate the way he looks.

Eli has style, that much is clear, but it's more of a clean-cut, all-black style. And it's obvious his suits are worth a pretty penny. His jaw is covered in short stubble, and he always wears expensive watches. But it's his eyes that look so light they're almost silver, and they are most striking against his rich, tanned Italian skin.

I've noted several other things about the mafia prince since I started keeping tabs on him.

One: He never brings a woman back to his place. No matter who the flavor of the month is, he only ever goes to their place, and he never stays the night.

Two: He is particular in the sense that if I were to move a picture frame a quarter of an inch from where he placed it, he'd probably quite literally kill me for it. Everything has an orderly place and purpose.

Three: He's as lethal about his dealings in business as the rumors say. I've watched him murder so many people for far less than adjusting his figuratively perfectly placed picture frame.

He removes his black suit jacket, the bulges and indents of his muscles flexing under his crisp, clean white shirt. He's also covered in tattoos. Tattoos you don't ordinarily see with the long-sleeved shirts covering them unless he rolls up the sleeves or unbuttons his shirt. He has none on his neck or hands, unlike his weird-ass friend Hawke.

If I didn't have to kill him, I would find him very attractive. But I know better than to take an interest in my targets.

Play with him. And when I give the order... end him. That was the request by my anonymous client.

So that's what I've been doing. It's not how I usually do things, but I couldn't say no to the money offered. I get paid a lot to kill people, but to play with Eli Monti, I get triple my standard price.

The money for this job is fair, considering the risk I take by not having the element of surprise. But it's what makes it thrilling as well.

My screen lights up with a new text message—another directive from my client.

Anonymous Number: Be at this event at 8 pm sharp. Masquerade.

It's not uncommon for hits to be made anonymously, and I don't have enough ethics or morals to care about who I'm killing, why, or who hired me when the money is deposited in my account.

I huff, irritated at the short notice and the fact that

I'll have to cancel my shift tonight at the restaurant. Not that I really give a fuck about that job.

More importantly, what am I going to wear? I ponder that as I pull out my pretty gold credit card. I mean, I suppose a beautiful dress is considered a work expense, right?

I smile and throw off the towel.

So, playing with Eli Monti is what I will do.

Until the time comes for me to kill him

THREE

ELI

My father stares down at his messenger with disdain. Blood pools around the man's head, and I continue to focus on my laptop screen as if nothing has gone amiss. The tension is palpable, primarily because of the thick file the messenger left at the edge of the desk.

"You know your mother doesn't like it when you get blood on the floors," my father scolds angrily. My scathing glare reaches his dark eyes, and we remain like that, the clock ticking ever so loudly through my parents' office.

Crue Monti is almost sixty-two years old, but he looks good. A few strands of silver shoot through his black hair, and his dark and depthless eyes, are just as mesmerizing now as they were when he was younger. People are either too stunned to look away from him, frightened by what he might do next, or avert their gaze immediately, submissively—their survival instincts kicking in.

I don't fear my father. I love him. Our bond is just a little different from most.

"Hawke. Ford. Come and clean up this mess," my father barks at my men standing outside the room.

"Yes, sir," Hawke says merrily as he all but skips in, an obvious screw loose. Ford silently follows.

"They don't answer to you," I grit out.

My father arches an eyebrow, and a smirk creeps onto his face. "You're in my house, son. Everyone in this house listens to me. And until you take over the business, I own every one of the lackeys you choose to hire."

"To be more accurate, sir, we're more like best friends," Hawke says.

"I apologize. My brother never knows when to hold his tongue," Ford adds.

I sigh and look away, my irritation growing. *These fucking idiots.* My father tolerates them, not like my mother, who has basically adopted them, but he's accepted that they're like annoying flies that won't go away.

Father takes a seat across from me. "Would you like to explain why you killed one of my men and haven't yet opened the file I specifically asked him to hand you?"

"I'm not going to marry any of these women." I glare at the file as if it'll scorch my skin even to pick it up.

I fucking refuse.

"There's nothing wrong with an arranged marriage. That's how your mother and I met," he says calmly, with a tone I know is anything but. It's only because my mother is somewhere in the house that he's on his best behavior. Lord forbid he gets in trouble because of me. Again.

He might be the most powerful man in New York, but my mother is the true figure to be feared. I love my mother, but I could never imagine a woman having that kind of hold over me. Ever.

Hawke and Ford efficiently drag the body out.

"No offense, Pops, but you're old as fuck now. Arranged marriages aren't a thing anymore."

"If you want to take over the business fully, it will be something you'll acquaint yourself with very quickly." I hold his stare. "Or you find a wife on your own. I don't give a fuck what you do with her besides fill her belly with a child. Do as you please, but you will *not* be the exception to family tradition."

My mother's voice cuts through the room. "He says

that, but what he means is you need to find someone who can match you and be your rock. There will be no other women outside of your marriage," she says with a warning tone as she walks through the door. I stand, and she gives me a welcoming hug. My father's jaw clenches; he's always jealous of anyone else who gets attention from her.

"You want me to retire, but you want our cold-hearted son to find love at the same time? You'll be waiting a while, princess," he says as he stands and adjusts his suit. He's always called her that, dotingly staring and longing for her in every capacity. My mother's gaze softens as she smiles and takes his hand.

She's dressed in a tight maroon dress, her caramel-colored hair falling in waves down her back. "You *will* retire by the end of this year. We agreed on this when you turned sixty, and it's far past that."

"And Eli will marry before the end of the year," he states.

My mother sighs and looks at me again. "I'm sorry, honey, but I agree with him. It's tradition."

Being born with mob ties on both sides of my family, I'm shackled by tradition and expectation. Sure, I can kill whoever I want with good cause, but make sure I pick a nice little delicate wife to have all their grandbabies. I snarl at the thought.

"You can go through the file later. We have a party to attend," my mother says, trying to dissipate the tension. "And would someone like to explain to me why the Ivanov twins are dragging a body around my polished wooden floors?"

A noticeable cold shudder runs over both my father and me, and I roll my shoulders uncomfortably. I wonder if he's about to snitch on me, so I clear my throat. "Would you believe me if I told you he slipped because of how well-polished the floors are?"

My mother shoots me a deadpan look, and I know I'm about to get an earful. I reluctantly sit down for my millionth lecture about the fucking floors.

their direction. I watch the scene unfold as Dutton grips the man by his hand and forces him onto his knees to apologize for even looking twice at his sister.

"Dutton! Stop acting crazy!" Billie screams as people circle around them.

"Apologize," Dutton grits out again.

This is when the sea of people splits and Eli strides in like a devil-masked God. Coming in at six foot four, there's no doubt in my mind he would've seen the unfolding of events and he just wanted to get closer.

Hawke throws an arm over Billie's shoulder. "Come on, Dutton. It's not that bad. Don't make the poor guy piss himself at his own sister's birthday party."

I try not to smirk as I take my first sip of champagne. The more I immerse myself in the madness of this family as a quiet bystander, the more amused I am. That's when every hair on my arms rises, and I'm acutely aware I'm being watched. The feeling is so heavy that I'm slow to lift my gaze from the groveling and apologizing man to a set of otherworldly eyes. Where he might take after his father with his strong jaw and perfect nose, he has his mother's almost silver eyes. And they're locked on me.

Eli doesn't break his eye contact even when Michelle tugs on his arm, begging him to stop Dutton from his craziness. I don't have siblings, but I imagine I would do the same if I did. As in break the man's hand, I mean.

But Eli seems to barely notice her as his all-consuming gaze slowly roams down my figure and then back up. I can feel it like a caress on my skin, as if with his stare alone he's physically touched me—a killer's gaze and mark.

I'm not here to tempt him. Although, in other circumstances, I'd have no issue cornering him. I'm here to blend into the crowd and figure out how I can fuck with him a little more. The laxatives are a last resort. I can't poison him yet. Besides, I'd prefer a bullet. So humiliating him is my next plan of attack.

When someone walks in front of me and breaks the eye contact, I take that moment to slip into the hallway beside me. Music is playing in the background as I notice a group of men on the left, snorting god knows what, in what appears to be a casual living space.

Caterers are busily attending to everyone's needs, and I make a point to mentally map out the Bedore mansion. I never know if this might be the place where I have to take the final shot. Knowledge is power, after all.

A woman bursts out of the door to my left and

barges past me. When I go to swear at her, I realize her dress is torn at the shoulders, and she's sobbing, running away scared. Looking into the half-ajar door, I see a man holding his nose and cursing. Another man who thinks he can take from a woman.

Not my problem.

I'm playing low-key tonight, I remind myself.

I plan to keep walking down the hall, but my feet lead me into the small bedroom, unable to help myself.

"Fucking stupid whore," he curses, then looks up. "Who the fuck are you?" he demands. But his tone changes ever so slightly as his filthy gaze roams over me. Sometimes, being a woman has its own power.

"I just saw a commotion and wanted to make sure you were okay," I say sweetly as I step toward him. A king-size bed is in the center of the room, closely positioned near bay windows that I consider throwing him through. It's only two stories, so he might not die. But even I'm aware that I'm at a disadvantage against such a heavy man.

"The fucking bitch broke my nose," he growls.

"Here, let me have a look at it." I tip my head and bat my thick eyelashes at him. He seems reluctant as if it's a weakness to show me his injury. "Maybe I can make it better?" I say sensually.

He smirks and removes his hand. There's barely

any blood; she must've just got a lucky elbow in, but had she not, who knows what might've happened.

"Oh, it doesn't look broken," I softly announce. As he goes to grab for me, I shift out of his reach and hit him with a right hook. Blood explodes as he squeals like a pig and stumbles back. "Now it is broken, you stupid piece of shit."

Fury bubbles to the surface at the thought of how many women he might've assaulted. I might not be able to kill whoever this fucker is, but a little broken nose never hurt anyone.

"You stupid bitch," he snarls, but it comes out muffled due to his fingers pinching his nose to stop the bleeding.

"Don't ever touch her or another woman again, asshole," I warn, peering down at him through my mask.

He grabs for his gun in his holster, which is probably the hardest thing he's ever been able to pull out of his pants. My body is ready to burst into action, except a trickle of danger keeps me in place.

It's not the man pointing a gun at my face that has my feet planted on the floor.

No. It's the monster who's walked in behind me, drawing the shadows of the room to him.

I don't even need to look at who it is because I can

feel the six-foot-four mass of muscle standing behind me.

"What do we have here?" Eli's voice slices through the room.

"This stupid bitch broke my nose," the man screams.

"And is that enough reason to point a gun at a lady?" Eli asks, and I internally roll my eyes as he puts on an act of being chivalrous.

The man seems gobsmacked. "But she's just a woman."

Eli steps around me, and I have to crane my neck to see what he's doing as he looms over the man whose hand is noticeably shaking, the gun no longer steady. The room is dark, only the light from the hallway shining in, and I imagine this fucker, who I now kind of feel sorry for, thinks he's being stared down by the devil himself. It kind of pisses me off because if Eli hadn't interfered, he would undoubtedly be looking at me with that reverence and fear instead.

"Please, Eli," the man begs.

"What did you call me?" Eli's voice cuts through the air.

The man gulps. "Mr. Monti. I don't know this woman, but she assaulted me."

Eli curls his hand around the collar of the man's

shirt, fisting enough material to slowly lift him to standing. "And does it make it better if a man assaults you instead? I know plenty who might take you up on that offer, but I'm not sure you'll like the items they use."

A cold shudder runs down my back. I've seen this man kill, but when he whispers threats, I must confess it's terrifying. His voice is so smooth and deep, it's like a lullaby. But one that only promises death.

And the man is too terrified to even lift the gun that's now gripped loosely in his hand, his arm hanging slack by his side. With a quick movement, Eli is behind him, his thick arm cording around his neck as his other hand grabs the gun. The man grapples, but to no avail, and the whole time, Eli stares at me, those ethereal eyes looking back at me like the devil himself in the dark as the hallway light seeps through to silhouette his frame.

My heartbeat kicks up as I suddenly realize my miscalculation.

I got cocky.

Taunting a monster like this is dangerous.

If it were an immediate hit, he would've already been dead.

But this... the closer I get, as per instructed by the client, the more lethal the job becomes to me.

This guy's a fucking nutjob. The man crumples to

the floor, and Eli lets him slip from his hold as if he's less than trash.

He looks down at the gun he's now holding, seeming underwhelmed, and then his gaze lands back on me.

Every instinct tells me to run.

Every reflex tells me to make sure I'm the only monster left standing.

Silence fills the room, and I remember my part to play as I look down at the man on the floor between us. I can faintly see he is still breathing, but instead, I innocently ask, "Is he dead?"

"No. But he'll remember this in the morning. You know how it is, an uncle of someone's who I don't want to piss off by accidentally killing him," he says matter-of-factly. But I know he doesn't care about things like that. If Eli wants to kill without reason, he does. Which means he's testing me.

I purposefully avert my gaze, trying to look as innocent as possible. "I-I don't m-much like violence. I should pr-probably leave," I stutter intentionally.

"Shouldn't you be leaving me a note with a kiss first?" Eli arches an eyebrow that has a scar, splitting it in half. As he speaks, he releases the magazine from the gun and tosses it aside. I realize he knows who I am, but he's toying with me and pretending to be unarmed.

"You're not even going to try and deny it? I must confess, the stutter was a nice touch."

Fuck, he knows exactly who I am. I could deny it all I like, but it's not going to get me anywhere with a man like this.

So, instead, I let the innocent act slip, not particularly being fond of it.

"It's just business. Nothing personal," I say as I carefully weigh my options. Then again, I've always acted on impulse. My only saving grace, I remind myself, is that I still have a mask on. "How did you know it was me?"

"Simply by the fact that you were ballsy enough to walk in here. Your height, the color of your hair..." He takes a step forward. "The way you hold yourself." He takes another step, and I take one back, considering grabbing the knife at my thigh. "But where you really fucked up was thinking you could hide your presence when you shine like a fucking beacon even in the darkness."

My heart stops at that.

The realization that I'm cornered.

I don't do well being cornered.

"Shouldn't you be whispering such sweet nothings to Michelle?"

"Michelle's not trying to kill me," he replies,

angling his arm above my head and pushing me against the wall—a luxury I allow him. My greatest skill is catching people by surprise, but I know well and truly he could suffocate me with one hand.

"She will no doubt kill you one day with all her flowery sweetness, I'm sure," I taunt with a smile.

His gaze bores into me as he hunches over, his elbow casually above my head. "Whose order are you here under, and what do they want?" he demands.

I casually shrug, not breaking eye contact. "I don't know. I just sign the dotted line for a paycheck. Please don't think you're that important that I care as to *why* someone wants you dead."

The corner of his mouth twitches. "A lot of people want me dead."

"Most likely because of your intolerable personality. But who am I to judge?"

"You'll be coming home with me tonight." The moment his hand goes for my throat, I grab the knife from my garter and slice at his torso. His reflexes are fast enough that I cut through his shirt and just barely scratch his skin. I can make out the glisten of blood through the cut in the fabric. He looks down curiously and then back up at me with a smirk.

"Unfortunately for you, knives are my favorite playthings."

I lunge for the door, but with lightning speed, he pulls out his own knife and throws it. The knife embeds itself in the wall beside the door I was about to escape through, and I come to a screeching halt.

Adrenaline pumps through me as I throw my knife into his left leg. He clutches his thigh above the wound, cursing viciously, and barely keeps himself upright. I curve a wicked smile, satisfied with my aim.

I'm startled when one of his men, Hawke, busts into the room with a blonde, his lips on hers as he hurriedly begins to undo his belt. He tears his attention away from the woman, belatedly realizing he's stumbled into something. Their entrance awkwardly breaks the lethal tension as I slip through the door behind him.

"Not quite." I hear the smooth voice of Dutton behind me. Before I can swing to face him, a cloth is placed over my mouth, and I know after the first inhale I'm royally fucked.

FIVE
ELI

I'm furiously tapping my finger against my leg, insufferably pissed off by a certain little smart-ass vixen who is currently tied up in an old warehouse in which I like to do some of my more unsavory business.

"I mean, it's kind of funny," Hawke says, breaking the silence. Ford and Dutton stare at him in disbelief, but the moment he meets my gaze, he simply chuckles and shrugs. "She got one up on you. Credit is due when it's due, no?"

When my silence continues, he sighs. "I'll remove myself from the room." And he does precisely that.

"I'll go and beat some sense into my brother," Ford says, excusing himself as well.

I choose to focus on the small hole in my thigh from her cute little knife wound that has since been stitched and bandaged. I'm currently waiting for little miss to wake up from the chloroform Dutton surprised her with earlier.

She mumbles under her breath, and Dutton peers down at her, a loose lock of hair shifting over his forehead. I don't like how close he is to her, so I clear my throat. This grabs his attention, and he looks over his shoulder at me.

"Why didn't you just kill her?" he asks.

"Because I would like to know who put her up to this little stunt."

"She's pretty," Dutton adds.

"She's wearing a mask," I deadpan. We could've easily removed it. In fact, Hawke had to display a discipline he's never known when I told him no one was to remove it. This is my prize to unwrap as I see fit.

"A mask doesn't hide her figure or—" Before I can cut him off myself, her massive gasp to consciousness draws both of our attention.

Her amber gaze scans the room as she fights her restraints. Her eyes remind me of a tiger's—wild and untamed.

"Motherfucker," she curses with a groggy voice. "Big mafia boy couldn't fight his own battle. Had to get his friends to help pin me down?" she snaps with as much tenacity as a wild animal caged with no way of escape.

I remind her of the words she used against me only hours ago. "It's nothing personal, just business, Kitten. Don't be upset because I took a much more effective approach."

She rolls her eyes as if I'm being a petty fuck, but she doesn't even know the meaning of the word yet. I want to smack the brat out of her. "It's come to my attention that you don't realize how serious this is."

She blows a piece of her hair from her eyes as she focuses on Dutton, and I don't like her looking at anyone or anything other than me, especially when I'm commanding her attention. When I'm in a space, people only look at me. Only give *me* respect. This little vixen should already be six feet under.

"I wouldn't call this serious. But I must confess, I'm used to doing the tying up, not the other way around."

Dutton's eyebrow arches and a sly smirk crosses his features. My glare warns him to be silent and that he better fucking wipe that smirk off his face. He immediately complies.

"I'm assuming pretty boy did the tying up. I can't imagine you being so delicate and patient," she says dryly.

I take three long strides until I'm looming over her.

I pinch her cheeks and pull, wanting to stop that sharp little tongue of hers. "I can be delicate," I lie.

She scoffs. Fucking scoffs. But when she focuses on me again, there's an undeniable fire in her amber gaze, something I want to break into a million pieces. Had she chosen to fuck with any other man, it might have worked in her favor. But she is shit out of luck here tonight. I release her cheeks. "Who sent you?"

She shrugs, even in the tight restraints, as if she's in the most comfortable seat in the room. "I told you, I don't know the name of the client. I just get a communication with the name of the target."

"And you're what, a trained assassin or something?" Dutton asks. My scathing glare has him realizing his mistake.

A slow smile crosses her fuckable, plump lips. It was only by chance that I noticed her tonight, and I still don't have any information on this woman. I still don't even know her fucking name. Dutton asking that question outright gives her that revelation.

"I couldn't possibly be," she says sarcastically. "I'm just a woman. I couldn't possibly be deadly."

I smirk at that, thinking of an ample number of women who people should be terrified of. "The wound to my leg might say otherwise."

"I was being polite. I could've aimed for your chest."

"So why didn't you?" I ask, twisting my features into an uncharacteristic smirk. "Don't tell me you've fallen for me already, sweetheart."

She seems to shrivel at my smile. "Hey, pretty boy, you're going to have to train him better at smiling because that shit is creepy as fuck."

In my peripheral, I can see Dutton is trying his hardest not to grin.

"Leave us," I say to him. He seems hesitant as he looks between me and Kitten, the tension palpable, but he makes the better judgment to excuse himself. Because I don't take disobedience well. The length of time it takes him to leave the warehouse sobers her up enough to realize the precarious position she's in.

I drag a chair closer to her and hang my hands casually over the back of it. I'm curious what she looks like. I can tell she has high cheekbones, come fuck me lips, and a sharp nose. I pull the knife from my pocket, and she swallows hard. Her jaw is clenched, and I can tell she's trying her hardest to save face. I'm impressed.

"Are you sure you want to die for this cause? I can be very accommodating if you tell me the truth. Tell me who sent you," I say as I casually lift the blade toward her face.

She's grinding her teeth but doesn't break eye contact. I can sense and smell the fear on her all the same, even if it doesn't break through to the surface.

"I told you I don't know," she responds tightly.

"Vengeful lies will have you winding up dead, Kitten," I explain. Curiosity gets the better of me as I slice the ribbon of her mask, and it falls to one side. My eyes widen slightly at my first glimpse of her.

Too beautiful.

Too tempting.

As most deadly things are.

And those iridescent amber eyes, despite the hint of fear flaring in them, refuse to look anywhere else.

A tigress indeed.

When she doesn't speak, I do. "What's your name?"

Her eyebrows crinkle in confusion. It's barely noticeable as she tries to mask her reactions, but very few things go unnoticed by me.

"I don't have any family to go after if that's what you're angling at."

My lip twitches. Beautiful and smart. But deadly being the most vital factor to remind myself of.

"I'll make you a deal. You tell me your first name—your *real* first name—and I'll let you go. Lie to me, and I'll kill you."

Her eyebrows bunch again. "And why would you let me go?"

"Perhaps I'm feeling merciful tonight."

She bursts into laughter, and it's the wildest, most unhinged, beautiful thing I've ever heard. "You're fucking with me, right? You're just going to let me walk out of here?"

"I'm a man of my word."

She looks me up and down. "Even though I put a knife in your leg and I'm still most likely going to try and kill you?"

She's either too honest or cocky to mention the fact that she'll still go after my life. Maybe I'm a sadist, but I feel hardly satisfied by this short-lived cat and mouse game. And I can't help but feel there's something more going on here. I need to figure out who the puppeteer is pulling her strings.

"I'll have you know, my mother shot my father in the leg on their wedding day, and they're still happily married. So a knife wound is nothing but foreplay to me, Kitten."

"Why don't you hand me the knife and let me tie you up, and then we'll see how much foreplay you can handle." The imagery her words conjure shoots straight to my cock.

Fuck me.

Where has this woman been all my life?

"Tell me your name," I demand.

Most sane people would do anything to survive, but this woman seems to be built as stubborn as they come.

Finally, however, she exhales, defeated. "Jewel. My name is Jewel."

I stand, pushing through the pain in my leg that is most certainly stirring a reaction in my cock. I have every belief it has nothing to do with the wound itself but with the woman tied up in front of me. With a clean slice, I cut away the ropes. I almost expect her to come out swinging, instead, she remains still, warily watching me.

"If I were you, Jewel, I'd make sure not to leave town. No matter where you run to, I will find you. You stay in town until I flush out your client." I turn my back to her and head for the door, satisfied with the way she looks dumbfounded and furious at the same time. I make a point to flip her knife in my hand as I walk out, deciding to add it to my collection.

"I'll have one of my men drive you home. Full disclosure: if you try anything on them, they will brutally murder you," I say as I look over my shoulder with a cruel smirk.

SIX
JEWEL

The smart thing would be to pack all of my shit and leave the country. But the undeniable truth is, I've never stepped away from a challenge, especially from a man. Especially one who I'm being paid a large amount of money to fuck with. Tonight was a failure. I contemplate the events as I stare up at the ceiling of the hotel room.

Of course, I wasn't going to let his thugs drive me straight to my apartment, so I booked a hotel in a different neighborhood. It should only be for a few days until I think of something. But does it really matter if he figures out where I live? I do believe Eli about one thing he said. If he wants to find me, he will.

I should've killed him. The moment I had the opening, I should've embedded that blade in his chest;

then, there would have been no way he could've followed me. Sure, his men would most likely haunt me for the rest of my days, but at least I'd have finished the job.

I stare at my phone screen, furious at my situation. My client hasn't sent me another message. The longer they have me stretch this out, the more my life is in danger. And besides, isn't it pointless now that he knows my identity? Well, he sort of knows; he only has a first name.

I sigh, ridiculously pissed, and hit one of the two numbers I have saved in my phone. Craig answers on the second ring. "It's late. Everything okay?"

"Hypothetically, what would you do if your identity was compromised on a hit?" I ask.

"I'd get the fuck out of there. I've never had it happen, though," he says cautiously.

Fuck. That means I've majorly fucked up.

Craig has been like a father figure to me since my dad died, and he's been a source of information to help me navigate strange situations in the business. But even I know this is a doozy. "Has your identity been compromised, Jewel?"

I consider his question.

I mean, technically, no.

Just a first name, right?

"No. I just had a close call, that's all."

"I don't like the sound of that," he growls.

"Yeah, well, it's high on my shit list too. Don't worry, I've got it sorted."

"Who's the target, Jewel? If there's even a slight chance you've been compromised, it could be a matter of life and death."

"Yeah, I know. Hey, I've got another call coming through, so I've got to go," I lie.

"Jewe—"

I hang up and call the only other number I have saved. Rory answers on the eighth ring, and before they can even complain about the time, despite the fact that they're a night owl, I blurt, "I need you to get as much information as you can on the Monti, Ivanov, and Taylor families. Dig further than the files you've already given me. Add in anyone else of interest I need to know about. You know I'll pay your price."

If we are going to play this cat-and-mouse game, I'll make sure to be fucking prepared.

Eli Monti made a mistake letting me go.

SEVEN
ELI

"Hey, that's her, isn't it?" Hawke says, nudging my arm. But I'd already caught sight of her from across the room the moment she stepped out from the kitchen. She's now leaning against the bar, wearing a short black dress and high heels, her long legs crossed at the ankles. I can't help but stare at those legs... so fucking tempting. She was equally tempting two nights ago in her black ballgown with the slit up the side.

Hawke and I stand at the entrance of the below-average restaurant while Ford parks the car. I haven't waited to be seated in a restaurant since... ever.

She looks exactly how I remember her. I purposely memorized every inch of her face and sketched it countless times. I sent one of the sketches and her first name to a family friend, Will Walker, who is a renowned tracker in our inner circle. He's eccentric, though, applauding my artistry and that perhaps I should've chosen a better path than following my father's footsteps. I don't know why he's suggesting it, considering he gets his hands just as bloody.

It took him two days to find her, and I've now discovered everything I need to know about this little vixen who stumbled into my life by her own stupidity.

"So what are we planning to do here again?" Hawke asks, leaning in. No one asked my intentions when I let her go, and Ford was the only one I trusted enough to drop her off without conversing with her, as I instructed. Hawke has a big fucking mouth.

I ignore Hawke because I don't answer to anyone, and besides, I haven't yet decided what I'll do with her.

A waitress approaches us, but it does nothing to draw my attention away from the lioness who is talking with the bartender. My teeth grind as I burn a hole in her back with my stare. *How has she not noticed me yet?* For someone who has heightened senses, I'm certain she must be ignoring me on purpose. I'm starting to wonder if it's a good idea to strangle the life out of her after all.

When the waitress offers a suggestive smile and

goes to speak, I interrupt her. "We will only be served by Jewel." She's taken aback and looks over her shoulder at her colleague. But she shrugs and leads us to a booth. She's speaking, telling us something about daily specials, but my gaze is focused on the lethal creature staring at her manicured nails while she waits for the bartender to make drinks.

She wasn't lying about her first name. Her full name is Jewel Diamond, which is funny, really.

"Anything else I can get you before I leave?" the waitress asks, still holding a suggestive smile. One that, unsurprisingly, Hawke reciprocates because he can't keep his dick in his pants. I don't judge; I just prefer to find the limited few women who can handle my tastes.

I don't even glance at the waitress as I ask, "How would you describe Jewel?" I put a fifty on the table and slide it toward her. When I do look up, she's smiling as she takes the bill and slips it into her bra.

"Well, she doesn't work for her tips. She's pretty cutthroat and probably not a great server, but she hasn't been fired yet," she tells me before she turns and walks away.

"She looks so innocent. Are you sure she's actually trying to kill you? This all feels pretty mundane to me," Hawke says just as Ford walks in and takes the seat beside him.

Hawke was more than a few drinks in the night of Michelle's party, but even he remembers watching me pull a knife from my fucking leg, a wound I've managed to hide from everyone as I consciously step through the little love bite. I refuse to show vulnerability.

If Dutton hadn't already been close and skeptical of her presence that night, she might've very well slipped away. So, yes, besides this little façade of waitressing, she is deadly.

But I not so subtly remind him, "She broke into my house, put a fucking rat in my drawer, and took photos of me fucking other women. I doubt she's innocent." I tap my finger on the table as I wait for her to notice us.

"So she has skills," Ford says. I resist the urge to punch him. "So why don't you just kill her?"

"I have my reasons." It's true a lot of people have tried to kill me over the years, and I often deal with them swiftly and efficiently. This situation was different; I needed a lead to find her client. If I kill her now, I've got nothing. And with tension building around the families as to who I might align with and take as a wife, it's very possible someone is trying to kill me to break an alliance and damage my family's reputation. It's exactly why I won't tell my parents that someone is after me. I will claw my way to the top, because in my mind, all of it is already mine.

Jewel turns finally, tray in hand, with four drinks balanced on it. The waitress we previously spoke to leans in and whispers something into her ear. Her gaze cuts in my direction, and I can see the raging storm flaring in those wild tigress eyes. I can't help the twitch of my lips, delighted in the palpable hatred she oozes when looking in my direction.

Her nose tilts higher as she walks in the opposite direction to deliver the drinks, nowhere near as friendly as the other waitress. Perhaps she wasn't so wrong about Jewel's personality.

I revel in the sound of her heels coming to an abrupt stop at our table.

"Has anyone told you two you look like Tweedledee and Tweedledum?" she asks the twins.

"What the fuck?" Ford hisses, offended, but Hawke laughs as he slaps his hand on his chest.

"I've been called worse," he admits.

Her mouth twitches at his response, and I fucking hate it. As if sensing the tension, Hawke clears his throat and quickly looks at the menu.

Her glare then cuts to me. "What can I get you? I don't think this establishment has much of what you're used to. Unless, of course, you like cheap whiskey and beaming hospitality."

Oh, so we're playing that game.

I suddenly pretend to be very interested in the menu. "What do you recommend?"

Her plump lips press into a thin line as that frown makes its disapproving appearance.

"Nothing, it's all shit."

"Your waitress friend was right; you're a shit server," Hawke says, and she turns to him and smiles. The skin over my knuckles turns white as I curl my hands into fists, irritated he's yet again grabbed her attention.

"Sure am, but your tip is automatically included in the bill. So it works. What can I get you three?"

"How about a side of rat?" Ford says, and her grip on the tray only momentarily tightens. But I give it to her, she's quick to recover. And I'm so interested in everything about this woman.

"Sorry, all out. But if you give me your address, I can have something personally organized for you," she deadpans. "You know, exceptional hospitality and all."

Hawke looks away, trying to hide his smirk. If the fucker wasn't snorting like an idiot, encouraging her, perhaps she would better be able to read the precarious position she's in, but I still think she'd be unfazed. Does this woman have a death wish?

Fuck me, even Ford seems mildly amused.

"I have a feeling you already know it," Ford says, shrugging. "I'd prefer if you start with kittens and puppies. That's where I started anyway."

Her jaw drops, and he looks up at her with a flat expression.

"That was a joke," he clarifies.

She scrunches up her nose, not entirely believing him. His humor is so dry that I'm not even sure if he's joking.

She sighs and props the tray on her hip casually. "I see Will was able to track me after all."

I lean in, intrigued by this beautiful and lethal woman. And I should not find anything sexy about a woman who leaves dead rats in my drawers.

"So you've done your homework." She does everything to not look in my direction. She's smart enough to know the twins work for me, but it doesn't make them any less evil or intimidating.

"Why do you sound impressed?" Hawke says out loud. He does that a lot—says shit in front of people he shouldn't.

"Don't be so flattered. It's part of the job. Do you think I'm truly dimwitted enough to involve myself in any way with the most powerful family in New York without doing research?" That irks me. She didn't say *me,* but my family. Aren't I her only target? If it's anyone else besides me that she's after, that changes this entirely, and I won't let her out alive. As if feeling the lethal tension beneath the surface, she looks me up and down with a frown, as if disapprovingly. "Now, if you would so kindly place an order before my other asshole customers start to complain, that would be great."

"I want a burger with extra bacon," Hawke says. We all look at him, and she seems shocked that he actually ordered. We all are.

She shrugs and says, "Okay, anything else?"

"Sit," I tell her, nodding to the empty seat in front of her.

"No," she replies with a sickeningly sweet smile. "And anything for you?" she asks Ford.

"Cake," he says. As I go to speak again, she turns her back on us and walks away, her heels clicking as she goes to the kitchen.

"You ordered fucking cake?" I bark at Ford, unable to unleash this rage within me from her ignorant behavior. "We didn't come to fucking eat; we came to interrogate her."

"Hawke ordered a fucking burger," he says defensively. "And you had the chance to interrogate her two nights ago and let her go free, so unless you plan on gunning down everyone here for more alone time..."

The elderly woman behind us gasps in shock, and I roll my eyes.

"Come on, it's not that bad, and besides, I'm hungry," Hawke says, tapping his belly and rubbing it. The man has the appetite of a fucking beast because he lives in the gym and eats everything in sight. "Don't get your panties in a twist because your woman won't do as you say."

The moment my gaze lands on him, he realizes he stepped too far. "I'm sorry, boss."

Fucking idiot.

"What else did Will find on her?" Ford asks, once again pulling his dumbass brother out of the line of fire.

I clear my throat, reiterating that this is a serious matter. She's got a hit on me, for fuck's sake.

So why the fuck didn't you kill her?

I'm irritated by my own logic.

"She's been on her own since she was a teenager, and her father was a sniper for the Air Force," I tell him, distracted as she walks back out with a tray of food and delivers it to the table next to us, not once glancing our way. The old woman who overheard our conversation is quick to ask for the bill and a to-go bag.

Jewel doesn't seem affected by our presence, and that irritates me more than I thought it would. Men fear and revere me. Women worship and throw themselves at me. This woman treats me with such contempt even with the knowledge I could and should kill her. Shouldn't she be more grateful to me?

"Oh, look, pretty boy made it," Hawke exclaims dryly as Dutton enters the restaurant. Dutton looks around the place as if it should be blown up immediately, and admittedly, I share his sentiment.

"Why are we here?" he asks, taking the seat Jewel was leaning against. The chair looks far too small for his broad shoulders.

"And she's back," Ford mumbles as Jewel comes over with a slice of chocolate cake and sets it in front of Ford.

"Oh, that's why we're here," Dutton remarks, unimpressed.

She folds her arms over her chest, unenthusiastic at the newcomer. My nostrils flare, and I think it has more to do with the hint of her musky floral perfume that wafts in my direction than anything else.

She smells like fucking dessert.

"Dutton, anything I can get you?" she asks, her hand going to her hip.

"Besides an explanation, no, dear."

"You and me both." She sighs miserably and then walks away, and he arches an eyebrow and watches her go.

"Stop staring at her ass," I grit, and the group falls silent.

"I'll have it known I was staring at the tenacious sway of the hips of the woman who clearly does not give a fuck that you're in her workplace. Do you want to explain why we're here?"

I don't know why I thought it was a good idea to invite these fuckers. I should've come on my own. We have other business to attend to afterward, though, so I thought a pit stop was a brilliant idea.

"I came here to give a distinct warning and make an evaluation of little miss assassin, but then these fuckers order dinner and dessert before I can finalize my threat." I cut Ford a look. "Are you seriously stupid enough to eat that? What if she poisoned it?"

"No problem, my dude," Hawke says nonchalantly. "One of the first things Anya taught us was to have a resistance to poison."

The table falls silent before Dutton daringly encourages him to explain. "Pray tell."

"Well, we built an immunity by poisoning ourselves over time, obviously." Hawke looks dumbfounded that Dutton even asked.

"You know, you really put into perspective how great my upbringing was," Dutton says casually.

Hawke chuckles. "As if any of us had a normal upbringing. Maybe that's why the only woman to make boss's cock twitch is the same woman who's trying to kill him."

"You just really don't know when to shut your mouth, do you?" Ford berates under his breath as he puts a spoonful of the cake in his mouth.

EIGHT
JEWEL

I considered poisoning them or, at the very least putting laxatives in the cake, but I must confess out of the group of them, I probably despise the twins the least. Mostly because they have a sense of fucking humor.

All four of them command the energy in the room. Other people stare, and the elderly couple beside them all but ran with their food but left a great tip on top of the one already billed, so I don't give a fuck. The other waitresses, however, have been watching them ever since the hot assholes walked in.

If only they knew all of them were killers.

But then again, who am I to judge?

A bad boy reputation isn't so sexy when they'll actually kill you to get off.

"That one with the dark hair asked about you and tipped really well to know," Sage, who is probably one of the only servers who talks to me, says. I've been here for almost a year, but I don't do friends. She's the only one I somewhat tolerate. So yeah, she's kind of the closest thing I have to a friend.

"What did you say?" I ask.

"That your service sucks," she says with a laugh.

"At least you didn't lie," I admit, grabbing Hawke's burger and fries from the pick-up window. I grab a steak knife with pleasure as I look over my shoulder to their booth. I don't need this job; I got it as a cover. But I had a feeling if Will Walker lived up to his reputation, and with the way Rory idolizes him like some kind of God, I knew it'd only be a matter of time until they found out my identity, which is why I did diligent research myself because I am not leaving until Eli has a bullet in his head and I receive the rest of my money.

The others are talking amongst themselves, mostly Hawke, who booms into laughter over something Ford says. Eli is still watching me, and it's fucking unnerving. He makes me want to squirm, and that's an unusual talent because I don't get uncomfortable easily. This guy must really fucking hate my guts because even as I've watched him fuck other women, he looks through them, not at them. Then again, I probably look at him the same way. But right now, I have his full attention. After all, we're preparing to kill each other. Literally.

"Wish me luck," I say to Sage before I turn and saunter back toward the table, refusing to let them intimidate me. If they're going to kill me, I'll go out swinging. I'm just upset I don't have my favorite guns to play with right now. And I'm down one of my favorite knives.

I push the plate of food toward Hawke and then stab the steak knife into the center of the burger, making a loud thudding sound. "Here's your burger, extra bloody."

Hawke's smirking as he looks up at me through thick eyelashes. He points at me and looks at Eli. "I can't help it, boss. I think I like her."

I smirk because I know for a fact, Hawke shouldn't be saying that out loud, and it gives me great satisfaction.

"Interesting that you took a liking to Eli," Dutton says to me, most likely trying to save Hawke's ass because Eli looks like he's about to kill him. "After our last encounter, any smart woman would've run for the hills." You can absolutely tell they're related. They're very similar in many ways. I guess that's what happens when you grow up close and are around the same age. I've seen photos of Honey and Dawson, who are a stunning couple. It makes sense they had two stunning children. But Dutton's personality has room for improvement.

"A liking, is that what you call it?" I ask him as Hawke reaches for his burger, and wastes no time biting into it. Ford has finished his cake and is watching me as well. "Or do you mean to say you don't think a woman would have big enough balls to stay for the challenge? I don't know how to break this to you, pretty boy," I say as I lean across the table, purposefully giving him a cleavage shot because he is, after all, only a man, but his gaze never drops from mine, "but I'm not like the women you men are clearly used to."

Hawke chokes on a piece of his burger. I don't give a fuck if they're involved with the mafia, underworld auctions, sex industry, or whatever, I won't be looked down upon.

"Oh no, don't be mistaken. We deal with a lot of dead women walking." Dutton beams at me with a challenge in his eyes.

I can't help but smirk back as we size one another up. It makes me uncomfortable how quiet Eli is, and yet his presence still demands my attention. So, I switch tactics. They want a damsel in distress; I'll give them that.

I suddenly turn to Eli. "You must forgive me, Eli." I rest my hand over my heart. "You are truly a man I have desired for so long I just couldn't keep my love for you a secret anymore, so I had to start leaving you gifts. I hope you don't think of me as some crazy stalker. I was just trying to speak your love language." I flutter my lashes at him, and his lip twitches.

"You're in love with me, are you?" Eli says dryly.

"Crazy, stupidly in love. Won't you forgive me?" I coo.

I'm caught off guard when he grabs my hand, which is still at my chest. I fight all instinct to fling him off because I now realize we have an audience as he looms over me when he stands. *Fuck.*

"I'm in love with you too. I want you to know that," he says sincerely, and it surprises me. I realize he's fucking with me, but a man with a face like that shouldn't be able to lie through his teeth so easily. And I never thought he'd actually join me in the game. I was hoping to make him uncomfortable and just label me as crazy.

"But we mustn't. It's a forbidden love, really," I reply, trying to yank my hand out of his. I feel Dutton's gaze on us the whole time, and out of the corner of my eye I see Hawke's and Ford's jaws drop. I'm wondering if they've never seen their boss act this way. I sure as fuck didn't think he would.

Eli grabs the back of my head, and his fingers thread through my hair. He forces me to look up at him. "Ahh, but nothing can keep us apart. You know I'll find you through heaven and hell." He leans in, and goose bumps erupt all over my skin as his hot breath wafts against my ear. "But we all know a path to heaven is no place for us, right, Kitten?"

I flash a smile and try to pull myself away from him, but his hold cages me.

My heart is pounding, and I glance back toward the steak knife until he suddenly speaks so loudly that I know it's for our audience.

"I love you, Jewel Diamond!"

Vomit.

My entire body locks up with repulsion as the onlookers cheer. He leans in again, and I'm unable to budge from his hold. To some, it might look possessively sweet. "Understand that any game you try to play, I will always best you. And if you ever break into my apartment again, I'll find where you live and slit your throat," he whispers, then pulls back, that smile etched on his face as everyone's cheers die down.

The other men at the table seem confused with what just transpired, but Eli only has eyes for me.

"And they say chivalry is dead," I remark snidely. "Now, let go of me, asshole."

"Not until you agree to meet me tomorrow night at Lucy's." His grip tightens, an unmovable force trying to dominate me. I wonder if he'd be so handsy if I still had that steak knife or one of my guns handy. As if following my line of thought, his lips curve a wicked grin. "That wasn't a request, by the way."

"Why?" I ask him. I know what Lucy's is; it's one of his family's clubs. One that he established the moment he turned twenty-one.

"Because I said so."

This time, I smile. "You really expect the whole world to stop and grovel at your feet, don't you?"

"I do quite like a woman on her knees, crawling to me, yes."

A flush runs over my body, noting our close proximity for an entirely different reason.

I've seen how he fucks. No remorse and no care.

I've photographed it.

Dreamed of it.

And that kind of hard fuck might knock some screws into the right place in my head because I seriously have to stop getting my nose out of joint around this guy.

"Are you two going to fuck or fight?" Hawke's voice breaks the tension.

"Both," Eli answers.

At the same time, I say, "Neither."

"Jewel, I need you in the back," Sage calls out. I stare at Eli with a raised brow, and surprisingly, he lets me go. I don't give him so much as another glance as I flip my hair over my shoulder and walk away.

This is fucking ridiculous.

I want to kill the man.

Not fuck him.

Right?

"I'll see you tomorrow night. Dress appropriately," he calls to me. I flip him off. Fucking asshole.

No man has ever told me I don't look good; I know I do. I spend a lot of money on my looks. I invest in myself—maybe not so much the clothes, but beauty treatments, hair treatments, I get massages, you name it. I love to do it, so I take that personally.

I wonder if I dropped another rat in his shoe if he might treat a girl differently.

"Thanks for the save," I say to Sage, who follows me into the kitchen.

"That guy's intense," she says, then adds, "I thought you said you weren't dating anyone."

"You're a fool if you're dating Eli Monti," my boss, Kelly, cuts in as she wipes down one of the counters.

I whip my head in her direction, surprised she knows who he is.

"Yes, we all know who he is. You would either have to be new in town or a fool not to know who he is. Never thought I'd see his type pass through here, but let me give you a word of warning, kid." My eye twitches at her calling me *kid*. "You've just had one of the most powerful men in this city declare his love for you. Don't be surprised if you have a target on your back."

I pick up the next plate of food, ignoring her and the concerned expression Sage regards me with. If only they fucking knew I was the reaper everyone should be scared of. And I'm the one used to putting the targets on someone else's back.

My phone buzzes in my apron pocket, and I pull it out to check the text message from my untraceable client.

> Anonymous Number: I want you to get close to the target. Before the final blow, tell me about his and his family's weakness.

This isn't what I signed up for. I signed up for a hit and a little bit of toying with Eli beforehand. But I'm already in too deep, and I'm certain whoever the fucker is who hired me and is paying me such a generous amount could just as easily put a target on me if I were to go back on our agreement.

"Don't worry," I say to the girls. "I can look after myself."

I always have.

NINE
ELI

"Why did you do that?" Dutton asks as we get out of the car. They'd all been smart enough to remain silent in the car, but my cousin has always had the uncanny ability to provoke me where the other two at least know where to stop.

"Do what?" I ask him.

There is no reason or rhyme to what I do. I do what I want when I want.

And he thinks because we're blood, it keeps him immune from my temper.

"You invited her to the club. Why would you do that?"

I look up at the elegant building that belongs to Edward Graham, a man with whom it would appear I have unfinished business.

When I don't answer Dutton, he sighs, frustrated. "Will found everything on her, you know that. Why are you pushing this? If your father knows someone has a hit out on you, he'll deal with it immediately himself."

I impose on his space, and Hawke and Ford have better sense than to get between us. My cousin is shorter than me, but he isn't deterred by the physical difference. Very few intimidate him.

"*I'll* deal with this. And if you so much as speak of this to my father or mother, I won't be lenient with you."

"Need I remind you that I don't work for you?" Dutton all but snarls.

"No, but you sure as hell like to get up in my business."

Dutton smiles, actually fucking smiles, like a wild man. "Fucking pussy whipped already."

I grab him by the collar of his shirt. "What the fuck did you say to me?"

"I don't repeat myself," he says, placing his hand over mine. "And as much as you're being an asshole right now, you're still my cousin, and I will always protect family. Even if you can't see clearly right now." He breaks my grip on his shirt and pushes me away.

I don't have to answer to anyone, but I remind him,

"Someone has a hit on me. I'd rather unravel which family is behind pulling the trigger, not the woman behind the scope. I can handle her."

"Keep your enemies close, huh?" Hawke says, trying to dissipate the tension. I adjust my suit, and Dutton brushes his light-brown hair back, not that any of it is out of place. His square golden ring shines in the light, and I remember the last time he clocked me with it. That ring has certainly busted my lip more than once.

"Besides, we're here for business," I remind Dutton, who cracks his neck to one side and then the other. This is a personal matter for him, too.

We enter the office space, which is a large twenty-story building filled with agents. I don't even spare a glance for the receptionist as we stride to the elevator and hit the button for the top floor.

It's a tight fit with all four of us, and I adjust the cuffs of my suit out of habit.

"I like her," Hawke blurts randomly from behind me. Dutton side-eyes him, and Ford nudges his brother. This fucker never knows when to shut his mouth or leave something alone.

"You can never read a room, can you?" Ford shakes his head in disapproval.

"What I'm saying is maybe you should marry her

so your father can finally hand everything over to you, and once you're done with her, knock her off if you're already planning on doing that."

"That's a fucking stupid idea, Hawke. Eli isn't going to marry a woman who puts fucking rats in his drawers and stalks him," Dutton barks back.

Ford cautiously asks, "So why does he look like he's thinking about it?"

And I do everything to refrain from smirking. Hawke's not the brightest guy, but sometimes that motherfucker is a genius. But I'm not sure if I want to deal with the hassle.

The elevator doors open, and I see Edward grappling with the phone. Most likely it's the receptionist advising him we're on our way.

"M-Mr. Monti, what a p-pleasant surprise," he stutters. The last time I saw Edward was at Michelle's party, and I had my arms wrapped around his throat after he tried to assault one of the women there.

I'm no hero, and I'm not here specifically for that. What I want is my money.

"I have the money. It'll just take one more day to transfer. Or I can give you the cash right now."

Hawke and Ford take either side of the door to ensure no one interrupts us, and I step toward his desk, evaluating the large room. It's flashy for a corrupt accountant, and it's good to see the money he owes my family has been going elsewhere.

Dutton stops at the edge of the desk, but I walk all the way around and look down on the fat little man whose eyes are black and swollen from the broken nose my tigress gave him. My upper lip twitches. She broke it well.

He scampers out of his chair and presents it to me. I sit, kicking my feet up onto the desk. I pull out a cigar and light it. Edward doesn't seem to know what to do with himself and stands awkwardly to the side, a foot away from me and Dutton.

"I have the money."

I smile and look at the boys, as if imploring them to get in on a joke. "The problem is, Edward, I shouldn't have to come in here personally to receive it or remind you. I only do reminders once."

"If this is about the woman from the party, I didn't know she was yours..." he says nervously.

I give nothing away. "Everything in this city is mine, Edward. Including you."

I've done my research on Edward, and he's a disgusting piece of shit who is underhanded and especially grotesque toward women. "Everyone and everything are replaceable, though, aren't they?" I add, and I swear the motherfucker is about to piss himself.

I find the button to the window shutters and press it, the slow pace of them dropping, agonizing the man in front of me as he turns a noticeable shade paler.

"I'll have the money to you by tomorrow. I swear," he promises.

"That's good, Edward. But as punishment, you will now give us a forty percent cut of your profits."

His jaw opens and closes several times before he says, "But it's only at twenty percent now, that's—"

With lightning speed, I jump out of my chair and pull out my new favorite knife, the one I stole from a certain little hitwoman. It all happens so quickly, and it's not until he's screaming that he understands what just happened. Dutton has him pinned back by the shoulders as I firmly hold down his arm, the blade smeared with blood from where I detached his finger with it.

My favorite color spreads over the table, and I relish the beautiful red glistening in the light.

"This isn't a negotiation," I remind him.

I hand the knife over to my cousin as I pick up my cigar again to take another puff.

I exchange places with Dutton, despite Edward screaming and trying his best to fight against us. I clamp down on his shoulders, cigar hanging out of my mouth.

"My cousin came here on business. But I came here for something personal," Dutton says, and the demon in him comes out to play. This is a side to him that not many see when the mask slips. He rips open Edward's shirt, revealing a hairy stomach.

"Please... P-please!" Edward screams hysterically.

Dutton smiles, taking pleasure in toying with him. "It's public knowledge I'm protective over my family. Especially my little sister. You remember Billie, don't you? You tried to, what would she call it... slide into her DMs?"

"I-I don't kn-know what you're t-talking about," he babbles on a sob, slowly starting to lose consciousness from the pain and shock.

"Well, she, of course, never saw that message because I deleted it. What isn't common knowledge is that I have access to all of my baby sister's messages. I'm quite protective, you see, and I've deemed you someone who needs to be taught a lesson about how you treat women."

His screams bounce throughout the room as my cousin casually and artistically starts carving "Pin prick" into his chest and stomach.

By the time we're done with him, he's sobbing under his desk, barely conscious.

"I don't want to come back here again," I warn him

as we make our way out, satisfied by the thrill but my thirst deeply unquenched for more blood. Discipline is a skill, one I've continued polishing. But even I need a release, and right now, the thought of Michelle repulses me; my cock only twitching at the image of amber eyes glaring at me with scorn and repulsion.

I smirk to myself, wondering how she'll cry when she chokes on my cock.

My hitwoman has turned into the perfect little distraction.

TEN
JEWEL

My hands run down my short, brown leather skirt as I stand in front of the building, staring up at the sign that reads Lucy's.

I shouldn't have come.

Any sane person would've packed their shit and left town by now, but I live by the motto better the devil, you know, than the one you don't. I have no intention of pissing off my client or having my first failed hit.

So here I am, walking into the mafia heir's den as if I'm a welcomed guest when I know I'm anything but.

A sliver of my midriff is on display between the hem of my tight white shirt and the waist of my skirt. The brown leather boots might be cute, but they also have a small knife hidden inside, just in case... Well, just in case shit happens.

Knowing I only have the bare minimum to protect myself with doesn't make me feel any more secure.

The security guard glances at me but says nothing as I stand there, looking like I'm building up the courage to go inside. In truth, I'm looking for any obvious escape routes other than the front door.

Maybe I shouldn't have agreed to this fucking hit.

Play with the target.

Yeah, it seems he's playing with me now.

"How long have you been standing here?" I turn to see Dutton approaching from the parking lot and pressing his key fob to lock his car. I make a point to remember which car is his and the license plate number.

He's dressed more casually than the last time I saw him, but make no mistake, he oozes money. And I'm not fooled by his charming, pretty-boy exterior. If anything, other than Eli, he's the one I'm most wary of. Turning back toward the club, I take in the impressively long line waiting to gain entry.

"I don't want to stand in that line," I reply, which is partially the truth.

"Your name is on the list," he says, stopping behind me. I glance over my shoulder at him. He's staring at me as if trying to figure out some complicated math. "Why did you come here?"

"Because I was asked," I say, though *asked* might not be the right word, more like commanded.

"I can't argue that my cousin always gets what he wants, but even you should have more caution. He *will* kill you, so why don't you explain to me who sent you, and maybe we can offer some form of protection?"

I shoot him a wicked grin. "Don't you think if I knew my client's name, I would've given it to you after you knocked me out and had me tied to a chair? No hard feelings, by the way."

"In all fairness, you threw a knife into my cousin's leg, so I think we're even."

"But let's not make it sound like we're coming to a truce, right?" I angle my head with a provoking smile. His eyebrows furrow only slightly. I can tell that, much like the other men around Eli, he's not sure what to do with a woman like me, and that in itself is satisfying.

Before he answers, I start for the door and security guard. "Raise your arms so I can pat you down," the man orders suspiciously. Most likely because of how long I've been staring at the building. I sigh and do as he says, but Dutton steps up behind me and pushes one of my arms down.

"If you want to live past tonight, I suggest you don't

touch Eli's guest." His voice is firm, and the security guard straightens and turns a noticeable shade paler. He's quick to step to the side and unhook the red rope.

On the plus side, it's nice to know Dutton's not only an ass to me but to everyone. Dutton walks behind me—more like guides me—into the devil's lair.

The moment the music hits my ears, I'm overstimulated by the number of naked women dancing on what appears to be hovering neon cubes. Clumps of wildly drunk people bounce and cheer, pour alcohol into one another's mouths straight from the bottle, and are basically fucking on couches.

It's not the "gentleman's club" style I was expecting at all. This is mafia on crack. I thought I dressed appropriately for this club, but it seems I'm wearing more clothing than most of the other women.

A woman walks past me with a tray full of various drugs. Two guys in a booth call her over and fish out some cash.

Dutton's hand finds my lower back, his touch feather-light, as if touching me will scorch him, but it brings me back into the room instead of being swallowed whole by its chaos.

"Move. He's already watching you," Dutton says, and I follow his gaze to the second level that overlooks the crowd. Eli is leaning over the railing with a drink in his hand. I see only a few people behind him, and they blur in the background, my attention drawn solely to his unearthly eyes.

Dutton removes his hand and makes his way to the stairs that lead up to the second floor, but I don't have it in me to follow like some good little girl.

I make a point to look away and lift my chin in a dignified manner, still able to feel his scorching gaze pinning me in place.

This might be his domain.

He might think he owns everyone.

But he doesn't own me.

He certainly doesn't control me.

So, I do what any sane girl does when she's drawn the attention of a monster.

I make my way toward the bar.

I'm not sure why I continue to put myself in these situations. Admittedly, I had so much fun following him and learning about who he was, but I didn't think the tables could turn so quickly. I mean, technically, I should have, knowing who this man is. I clearly underestimated my target, and that was a foolish thing to do.

When I reach the bar, I intentionally lean against it, bending over, fully aware that from his angle, he'll be able to see the bottom of my ass beneath the skirt. I choose to work with my assets because they're just as powerful as any weapon.

He may be better at this game than me, but he's a man, and I am a woman in a short skirt who is used to getting her way.

"Can I buy you a drink?" I don't bother turning to look at the man offering to buy me a drink. I couldn't care less about him. If I wanted a drink, I'd buy it my fucking self.

"You want a drink or what?" he says impatiently. This time, I do turn to look at him. His thin lips are pulled back in a sneer, and his hair is so slicked back by gel that I wonder if the tightness of it is affecting his features. He's clearly trying way too hard to impress. Little does he know he's failing, especially regarding how to speak to a lady. I try not to laugh at that thought. *Me? A lady?*

I don't even waste my breath on him; just simply shake my head no as I turn to get the bartender's attention.

"Fucking skank," the overconfident asshole seethes.

"What did you just say?" I ask, now turning to give him my full attention. He looks me up and down, making me feel dirty with the action.

"What, you think you're too good for me? I offered

to buy you a fucking drink, not ask you to suck my cock, you rude cunt."

I scoff at him.

"First of all, I would never suck your cock, and I pity any woman who does. Second of all, 'cunt' is a lovely word, so don't use it as an insult when it's a cunt you want. Unless you prefer the sausage, that is," I snap back, angling my head to the side and waiting for his reply. He spits in my face. The second that filth touches me, my body works on reflex, reaching out for the half-empty glass on the bar. I smash it across the side of his face, and it fractures into a dozen pieces. He doubles over, barely catching himself, shocked. Then, with great satisfaction, I watch as the anger takes over like he can't believe a woman hit him with a glass to his fucking ugly-ass face.

"That's no way to speak to a lady," I tell him calmly. Glass litters the floor between us, and I shake off a small piece that landed on my boot.

His hands ball into fists, and the shock of what I just did now hits him hard.

"You fucking bitch!" He lifts his hand, ready to hit me, and my body hums with delightful anticipation. I'm going to fucking ruin this guy. But as he goes to swing, another hand catches him by the arm.

The newcomer's wrist sports a very flashy watch, and his forearm is covered in ink. While I don't know every tattoo the man has on his body, I know those hands belong to Eli Monti.

"I think it's time you leave," Eli says. "My men will show you out." He nods to the security guys who have followed him to the bar.

The dumb fucker hasn't even noticed who's speaking to him, his gaze pinning me with a glare. I confess I feel his frustration since my fun has been cut short.

"How about no. Remove your hand so I can teach this bitch how to treat a man—" The idiot pales as he finally looks up at Eli, recognition dawning on him.

Eli casually steps in front of me, twisting the guy's hand as if to shake it. He brings the man into what looks like an embrace from behind as he whispers something into his ear. The man grunts in what looks like physical pain as a vein pulses at his temple. He nods frantically at whatever Eli is saying.

"I'm—" The man gasps. "I'm s-sorry." He barely gets out the words.

Eli releases him and shoves him as if he's no more than filth. The man stumbles over his own feet, but as he tries to stand, I realize he's holding his stomach. I look down at Eli's hand, where blood glistens on the knife he's holding.

"Is that my knife?" I demand angrily. I've been wildly pissed that I lost it the night I threw it at him.

"Wouldn't most women ask if I stabbed the man instead?"

"Well, that much is fucking obvious. Give me my knife back."

The corner of his lip tilts. "No. This is mine now. And shouldn't you be apologizing for smashing a glass over someone's head in my establishment?"

I cross my arms over my chest. "It was an accident. My hand, which so happened to have a glass in it, slipped and *accidentally* hit him in the face. And I don't need you to defend me. I can handle myself," I say, flipping my hair over my shoulder and leaning over the bar. "But now I'm really fucking thirsty since your presence, as usual, puts me in a mood."

He leans in, and I hate how acutely aware of his body heat I am. Of the harsh, intoxicating smell of his cologne. My nostrils flare, and I hate the fact I like how good this fucker smells. I nudge him away. "You're too fucking close. And shouldn't you smell like melting skin or maggots or something?"

This time, he does smirk as he holds his hand out expectantly to the bartender, who hands him a white cloth. Then he begins wiping down the bloody knife as if it's the most normal thing to do at a bar. "So you like how I smell?"

I look up at him, dumbstruck. "Wow. You really do love yourself, don't you? Also, your bartenders are shit servers."

That grabs the attention of one of them, and they give me a death stare. I shrug. "What? You haven't once asked me what I want."

"You're bleeding," Eli states.

"What?" I'm startled as he grabs my hand and stares at the small cuts on my palm. Fuck, I hadn't even noticed.

"Fucking hell. Hey." I wave at the bartender with my good hand. "Can I get another one of those cloths?"

Eli grabs hold of my wrist, assessing the wounds in the dim light. I'm startled by his firm grip, yet his eyebrows furrow as if concerned by the damage.

"Look what you went and did." He drops my hand and reaches over the bar for a napkin before he lifts my hand again.

"Does this mean I can go home early? Since I'm wounded and all?" I ask innocently.

"No, you'll stay for at least an hour. And moving forward, the only one to hurt you will be me."

I look at him, once again dumbstruck. "Wow. So romantic."

"Do you want romance, Kitten?"

My face naturally twists of its own accord. "Keep that shit to your blonde-haired girlfriend; she seems like the type to enjoy it."

"I don't do girlfriends," he states. "Now, you're coming upstairs with me so we can fix this."

I lean in, my boots giving me some height as I stand on my tippy-toes to reach his ear. "I'll give you a heads-up. I don't respond well to being told what to do."

His mouth grazes my ear, and I can't help but momentarily sink into the undeniable intoxication that this asshole radiates.

"I know you want to be forced into submission, sweetheart, so your sharp little tongue can wag all it wants. I'll cut it out if I have to. And then I'll shove my cock so deeply down your throat, you won't know if you're choking to death on my cock or your own blood."

A shudder runs down my spine. The threat and the visual it conjures is terrifying, and yet there's a warmth that floods to my core.

I pull back and grin at him, really appreciating the lines on his face. "You're so beautiful." I slowly lift my good hand as I press one fine-tipped nail to his forehead. "And you'll be prettier with a bullet between these brows."

The fucker has the audacity to actually laugh.

It's as equally unhinged as it is beautiful.

ELEVEN
ELI

Most women would run for the hills or, at the very least, flinch at my provocation. Not this woman, though. She's currently sulking in my private booth, stabbing at her drink with a straw as if it's personally offended her.

I plucked out the two slivers of glass embedded in her palm and thoroughly bandaged it. Other than a few shallow cuts, her hand was fine. She'd even had the effrontery to say "it was nothing" under her breath more than once.

But it was everything. No one has permission to make this woman bleed but me.

She throws her hand up, exasperated. "Can you stop looking at me like a creeper and tell me why the fuck I'm here?"

"Are you going to share with me who your client is yet?"

She throws herself back into the leather seat, arms folded over her chest. She hasn't had one sip of the drink one of my men brought her. She crosses her legs, and a tic jumps in my jaw as I see a flash of red panties.

Jesus Christ, I'm falling from grace if the mere glimpse of underwear can get me off these days. I adjust my crotch.

"Sit here," I tell her, not liking the way a few of the club members have a clear view of us. I could tell them to leave so we have this space to ourselves, but I'm not accommodating her, and besides, Lord knows what I'll fucking do to her if left alone. I'm still not sure if I want to kill or fuck her. Both, I think.

"No," she replies, looking over her shoulder at the others.

"Look at me," I growl as I take a puff of my cigar and spread my legs wide. Her gaze doesn't miss the adjustment, and I quite like that. Whether she wants to admit it or not, she's just as drawn to me as I am to her.

Hawke's booming laugh echoes over the space as he entertains two blondes, one on each knee. Dutton is here somewhere, and it's not often Ford doesn't follow his twin, but he's nowhere to be seen tonight.

She looks at her phone as if to check the time. Frustrated by her ignoring me, I stand, looming over her, and circle around the booth. I sit on the wooden table and put my glass of whiskey and cigar down beside me. I push my legs between hers and splay them out, giving me a perfect view of those red lace panties.

To her credit, she doesn't flinch, and her gaze is unmoving. "I'm not going to kill you tonight," I tell her.

"That's nice to hear. Can't promise you the same thing," she replies bitterly. My smile is slow and sensual.

"I want you to sit on my cock like a good girl."

This time, Jewel's lips curve into a sultry smile, and I've known from the moment she walked in with that short little skirt that she was playing a dangerous game with me. "Aren't you the least bit curious?" I ask. I can see by the fire in her gaze and the way her body responds to me when I force myself into the space that she is in.

"And then, can I kill you afterward?" Her tone is overly sweet.

I lean forward with a smile, slowly gliding my rough thumb along her collarbone and up to her jaw. I expect more fight from her, but that calculating gaze is letting me close, most likely because she's ready to stab me again, but I won't fall for the same trick twice. I curl my fingers through her hair. The point of her being here was so if any insider is behind this hitwoman's paycheck, they'll know I own her now.

But having fun with her in the meantime might release some of this tension that's been bundled in my balls since first meeting her.

Her fingers twitch, and I can tell she's contemplating if she should use whatever sneaky little weapon she most likely has on her. "I demand a taste."

"And what makes you think I'll give it to you willingly?" she snaps, breathing heavily as I inch my face closer.

My cock throbs at her venomous tone.

I lean in and brush my lips against her jawline. My fist tightens in her hair as my nostrils flare at her light, flowery scent with something deeper and richer beneath, much like her temperament. It's like the mask of temptation before the true she-devil shows herself. "I think it's the unwillingness part that makes you want it even more."

Her body naturally leans into me, and I smirk, satisfied by the reminder that as much as she fights it, she fucking wants me. And if she thought walking in wearing an outfit like this was going to be my undoing, she was correct.

I stand up, adjusting my semi-hard cock at her eye level. I stare down at her come-fuck-me eyes and slightly parted red lips. Rubbing my thumb along her plump bottom lip, I'm mesmerized. Her breath hitches, and I can tell she's crippled by the tension just as much as I am.

That's when I notice her hand slowly creeping toward her boot. It happens so quickly. As she reaches for what I'm assuming is a hidden knife, I grab her hand. I twist her body and pull her down with me so she's on my lap, her back against my chest. She lands on my cock so firmly I'm certain I almost puncture a hole through my pants and her skirt. She lets out a low *oomph.*

I have her arm pinned to her side with one hand, and my other is wrapped around her throat. I breathe in the scent of her shampoo, intoxicated by the scent. Or maybe it's the thrill of this woman yet again trying to stab me. Her throat bobs beneath my firm grip.

"It'd be easy for me to break this slender neck of yours," I warn, holding back a growl as her ass wriggles against my cock. There's no fucking way she doesn't know what she's doing.

I run my nose along her shoulder. Despite having her pinned, there are many ways she could try to fight her way out of this. And although we're in a room full of people, I'm appreciative of the fact I have my back to them—something I never do—just so none of them can see her flushed, aroused state.

I look at the glossy black wall in front of us. It gives off a bit of a reflection, showing me her expression, but not clearly enough for others on the other side of the room behind us to see.

I can see her peering at me through the shiny wall reflection, barely.

My little toy.

My fucking temptation.

Potentially my undoing.

My cock pushes angrily against my pants. "I'm starting to think you really do want me to kill you with how hard you are," she breathes, trying to keep face.

"I can be a generous man," I reply. "As long as you sit like a good girl."

I loosen my grip around her throat, waiting for her to move, almost begging for it. I enjoy pinning this woman down. I find it almost cute the way she tries to kill me. When my hand hovers over her collarbone and she still hasn't done anything, I let my fingers feather along the tops of her breasts. She takes in a sharp breath, and I can feel the arousal radiate off her as if I'm already buried deep inside of her.

I cup her breast, testing, waiting for her to try and smash my nose with the back of her head. But it only adds to the thrill. *How far will she let me go? How much does she want it?*

I squeeze her tit and twist. She hisses, but her body arches further into me, that demanding little ass still wriggling against my cock.

Fucking hell.

"These perfect tits," I whisper into her ear, waiting for her quick tongue to lash me with a reply. But when she remains silent, a male pride fills me. I'm still watching her in the vague reflection from the glass wall. I gently release her wrist and skim my fingers down her skirt. When I drift them back up, she lifts off me just enough so I can pull the skirt up higher.

The moment my fingers touch the lace of her panties, I realize with satisfaction that she's already fucking soaking.

Fucking beautiful.

"You want this, don't you?" I purr into her ear.

When she doesn't respond, I twist her other tit, and she snarls under the savage contact.

"You're already soaking wet for me."

"There was a handsome guy down—"

I move my hand from her breast and wrap it around her throat again, cutting off her airflow. I begin to circle her tight bud through her panties. "I suggest you never mention another man to me again. As of now, you are my property until I decide to discard you. Do you understand?"

She can't speak, but she can nod. She doesn't attempt to do either. But she also doesn't try to free herself from my hold.

I slip my finger under the edge of her panties, dipping into the warm flesh that welcomes me. She moans and sinks back against my chest, and I can see the redness flush down the back of her neck from her lack of air supply.

"Do you like that, Kitten?" I ask, pumping my finger into her.

She moans, and I'm dying to replace my cock with the two fingers now working her slick pussy.

"Tell me you want it," I coax as I loosen my grip.

After catching her breath, she admits, "It appears you might be useful for something after all." Then she moans, and I smile as I slip a third finger into her, slamming into her pussy. She's wriggling against my palm, thirsty for more. Thirsty for my cock.

Fuck, she feels even better than I could've imagined, and I'm pumping into her with my fingers, almost in disbelief at how wet she is for me.

"Sir!"

My cute little killer freezes at the sound of my new bodyguard coming to a stop behind us.

"Fuck off!" I grit out, but it's too late. Jewel has already broken free of my grip, shimmying her skirt down as she steps out of my reach.

I glare at the new guard, whose eyes widen when he realizes he's just triggered his untimely death.

"Anyway, that's been an hour, asshole. Thanks for patching up my hand." She makes a break for the staircase.

"You're not going anywhere," I growl, adjusting my rock-hard cock, as she looks over her shoulder with an antagonizing smile. I would usually break kneecaps if someone gave me that much sass.

She has the tenacity to wink at me before she flees down the stairs.

"Is everything okay?" Dutton asks as he climbs the last two steps.

I run a hand over my jaw, my cock painfully straining, as I wave the security guy over. He's hesitant to obey.

"I'm sorry, sir. I thought you'd want to know that some young guys broke out into a fight and started stabbing one another out in the alley, and—"

When he's close enough, I grab the gun in his pants and shoot him dead center in the forehead. A scream sounds from behind him, and one of the blondes crawling all over Hawke is startled to sobriety. He jumps up, attentive and ready for action.

"Clean this shit up," I bark, throwing the gun near the man bleeding all over my floor. Hawke glances between Dutton and me as if looking to be clued into what happened. Without further instruction, he starts yelling orders to other guards.

The partying around us continues, but I'm so fucking frustrated I think my cock is about to split in two.

Fuck.

She slipped straight through my fingers. I bring said fingers to my lips, licking them and enjoying the flavor. I can't wait to taste her again.

Dutton stares at me as he inquires, "Did you learn anything about her?"

The only fucking thing I learned is she's fast. And that she just so happens to wear my favorite color.

Red.

I grab my cigar from the table and light it as I contemplate my next move. I didn't expect her to let me touch her... or for her to affect me the way she has.

Mark my words: before I kill her, I will fuck her just to get her out of my system.

"Not yet. But I will."

"And, Dutton, a word of warning. Don't ever touch her again." I think of the moment he placed his hand on her lower back when they entered the club. I've never wanted to kill my cousin as much as right then in that moment. I've never been in the habit of sharing my toys.

I'll unravel that sweet little cunt of hers like it's my personal present from the devil himself.

Suddenly, Hawke's idea of marrying her for convenience doesn't sound too bad.

TWELVE
JEWEL

I'm out of my fucking mind.

I'm out of my fucking mind.

I'm out of my fucking mind.

As I race down the stairs and out of Lucy's, I know I've crossed a line. But I'll be fucked if there was any way I could stop it.

Fuck, just the reminder of what happened causes a hot flush to creep over my skin. It takes me two full blocks to realize I'm still running away from him. I stop dead in my tracks when I notice I'm not being chased.

My breath is shaky, and I brush my sweaty hands over my skirt. *What was I thinking?*

I was no better than a horny man because the moment he had me pinned, something fried in my brain. My wires got crossed and… Fuck, why is he so attractive?

This has to be part of his plan.

I thought I was toying with him, but that sure-as-shit got flipped on its head. I tap my finger against my lip, not at all okay with this change of events. My skin is still tight over my body, and I close my eyes, welcoming the cool breeze.

He's a beautiful monster, indeed, and I'm fucking soaked because of him. Had it not been for his guard interrupting us, I probably would've let him fuck me then and there, even with an audience behind him.

I bite the tip of my nail. This just won't do.

And then a dazzling idea comes to mind.

When he threatened me two days ago, he said if I were to break into his apartment, he'd slit my throat… but he said nothing about his mansion.

I smirk as I check the time on my phone. Ah, but the night is young.

I beam at the thought of fucking with this guy just as much as he fucked with me tonight.

I sure as hell won't be falling for that again.

THIRTEEN
ELI

I'm going through paperwork at my desk at Lucy's when my father walks in, his second closely following him. My father signals him with his gaze alone, and he closes the door. It's irritating, the way my father still acts like he owns everything.

Technically, he still does. Until he hands it over to me, it's only a matter of time before he does it, even if I don't have a wife, because my mother is sure as shit pressuring him to retire.

"Whiskey's there." I point to the bottle at the edge of my desk. He picks it up and smirks at my exquisite taste.

I look at my watch. It's two in the morning. "Isn't it past your bedtime, Pops?"

He doesn't even acknowledge the smart-ass

comment, and I try to hide my own smile. My father is as straight-laced as they come. His humor is… well, it's on the border of non-existent and dry, and I'm almost certain he might be a psychopath.

In this, the apple didn't fall far from the tree.

"I was just finishing with some business before heading home. Did I hear correctly that you cut Edward Graham's finger off and carved a message into his chest?"

I don't look up from the paperwork I'm signing off on. "No. I cut his finger off and doubled our profit. Dutton carved a message into his chest."

My father nods approvingly. "That one is full of surprises, isn't he? You did well doubling the profits."

This catches me off guard. My father very rarely praises me. It's cause for alarm in itself. I give him my attention now. Over the last two years, I've taken the lead on sixty percent of his businesses, and I handle most of his indiscretions. Slowly, he's handing me over the empire I've continued to build upon, but he still holds enough of the reins because of that archaic marriage stipulation.

"Your mother is adamant I have a party for my birthday," he says grimly. We both sigh at that. My mother is probably the only thing that keeps us from losing all of our humanity. Neither of us cares for moments of celebration, but we both indulge her because we love her. She deserves her every demand. "I'd like to announce my retirement then to make your mother happy."

Tension ripples in the air. Because what goes without being said is that I will have to be, at the very least, engaged by then.

His birthday is in three months.

"If you haven't found someone of interest by then, I'll also be treating it as a matchmaking event."

"Multitasking at its finest," I growl. "And does Mother know about this?"

"Of course not. But are you going to tell her otherwise? Will you ruin the pleasure she gets in party planning because you can't pull your head out of your ass?"

I clench my teeth.

"I love you, son. And I'll kill anyone who interferes with you or this family in any way. You are my heir and the second love of my wife's life."

"I'd say her first love," I correct.

He gives me a scathing look, his dark eyes promising payback in my future, and I smirk. "Don't get smart." He's always jealous of my mother loving anyone else. I'm actually surprised my own father didn't try to suffocate me as a baby with how much attention she gave me instead of him.

"Back to the topic at hand. Whether you think I'm being unfair or not, there is a code. You understand this more than anyone since you'll be the next head of this family. No exception is made, not even for you. There wasn't one made for me, and I will apply the same rules to you."

"And if I don't have someone by your old-man party?" I jest, always wanting to get under my father's skin.

He throws back the rest of the whiskey, admiring the empty glass. "Then your mother will be upset, and I will remain in charge for many more years to come." I know he'll force my hand before he upsets my mother.

"I may not be nurturing, but if there's one thing I've instilled in you, it's that you'll do what needs to be done. Don't agonize over this one caveat. Take an obedient wife and rule over New York. It's as easy as that." He stands and places the glass down.

He steps toward the door but pauses. "Also, I received your gift."

I grin. "The new car? What do you think?" I had it custom-made for him and oversaw the specifications myself. The car is fucking sexy.

"Just don't tell your mother about it. Wouldn't want her to know I go over the speed limit or anything," he says dryly, and I chuckle. The corner of his mouth tilts up as he excuses himself.

I'm left alone in the office, his words swirling in my head.

"Take an obedient wife and rule over New York. It's as easy as that."

Why does that thought make me want to vomit?

Because there's no fun in that.

My mind drifts to a pair of amber eyes and the memory from earlier tonight of holding her in place against my cock. I would much rather force my wife into submission than have her come willingly.

EVEN AFTER I leave the club, I can't stop thinking about the way she melted against my palm, fucking herself on my fingers. I should've killed her the moment I first cornered her in that room at the party. But I find her very intriguing, not just because she's an attractive woman but because of her very blunt and cold personality. I can tell she doesn't like it when men touch her. She tensed up when Dutton placed his hand on her back, and she always puts space between herself and anyone else, as if it personally offends her when someone gets too close, which is precisely why I do exactly that. I want to force her to crumble into defeat and submission. I remind myself it's just business to use her as a pawn to flush out whoever is targeting me. But now, the intrigue is far outweighing the logic.

I'm not sure how long I'll keep her alive, but even Will has drawn a blank on who might've hired her. She's either very fucking good, or her client is very lucky. I can't work out which one it is.

That undeniable curiosity has me driving past her apartment at three in the morning. I park along the curb, surprised to find her shadow moving across the curtains.

I consider the things my father said, and at no point was I even tempted to tell him about my precarious situation. If my father knew anything about it, his advice would be very simple: kill her. In fact, he'd probably try to do it himself.

My phone lights up with a text message.

> Stalker: Do you plan to come in and leave me love notes? 💋

I can't help the smile that tugs my lips. Is that what she calls the notes she leaves stabbed to my door? I guess she did leave a kiss mark, so maybe that's her definition of a love note. It also doesn't surprise me that she knows I'm parked outside her home. I don't care much if she bugged my car or just has phenomenal security outside her window. It's not like I'm exactly hiding.

I reply to her message.

Me: Would you like a love note?

Sincerely,

The man who left you soaking wet.

I look back up to her window. Only a few seconds pass before she pulls back her curtain. And despite the distance, I notice the scornful glare she shoots me. She flips me off with her bandaged hand, and my upper lip twitches, amused by her incessant urge to piss me off.

I like the spice she has in her. When I was watching that man talk to her at the bar, I could see her demeanor change completely. It was like she went from being a seductress to a lethal killer. I haven't seen anything like it in a woman in a very long time. Anya Ivanov, the twins' adoptive mother, is the only woman I have ever seen switch so quickly and completely, but then again, we always knew she was a little crazy. And although the twins aren't biologically hers, they definitely take after her.

Her face is illuminated as she looks down at her screen, and then my phone lights up with another text.

> Stalker: I would love one since I've left you so many. By the way, which man is this? Sorry. 💋

After I read her message, I look back up, but she's already closing her curtains, and then the lights switch off.

Although she's being a smart ass, I contemplate leaving her a "love note" to return the favor of the dead rat.

A love note. Can't say I've ever written one of those before, but if her love notes are anything to go by, I'm sure I've got this in the bag. I sit parked outside her apartment for another thirty minutes, contemplating welcoming myself into her apartment.

Then again, this cat-and-mouse game isn't so fun if I trap her so easily in her own home. I can come back anytime.

I decide to drive to my mansion. It's only a thirty-minute drive from the city, and it gives me time to consider my next hand to play, as well as my father's words.

When I arrive home, I undo my tie as I approach the entrance. One of my guards stands at attention, and I throw him the keys to my car. My home is quiet at this time, and it's nice to see neither of the twins has crashed here for the night. Sometimes Hawke likes to crash at my house simply because he thinks the gaming is better in my cinema room. It's just an excuse for him being bored and constantly needing to be around people.

Unless we're conducting business, I usually let them have the weekends off, much to my father's dismay at me not having constant security.

I begin to undo my top buttons as I walk to my bedroom and open the door. The moment I enter the room, something feels off. Someone has been in here. I slowly grab the gun from my pants, and when I switch on the light, I find it empty.

An ominous object catches my attention. A knife has been punctured into the middle of my bed, pinning a scrunched-up note to the mattress.

Anger floods me at her ability to sneak into my space once again, yet my dick twitches at her cockiness.

When I open the note, the first thing I notice is the red kiss mark. Those fuckable little lips acting as a calling card.

This was most likely what she got up to tonight after fleeing my club.

I liked your watch collection. Hope you don't mind that I borrowed one or twelve.

I crack my neck as I head into my closet and contemplate her last text message.

> I would love one since I've left you so many.

Everything looks just as I left it a few days ago until I open a drawer and notice my entire watch collection is gone. I don't like sharing things, let alone someone disrupting the orderly way I place them. But I'm equally impressed. Either way, I'm going to have to install those fucking cameras because of her.

I walk into my private bathroom and pull my shirt over my head. When I've removed it completely, something catches my eye. I approach the marble counter, where my aftershave, comb, and toothbrush are. My left eye twitches as I adjust the aftershave into the right position. *Did she go through my bathroom?*

I scan the room, checking if anything else has been moved, and that's when my attention is drawn to the corner behind the toilet.

She's not even trying to hide the fact that she placed a camera there, and so I smirk with a brilliant idea. If this is the game she wants to play, then we can play it. I free my cock and begin to fist it while facing the camera, thinking of how tight her little pussy was wrapped around my fingers tonight.

I don't know if she's watching this now or if she will when she wakes, but I'll make sure she doesn't forget me, especially when I've made my mind up that I'll bury this cock in her one way or another. However, when I kill her is still undecided.

FOURTEEN
JEWEL

I don't work today, so I decide to read up on the extra files Rory sent me on any public business announcements or obvious relationships Eli Monti has. I've become obsessed, primarily due to the fact that my life literally depends on it.

On my days off, I'd usually be at the gun range practicing. It's the only time all my busy thoughts are silent, and I have one thing to focus on. Just the target. I know I'd be too distracted for it today, and it'd only infuriate me more, most likely throwing off my aim. And I outright refuse to have anything less than perfect aim.

Eli has gotten under my skin. I don't usually dance with my targets. Hell, I usually don't even talk to my targets. And I certainly don't let them put their hands beneath my skirt and ride their fingers to a very frustrating missed climax.

I only received one text from Eli after he sat outside my apartment for almost an hour last night. It not-so-cryptically and simply stated, "Delivery." Two minutes later, there was a knock on the door.

It caught me by surprise this morning when he sent food to the apartment. Not only breakfast but a hot chocolate as well because he must know I think coffee tastes like the devil's piss. I'm not sure what his definition of a love letter is. But sending a woman food is pretty fucking close. Not that I would accept it. So when Jenny received it at the door, I told her it was from me to her. A total fucking lie. Because of her shocked expression, I had to explain further that I felt guilty for borrowing her heels without asking. I didn't feel guilty at all. And if anyone in this apartment was going to get food poisoning, it wasn't going to be me.

Not that I wanted her to be murdered, and I was ninety percent sure Eli was above doing something so sly. Not because he had morals or a conscience, but I'm certain poisoning me wouldn't give someone like Eli satisfaction. No, Eli is definitely the type to choke me to death with his bare hands. Or something else just as up close and personal.

Although the thought did cross my mind that if

such an unfortunate thing were to happen, at least I could totally steal those heels back.

I stop reading the files to check my phone again. I would have thought by now he'd have contacted me about his admirable watch collection that is... well, not so impressive now. I pull up the surveillance cameras I placed in his mansion last night; there are three in total. One in the bedroom, another in the private bathroom, and the last in the walk-in closet. I rewind the footage, certain he went back to the mansion last night.

It's a gamble, really, but I had to get under his skin as much as he has mine. While I was there, I also looked for information that my client might want to know about him, but the asshole is as clean as he is ruthless.

I grin like a Cheshire cat as I roll onto my stomach on my bed and kick my feet back and forth. I love watching him discover his missing watch collection. I look at the box in the corner of my room where I threw the thousands of dollars worth of watches like they were less than garbage. I still don't know what I'll do with them; that wasn't the point.

Perhaps provoking the monster who's promising to kill me isn't the smartest thing to do, but since it's part of the game I've been hired for, I remind myself it's necessary, and I'm not doing it simply to piss Eli Monti off. I'm doing it because it's a job.

My smile slips, and my heart falters as Eli steps into his bathroom and begins peeling off his shirt. My mouth goes dry as I scan over the intricate pattern of black and gray skulls and dragons twisting through one another across his back and down his arms. His chest and stomach are completely covered in ink, and I can't help but appreciate the finery of it.

That's when he looks directly at the camera, and I gulp. He saw this last night, so why hasn't he mentioned it yet? Why has there been no consequences? And then he smirks at the camera as he slowly undoes his belt. I can't look away as he pulls out his sizable cock.

I've seen it many times before, specifically when he's fucked his lover, Michelle, whom he hasn't touched since almost a month ago. I stare, mesmerized, as he fists himself and pumps, staring into the camera the whole time.

That son of a bitch is fucking with me, and yet I can't look away, imagining what it might feel like to have him inside me. I fantasized about it nudging at my entrance last night when I sat on his lap. Heat spreads up my body as I recall his hand around my throat.

Fuck.

I jump, goose bumps erupting over my skin, as three defiantly loud knocks come from the front door. I immediately close my screen and hurry from my bedroom, but Jenny has already beaten me to the apartment door. She twists to look at me, her expression a mix of shock and suspicion. No doubt because of the asshole with a sultry gaze staring at me from the other side of the threshold as if it's his God-given right to show up at my apartment.

Shit.

And to make a point, he steps inside before being welcomed in. He scans the room, most likely because it's smaller than the bedroom he grew up in.

"Umm, hello?" Jenny says in a high-pitched voice. Eww. Why do people go gaga over this man? Yes, he's attractive, there is no denying that, but shouldn't she be more concerned with the man barging in without introduction?

"Jewel." He says my name, ignoring Jenny, as his ethereal gaze lands on me again. In the daylight, with the sun shining through the windows, they look almost silver, much like his mother's. It's bizarre to see him in the daylight.

I cross my arms over my chest, conscious of my pajama shorts and tight tank top that clings to my naked frame. He seems to notice the same. I lean my shoulder against wall.

"I thought the devil only works at night," I say dryly.

Jenny's mouth drops open. "You're here for Jewel?" she says in disbelief. Come on, he clearly looks dangerous. She'd have a fucking coronary if I told her this man's an outright killer.

Eli glances over his shoulder at her as if noticing her for the first time. I don't like his casual outfit, which still consists of a long-sleeved button-up shirt to hide his sinful tattoos and a body that isn't fair for anyone to witness because once seen, you can't unsee it. I can't not compare it to all the men that came before him and they don't even come close. And I hate adding to his God complex, which is why I'll never admit it out loud.

"Yes, I'm dating Jewel and thought I'd come by for a quick hello between business meetings. And you are?" Eli flicks her a charismatic smile, and I want to gag at the monster playing housecat. Jenny blushes the moment he offers his hand, and she takes it. She looks equally awestruck and confused.

Yes, it's so unfathomable to believe me, the person who stays in her room other than to go shooting or to work, has a boyfriend.

I don't even attempt to dispute him because poor

Jenny can't take any more confusion right now, but I narrow my gaze, unimpressed by his antics.

"Did you forget I was coming over, Kitten?" he asks sweetly.

A shudder of revulsion rolls through me at the pet name.

"Kitten?" Jenny says, baffled, as he removes his hand from hers. I can tell by the way he's looking at it that his particular immaculate self most likely wants to scrub his hands.

"Let's get this over with," is all I say as I lean my back against the wall to make space for him. Not that it's enough, considering the width of the fucking man.

He seems amused as he stares down at me while walking past. Then he grabs me by the wrist and pulls me into my own room, closing the door behind us.

The moment the door closes, he drops my wrist and glances around the very empty space. I have nothing personal in here, apart from a few books and a photo of my father and me. When he notices the photo, he picks it up. I don't like him studying it so intently, but it's no liability, either. The only thing really worth anything is the box in the corner, and the only thing hiding the contents is the thin cardboard lid.

The longer he stares at the photo, the more uncomfortable I become, not because he's in my room but because I can't stop my gaze from tracing down his shoulders and back, imagining the video I was watching only a few minutes ago. The heated flush returns to my cheeks with a vengeance, and I'm fucking furious he has this type of hold over me.

"Your father is dead, correct?" he asks, breaking me from my thoughts.

"Yes." I step away from the door and place my hands behind my back. I'm just grateful I don't store my guns here. They're the only possessions of mine that mean anything to me. So, giving him access to this room is nothing. He can burn it down for all I care; everything is replaceable.

"And your mother?"

"I'm sure you know all the details, so why are you here?"

"Did you like the food I sent?" he asks, putting my photo back down and then wandering around the room. He runs a finger along the window sill as if looking for dust. *Prick.* I might not own much furniture, but I'm not a slob.

"No, I gave it to Jenny," I tell him. "I'm vegan."

"Liar," he says as he trails his hand along the wall and stops at my dresser. He opens the first drawer and pauses as he stares down at the array of colorful lace.

He pulls out a red G-string and holds it up with one finger.

Still holding my underwear, he asks, "Should I take these?"

"Why would you want to take them?"

"So when I fuck Michelle, I can think of you." Red-hot anger and some other emotion—jealousy, maybe? No, it couldn't be that—flash inside me. It pisses me off that his sudden mention of Michelle has any effect on me. He smirks when I don't respond to his antics, and he slips my underwear into his pocket and closes the drawer.

"I thought I'd stop by and return the love letter," he says, coming to a stop in front of me.

"No dead rat?" I ask, folding my arms over my chest as he fishes a note from his pocket.

"Do you want one that badly?" He looms over me, and I grow uncomfortable at the way he looks down my chest, his gaze seeing all of me.

"Not particularly." I refuse to look away from him, meeting his gaze as if it does nothing to me.

He bends down slightly so his hot breath is against my ear. "Have a good day, Jewel," he tells me as he places a perfectly folded note into my hand. "I'm sure I'll be seeing you real soon."

I look up through thick eyelashes as he straightens

to his full height again and I point to the door. "You're starting to get awfully needy."

He chuckles as he turns to go. "Some might call me attentive."

"I've never asked for your attention," I remind him.

He freezes with is hand on the door handle and looks over his shoulder. "You don't need to, sweetheart. Your body tells me all I need to know about what type of attention you need."

I stop my jaw from dropping as he lets himself out.

Arrogant asshole.

Jenny is busily scrubbing a pot in the kitchen as she watches him leave. "Bye!" she calls out, but he doesn't acknowledge her or even look back at me. The moment he lets himself out the front door, I slam my bedroom door before Jenny can ask me any questions.

Fucking asshole.

I open the note he placed in my hand.

Jewel,

If you want your guns back, you will come to my mansion at eight o'clock tonight. Use the front door for once.

Sincerely,

The man whose cock you're going to come all over.

My hands are shaking so much I almost tear the note in half.

My guns? No way.

How could he possibly know where they are?

The next hour is a blur as I quickly change and drive out to the storage unit I've rented under a fake name to keep my guns safe.

I'm warily looking over my shoulder as I all but speed walk down the hall full of roller doors until I find my number. He couldn't know where I store them, could he? Fear grips me so profoundly that even on the drive here, I couldn't talk myself into any sense. He's just fucking with me. He has to be. But it's something I can't leave to chance.

And so help me, God, he better not have one of my fucking guns.

They're like my babies.

In fact, if I were to ever have kids, I'd sell them all to him in exchange for my guns.

When I finally reach my unit, I unlock it, lift open the door... and find it empty inside. My stomach grows heavy, and my heart feels like it's stopped. Everything goes quiet as the reality of my situation sinks in. I take two steps inside and stumble to my knees.

No.

This is all I had.

I've never felt so exposed.

Vulnerable.

All I have to remember my father is gone.

My guns were my point of living.

A hollow emotion grips me, one I try to push away because I don't do emotion. I haven't since my father died.

This is all I have.

My mother shunned me and walked out.

And my father left me too.

This is all I've ever had since then to give me purpose.

It's what I'm good at. But what kind of hitwoman am I if I let some asshole steal them so easily?

"This means war, motherfucker," I grit out angrily, for the first time starting to create a personal vendetta against this guy.

First, it was just business.

Now, it's personal.

I'll enjoy it when I bury him six feet under.

I stomp from the empty space, then slam the door down and scream, the echoing sound, a chaotic promise to retrieve my precious property.

My eyes burst open with focus.

Fuck him.

Now, we play.

FIFTEEN
ELI

"Get the fuck out of my house."

"Come on, my dude, don't be like that." Hawke groans in complaint, not even bothering to look over his shoulder at me because he's so invested in some shooting game on the screen. I swear, the single worst thing I had built into this mansion was the cinema room. I never even use it. But it's somehow turned into a hangout for whoever the fuck wants to come around.

I stare a hole into the back of Billie's head. She's another unwanted guest. "Does Dutton know you're here?" I ask, irritated. Dutton is many things, but he's especially protective over his sister.

"No, and I want it to stay that way," she says, then snaps, "Are you fucking kidding me, Hawke? I thought you said you had my back."

"Stop being a princess. Not my fault you're a shit shot."

"Maybe you should practice more in real life, and you'd be more useful with an actual gun," Billie bites back as she flips her long honey-colored hair. She's striking, with features very similar to my aunt Honey.

"I don't disagree," Ford says as he focuses on the portable chess board he's playing on the floor against Hope. Hope is rarely here; her heavy studies and traveling abroad keep her away from home. With a famous mother like Lena Love and a father like Alek Ivanov, who partly runs the underground auctions of New York, it's fair to say she's both aloof and guarded.

She tucks a loose strand of vibrant red hair behind her ear and pushes up her glasses as she asks, "Shouldn't you be studying anyway, Billie?"

The two attend the same college, though virtually most of the time, considering their busy lives and influential families.

"I could say the same to you. Where's your overbearing father?" Billie jokes.

"Out on a job. Gave me a few hours to fly the coop," Hope replies as she moves her next piece. Ford looks at it appreciatively.

Hawke gets killed on screen and loses his shit,

throwing the controller. Billie chuckles, and he pounces on her within seconds.

"That's not funny," he growls playfully, tickling her ribs.

"Fuck off. You deserved that, asshole." She laughs. My left eye twitches, and my last fucking nerve snaps.

I pull out my gun and shoot twice into the ceiling. Hawke and Billie break apart, and he's covering her body with his within seconds. I bet any money that if Dutton were here, he'd fucking string Hawke up by his ears for even touching his sister.

"What the fuck, man?" Hawke snaps. The other two seem unaffected but look up from their game.

"Get the fuck out of my house," I repeat as I grit my teeth.

"I don't see what the problem is; you don't usually care," Hawke says, exasperated.

Ford begins packing up the portable chess table. "He's always cared, genius; he just usually hides in his library to focus."

"Get off me, you oaf," Billie says, shoving Hawke off. He's three times her size, yet she kicks him off with ease.

"That hurt my feelings," Hawke says, rubbing his chest before turning back to me. "What, you got some big date or something?" he mumbles. I take a step to the side, pointing to the door. His eyes go wide.

"Do you?" he asks, now in total bewilderment.

"I don't date."

Billie mockingly says under her breath, "I don't date. I fuck. Me, man."

"You looking to leave in a body bag?" I ask her as she passes me.

She taps me on the shoulder with a smile. "Not unless you want to explain to our parents why you killed your sweetest cousin. Might not go down well at the funeral."

I barely restrain a growl.

Ford ushers them all out. Hope is nice enough to thank me for my hospitality despite no invitation going out to anyone. It just so happened that once I was done with business and returned to my estate, the twins snuck off as I went into the library, and when I went to kick them out, somehow, the girls had joined them.

I stop Ford at the door, my hand hovering in front of his chest. In a low voice only he can hear, I ask, "They didn't see the body, did they?"

I don't usually make a mess in my house, but as circumstance would have it, we got a little careless with a newcomer from a motorcycle club in Boston who thought it would be a good idea to try and infiltrate us. Let's just say he didn't make it past the week.

"What body?" Ford asks, feigning ignorance.

I nod once and watch them as they leave. There's no way in hell I want any of them here for what's about to go down. I'm certain a beautiful and furious woman is about to attempt to rip me to shreds. And I can't fucking wait.

SIXTEEN
JEWEL

His house is lit up like a fucking Christmas tree. I'm beyond ready to blow it up with how painfully welcoming it is, and I know it's purely for me. Despite him technically inviting me, I refuse to waltz in like a guest. We're anything but friendly.

I know the layout of this house; I made it my personal fucking mission. Now I just want to remind him, yet again, that I can break into his home anytime I want. I scan the usual spots, knowing well where the cameras are positioned and how not to set them off.

He's always had security on the outside of his house; on the inside I get to wreak unchecked havoc. I wait until the security guard takes his cigarette break, and then I sneak in through the side garden, which is a minor blind spot. When I reach the door leading to the garden's courtyard, I quickly pick the locks and sneak into the only room that doesn't seem to be lit up.

"So that's how..." I freeze at the voice and am caught red-handed by the light switch flicking on. Eli is leaning against the door frame. "I told you to use the front door."

"I don't give a shit what you told me," I snap, crossing my arms over my chest.

He stands there, tilting his head and staring down at me through his eyelashes. I should just kill the motherfucker right now and be done with it, but how the fuck will I get my guns then? It would be satisfying, though.

"If you kill me now, you won't ever get your guns back."

My jaw falls open. How did he know that's what I was thinking? He pushes off the doorframe. "It's written all over your face, Kitten. You might be good with a gun, but subtlety is not your forte." He turns his back to me. "Come, let's eat. I made us dinner."

I scoff, grumbling under my breath, "Come, let's eat in my evil lair."

He turns, appearing offended. "What is it with everyone mimicking me lately? I don't even sound like that."

I flick my hair over my shoulder. "Have you heard your own voice? You're kind of fucking annoying."

He turns again, trying his best to hide the smile. "Someone is sensitive about their guns being taken."

My fingers curl into my palms until his previous words finally hit me. "Wait? You cook?"

"I do. Now, fucking move," he grumbles and reaches for my hand. I pull away from him. This motherfucker might have me here willingly, but that doesn't mean he has permission to touch me. Especially when I'm fucking furious.

Remind me why I haven't killed this motherfucker yet.

Oh, that's right, because my client still wants him alive.

That makes this asshole one lucky bastard.

It's the fragrant aroma that hits me first as we enter the kitchen, and I try not to show my surprise. *Is this guy just good at fucking everything?*

"Sit," he instructs, without so much as looking in my direction. I bite my tongue to keep from grumbling under my breath again.

I take a seat at the island, sweeping my gaze around the grand kitchen. I hadn't made it this far the last time I broke in. I'd only crept up to his bedroom. I hate the fact his home is beautiful. But it also feels empty. Probably because of the soulless asshole who owns it.

I wonder if my guns are hidden here somewhere.

I twist and look over my shoulder, trying to peer out the doorway that seems to lead into a dining space.

"Your guns aren't here if that's what you're looking for," he states casually as he plates up what looks to be chicken smothered in a cream sauce and vegetables on the side. Well, don't we have a fucking Michelin chef in here.

"You get that out of a box?" I snidely remark.

"In my family and heritage, you say thank you when someone serves you food."

"In my upbringing, you don't steal," I snap back.

He pauses mid-scoop with one eyebrow raised, that scar splitting through it. It's disgustingly beautiful to see this deadly god of a man do something so fucking mundane while still well-dressed and perfectly put together.

"You stole my watches first."

I go to speak but immediately close my mouth.

Fuck.

He has a point.

I have to look away when his arrogant smirk kicks up again.

Fucking asshole.

"If you want your watches back so badly, I'll even spit polish them before I return them. Just give me my guns back," I say, getting irritated. One of them was my father's. I should kill him now, fuck the contract. Those guns are my life, and nothing can replace them.

"You seem to really care about your weapons. Let me guess... a gift from your father?" The aroma of the food wafts under my nose, and I have to give credit when it's due; it smells fucking amazing, which only pisses me off more. He called me over for what? Fucking dinner? At my silence, he seems proud of himself. "Okay, so I did hit home. Maybe they were your father's."

"I hate you," I mumble. The corner of his mouth tilts up at that as he carries the plates toward the dining room, where a pre-lit candle stands in the center of the table.

Vomit.

When I make no move to join him, his voice carries between the rooms. "Jewel, you'll only make this harder on yourself."

I hop off the stool, knowing he's right. He has to have a reason for me being here; it can't be to just wine and dine me. The room is just as beautiful as the rest of the mansion I've seen so far and just as soulless. Or maybe that's because of the monster standing at the head of the table, pulling out the chair beside his and waiting for me. Between the two dishes is a bottle of white wine, and he pours us each a glass.

"Sit," he says without looking up at me. I'm uncomfortable by the ambiance that seems to swallow us whole. The dim lighting, the candle flicking back and forth in the center of the grand wooden table that could seat twelve people. I feel so small in his home, and it mostly has to do with him leaving me unarmed by taking my most precious items. I shouldn't be here. I should not be dining with my target. If Craig discovers this, he'll have a fucking heart attack.

I drop into the chair, arms across my chest. He seems amused as he goes to place the napkin on my lap, but I snatch it from his hand.

He takes his seat at the head of the table, and I dreamily look at the sharp knife positioned beside my plate. Then again, a fork can be used as effectively as any weapon, I suppose, especially if it's going into those beautiful fucking eyes.

"Eat," he commands.

"I'm vegan." I lean over to grab one of the small bread rolls from a basket.

"Liar. You think I haven't seen photos of you eating sauced ribs and the like?"

I shrug. "I just enjoy licking off the sauce."

"That's not vegan. And I'll have you know, my mother is vegetarian, so if you want to play that game, I can easily accommodate you. We can do this dance all fucking night."

This guy wants to fucking dance?

He took my guns and invited me over for dinner like it's the most natural thing in the world. This guy is under my skin, and the rage begins to bubble over within me.

Why the fuck is he starting to get pissy with me when he did me dirty?

My fingers curl around the knife as I stare at the vein in his neck.

"I wouldn't if I were you," he growls out.

It snaps the last of my restraint as red hazes my vision. I lunge across the table, my blade to his throat. He grabs my wrist at the last second, so the knife barely hovers at his jugular.

"How many times do I have to tell you I don't take orders? Especially from assholes like you." I push against him with all my strength, but he easily keeps me in place, that lethal edge crossing his gaze.

"This is nothing but foreplay, Kitten. And if you keep acting like this, I'll restrain you and fuck you with this very knife. My patience will only hold out so long." He leans into me. His lips are so close to mine, his hot breath washing over me. "If you want your guns back, you're going to sit down and shut the fuck up, understand?"

We stare for a moment longer, his firm grip around my wrist holding me in place. I fucking hate this man with everything I am. But he has the only thing of value to me. The red haze dissipates, and I slowly retreat, taking the knife with me.

He adjusts his crotch, and I can't believe this mother fucker actually gets off on this shit. Then again, he definitely has a screw loose, so it's not that much of a surprise.

He nods to the food in front of me. "Eat."

I grudgingly put the knife down and stab my fork into the piece of chicken. The moment it hits my mouth, I stifle a moan so he doesn't know how good it is. That's all his ego needs—a boost from me.

"Good, right?" He takes a mouthful of his wine as if we're having the most civilized dinner together.

I say nothing and take another bite.

"I like that you dressed up for me. Do you wear your leather often when you break into my house?" he asks, admiring my attire. I hate how it elicits goose bumps along my skin, and I can only think about the way he handled me the other night.

"Yes."

"Damn, next time, bring your leather whip. I'm sure we could have some fun."

I glare at him when I puncture a piece of vegetable, and he seems to enjoy the way he so easily riles me.

He takes another bite. The silence stretches and stretches and stretches, my frustration teetering on the edge again.

"You don't plan to give me my guns back, do you?" I ask.

"I do, but first, you have to do something for me."

"And what is that?"

He nods to the food, and I take another bite. Chewing it, I wait for him to speak.

"Wine?" he asks, nodding to the two full glasses on the table.

"No, you probably laced it with something."

A knock sounds on the door. "Come in," he commands, and the double doors open. Two of his security guards enter, dragging in the man I'd smashed over the head with the glass at Lucy's. His clothes are covered in blood, and he looks like he hasn't changed them since that night. His face is beaten up, so he clearly, didn't leave the club unscathed, and I'm wondering if instead of escorting him out, they trapped him in some little dungeon.

When his eye—yes, only one because the other is

swollen shut—finds mine, he moans something that sounds like an attempted apology. I look back at Eli, who is watching me expectantly.

"You remember our friend, right?"

"Yes," I say, slightly confused as to why he's even here. He's a nobody. *What is this, some knight in shining armor bullshit?*

"Good." Eli reaches under his suit jacket and pulls out a gun. His gaze remains on me as he aims it at the man and shoots him in the chest twice. The man crumples to the floor, dead, most likely put out of his misery from whatever satanic torture he was going through up until now. "I told you last night that you now belong to me. And that means in every sense of the word. If someone moves against you, I take it personally. If someone so much as looks in your direction, I'll remove their eyes and feed them to them."

The man is twisted in thinking this is what I meant by a love letter, and the declaration is far from gentle poetry. But if Eli is good at one thing, it's making a point.

"Now, Kitten, let's discuss a deal. One that might get you out of this alive." He puts the gun on the table within reaching distance from me and starts to eat again.

SEVENTEEN
ELI

The unfortunate man who thought he could provoke my property gets dragged out. We continue to eat as she stares at me with that less-than-grateful expression. Taking a sip of my wine, I lean back and take her in.

"What do you want from me?" she asks.

"I want you to marry me," I say matter-of-factly.

She scoffs, and it looks as if she's about to laugh until she notices the serious expression on my face.

"Marry you?" She shakes her head in disbelief. "That's definitely never going to happen." She goes to stand, and I tap the table twice.

"You'll sit down if you ever want to see those guns again," I say curtly. She freezes as if suddenly remembering why she came here in the first place.

She reluctantly lowers back on the chair.

When Hawke first suggested the idea that I marry her, the others thought he was an idiot. And although I don't disagree with them about that most of the time, this might be his greatest idea. It's so crazy; it might work. This little tigress might be the answer I've been looking for all along. I can keep her close, flush out her client, and inherit my family business all at the same time.

The kingdom will finally be mine. And I'll decide how to deal with my new wife afterward.

Punish her. Definitely punish her.

"I don't want to marry you. I don't even like you," she scoffs.

"That's perfectly fine; you just have to pretend you do around my family."

"Your family?" she chokes out.

"Did I stutter? Yes, my family."

"Are you that out of your fucking mind? I'm the person who, at any moment, is going to kill you. I don't like being in the same room as you, let alone marry you. How about we agree I make your death quick, and in return, you give me my guns back now."

Her attempt at negotiation is amusing, and I try not to smile. Jewel is one of few who can actually keep me entertained. Her quick wit is attractive, and her delusion of having any control of this situation is... cute.

Reaching into my pocket, I pull out a box, then slide it across the table to her. She immediately looks like she wants to puke.

"Marry me, and I will return your guns four months after."

She shakes her head in absolute shock. "You're out of your fucking mind if you think we can survive playing happy couple for more than a day. Why don't you marry princess Michelle? She seems submissive enough to be your type."

A wave of irritation rolls through me at the mention of Michelle. I don't and have never, cared for the woman. I haven't even seen her since this infuriating little tigress came into my life as subtly as a wrecking ball.

But she's disposable, I remind myself. That's the *only* reason she's perfect for this role. At least, that's what I keep telling myself.

"My type is irrelevant. I have an objective in mind, and you are cornered with no other place to run. This isn't a negotiation. This is an offer for you to stay alive for another day."

I can see her sorting through her options in her head. Good, she is, at the very least, an intelligent woman. She'll know what's best for her.

"You could just kill me after the wedding," she says, giving me a shrewd look.

"As you could kill me before the wedding. Come now, Kitten, doesn't this sound thrilling? Don't you want to dance with the devil a little before you get married?"

The mere mention of marriage has her turning a shade paler. She seems just as averse to the concept of legally tying herself to someone as I am.

"It seems like you'd be getting a lot more out of this than I would. Your father won't hand over the business to you until you're married. So why do I have to wait four months for my guns?" Her gaze flicks back to the box between us as if it's burning a hole in the table.

The less I tell her, the better. After all, I don't actually want her to have inner knowledge of my family's business; however, a small piece of information won't harm the objective.

"My mother let it slip that the rights to the business don't get handed over until three months after the marriage. So, four months of pretending to be a good little wife will ensure you and I both get what we want out of this. I'll even pay you two million for your time to show my generosity."

"Fifteen," she quickly replies.

"Done."

"No, sorry, fifty." She crosses her arms over her chest, pushing her breasts up as she does, and I know it's intentional. Unfortunately for me, it has it's intended effect in that tight fucking leather she's wearing. Leather, I'd do anything to cut into right now. I clear my throat, wishing I were adjusting my cock instead, but I refuse to show her the hold she has over me.

No woman has ever affected me like this.

They've always served as a means to an end. But I've never... yearned for a woman before. That can't possibly be the right word to describe this. I just simply need to fuck her before our wedding day to flush her out of my system.

"Done. I'll transfer half as an engagement present and the rest on the wedding day once you're my darling wife. But you won't get your guns back until we're done."

"I hate you," she snarls as she stands and glares down at me. I quite like the scornful expression, knowing I've ruined my soon-to-be wife's fucking day.

"Oh, and will you be a good fiancée and tell me who's hired you to kill me? When you find out, that is."

She smirks. "Dear, sweet husband-to-be, I can tell you already that our strength is not communication."

"Then what will it be?" I ask with an arched eyebrow.

She places her hand on the ring box and pulls it toward her with a twisted smile.

"Tolerance, at the very least. Personal space at best." Her smile drops, unsheathing the feral expression beneath. And she takes her leave.

I stare at the tight leather wrapped around her curves as she saunters out, and I smirk.

This might actually be fun.

EIGHTEEN
JEWEL

The ring box mocks me from the end of my bed. I sit cross-legged in front of it. I haven't dared open it yet because that just feels like it will be the nail in the coffin. Even though I agreed to marry him, sitting here alone in my apartment makes it all feel surreal. How stupid am I? Why did I even think for a second I could compete with men who have been playing mind games all their lives?

"Jewel." A knock comes at my door, and I'm tempted not to respond to Jenny. I sigh, perhaps grateful for the interruption of my spiralling thoughts.

"Come in."

Jenny's head pops around the door. I haven't spoken to her since Eli first walked in as if he owned the place yesterday. I have my head in my hand, most likely with a visible thundercloud looming above me. Her gaze falls to the ring box, which I've been staring at for a good hour, and her mouth falls agape.

"I didn't know you were in a relationship."

"Neither did I," I mumble under my breath.

"He seems nice. A little bit of a handful for you, though. I didn't think someone like him would be your type."

"And what do you mean by that?" I do very little to mask the snideness in my tone.

"Just... you know. He looks like someone who has a lot of money and fancy things. You... don't. That's all."

I laugh. "Just to make things clear, I'm out of *his* league, Jenny." The only way the asshole has half a shot with me is by blackmailing me.

"Oh yeah, totally." Her tone says I'm delusional. "Anyway, flowers were delivered for you." She pushes the door all the way open, and she's holding a bunch of beautiful, vivid yellow sunflowers. I grind my teeth as she comes in and hands them to me. They were my favorite flower as of thirty seconds ago. "So, it's serious, then?" I take them as she nods to the ring box.

"What?"

"Your relationship. Do you plan to move out? Because if you do, I need to know."

"Thanks for the flowers, Jenny," I say, my throat constricting. The ring feels like a bad omen. This fucking ring is a noose around my neck. Whether it's Eli, the neighbour next door, or fucking Santa Claus, I don't want to be owned by anyone, even if it's fake.

Jenny makes the smart decision to leave, and the door clicks behind her. I open the card.

Wear the ring.

In the coming days, we will announce our engagement.

Congratulations on landing the most eligible bachelor in New York.

Sincerely,

Your soon-to-be husband.

I crinkle the note, and within seconds, I'm growling and screaming as I tear it up into tiny pieces. Which is frustratingly hard, considering how thick the fucking paper is. My fraying nerves snap, and I throw the flowers and ring across the room.

This guy thinks he has a fucking collar around me. And even if he might have the means to kill me, I refuse to be told what to do or to be treated submissively. Maybe it's the serious aversion I have to commitment, but I can't even fake it at this point.

He's stepping into my space, and no matter how much distance I try to put between us, he's caging me more and more.

I bite the edge of my nail, thinking.

I need out of this room. Right now.

Looking down at my phone, I read the message from my client from two weeks ago. No updates. No further instructions. Nothing.

My phone pings with a new message, and it's like the ray of sunshine to push away these dark clouds. I never saved Sage's number on my phone but she tries to text me from time to time. This one, for once, grabs my attention.

Agreeing to join her might be reckless. But that's my middle name.

As luck would have it, it's just the reminder I need that I'm not someone's property and I can still do my own thing.

> Unknown Number: Jewel, please help. I'm supposed to meet up with three guys with some of my girlfriends, but they just bailed on me. You said you're still single, right? Please come just as a filler. I really like one of the guys. I'll make it up to you and take your shitty shifts. 🙏

I know she's desperate if she's messaging me as a last resort. But the timing couldn't be any better. So I reply.

Me: Sure. Give me the time and place.

NINETEEN
ELI

Not even twenty-four hours out of my sight, my fiancée needs to be taught her first lesson.

"Do you want to tell us what this is about, boss?" Hawke asks from the passenger seat. Ford is driving and staring at me through the rearview mirror as I check how many bullets I have in my gun.

I had every intention of dealing with a business partner who'd gone stray, but the moment I was notified Jewel went to some run-down Chinese restaurant and is sitting across from three men, I saw red.

"No. Just be ready for cleanup."

I'm thinking clearly, I know that.

It's the most clarity I've experienced in a long time.

When I claim something as mine, it is deeply, irrevocably my possession.

Jewel will learn a lesson tonight: If she chooses to see other men, then she might as well be the one pointing the gun at their heads.

Ford pulls over at the curb, and I step out of the car without so much as giving them a second glance. I adjust my suit as I storm inside the restaurant. There aren't many people here so late in the evening. A hostess approaches me, but the moment she sees the gun in my hand, she screams and runs into the kitchen. Customers begin to scatter out of the shitty restaurant.

Laughter catches my attention, and I turn toward the head of auburn hair in the private section of the room. It's her friend Sage's laughter, and some guy is smiling across from her, brushing his thumb against hers.

My little tigress, however, seems less fierce than usual. She's throwing back a drink with three empty glasses beside her. The two men across from her greedily stare at her despite her dismissive attitude toward them.

I barrel up to their table, and Sage screams. Jewel looks up in a daze, and then rage quickly sparks to life in her eyes.

"You're not invited," she snarls.

I offer a tight smile. "I am wherever my fiancée is."

That's when her gaze drops to the gun and realization sinks in. "Don't you fucking—"

I aim for the first man on the left and shoot him between the eyes. Sage screams again as Jewel jumps over her. By the time I've shot the second guy, she's standing in front of the remaining two protectively. Interesting. I didn't take her to care much about her colleagues, but apparently, even she'll draw a line somewhere.

"Are you out of your fucking mind?" she growls, and if ever she's looked like a protective tigress, it's now. I can only imagine how fiercely she might protect her own.

My fiancée.

I wonder what it might feel like to have that same loyalty.

I try to shake the thought away, along with the humming in my veins. I don't entirely understand it. But she's mine, and no one will so much as look at her.

Her friend is sobbing behind her, and the remaining man seems perplexed as he mourns his friends but tries to also cower under the table.

"Ah shit," Hawke says behind me, finally understanding why we're here, but I don't pay him any attention. I'm completely focused on the furious, amber-eyed woman sneering at me.

"What do you want?" she asks.

"Out. Now," I command.

Her gaze narrows on me, but she straightens her spine and approaches me. I notice the slight wobble of her walk. *Is she drunk?*

She follows me into the main room, where almost everyone has cleared out. Ford is offering compensation to those who remain—most likely the owner and a few staff members. Hawke quickly steps into the room we just left.

She snaps at me. "Do you—"

I shove her against the wall with my hand around her throat. She doesn't seem surprised if the knife at my balls is any indicator. She lets the tip of it dig into my inner thigh. My cock twitches, thinking about her tracing lines into my skin. My gaze drops to those fuckable lips. The way they part and her hot breath mingles with my own.

I want her.

This fiancée of mine needs to be taught lessons.

Punished in a way only I can deliver.

My blood is pumping with adrenaline as our lips inch closer.

The urge to take her and make her mine courses through my veins.

She smells of alcohol so strongly I can almost taste it on my own tongue.

"Jealous much?" she snarls.

"I don't share," I bite back, unable to contain the fury swirling within me. There's an underlying emotion driving it that I don't entirely understand but refuse to look further into. "You won't pull this little stunt again, do you hear me?"

She hiccups, her throat bobbing under my tight grip. "You don't own me."

"I do in every sense of the word unless you want more people to die around you. We're not playing anymore. You are my fiancée, and you *will* be obedient."

She laughs hysterically as if the word *obedient* itself puts her in a delirium.

"Jewel?" Her friend's voice slips from the door. She's in shock. "I'm going to go home."

I angle my head toward her and the man at her side. Hawke is standing behind them, efficient and effective in his threats and damage control. Ford has most likely bought out the owner for their silence and explained the consequences if any of this were to leak.

Jewel remains silent, her mouth opening and closing as if she can't seem to think of what to say.

When her friend begins to walk out, Jewel pins me with a glare. "If you so much as touch her..."

"I never wanted to be here in the first place." I sneer at her. "You did this."

She scoffs and pushes at my hand. I roll my shoulders and step back, uncomfortable with not touching her. It's as if I have to leave my mark. Make her truly understand who she belongs to now.

"Emotional warfare doesn't work on me, asshole." She hiccups.

"We had an agreement," I grit.

She pops one hand casually on her hip. "I conveyed to you that I don't do well with being told what to do."

"Then you better learn pretty fucking quickly. Now, get in the car."

A wild storm brews in her eyes as she weighs her options. But I am not to be trifled with right now. On other occasions, I was lenient with her; some might even call me kind. But right now, I will have my way, no matter what.

It's as if she recognizes that because she mumbles a complaint under her breath as she walks to the front door, with a slight sway to her step.

Hawke gives her a sympathetic expression but says

nothing as I pocket my gun and follow my stubborn fiancée.

TWENTY
JEWEL

Adrenaline courses through me as my mind tries to wrap itself around what just happened. Perhaps other women would be horrified by what they just witnessed, but I'd become desensitized to death a long time ago.

I wasn't even having a good time, and the evening was lackluster at best. I hate to admit it, but the asshole knows how to make an entrance. It wasn't fair to involve Sage and the guys, though. I didn't think he would act so crazy that he'd happily waltz into a restaurant and gun down whoever he pleases. I'll definitely have to make it up to Sage and offer to at least pay for her therapy. And this confirms one thing: he's watching me.

He doesn't so much as look at me as he opens the passenger door. His scent has deep earthy notes. I don't like the way it does something to my brain; it brings me back to only moments ago when he had me pinned against the wall, and I'm almost certain he was going to kiss me. And I'm ashamed of my lack of fight.

Did I want him to kiss me?

Definitely not.

Another two cars pull up behind us, and two men in suits step out and walk into the scene of the crime. Efficient much?

I slide into the leather passenger seat, looking around the car. It's nice and stylish, that's for sure, but it's just a shame about the company sliding in beside me. He pulls away from the curb and begins driving, the tension palpable. He readjusts his suit jacket, and we remain silent for several minutes.

When he breaks the silence, I'm confused. It's as if this man has an on-and-off switch. He pulls into a fast food drive-through and stops at the ordering box. "Burger?" he asks me. I never would've imagined someone like Eli, raised using golden cutlery, being familiar with fast food. But I'm starving. I might not want to dine with this asshole, but I'm certainly not health-conscious enough to ever say no to a burger. I nod, and he orders us the same meal.

We're quiet as we continue along the drive-through and collect our meals. He leans over, opens the glove box and hands me a wet wipe for my hands before he grabs one for himself. I try to hide the smirk because despite this killer getting bloodied all the time, he has an underlying obsession with perfection and cleanliness.

He hands me my burger and places the bag of fries between us. I take a bite, watching him. Witnessing him doing something so mundane is strange, especially straight after he decided to go on a crazed killing spree.

The burger hovers at my mouth as I look at him. "Were you jealous tonight?" It's unthinkable, really, for a man like this to even have emotions, let alone one so childish as jealously. But I certainly didn't expect him to kill two guys just for talking to me. That was a miscalculation on my part.

He wipes his mouth before he speaks, the burger already almost gone. "No. I wasn't. You're my property. My fiancée. You will not socialize with other men unless I'm with you."

As if truly seeing me for the first time, he looks at my ring finger, and a slight frown appears on his face. "Why aren't you wearing your ring?"

"How's your leg?" I ask, changing the subject. "And besides, I'm sure our nuptials aren't going to end your side shenanigans, so why shouldn't I be able to fuck whoever I want?" Not that I wanted to fuck either of those men in there.

"I won't be fucking anyone else during our time together, Kitten. And I'll have it known, I'll gladly fuck you."

"Why? Because I'm the only woman daring enough to put a blade to your throat as we do the deed? Really gets your rocks off, doesn't it?"

"If a declaration of sorts is what you're after, then you can come with me as I cancel previous commitments."

Fuck me, this guy is so business-oriented. Everything sounds like a transaction.

"With Michelle?" I ask. "Won't it upset your relationship with her family if you choose me over her?"

"You are to be my wife, not her. People will accept it." He says it like it's a known fact.

Around a mouthful, purposefully to piss him off, I speak. "You can keep her if you want. I won't be fucking you."

"We shall see," he says, pulling out of the parking lot. "You're also slightly tipsy, so you're not thinking straight."

I roll my eyes. I don't need to hear that from the asshole who just shot up a Chinese restaurant.

TWENTY MINUTES LATER, we pull up at an address I know well, mostly because I've staked it out twice already when I first started stalking Eli.

He gets out of the car and walks around to open my door. He holds his hand out expectantly, but I ignore it and cross my arms over my chest.

"We're not at the hand-holding stage. And you can do your breakups on your own; it has nothing to do with me," I snidely say.

"It has everything to do with you. Michelle needs to see you, or she won't believe I've moved on."

"So, send her a photo," I reply, stubbornly remaining in the car. "I don't really give a shit about your personal drama."

"Funny, considering you seem to be the center of my drama right now," he says bitterly. "She and I were never in a relationship. Tonight will be the first official fiancée task you're given. So you best remove yourself from that seat before I drag you out of it by your hair."

Heat flushes to my core at the thought of him tugging at my hair, and I curse under my breath at my fucked-up body betraying me. Maybe it's because I'm still tipsy. It has to be.

"Sorry, Romeo. But you told me I only had to

impress the in-laws. Keep walking, I'm tired of your macho shit tonight," I say, not looking at him. When he doesn't leave right away, I glance up at him. "Unless you're going to pay me to put a hit on her, then—"

"You're intolerable." He curses and then storms away, leaving the car door open.

"That's what I've been telling you!" I shout out after him. I'm quite enjoying the fresh air, so I leave the door open. I pull out my phone and start a message to Sage to check up on her. I know she's seen some shit in her past, or so she's told me at work, but I don't think that kind of trauma covers witnessing a murder... or two. It's fair to say she'll never see that guy again, and I don't think a "get well soon" card will exactly cover it.

I glance in Eli's direction as he knocks on the door. Michelle has a charming three-story apartment on the water. She has good taste; I'll give her that. She probably didn't have to work a day in her life to get it, though.

I don't think Eli is one to apologize, but his father has a good relationship with Michelle's father, so he's most likely doing this out of respect. Not that I think Eli understands the meaning of the word.

In my peripheral view, I watch as she opens the door, surprised but delighted to see him. She immediately reaches for him, attempting to wrap her arms around his neck to pull him in, but he stops her.

I don't like the ugly smugness that rises within me, knowing that if I weren't in the picture, he would be up there fucking her.

Turning away because I don't like the way that makes me feel, I look back down at my phone. Michelle's voice raises, and she starts yelling at him. I ignore it.

I even contemplate calling Craig tonight since he's the only one who cares about my whereabouts or if I'm alive. Though if he knew about my current shitty predicament, I know he'd come to town looking for me himself.

My life is not interesting. I have no one to share it with. I wonder if that's exactly why Eli chose me. We only have to convince his family. I'm discardable. The moment I'm in the equation, I'll be out of it, and no one will think twice about it.

"Her?" Michelle yells furiously, stepping partway between her apartment door and the car. She looks at me in disbelief and then at Eli as if he's gone completely mad. I hate that I agree with her on that until I don't like how the bitch scrunches up her nose in disgust when she looks at me again. Then Eli moves, so he's blocking her view of me.

"Her? Really, Eli, you could do better. What could she possibly offer you that my family can't?"

Eli looks over his shoulder at me as if inquiring if I'll defend myself. I don't give a flying fuck what she thinks or says. Ain't my drama. I look back at my phone, but the moment he turns to speak to her again, I peek over my phone at them. I can't fucking help myself. I just wish I had popcorn. Instead, I pick at some cold fries.

"Michelle, you knew this was temporary. It was never going to work out. I liked to fuck you, that's all." Her mouth opens in shock, and then her hand goes to her hip as she pins him with a glare. I totally should not be here for any of this.

"Fuck me? You did more than fuck me, you asshole." I can't help but laugh at the use of the word asshole. Does everyone in his life call him that? "You think that's funny? You steal my man and think that's funny?"

"You can have him," I say around a mouthful of cold fries, knowing it pisses her type off epically.

"Now, Kitten, we don't share, remember. Or do you have to learn that lesson again?" Eli says with a raised brow.

Is that why he's doing this dramatic breakup thing in front of me? To show me... loyalty?

Monogamy? I almost choke on a fry. Me. Him. The two people in the world who are not built for that shit.

"You know he only fucked me a few weeks ago, right? And now you're engaged to him! Have you no shame?" she screams as she takes a few steps forward.

I pin Eli with a stare. What would a good wifey be expected to do at this moment? Because right now, I want to break her precious little nose if only to dull the headache she's creating.

"I'm aware," is all I say.

She scoffs. "Well, it won't last because you have nothing to offer the Monti family." She glares at Eli with tear-reddened eyes. "And then you'll come crawling back, and I might not be so nice as to take you back." She flips her long hair over her shoulder and walks toward the security guard, who now hovers at the door.

I wonder if she actually did love him and if I was just involved in breaking her heart. Then again, she never made a fuss about *him* leaving her but made a deal about the *Monti family*.

"Stop looking at her like that," Eli says as he approaches the car, seemingly unfazed.

"Did you care for her at all?" I ask as he comes to close my door.

"I liked to fuck her. Care? That's a strong word. I care for my family, that's it."

"So you wouldn't care if I walked in there right now with *your* gun and shot her point blank in the head?"

He scratches the stubble along his jaw contemplatively. A devilish smile works his lips as he leans into the car, his lips inches from mine.

"Would you fuck me after?"

I scoff at him. "No."

He shrugs and says, "Worth a shot," before closing the door.

When he reappears and sits in his seat, I say, "You have no shame."

He seems amused by that until I put my feet on the dash to feel more comfortable, and all his humor vanishes. "Remove your feet from my dash at once."

I sigh as I roll my eyes.

And the asshole is back.

TWENTY-ONE
ELI

Besides the blood on her polished floor, it's been a while since my mother has lectured me.

"You were reckless, Eli," she says, biting the edge of her nail. I know this lecture is going to be particularly bad because she came all the way from her firm this morning right before a big case. She's dressed in a business suit, and right now, I wish it were my father because there is nothing worse than my mother looking at me with disappointment.

My father sits comfortably across from me, almost smug that it's me getting in trouble and not him. They both barged into my apartment twenty minutes ago, waiting for their coffees first before blasting me.

She throws her arms in the air. "Are you even going to explain why you thought it was a good idea to shoot up a public restaurant? Do you know how much paperwork I've had to cover this morning just to solidify that your payoffs last night are ironclad?"

My father smirks behind her. Yeah, of course, he does because we both know that money and threats speak volumes, but my mother ensures everything is contracted and legally, or in some cases not-so-legally, binding.

Hawke and Ford are standing outside the room, and I know they're confused about last night. Hell, I can't even put a particular reason behind it. Not a sane one any way.

"I was teaching them a lesson," I simply say.

"The restaurant owners?" My mother arches an eyebrow.

"No, an... acquaintance."

I can see the cool calculation in both of their gazes. The problem with having incredibly educated and crafty parents is that you don't get away with much until you learn to be better than them.

"This doesn't have anything to do with Mr. Bedore calling me up about his daughter in hysterics after you broke up with her, does it?" my father asks.

"They were never dating," Mother says quickly, switching to my defense. Then she looks at me. "Wait, did you...? Why? Is this acquaintance a woman?"

My father perks up with interest now. It would be easy to tell them about Jewel, but something in me wants to keep it quiet, if only for another few days. To keep her to myself and assert complete dominance before I introduce her to my family because the moment they know about her, they'll start snooping, and I need to make sure Jewel thoroughly understands her part to play. If my parents know I'm tricking them with a marriage of convenience just for the business, it won't go down well.

"No. And did we not discuss a while ago that my business is my business?"

"If it's a woman, I think you should know they don't take kindly to shoot-ups in the middle of restaurants; it has no woo factor," my mother says, pinning my father with a disapproving glare.

If only she knew the woman in question lit up like a Christmas tree when she saw blood. Although, perhaps last night, she wasn't particularly fond of it.

"I disagree," my father says. "Lessons are to be taught. The most effective way is to scare someone into submission. If they know there are fates worse than death, they'll comply. Don't tell me you're still mad about me killing your boss, princess. That was almost thirty years ago."

She shakes her head disapprovingly and then takes

a sip of her coffee. "He is not the only person you killed because they got too close to me, Crue. What about the date I had before we were even together? You killed him in my apartment when I brought him home."

"And I'd do it again." His hands grip the chair tightly. Interesting. It's rather obvious who I take after in matters of conveying ownership.

She throws a hand in the air and looks at her watch. "I really have to go. This is a big case today, but this conversation is not over." My mother places a kiss on my cheek. Although she doesn't personally take too many cases nowadays, as she and my father have stepped into semi-retirement, she can't help take over the ones that excite her.

"Give us a moment," Father says to her. She looks between us and then takes her leave.

"If this is about the marriage thing, I—"

"Good job," he cuts in, and I'm stunned. "I would've done the same thing." I wonder then if he already knows about the little she-devil I've got on a leash. My parents are particularly good at discovering my secrets even before I'm ready to expose them. "I want you to take care of someone for me this evening."

He slides over a note. "He's late on payments." My eyebrows furrow when I look at the name. This is a business partner my father has been managing since the guy first stepped into New York. This task brings me an inch closer to the empire being entirely mine. "And don't worry about the Bedore family. We are kings in this city, and other families can only gain from us. Just don't stress your mother out."

I don't need to hear that from the man who has most likely given her more headaches than I ever have. But that's what it is to be the wife of a mafia head. I toss the note back and forth in my hand, considering. Maybe I should be putting my fiancée through some trials of her own with the same hardships.

TWENTY-TWO
JEWEL

I'm grateful Sage was surprisingly calm about the situation and didn't tell anyone at work about it. I've learned to go without friends all my life, and it wouldn't be difficult to stay that way, but while I'm in New York I'd like to keep at least one.

I'm so used to coming in and out of people's lives that it makes sense to not become attached. It's six in the evening when I return home from my shift, so I decide to call the only person who is irreplaceable to me. I put it on speaker as I shuffle out of my work clothes and put on some comfy jeans and a loose tank top. I fling my bra across the room, finally free.

Craig answers on the first ring. "Lonely in the big city, kid?"

"No, I just wanted to make sure your brain hasn't

rotted from all the television you're watching these days." I sit on my bed and cross my ankles. He chuckles, and I can't help but smile.

My room is still a mess from yesterday. The sunflowers are scattered about, and the ring box glares at me from the corner of the room. I should probably pick both up. "I just got myself into a predicament," I admit as I start biting the skin around my nails, an old habit I tried to kick but can't seem to do. Especially lately.

"Hopefully not boy trouble." He laughs, and I stay silent. "Oh."

"Yeah." I sigh. "Boy trouble is the worst." I roll my eyes. But "boy trouble" doesn't seem to define what's going on between me and Eli.

"His name?" Craig asks, and I can just imagine him walking over to his computer now, ready to search for everything he can on the man. But I have a feeling Craig won't have to do much research. I feel the weight of his name on my tongue. I'm nervous to say it out loud because it's as if I'm admitting to how much shit I've gotten myself into.

Last night, I was tipsy. Now I'm sober. The last forty-eight hours have been a whirlwind, and I can't help but feel I'm being further backed into a cage.

"Eli Monti," I finally say.

His breathing pauses.

"Jewel," he growls out.

"I know."

"He's your target. Why are you involved with your target? You know better than that."

"He stole my guns," I say the words in a rush because he's the only person in the world I can trust to have my back no matter what. He's the only other person who knows how important those guns are to me.

"How did he get hold of your guns? Did he find out you were hired to kill him and is blackmailing you to turn on your client or something?" He sighs. "You got messy on this one. Why didn't you just take the shot when you had the chance?"

I haven't told Craig the full story about what the client requested—that I toy with Eli and gather information about his family. I'm barely floating through the situations Eli drags me through, let alone having the time to think how the fuck I'm going to get out of this mess.

"That's not all," I say, swallowing and glancing back over to the ring box that I haven't yet opened. The moment I say the next words, I know it'll be set in stone. That I'm royally fucked. "I'm engaged to Eli Monti."

I hear something drop, and know he's already pacing the room. I bite the skin surrounding my nails, holding my breath. I know his mind is working busily, just like mine, but I haven't had time to fucking think. Eli Monti is all-consuming.

"How? How can you be engaged to this man?"

"He stole my guns, and in order to get them back, he wants a contract where I marry him. He'll pay me as well... fifty million dollars."

"Fucking hell, Jewel, you should have put the bullet in his head the minute he discovered your identity. Fifty million isn't a small amount, but is it really worth marrying into a mafia family? And you'll have a target on your back for reneging on your client's terms. It'll ruin your career. Just kill the fucker and forget about the guns. I have one of your father's guns here. I'll let you have that."

"It's not his favorite one, though," I say quietly. No, his favorite is the Barrett M82. It's the same sniper rifle I've used for all my long-distance shots. Defeated, I admit, "He also stole one of the knives you gave me for my birthday last year."

"I don't give a fuck about the knives, Jewel. And your father wouldn't care about his guns either. His favorite were the guns that kept you safe. Not when they're putting you in danger."

I wipe my eyes even though there are no tears coming out. The last time I cried was at his funeral, and I'll be fucked if I let a man like Eli Monti push me so far into a corner to break me all over again.

I know something like my guns might seem silly to others, but they're literally all I have. I didn't have a happy upbringing. I had a mother who looked at me with disgust and a father who taught me how to survive in a man's world. And then I was left behind to make my way through that world. There is no one and nothing left for me.

Only that gun collection... and Craig.

"End it. Don't dig yourself deeper," Craig says carefully.

I feel tired. It's been so long since I've actually made a kill shot that I miss the empowering buzz. I feel less than mortal lately, and it fucking sucks. But one thing I adamantly cannot do is let anyone else win. I'll die with my fucking pride. I won't back down just because Eli thinks he can take from me and control me. I roll my shoulders defiantly. No man will break me—especially not a Monti.

"I want them, Craig. I'll do the job, and once it's done, I won't ever come back to this city," I say more to myself than him. I love Craig, and I usually take his advice. But the guns? They are non-negotiable. And I hate that Eli figured that out so quickly.

"Use those brains your father gave you. Don't be reckless," he implores. I smirk at that because we both know reckless is my middle name. A knock on the front door startles me. Jenny isn't here to answer it, so I jump off my bed.

"Thanks, Craig. I'll keep you updated. If you don't hear from me, I'm probably dead."

"That's not even funn—" I hang up on him as I open the door, and my stomach drops through the floor. *What the fuck?*

The woman standing before me wears a pinstripe suit and black heels, and her hair is perfectly tied back. Those almost silver eyes stare back at me, and I'm in shock as I look at the powerful woman who was on the television only hours ago, discussing matters of her recently closed case.

Rya fucking Monti is standing at my door.

Her gaze sweeps up me, though it gives nothing away. "Jewel Diamond?"

"Speaking." Embarrassment rushes through me. "I mean, yes, that's me, ma'am." *Ma'am? Why the fuck am I calling her ma'am?*

She quirks a tight smile.

If I thought Eli was intimidating, he has nothing on his mother.

She steps into my apartment without invitation, which is apparently something that must run in their family.

"Do you know who I am?" she asks, looking around. She doesn't seem as amused as her son was only days ago when he first walked in.

Fuck, why is she here? Does she know about the hit on her son?

"Yes." I nod. "You're Mrs. Monti."

"Good. And I know who you are. So, why are you marrying my son?" Her heavy gaze slides back over to me and then down to the bare ring finger on my left hand.

Shit. Talk about putting a woman on the spot. How do I tell her I'm only marrying her son because he offered me a large sum of money and he stole all my guns? I'm sure that's not the story he wants me to tell her. And to be honest, I hate lying, but it's something I'm going to have to do if I ever want to see my guns again. It doesn't make it any easier to square up against this woman who oozes intimidation and a cunning intellect.

Or maybe it's because I've never had to deal with anyone's mother.

"He asked me," I say simply, which is the truth, so technically I'm not lying.

"Yes, I gathered that much. But it's unlike my son to keep secrets. Especially of this magnitude. Are you the reason he killed two men in the restaurant last night and finally got rid of the Bedore girl?"

I try not to show my surprise at her clear dislike for Michelle. Okay, maybe I could like Rya a little more as a badass bitch. But right now, as the mother of my... fiancé, she's really busting my balls.

When I don't speak, she considers me. "My son, although headstrong, is not usually so reckless. Or he's better at hiding his misdeeds."

"That's a polite way to say his murders," I joke.

A silence fills the air, but the corners of her lips twitch.

"Would you like to explain how you found this address, Mother?" Eli's voice booms from the doorway.

Oh, fuck me. Is this family reunion day? I don't know if I can handle Eli Monti in here as well. I should've shut the door behind her, but I didn't think she'd be here for so long.

Rya picks at an imaginary piece of fluff on her suit jacket.

"You were acting strange this morning, so I looked into it, and it led to me discovering a recently purchased ring and this address you've now frequented more than once. Including last night. And it would appear Jewel hasn't denied being your fiancée, which confirms my suspicions." Damn, I walked straight into her confession without even realizing it. How am I feeling like the misplaced one in my own home right now? "Why didn't you tell us you were dating someone, let alone how serious it is?"

This time, her gaze lands on her son, and I can see the hurt there. I say nothing as Eli walks over to me and slides his hand around my back. I want to throttle this asshole since he's the one who put me in this uncomfortable situation in the first place.

"Jewel and I wanted to enjoy a few days together in peace before the chaos unfolded," he lies.

She seems somewhat sympathetic to the issue. But not so much so that she didn't take matters into her own hands. "I wanted to meet her." Her gaze flicks to me and then back to Eli. "To make sure you aren't making a mistake. You know what it means to make this public."

I should be offended, but I'm not because I know it has nothing to do with me and everything to do with the amount of pressure they must carry with the Monti name. I still don't give a fuck.

"You think I have the capability to make a

mistake?" he asks. I scoff at that, and both of them turn their attention to me. My eyes open wider when I realize my noise was audible.

"No, son. I know I raised you right. But not everyone has good intentions," she says matter-of-factly. And I can attest that I am the definition of not having good intentions toward her son.

"Next week, we'll set up a dinner. You can sit down and grill Jewel all you want. But for this week, Mother, we want it kept private. Just to enjoy each other before everyone else takes hold." He leans in and kisses his mother's cheek. When he pulls away, she nods her head agreeably.

"Pleasure, Jewel. I look forward to getting to know you. I'm sure you're aware that our family is... a little different."

"Oh, I can tell how different your son is," I reply with a sweet smile that doesn't reach my eyes. Nevertheless, it seems to humor her, and she takes her leave. The moment Eli closes the door behind her, he grabs my left hand.

"Why aren't you wearing the ring? Please don't tell me you hocked it with my watches."

I pull back my hand. "I'll have you know, I have better things to do than admire all the pretty things I steal from you. I don't orbit around your existence."

"Jewel," he growls. "Where is the ring?" He storms past me and into my bedroom. I sigh, my shoulders sagging. Here, I thought I'd have a delightful evening with me and my vibrator. "On the floor? Really? And why are these flowers scattered all over the place? Are sunflowers not your favorite anymore?"

He's making a fuss in my room as he basically starts cleaning it. I lean against the doorframe, smirking at the way he's all flustered. If I keep acting like a slob, he might break the engagement off just for that alone.

He shakes his head, frustrated with the mess, and opens the box in front of me. It's the first time I'm seeing the blue square-cut diamond that's twice the size of my fingernail with a white gold band. Damn, that's excessive.

He reaches for my hand, but I immediately pull back. "Jewel. A deal is a deal, is it not?" he asks, raising a brow. A shiver runs down my spine, and I feel like I'm breaking out in a rash.

I don't want it.

I know it's a façade, but even so... I don't want to belong to anyone.

"Now that my mother knows about us, it'll only raise suspicions if you're not wearing a ring. Fight *with* me, not *against* me, if you want your guns back," he says. I try to swallow the lump that seems lodged in my throat.

"Get on your knees," I find myself saying.

"Sorry?" His eyebrows shoot up. It's as if the command is so foreign, and he's never had a person in his life tell him what to do. So I lean into it comfortably.

"On your knees. If you're proposing, you'll do it properly," I tell him, hoping my demand will be enough for him to end this ridiculousness.

He seems to contemplate the power play for a moment, then slowly drops to his knee, and my heart stops. Eli stares up at me. He opens his mouth and then closes it. Just when I think he won't do it, he clears his throat and looks at me with determination. He holds my left hand in his as he lifts the ring between us. "Jewel Diamond, would you do me the honor of becoming my wife?"

I can't breathe. And for once, he actually asked. Didn't command or demand.

"I'd rather not," I say, attempting the most neutral tone possible and failing miserably.

His jaw tics. "Work *with* me here, not *against* me," he says again as he slides the ring onto my finger. I expect to go up in flames the moment it touches my skin, but nothing happens. In fact, I can't look away from it. I also notice the way Eli strokes my hand as if trying to offer comfort.

It might as well be a collar around my neck.

"Would you like me to do something else while I'm down on my knees in front of you, *fiancée*?"

I smile as I feather my fingers through his hair and pull him up so he's standing. He chuckles as I tug on his hair. "No. I would like you to leave now, *fiancé*."

When I release him, he takes a step back but doesn't leave. I'm too preoccupied staring at the ring to berate him about it.

He sits cross-legged on my bed expectantly.

"Get your boots off my bed; that's disgusting." I smack his foot.

"It's not so nice, is it?" he cockily says, and I realize he intentionally did it because I put my feet on his dashboard last night. "We need to get our basics in order before we publicly announce our engagement. My parents have been wanting me to marry for a while now, but with how suddenly I've organized this myself, they might be slightly suspicious. Under no circumstances can they know this is a temporary arrangement. We need to get our story straight before dinner with my family because they *will* grill you."

"I know enough about you," I state. "Where you like to go, who you like to fuck."

He grabs my wrist with lightning speed and pulls me onto his lap. His fingers feather through my hair and then twist, keeping me in place.

"Yes, we've established how you like to watch," he says in a gravelly voice, and I try to slow my racing heart. My fake fiancé shouldn't have this kind of effect on me, especially because I hate everything about him.

His cock thickens and gradually pushes more firmly against my ass. Electricity dances along my skin as I think about how he had me pinned against the wall last night. How his fingers felt inside of me at Lucy's. My gaze dips to his lips. *Nope, I can't do this again.* When I look back into his eyes, I realize he's staring at my lips as he says, "What's my favorite meal?"

I can't even think straight as his cock continues to strain against his pants and against me.

"How the fuck am I supposed to know?" I whisper.

"One day, it'll be your cunt," he says, and heat flashes straight to my core.

It'd be so easy. Too easy to slip into this tension and let him ravish me. But I can't let him win.

Can I?

"You wish," I say, but it's barely a whisper.

He kicks up an arrogant smile as he loosens his grip around my hair but keeps me in place. His hand trails to my exposed midriff and finds the edge of the tattoo.

He runs his thumb over it, and goose bumps erupt over my skin.

"I cooked it for you the other day," he says distractedly, clearly more interested in my tattoo.

"The chicken?" I ask, and he nods.

I wonder what it would be like if his fingers trailed lower if I just gave in to this tension and got him out of my system.

"My grandfather used to make it for me." I remain silent, and he meets my eyes, licking his lips. "What's yours?"

"I'm vegan," I say with a grin.

A slow smile spreads on his face, and it's hard to believe this man is a monster. Something so brilliant and beautiful is truly criminal. "You're such a fucking liar."

I swallow hard.

"Cinnamon roll," I admit, unsure where to put my hands. I don't want to put them anywhere on him because I'm not sure if I'll be able to control myself, so I put them on my legs, and I hate how submissive it makes me feel. He seems to notice.

"Why?" he asks.

I sigh, uncomfortable with all the questions. "Do we really have to do this?"

"Yes. Unless you plan on fucking this up for the

both of us and not getting your guns back." And the asshole has come back with a vengeance. All my curiosity about his very hard cock pressing into my jeans is gone. But I suppose it doesn't matter telling him this much. It won't do anything to hurt me.

"My father would take me out on Saturdays for shooting practice. He would get a coffee for himself and a hot chocolate for me, and the cinnamon roll would be a treat we shared. My father was strict when it came to eating clean and nurturing the body. So every time I think of the cinnamon roll I think of a treat and my time spent with him."

I grow irritated at the idea that I'm becoming more vulnerable around him bit by bit.

I hate that I told him that.

I hate that I took this job.

I want my guns back, and I want to leave.

Fuck this city, and fuck Eli Monti.

"You get these hard lines on your forehead when you're mad at me, did you know?" He lightly flicks my forehead. I swat his hand away and flip him off.

"So why don't we make a lasting memory? Join me for a job this evening."

"I'm busy." I go to push off him, but he holds me in place. He grabs my jaw, and his thumb strokes against it gently. And I know I'm royally fucked with Eli because I should not be attracted to the man currently holding me prisoner in his arms, let alone sitting on his *very* hard cock right now.

"What if I told you it involves guns?" he asks in a mischievous tone. I can feel the excitement light within me, but try my hardest to cover it.

"What job?" I ask nonchalantly. His rough thumb trails over my bottom lip, and I inhale a sharp breath.

"Just a boring debt collection."

I roll my eyes. "How very mafia of you."

"How very smartass of you. I'll even reward you with a gift of your liking."

I lean back skeptically. "What's the catch?"

"You're my fiancée; there is no catch."

"The catch is being your fiancée," I sass back.

The corner of his mouth tilts upward just a bit. "You can't tell me you're not the least bit curious about mafia things, Kitten." He leans in and inhales my scent. "You reek of recklessness and poor choices."

I can't help but chuckle as I push against him. "Aww, my fiancé really sees me. Still sounds stupid if you ask me."

"Yeah, well, I didn't. You might want to put those tight leathers on again." He slowly pushes me off and heads for the door, adjusting his cock on his way out, expecting me to follow him. I wring my hands in the air, wanting to throttle this asshole. Then the ring catches the light, and I'm reminded all over again of the horror show of being someone's fiancée.

I stare at his broad back as he looks around the living room once again. I guess he's used to people following him and still hasn't realized I'm not the type.

TWENTY-THREE
JEWEL

I followed, not because I wanted to but because my life literally hinges on it.

I need to learn more about Eli and his family if I intend to get myself out of this situation. That, and I figured it didn't hurt to blow off some steam, assuming Eli wasn't lying about there being some kind of gunplay. That usually brings my twitchy nerves to a standstill.

I also know tonight is when he usually conducts business at Lucy's, which might give me time to slip into his mansion and see if I can find my guns. He's hiding them somewhere, and that seems like a good place to start searching. Tonight would also usually be when he'd go and pay his fuck buddy a visit, who I can assume isn't happy about the ring on my finger and the bold declaration he made last night.

Then again, he's a man with needs, and I'm hell-bent on ensuring I'm not the one taking care of them.

Our car ride is filled mostly with him providing me with his likes and dislikes. And I answer some in return, as long as it's something that doesn't go too deep. The questions that feel too personal, I just don't answer.

Without warning or context, Eli pulls over to a seafood restaurant on the wharf. It's the only one here, and at five in the evening, it still seems closed. Only a few cars are parked outside, which most likely belong to employees. I immediately get the sense this isn't an ordinary restaurant.

Eli leans over and puts his hand between my legs with an arrogant smile. I don't even flinch as he pulls a small bag out from beneath my seat. When he unzips it, I see an array of guns and knives inside.

Well, fuck me. I wish I knew that was under my seat this entire time because I might've blown his brains out on the way here, especially for that arrogant smile he's sporting as if knowing my train of thought.

"Take this, and don't be too tempted to use it on me, Kitten. Be prepared for my family to hunt you down and kill you if you do. And trust me, they will find you no matter where you are." He hands me a gun, and I slip it into the waistband of my jeans. I purposefully didn't wear my leather, now that I know how much he appreciates the view. I couldn't come entirely willingly. "Besides, the moment you turn against me during our little treaty, I will destroy your guns."

"You can't do that if you're dead," I remind him. It's as if this fucker keeps forgetting that I've been hired to kill him. However, I can't say I won't hesitate when the order to take him out finally comes... just because I really need my guns back.

"Ah, but I can. I've ordered the twins to take care of it if something happens to me," he says as we step out of the car.

"Of course, you have," I say with an eye roll. He circles the car and stands in front of me, squeezing my cheeks in his hands.

"Roll your eyes at me one more fucking time, and I will spank you," he warns.

"Keep touching me without permission, and I'll make sure to put laxatives in your drink next time," I bite back, though it's barely understandable because of how hard he's squeezing my cheeks. He kicks up a smile.

"This might get a bit crazy, dear. Consider this your first wifey trial." He releases my cheeks, and before I can reply with a smart-ass remark, I notice the shift in his demeanor. Any type of playfulness is gone, and the monster has come to the surface.

Okay, we *are* on some serious mafia business shit.

He strides toward the restaurant, and I follow, not entirely sure what to expect. Are we just here to scare some people? Trade some things? Anything is possible with Eli Monti.

A bulky man, who is definitely not a host, opens the door for us. It's clear he's some kind of security guard, and as I do a sweep of the room, there is no doubt in my mind that we've just walked into some kind of thug den. However, it is an actual restaurant. Smoke assaults my nostrils, and when I look back at our only means of escape, I realize the windows are blacked out. That explains why you can't see in.

Eli walks straight up to the three large men sitting at a table playing poker. I trail six steps behind him, and the slight buzz of adrenaline fills me.

I hate to admit it, but Eli knows how to woo a woman.

The thrill of not knowing what we're about to get ourselves into drives excitement and anticipation into me hard, and I beg for there to be some kind of action. Some sort of release from the mundane life I've become stagnant in over the last month. Well, until a certain mafia heir made it his mission to turn my world upside down.

The men playing cards look up at him, and then, just as quickly, they dismiss him, as if he isn't one of the most powerful men in the city. From everything I've gathered from watching him, he is just as deadly as his father. But from the way they're treating him, it's as if they aren't pleased he's here instead of his father, and I have an acute sense that it has something to do with his age.

These men look well into their sixties.

"Boy, why did you come?" One of them finally addresses him, still with a lack of respect for not meeting his gaze. The old man brings a glass of golden liquid to his lips as he studies his hand of cards.

"Well, Dee, you owe money, and you're overdue," Eli replies.

The man named Dee huffs out a puff of smoke before putting his cigar out and finally turns to Eli.

"You've been coming in here for years, doing your daddy's dirty work. And I pay, do I not?"

"You do, but you always push your limits. And, frankly, Dee, the only reason I haven't put a bullet in your head yet is because my father asked that I don't. But I want to make something very clear; he isn't in charge right now."

Dee seems amused by this as he snorts a chuckle. "What, have you hit puberty or something, boy?" Dee clicks his fingers, and two men—clearly not chefs—come out from the kitchen on the right and advance toward Eli. The two security guys who were hovering around the door move in on us from behind.

Adrenaline comes in short bursts as my heartbeat picks up speed. Holy shit, we might have a fight on our hands after all. There is a different thrill to close combat. I prefer long distance because it ensures my safety while providing the same level of satisfaction in killing someone at close range. But close-up evokes an entirely different type of high. Because my life is on the line. I wish I wasn't into it, but it's when I feel most alive.

"I don't take kindly to threats in my own home," Dee explains as his men advance on us.

Now, the other two men at the table finally give us their attention, but they don't seem concerned, just curious about the scene currently unfolding.

The mistake the security guys make, however, is only targeting Eli. Only one them even spared me a glance, dismissing me just as quickly. It's always the same; men don't take me as a serious threat until it's too late. One of the men who walked out of the kitchen raises his gun to point at Eli's head.

"Perhaps there needs to be a change in the Monti hierarchy if you're next in line. You need to show your elders respect. I should kill you where you stand," Dee says casually, as if he's offering some kind of great insight.

"But then you would make my fiancée very mad," Eli replies, and it's then they seem to actually take notice of me. Dee's eyebrows dip in puzzlement, probably because of my sudden introduction and how irrelevant he most likely finds it. Again, he might find out too late his mistake of overlooking me.

"Sorry, you picked a dead man walking, sweetheart. We'll be sure to bury you together."

Eli looks over his shoulder at me expectantly, seemingly unfazed, with the gun to his head.

"Fucking hell, do I really have to join in?" I ask exasperatedly. I'm not above being involved with mafia business, but my father would be rolling in his grave with what's about to happen. And, as usual, there's always a risk to my life. That's why my heart is pounding in my chest, and my breathing deepens as the tingles begin to shift over my body.

Target. Target. Target.

"You want your guns, don't you?" Eli asks, smiling.

I want many things. My guns, especially. But right now, I want to walk out of here alive. My body ignites with the killer instinct that my mother always disapproved of. The part of me that I was told was unnatural and vulgar. That society would frown upon. My father encouraged it, though he tried to direct it in a military fashion. Maybe I was a disappointment to both of them. And yet, this man is coaxing it out so effortlessly. It brings a sadistic smile to my face that I don't entirely understand. I finally look back to the man in charge.

"I'm sorry, Mr. Dee, but unfortunately, I still have use for my fiancé." His forehead furrows in confusion before I lift my gun, and chaos explodes.

TWENTY-FOUR
ELI

I had a feeling she was lethal, but seeing her in action makes my cock hard, even when I have a gun pointed at my head. Watching the quick change in her personality is the sexiest and most powerful thing I've ever seen. In the blink of an eye, she goes from an unassuming female to a feral animal and she raises the gun with a sickly-sweet smile.

The moment I see her gaze light up with killer intent, I match it. With lightning speed, I grab the hand holding the gun to my head and steal the weapon, a basic maneuver that catches him by surprise. I hear the first shot go off as she takes out the man to my left and then spins to the one closest to her. He doesn't even have time to get his gun out before he drops to the floor.

I put the barrel of the gun to the head of the man who held it to mine and pull the trigger. As the two elderly men beside Dee pull out their own guns, I shoot twice, hitting them each in the center of their forehead as Dee cowers.

I twist around to cover Jewel's back, and we shoot at the same time, one of us hitting the man in the chest and the other in his head. Within seconds, the only three remaining alive in the room are my fake fiancée, the old man who thought it was okay to undermine my authority, and me.

Her gaze sweeps the room, and when she turns toward me, we immediately raise our gun to one another's head. Those amber eyes light up with the savage nature of the tigress I often see within her, pacing back and forth, waiting to be unleashed.

So fucking beautiful.

So fucking mine.

"I'm so happy you're going to be my wife," I say with an arrogant smile. Fuck me, my cock is rock hard, and I need a release. The scent of blood fills the room, and all I want to do is drive hard into her pussy as we roll around in the carnage we've just created together.

"Fuck you," she spits back. I can sense the adrenaline coursing through her veins. It's a test, really, because I've intentionally turned my back to Dee, wondering if she will truly cover me if he pulls out his own gun. Her gaze drifts over to him enough times for me to suspect the answer may be yes.

I step into her space and slowly lower my gun. "I'll take that back now," I say as I go to pluck the gun from her hand. She's hesitant to release it as if I'm taking away all her fun. And I only want to pull her closer to me. To suffocate and consume that wild creature within.

"How can I protect you if I don't have it?" she asks with a sinister smile.

"It's not him I am concerned about turning my back on," I confess as I take it from her. She inhales a sharp breath as if surprised by my praise. "Besides, I never needed protection. I could have taken them all. But I had to test you, Kitten."

"You're such an asshole," she mumbles as I turn back to Dee, who is staring at his men lying dead on the floor.

If only she knew how much I loved the way she calls me that. "You can head for the car now, Kitten. I'll finish up here."

She throws her hand in the air, clearly pissed, and I can understand her frustration. I know what it's like to be on a high with no targets left to release it.

"This is bullshit. You owe me a new outfit now; I'm

covered in blood," she grumbles as she exits the building. I stare after her, a cord in my neck straining with how far my neck twists as I watch her tight ass walk out of the restaurant.

"Now, I'm going to make this extremely quick. You deal with me now, Dee. If I choose to kill you and your family, I will. What you said today about my family was blasphemy. But I'm willing to overlook it as long as we come to a fair agreement." I'm not actually willing to overlook it. I intend to kill him. But first, there's money to be made. Once the agreements are made and signed, he'll be dead within the week.

I don't pardon treachery or disloyalty.

My lethal edge is only diluted by the fact that I want to keep this short so I can bury myself in the woman who is waiting for me outside. A gentle buzz hums under my skin, singing my praise and victory.

"Anything you want," he says quickly as he looks at his deceased partners with wide eyes. If memory serves correctly, I think they were his cousins. Doesn't matter.

"Excellent. As of today, we take sixty percent of your current dealings, and for any new businesses you conduct, we will take thirty percent."

"That's extortion!" he snaps.

I raise the gun to his head. "A dead man can't complain from the grave."

His bottom lip wobbles, and rage fills his expression. He clears his throat. "Very well. A word of advice, boy: Making enemies along your path is not the way to go."

"Who said we're enemies, Dee? I just don't give leniency, and I like money."

What perfect timing considering I recently discovered he's gone into business with a motorcycle club in Boston, The Boston Delinquents that I have every intention of digging into their money streams.

"I'll send the details over, and I very much suggest you don't do anything rash. No matter how many men you have, I'll bring an army to destroy everything you own and love. It'll be more than just me and my fiancée coming to clean up this mess if there's a next time."

He goes to speak but thinks better of it and says nothing.

"Now, if you'll excuse me, it appears I have to take my fiancée shopping because your men's blood got on her clothes."

TWENTY-FIVE
JEWEL

The moment Eli steps out of the restaurant, I shoot. The window closest to him explodes, but he barely flinches. I quite like the gun that was left in the bag under my seat.

It's dark and eerily quiet in the parking lot, but I can still see the unimpressed look he gives me and hear the waves crashing on the shore in the distance.

"If you were going to kill me, you wouldn't have missed," he states confidently, his long strides eating the distance between us until he stops directly in front of me and grabs the wrist of my hand holding the gun. He slams me against the car, and I'm startled but fight against him in equal measure. Adrenaline zips through me, and the air crackles around us as we battle for dominance. He pushes his hips against me, and my lips part in surprise at the bulging pressure of his cock behind his pants.

"Did you have fun in there, Kitten?"

"A little heads-up would have been appreciated," I say, trying my hardest to ignore the tingles erupting along my skin.

"See how fucking hard you make me?" he growls. A pool of heat floods my core, and a low rhythm begins to hum between my thighs. His gaze skitters over my features, and then he steps away. "I don't want anyone else seeing you flushed like this. Get in the car."

I'm surprised by the sudden switch. Wait. Did I want something else to happen? My body is a confusing, flustered mix of need and excitement. Where shooting usually gives me a high and then a calm, relaxed feeling, I currently feel like I'm on fire with no way to put it out.

I take my seat and buckle the seat belt, fidgety in the car because of the endorphin rush.

He doesn't even bother with his own seat belt as the car fishtails on the slippery road as he takes off.

"I can see the look on your face. You get a high after killing, just like me," he says.

My gaze dips to his cock. "I don't," I lie. He's driving at such a fast speed, I have no idea where he's even taking me, but I can't stop looking at him. My body is coated with a buzz that I can't shake off, and it has something to do with this powerful man beside me, pushing against me with a level of tension I've never competed against.

A natural born killer.

"Are you sure? Because if you're anything like me, fucking after you kill is the best damn high."

"I'm not fucking you." But it's barely a whisper, and my thighs clench together automatically. He definitely notices it, and I can hardly push down the lump in my throat. I'm fighting against myself now for every fiber of control. What fucking spell has he put me under?

I have never fucked anyone after firing my guns. And the men I've fucked in the past have all been one-night stands.

"Well, I would like to fuck you," he states, sharply turning the car. We veer off the road, and he slams hard on the brakes before we hit a line of trees. He turns to me then. The moon beaming down, and the dim interior lighting cast an unholy shadow across his features.

He's as terrifying as he is beautiful.

My heart is pounding, and I can't look away. My pussy is throbbing, and I'm crippled under his intensity.

"Can we call a truce for ten minutes?" he asks breathlessly.

"A truce?" I question, staring at his lips.

"A release," he promises. "Let's finish what we started that night at Lucy's before you ran like a coward."

I internally tense at his provocation. Before I can speak, he orders, "Get out of the car." And then he's hefting himself out of his seat and rounding the hood, rushing to open my door. I realize with sudden clarity that the palpable tension I felt before wasn't one-sided. The only reason he drove us farther down the road was so there would be no threat if we were distracted.

My heart is pounding in my chest. My head logically knows I should fight him on this. If I give in, I'll only be giving him what he wants. Handing over my power. But another side of me thirsts to feed off him. To taste a man that powerful and have his carnal urges dance with mine. I've never been with a man like him before, and I have the sense it'll ruin me.

Hell, I'm already ruined.

He holds his hand out to me, and I try to moisten my mouth, the buzz from the kill still at an all-time high. I'm not thinking straight as I unclip the seat belt.

"You owe me a favor if I do this," I say.

He smiles wickedly. "Forever negotiating. I'll give

you anything but your guns. Now, put your lips on my cock." He takes my hand and yanks me into him. The calm rhythm of the ocean waves in the background and the moon shining down on us are opposite to the carnal tension crackling between us.

I should run.

His hand grips tightly onto my hip, and he slams me against him so I can feel his erection. A small moan escapes me, and I'm crazy to think I could pull away from this now. He pins me against the car, his hand scooping under my ass as I balance on top of his cock. For a moment, we just stare at one another, unsure of what to do. Some kind of new awakening happening in both of us.

It's hard to think clearly through the haze of desire, but I'm certain of one thing: I want this man.

Even though I shouldn't.

"Don't take it personally when I have to kill you, okay?" I say breathlessly.

His fingers possessively feather through my hair, and he holds me captive with a devilish smile. "You can try to kill me as many times as you want. Nothing is keeping me away from this pussy that belongs to *me*."

And then his lips are on mine. An explosion of stimulation bombards me as his primal nature meets mine. His tongue presses against mine, and I'm caged entirely, forced to take him. All of him. It's not just a kiss; it's an utter claim.

I wrap my arms around his neck, pulling him closer, a small moan escaping me.

I want him.

I need him.

I need him to calm this fiery buzz under my skin. Everything he touches comes to life. Our mouths are so desperate for each other, it's like we're fighting over the same pocket of air.

Fuck. I'm in trouble.

Heat pools at my core as I fight him for dominance in our kiss. I'm shoving up his shirt when I feel cool air on my back as he carries me around to the hood and lays me down on it. He doesn't break the kiss as he discards his jacket, throwing it to the ground.

I lift my hips as he undoes my jeans. I desperately unbutton his shirt, praying he can calm whatever this reckless energy is within me. I'm feeding off him like he's the only solution.

Our lips break apart as he yanks down my jeans and drops them next to his jacket. He stands over me, his shirt and hair a mess, as he stares at me like a rabid beast. His nostrils flare when he notices the red lace I'm wearing. My gaze lands on the small sheath strapped at his hip, and he notices.

"Are your claws not enough, Kitten?" he taunts, slowly undoing his belt, teasing me with a leisurely pace I can't stand. "Show me those beautiful tits."

"How certain are you that I won't kill you?" I ask with a wicked grin as I remove my top, revealing the matching red bralette.

He removes the sheath and then his shirt. He continues holding the blade as he pushes down his pants and my pussy floods at the sight of his thick cock. I've seen his dick before—even taken numerous photos of it—but it's not until this moment, with him standing in front of me, that I get my first up close and personal view of it. He's massive. Veins aggressively bulging under smooth skin.

He purposefully and slowly unsheathes the knife, and my heart rate picks up with the unknown mixture of excitement and danger. I hitch my feet farther up the front of the car so he has a clear view of my soaked panties. He steps between my legs, his gaze sweeping up my body.

"You're so fucking beautiful."

My heart falters in surprise.

His thumb firmly presses against the neon blue tattoo on my hip as he stares at all of me as if memorizing every inch. His hand wraps around my waist and grips me tightly as if he's unable to contain his strength.

He raises the blade to the same hip as the tattoo, and I inhale as I watch him slice it through the thin waistband of the panties.

He intentionally pricks the tip of the blade into my skin, and I suck in a breath as a trickle of blood blooms on my skin. I'm so attuned to his every caress, the pinprick momentarily the only thing I can feed on, feeling like a release in itself.

And then he flips the knife in his hand and catches it with ease, offering it to me by the handle.

"I don't think you're ready to kill me yet, Kitten," he says as he holds the knife out to me.

I curl my fingers around it slowly. Everything about me feels so wrapped up in him, as if I don't know where one of us starts and the other ends because Eli is an enigma. An entity I know I shouldn't be drawn toward but undeniably am.

As he leans over me, I raise the knife very slowly to his throat, and a sensual smile spreads over his lips. "Why don't you drop the knife, Kitten, so that I can have my taste."

I make no move to do as he suggests. And he just leans over farther, edging his throat along the blade. I watch, mesmerized at the small red line that appears at his jugular. But it's his eyes that draw me back in —a striking silver in the moonlight.

"Something tells me you don't want me to remove the knife."

He grins arrogantly as his fingers trail up my inner thigh, and a shudder rolls through me. His lips brush against mine once again, pressing himself harder against the blade in the process.

"I'm almost certain you don't want to fuck a dead man tonight."

"Then don't die," I sass back, then sharply inhale as he stuffs my pussy with two fingers. His lips crash against mine as he takes my breath, and I'm stimulated by the two new pressures: thirsting, craving, and needing an outlet. All this energy buzzing inside me needs to be purged, and I know Eli is the only one who can take it.

He bites at my lip as the knife knicks him again, a slight growl coming from him, and I moan, hungrily wanting and needing more of that. I edge the knife in deeper, and when I do, his other hand wraps around my throat, cutting off my air supply in warning to not dig any deeper.

I'm being consumed by him as he breathes hotly against my lips. "Look how fucking wet you are for me already, Kitten. Such a good fucking girl."

He steps out of my reach, and I snarl in irritation until my gaze locks on his very hard cock as he begins to stroke it. Blood trickles down his neck as he grabs hold of my ankle and yanks me down the front of the car. I almost fall off, but he raises my ass in the air as he hovers at my entrance.

"Do you want this cock to fill you?" he asks, still lazily stroking himself. My pussy is pounding to be filled, and I'm not so much of a saint that I can ignore my bodily desires.

"Yes," I confess.

His eyebrow arches, beautifully split in two with the scar. "Such a fucking good girl." He rubs his cock against my folds, and we both stare in bewilderment. How the fuck is he supposed to fit inside me?

"Did you have fun killing all those men today?" he asks as he spreads my juices over his erection. I breathe heavily, my body shaking with adrenaline.

"It's written all over your face. We are the same, Kitten, whether you like to admit it or not. The thrill of the kill. The energy of the high. Needing that release afterward."

"It's a truce only this once," I breathe, wriggling restlessly, trying to edge him into me.

He kicks up an arrogant smile. "You keep telling yourself that, Kitten." He grabs my hip, and I hold my breath. "Look at me when I impale you with my cock," he demands, and I do exactly as he says.

The pain is so sharp and explosive that I grunt from the sheer size of him. I wrap my arms around his neck for support as he holds me in place. This fucking man. This enigma. I can't stop staring into his eyes because it's like he sees every bit of me, and that's as terrifying as it is exhilarating.

He pulls out and then hits the same spot again, triggering another hiss that quietly falls into a moan. He takes my lips again, and the fucking becomes desperate as we devour one another's grunts and groans. I don't usually kiss, but this otherworldly god demands his tribute.

The blade in my hand knicks his shoulder, and he hisses as he bites my lip, dragging his teeth along it as he pulls back. He stares down at me. I can taste blood on my tongue as a silent communication passes between us.

I adjust my hand, holding the knife, hooking it around his side, and angling the blade toward his back. "Do you like this?" I ask, dragging the tip from one shoulder to the other. He grunts, his pupils dilating, and he looks like he's about to kill me.

But then his hips pull back and then thrust forward once more, impaling me again. I choke out a cry and drag the knife against his back again. He growls, slamming into me again, and then his lips are back on mine.

I can't scream as he devours my mouth. A mix of pleasure and pain has me bucking my hips into him. My hands are working on their own, leaving small cuts down his back as he impales me again and again. My toes curl as he drives into me harder and harder.

He's unhinged.

A monster sending me over an edge I never knew existed.

"F-fuck."

"Scream my name!" he demands, biting at my lips again. I don't know if it's his blood or my blood anymore. And I can't even string my thoughts together as he buries himself deep inside me. His hand wraps around my throat, cutting off my breath, and I limply take his thrashing.

"Say my name!" He curses, driving me into oblivion.

"Eli," I barely gasp. His grip slackens, and he kisses me again as if in reward. I'm on the edge as I carve one more line down his back. He grunts into my mouth, his hips rolling into me.

"Eli!" I scream, snapping as I finally crash over the edge, and he's holding me, supporting me as my body convulses on its own. He impales me one more time and curses under his breath as he begins to release inside me.

I'm riding the high, holding on to him for dear life as the crash comes in waves. I've shattered into a million pieces. The adrenaline that was once holding me together, is replaced by the very monster I shouldn't be fucking.

Eli holds me as I cling to him, coming down from the peak of ecstasy. We stare at one another for a moment, an unnerving and dangerous energy crackling between us again.

I promised myself it would only be once.

A truce only for today.

But I'm unsure how to keep that promise when I've never been fucked to within an inch of my life like this, and something has never felt more right. For the first time in my life, I feel grounded and like I'm where I'm meant to be. And I have no idea what that even means.

Especially considering the bloody mess we've made of one another.

We're both still breathing heavily as some kind of reality snaps us back into place, and I push against him as quickly as he pulls out.

I search for my clothes, ignoring his arrogant grin as he fastens his pants and belt.

I don't want to acknowledge what just transpired between us, but whatever it was, it satisfied my immediate need for release but replaced it with something else entirely—addiction. Because I already want more.

"I'm clean, by the way," he mentions as he bends over to collect his shirt. "I don't usually fuck without protection."

"So why—" My mouth snaps shut as I take in the carnage I caused. Two thick lines carve his flesh, and smaller ones add to the trail of blood dripping down his muscled and tattooed back. "I'm so sorry."

I'm mortified. Why did I do that?

"Don't be." He shrugs, then leans into my space, planting his hands on either side of me. "Next time, just make sure to do your duty of care." His muscles bunch and I'm hypnotized for a moment by the dangerous beauty of this man.

I click my tongue. "There won't be a next time."

He smirks as he brings his hand to my throat, applying pressure. It causes another buzz to come to life under my skin. His callused thumb delicately brushes over my jaw and rubs against my lips. He withdraws his thumb and looks down at the smudged blood, now painting the digit. "We shall see, Kitten," he remarks before he takes the thumb into his mouth and sucks.

TWENTY-SIX
ELI

"Married?" Dutton questions loudly. "To the woman who's trying to kill you?"

"Don't sound so shocked," I say as I remove my shirt and dump the bottle of water over my sweaty body.

Dutton and I have been throwing a few rounds in my home gym. Usually, Hawke and Ford would train with us too, but I have them out cleaning up the Dee mess. They were unimpressed by the fact that I didn't take them as backup. But I don't answer to them; they work for me.

I check my phone to ensure they've received the money without a hitch, and proceeded with the document exchange to begin the new contracts with Dee. I eagerly await to see what he already has in motion regarding the motorcycle gang, The Boston Delinquents. The moment I have the details, I have no issue with doubling back and removing Dee from the equation entirely. He offended my family, and people don't survive that shit.

"Shocked? Weren't we only having a conversation the other day about figuring out who hired her and then getting rid of her? Do your parents know about this?" he demands.

I look up from my phone. "It hasn't been publicly announced, but my mother did decide to appear on her doorstep a few days ago."

Dutton throws his hands in the air. "And then you decided to have a little shoot-out with your girlfriend against Dee and his men *without* Ford and Hawke. Have you lost your goddamn mind? She could've easily killed you then."

"I've heard tests of loyalty are healthy for any relationship," I say dismissively.

He laughs then, the sound both chaotic and lethal. "*Relationship*? What the fuck are you on about? You don't *do* relationships."

"It's a means to an end. I can marry her, wait out the three months until I'm officially named head of the family, then decide whether I dispose of her permanently or pay her out and send her off so she can start a new life."

Dutton stares at me incredulously. "Why are you going so far for this woman you barely know? And why am I repeating myself? She has been paid to kill you. This jeopardizes not only your life but your family as well. What if her client decides to kill not only you but your parents as well?"

"I won't let that happen. Trust me when I say I have it handled." I throw the empty bottle down, the rage I expelled while working out now piling up again. I love my cousin, but he's the person who gets most under my skin. We're close in age, but that doesn't mean our perspectives and goals are the same.

I turn my back to him and pick up the towel to wipe over my face. "What the fuck happened to your back?!" he exclaims. I freeze, having forgotten about the wounds there. The moment she started carving up my back, I fucking reveled in it. Savored every squeeze of her tight pussy that was barely able to fit me inside.

The intensity of her gaze and needy, spiteful kisses. The knife down my back was fucking heaven. It created an uncontrollable sexual buildup I'd never experienced right before I blew into her, filling her with my cum.

There was something carnal about fucking her, and

I'd do it again and again, even if I'd have to re-ink the lines of every single tattoo on my back. It was fucking worth it.

I look over my shoulder with a smug smile. His features harden.

"You're a sick motherfucker, you know that?"

"I'm not the only one into some depraved things," I remind him. "Remember how you choked out your last lover? You're lucky she survived."

He looks away. "It was an accident."

"Keep telling yourself that."

"Is that how you got the nick to your throat? I don't think any family dinner with your parents is going to go over well if you keep appearing with knife wounds."

I shrug, done with this discussion. I've burned off enough of my excess energy to get me through the day. I haven't seen Jewel since I dropped her off almost a week ago. And that's specifically because I've taken time to sort out family affairs, contracts, and what some might consider a date for tonight. Jewel just doesn't know it yet.

My fiancée is hellbent on not replying to most of my messages, but I seem to get a bite on the few that really antagonize her. And when I send her gifts, she often sends photos of them in the trash. Unless it's a specific piece of jewelry or lingerie set that she likes the look of. Then I don't get a reply at all. Her silence is as good as a thank you.

"I don't like it. You've done some dumb shit in the past, but this is too much. Her pussy can't be that golden."

I turn on him then, sizing him up. "How about you keep my fiancée's pussy out of your mind, or we're going to have a problem."

His eyes narrow. He shakes his head with a condescending smile. "You know what, motherfucker? For someone who's talking about this woman being disposable, you seem awfully attached, calling her your fiancée. So don't let me interfere with you potentially fucking up your life and getting yourself killed. I hope she's worth it."

A tic jumps in my jaw as adrenaline resurfaces, and that roiling anger that's always close to the surface wants to rear its ugly head.

"If my parents find out this is a fake marriage, I'll know it's because of you."

He looks over his shoulder with an arrogant expression. "Oh, don't you worry, it won't be me fucking this up for you. You can manage that shit all on your own. Just don't come to me for help when it blows up in your pretty-ass face."

He takes his shit and leaves. My knuckles turn white as I clench my fists. Motherfucker.

I know exactly what I'm doing, and I don't need his permission to do shit—especially considering his sly deals and management of his own business are less than moral.

I look back at my phone, approving of the quick work of my men. Ford and Hawke are on their way with the goods, and that means I can focus on treating my fake fiancée to a little date tonight. One she won't be able to refuse.

I have every intention of showing her off like a trophy wife because whoever can afford a hit on me is most definitely someone in or close to our inner circle. Unfortunately, it's hard to tell who because I've pissed so many people off.

Once they know she's mine, they'll falter, perhaps reveal their hand or change their tactics.

In the meantime, I get to spoil my soon-to-be wife.

TWENTY-SEVEN
JEWEL

Bang!

I let my breath flow out with ease, satisfied with the dead-center shot. I reload the gun. I've been here every afternoon since the shootout with Eli at Dee's. My nerves have been on edge ever since I was fucked to within an inch of my life by the mafia heir. I haven't been able to shake it out of my memories or shake him out of my head. My skin grows tight over my muscles, a warmth flooding my core at the mere thought.

"Motherfucker," I hiss under my breath as I try to focus my mind. I aim again, breathing in and out slowly. Everything becomes still, and I'm completely and utterly in control again.

Bang! Bang! Bang! Bang! Four shots go off for the four targets. Three are perfect bullseyes. The last one is slightly off-center. "Fuck," I curse, removing my ear protection. This is frustrating beyond measure.

"Inappropriate thoughts hindering your aim, Kitten?"

I spin around at the voice, and a wave of fury washes over me. "What are you doing here?" I demand. How long has he been standing there?

Eli kicks off the wall, looking immaculate in his fucking suit. I try to ignore his imposing presence, but it's fucking hard when the man comes at six foot four and is built like a fucking house.

"I'm not chasing after you for some mafia fun bang shit," I say, assessing my gun as if that was the problem with my aim.

"Mafia fun bang shit?" he repeats lazily as he leans against the screen between me and the empty stall beside me.

"How did you even get back here?" I ask. I make a point to hire the entire range every time I'm here. Simply put, I don't play nicely with others, and I've experienced enough mansplaining on how to use a gun that I now make sure I have the place to myself—I have more than enough money to cover it.

When his smile kicks up, it's answer enough. Because Eli Monti pays, persuades, or threatens to get what he wants. "I want to take you somewhere special."

"Hard pass." I put my ear protection on again and roll my shoulders, breathing with ease as I focus on the six new targets. I breathe in and out, my hand steady. Six rounds go off, all perfect shots. My lip twitches arrogantly, the slight tingle of adrenaline dancing beneath my skin, but it's nothing like the high of the other night.

When I remove my ear protection and look to my right, I notice Eli frowning down the line of his range. I sigh but can't help but be curious, so I lean into his space. Motherfucker is a decent shot. Out of the six rounds, four are dead center. It gives me smug satisfaction to know I'm a slightly better shot. As I should be, considering it's my fucking job.

He's looking at his gun as if it's rigged. I sigh. The enjoyment of being alone here is gone because Eli won't leave of his own accord.

"What do you want, Eli?"

"A date. I promised you a reward and a favor. I can manage both tonight."

"That seems awfully cocky, don't you think? Very few things excite me. Especially when they come from a man."

He leans in, his hot breath against my ear, flushing

me with an immediate fever. "I think we both know that's a lie. Especially when your fiancé is involved." He makes a point to look down at my left ring finger. I've kept the ring on, though I still haven't gotten used to it.

"Does it involve food?" I ask, realizing I've only eaten a protein bar today.

"It can on the way, but not at the function."

"The function?" I ask, looking down at my jeans and midriff-baring tank top.

"I have a change of clothes for you in the car."

I scoff, but before I can argue with him, he says, "I promise you'll love what I have for you, my sweet fiancée. It's something that will exceed your expectations."

I fold my arms over my chest. "Very doubtful." And yet I follow him out to the car. He seems smug about it. As we walk out from behind the counter, Laurence seems to be avoiding my gaze, most likely embarrassed by whatever type of payoff was made for him to let Eli through. Though Eli most likely just walked straight through anyway.

"What, you just want me to leave my car parked here the rest of the day and overnight?" I demand as I stare at my yellow car. Other than Eli's slick black sports car, it's the only car in the lot.

"I'll have Hawke and Ford drive it back to your apartment."

I shake my head, furious with this man's ability to always have everything go his way. And I want to fight and argue with him about it, but I've come to realize that while I'm stuck in this shitty position of fake marrying the mafia heir, I have to pick my battles.

And this is not a battle I need to fight.

He opens the passenger door to reveal a black bag on the seat. He pulls it out and hands it to me expectantly.

"How do you even know you have my measurements right?" I ask as I take it.

"I know everything about my fiancée. And besides, I have a photographic memory."

I look at him, and heat floods my core at the insinuation. *A photographic memory from the other night.* I wonder how I looked to him, sprawled on the hood of his car. *This* car.

I'll have to make a point to light it on fire.

I zip open the bag, revealing a tight black dress. On the seat is also a set of strappy black heels and two boxes of what I imagine to be jewelry.

"You know this shit doesn't woo me, right?" I say, not entirely opposed to the grand gifts. After all, once I put a bullet in his head, I can sell them. In fact, I might be inclined to hock them while he's still alive just to piss him off.

"Perhaps not, but where we're going will."

There's a chance the dress might not fit, but I very much doubt that. The parking lot is empty, so I begin to peel off my shirt, and then I notice Eli watching.

"Avert your gaze," I warn him. I might not have my preferred guns right now, but that doesn't mean I'm not carrying. I always carry a knife with me.

"You want me to avert my gaze after I fucked you like a filthy animal only a few nights ago?" he deadpans.

I tilt my nose higher. "We had a momentary truce. We don't anymore."

He chuckles but, surprisingly, turns his back to me as I shimmy out of my jeans. I'm wildly pissed when the dress fits perfectly. I strap the heels on, and when I open the boxes, I gasp quietly. Fuck, these definitely cost more than my car. Hell, more than six months' worth of my rent, most likely.

"Do you like diamonds?" he asks as he turns and picks up the diamond necklace. I'm in shock at the size of it. He steps behind me and instructs me to lift my hair. I do as I'm told... for once. His warm fingertips brush over my collarbones and then move to secure the necklace in place. His knuckle brushes down the back of my neck when it's clipped up, and my breath hitches.

I hate how this man has a hold over me. I don't understand it. Can't fathom it.

I turn to face him, and he's watching me carefully as I look up at him through thick eyelashes.

He swallows. "You should wear your hair up."

"You should fall out of the habit of telling me what to do," I snap back as I drop my hair and reach for the matching earrings. I can't believe I'm crazy enough to do anything or go anywhere this crazy fucker suggests. But I must confess, I'm kind of curious now.

TWENTY-EIGHT
ELI

The irony of her last name is not lost on me. Because Jewel is a diamond in many ways, but she'll look so much better with my last name instead of hers. I keep that thought to myself, of course, because it was hard enough getting her to wear the fucking ring.

She's grumbling complaints in the passenger seat after touching up her makeup and hair. Not that she needs to; she's stunning as it is. "This better be worth it."

I can't help the arrogant smile that touches my lips because I know she's going to fucking love it. "You love picnics, don't you?"

I feel the sensation of her hateful glare boring into the side of my head and the unspoken promise of a thousand deaths if that's what I have planned. I laugh, unable to stop myself. She's too easy to rile up, especially at the mention of anything romantic or commitment-related.

We pull into one of Ivanov's estates. Hawke and Ford's adoptive parents, Anya Ivanov and River Bently run the underworld auctions within the city alongside their uncle, Alek Ivanov. Alek and River primarily run the gun auctions. My family has worked with them for years, establishing a friendly agreement. None of them are ready to retire, and I'm certain Anya will take her jewels to the grave, but her riches and business will go to the twins.

Jewel's eyebrows crinkle slightly as she assesses the wealthy clientele making their way up to the mansion. The majority of those who attend these auctions are men, and most of them are intimidated by the red-haired woman standing at the door, welcoming everyone with an insincere smile.

Anya Ivanov, who is nearing her sixties, is not a woman to be trifled with. So I'm certain Jewel will like her very much.

I step out of the car and round the front before the valet can offer his hand to Jewel. I hold my own hand out to her, and she unenthusiastically takes it and steps out. "Remember to pretend to like me. After all, you are my soon-to-be wife."

"You're really looking forward to an untimely death before the wedding, aren't you?" she threatens with a sweet smile. I return the smile as I hook our elbows so I can escort her.

Anya sneers at the back of the person she just so "kindly" welcomed into her home. "Disgusting choice in shoes," she says when her husband steps out beside her.

"Eli?" River says, surprised to see me. He steps up to us and takes my hand. His father and mine have been doing business for many years now. River is known for shipping high-quality weapons into the city. I don't know much about his and Anya's marriage, but from what the twins told me, he blackmailed her into doing business with him; she tried to kill him multiple times, and then they somehow fell crazily in love. "I wish I knew you were coming tonight."

"I was hoping you could make room last minute for me and my fiancée," I say, motioning to Jewel.

"Fiancée?" Anya says over River's shoulder, basically pushing him out of the way to get a better look at Jewel. "I haven't heard this." She sweeps her gaze over Jewel, and to her testament, Jewel isn't intimidated. And then Anya zeroes in on the ring and necklace. Anya is known for her love of jewels. "Well, it would appear the boy has good taste at the very least," she notes, taking my fiancée's hand and peering closely at the ring.

"I wish she looked at the ring I tried to hand to her all those years ago in the same way," River jokes from behind her. She gives him a pointed glare.

"You were lucky I married you," she's quick to remark.

"This is Anya Ivanov. She runs the auctions with her brother, Alek. She's also Hawke and Ford's mother."

"Adoptive mother," she corrects. "Those little shits would have more manners if I'd trained them from the very start." But her tone has softened. As terrifying as this woman is, she would kill anyone who spoke poorly of them. Except for herself.

"I think they learned most of their poor behavior *after* meeting you," River jests.

The corner of her lips tilt into a smile. "Are my thugs of sons with you tonight?" she asks, looking over my shoulder and dropping Jewel's hands.

"Not tonight. I wanted to have some alone time with my fiancée. She has a fondness for guns, so I was hoping to treat her to some gifts this evening."

Anya's gaze slides back over to Jewel, mischief glittering in her expression. "A woman who can handle herself is always welcome through these doors. As long as you promise me the moment Mr. Monti makes you feel less than, you'll put a bullet in his brain."

Jewel actually laughs at that. "I can absolutely promise you that. The still-healing knife wound to his leg can attest to it."

Anya's expression breaks into a wicked smile as she turns to me. "I like her."

River pulls her back by the shoulders. "Please don't give my wife any more ideas."

"There might be hope for the new generation yet," she says over her shoulder. "Come. I'll personally escort you to the auction. Be a good husband and greet our guests, River."

Jewel leans into me and whispers, "She's kind of terrifying, but I love it."

"Of course you do," I reply, not at all surprised.

"And you don't have to treat me to guns. Just give me my father's back."

I pat her hand. "You know I won't do that. But it doesn't mean I can't treat you until then."

"Does your father know you're here tonight?" Anya asks casually. "It's been a while since I've seen Crue. Is he halfway into the grave yet?"

I bite my tongue. There are only a few people who get away with speaking about my father dying. Anya is one of those few.

"No, but he'll be retiring soon. After our marriage."

"Oh, yes." She stops at a barrier of red curtains. "I forgot about the archaic marriage rule you have in your family. I'm lucky my sons choose to simply fuck like rabbits and not bring anyone home. I definitely don't want to deal with little wet blankets as sons."

Jewel tries to hold in her laughter, and I try not to let it infect me the same. Anya pulls back the curtains, and her twin, Alek, stands there, watching the night's crowd. He adjusts his gloves as he glances over at us. His expression doesn't change when he notices me.

"Mr. Monti and his fiancée, Jewel, are here to bid on some guns. Give them our table for this evening since we don't have any available space," she tells him.

He nods and starts walking. We follow in silence. Alek is known for his lack of communication, and the gloves he always wears have been a mystery to many. The only people he will touch or let touch him are his wife, Lena Love, who is a famous singer, and his daughter, Hope.

Jewel's eyes widen as she looks around the room, taking in the tables, each with a single candle in the middle to illuminate them. A main stage is positioned at the front of the room. I've been to a few of these auctions. I also supported Dutton when he conducted his first virginity auction a few years ago after taking over the majority of Dawson's more lucrative businesses.

Alek stands beside a chair and pulls it out for Jewel. He looks bored, and I know it's only because of our families' close ties that the killer is even pretending to have any manners. The elder Ivanov twins are wild cards. Then again, other families say the same thing about my own, so who am I to throw stones?

When Alek leaves and I sit beside Jewel, she leans into me. "Isn't he married to Lena Love?"

I'm not surprised that she's done her research on my family members, close friends, and our dealings with both. But I don't like it either. I drag her chair closer to me and pull her to sit on my lap.

"Is this really necessary?" She tries to break from my hold.

"Extremely. Look around you," I say, brushing the back of my finger against the pulse at her neck. Her breath hitches, and my cock begins to thicken, with her simply sitting on my lap. "Everyone is watching you."

She looks around and then, as if not even realizing, wraps her arms around my neck as she says quietly, "They're not looking at me. They're looking at you."

"They're looking at *us*," I correct her. Attending an event such as this is a public announcement of my engagement. I make a point to hold her hand to my lips and slowly kiss the ring. Realization dawns on her expression.

"Did you bring me here to show me off like some brood mare?" she hisses under her breath, looking wildly pissed.

"No, I brought you here to let you buy whatever you like. Some women might like jewels. Others lingerie. But you, Kitten, love guns."

She looks around again. "And remind me why I have to sit on your lap for that?"

"So you're reminded of the gun you're sitting on that's kindly paying for all these gifts."

She laughs then, and I hate every fucker who turns our way and looks at her. "Did you really just refer to your cock as a gun?"

I thread my fingers through her hair possessively and pull her lips closer to mine. "I don't know how long I can contain myself if the word cock falls from your lips again." I rub my thumb against her lips thoughtfully.

Her gaze intensifies, and I can't look away. I want her again. But I want her to come to me willingly. To crawl to me and show her loyalty.

Some of the most powerful and lethal men in the city are in this room tonight, but it's her I can't look away from. She's more lethal than all of them combined.

An announcement is made that the auction is about to start, and she pulls away. That's when we notice a waitress wearing lingerie, standing a few feet away, seemingly too nervous to interrupt. *How long has she been standing there?*

"Drinks are on the house," she says with a smile, unable to meet our gaze. She places a whiskey on ice and a champagne flute down in front of us.

An announcer steps onto the stage, leading several men wearing suits and carrying briefcases. They each place a case on separate tables, then flick open the locks and lift the lids to reveal the weapons inside.

Jewel leans forward, her eyes growing wide, and I grin as I watch my fiancée light up like it's Christmas Day.

No, jewelry and lingerie are definitely not going to woo my fake fiancée. But anything that could kill me will.

TWENTY-NINE
JEWEL

Ten million is how much tonight cost my fiancé, and I'm not the least bit sorry. Especially not with the two gold-plated guns I'm now gleefully holding in my lap as we leave the Ivanov's estate. They were the only ones I could walk away with today. The others I giddily bid on to be delivered to the Monti mansion, and Eli promised to wrap them in a bow and hand them to me. *Fuck the bow, just give me my guns.*

The gold plating, although seemingly impractical, I fucking love.

I love them so much that I've allowed him to stroke the inside of my knee the whole ride home. And I try my hardest not to focus on his fingers against my skin.

When he pulls over at the front of my apartment

building, the tension between us is palpable. I make a point to study one of the bullets.

"Tomorrow night, I want you to meet my parents," he says.

I swallow as I polish the bullet with my thumb. "You're really set on this, aren't you?"

"A deal is a deal, is it not? You play perfect fiancée, and you'll get your money and your guns back. After meeting my parents, we'll start planning the wedding. The sooner it's done, the better, wouldn't you agree?"

A tightness constricts my throat as the wild thought of walking down an aisle to anyone suffocates me. He's acting as if the fact I have a contract to kill him isn't relevant anymore. I open my mouth and then close it again. I can't even speak. I clear my throat and frown at the bullet as if it's the problem I have the issue with. "I have a shift tomorrow."

"Come after." It's not a request. His grip tightens on my knee, and I can't help but look at him now. "Can I come up?"

My eyebrows raise in surprise. "You ask for permission now?"

"I've had someone berating me that I shouldn't tell but ask."

I scoff at that. "You just literally *told* me I *have* to meet your parents tomorrow for dinner."

He takes the bullet out of my hand, and I watch it with keen interest as he rubs it against my lips, mesmerized. I don't know why I'm so fascinated, but I am. What Eli lacks in words, he sometimes makes up for in touch. If I were a woman capable of love, I'd think the way he's looking at me is as if he's a man torn between lust and love. But neither of us is capable of that.

As if to prove my point, Eli slowly presses the bullet to the seam of my lips. The tip of it enters, encountering my clenched teeth. "You're so fucking beautiful," he breathes, pushing the deadly object with just enough pressure to force me to unclench my jaw and let him in. My tongue curls around the warm bullet, and he leans in, his thumb now caressing my jaw.

I can't look away from his all-consuming gaze as he searches mine. What he's looking for, I'm not entirely sure. I freeze as he brushes his lips against mine, and then his tongue is there, nudging against mine, demanding, imposing as always. Our tongues wrap around the bullet, battling for the upper hand.

I push it into his mouth as he pulls me over the middle console, and I awkwardly straddle his lap. He moves back his seat so there's enough room for me. A small moan escapes me, and his fingers dig greedily into my ass cheeks in response. Heat floods my core as I rub along his erection, hungry and depraved.

I pull away with a pant, searching his eyes. He spits the bullet to the side, lifting my dress to my waist.

"What if someone sees us?" I breathe.

"You don't fucking care," he growls as he grabs the back of my neck. "Besides, the windows are tinted." He pulls me back in for a kiss, but I resist him. He looks confused.

My pussy is throbbing, and I want so badly to impale myself on his cock. "I'm still going to kill you," I tell him.

"So you keep saying." He raises an arrogant brow as his thumb trails over the lace of my underwear and begins to circle my clit. *Fuck.* My body naturally arches toward him. "But not tonight."

He pushes my panties to the side and thrusts a finger inside me. My back bows, and I moan as I ride his hand. "We can have a truce, but only for tonight," I whisper, chasing my own pleasure.

"Call it whatever the fuck you want," he growls as he inserts another finger, and I groan in pleasure. I'm soaking wet. When I look back down at him, he leans forward, crushing his lips to mine, biting and sucking.

I desperately begin to undo his belt, hungrily

needing a release from the adrenaline that spiked from the tension of being in this car with this man.

"So aggressive." His tone is one of approval as we both awkwardly lift to shove his pants enough to free his cock.

"Shut up," I breathe, slapping my hand over his mouth and impaling myself on his cock. "Oh fuck!" My head drops back, and Eli bites down hard on my hand.

Fuck. Fuck. Fuck.

I begin riding him, my hips rocking back and forth, as I take my rightful fill. I move back a bit too far, honking the horn accidently, but I don't give a fuck. Eli's hand snakes around my back, pulling me closer, and I moan as the pleasure intensifies with the change in angle. His teeth clamp down harder on my hand, most likely hoping it'll become too painful for me to keep silencing him. But it's not enough to deter me. In fact, I fucking love it.

When he applies even more pressure, I curse and finally remove my hand, realizing he's drawn blood. It smears his lips, and I'm as horrified as I am turned on. There's a beat between us when we assess one another's approval.

He pulls me in closer as I continue riding him, and

his lips find mine again as if his life hinges on it. I can't stop moaning even as I taste my blood on him. His hands wrap around my throat, pressing the stones from the diamond necklace into my skin and cutting off my airway.

Fuck.

I keep rocking against him, and his thrusts match the rhythm I set. I can't breathe. And yet, the light-headedness is adding to my high.

My legs begin to shake as I reach a new, higher peak. He greedily kisses me, taking and taking until I fall over the edge. I can't even scream as the wave washes over me, and I come on his cock. He lets go of me then, and the rush of air and pure bliss hits me like an avalanche.

He holds me in place as he jerks inside me, filling me up. His intense gaze keeps me grounded as I slowly rock my hips back and forth as I come down from the high.

Blood is smeared on his lips—and most likely mine—and my hand. I should be mortified, but there's something untamed and carnal about fucking this man. Like he pins me down, marks me, and breaks me, and I get off on the high every fucking time.

"You enjoy milking my cock, don't you, Kitten," he says with an arrogant smile.

I mirror his smile. "It's the least I can do, fiancé... before I kill you."

His smile grows bigger, and I wonder if anyone gets to see this side of Eli. In all the photos I've seen of him, I've never seen him smile like this, so beautifully and openly.

My hand raises to his face, and I rub my hand against the scruff of his jaw as if petting him.

He seems perplexed by the tender touch, and even I don't know why I feel so moved to do it. Aftercare is not my specialty.

I snap into a sudden realization. Aftercare? What the fuck am I thinking?

I lift myself off him and quickly scramble over to the passenger seat, pulling down my dress and adjusting my panties.

"Truce is over," I say, my heart hammering and strange emotions I'm not entirely comfortable with, wanting to explode out. He's chuckling, amused by my quick switch, as I place my golden guns in their case and practically jump out of the car.

"Aren't you forgetting this?" he asks, holding up the bullet.

"I was hoping you'd choke on it. Keep it as a memento, asshole," I bite out, slamming the door as he laughs.

I cut across the parking lot to my apartment building, focusing on the clicking of my heels as I walk.

Shit. Shit. Shit.

What am I feeling right now?

Why do I feel like this?

I hit the button to the elevator more times than needed, but when the doors finally close, I hold the gun case close to my chest and thump my head on the wall with a sigh.

A momentary truce, huh?

Meeting his parents?

Fuck, is this becoming real?

I pull my phone from my small clutch, noticing a new text message from my client that came in two hours ago. I feel the life drain from me as I read the words.

> Anonymous Number: Meet one of my men in this location tomorrow evening at eight to exchange details on the Monti family. Don't be late.

"Fuck." The glint of my engagement ring catches my eye, and I swallow. I bite at the tip of my nail. The longer I prolong the hit, the longer... Well, I'm not entirely sure what I'm feeling.

The elevator doors open, and I hide any emotions

that might be showing on my face. I'm a lethal hitwoman, for fuck's sake. And no man will be my downfall.

I remind myself of that as I step into the hallway with my two golden guns.

THIRTY
ELI

"Married?" Billie says, baffled. Dutton, Hawke, and Ford are sitting behind her. She turns to Dutton. "How could you not tell me this?" she asks accusingly.

His hands are folded over his chest, and he shrugs. "I only found out a few days ago."

"Isn't that kind of big news? Who is she? It's not Michelle, is it? I can't stand her."

"And what are you going to say if it is?" Hawke asks, laughing. She goes to speak but closes her mouth. My cousin is, unfortunately, a dumbass, much like Hawke. Neither of them think before they speak.

"It isn't, right?" She winces as if she's put her foot in her mouth.

"Absolutely not," my mother calls out. "My son has some taste."

"At least your son seems interested in a relationship; mine just seems to drift from bed to bed," Aunt Honey calls from the kitchen.

"Why am I now being targeted?" Dutton shouts. Hawke and Ford laugh as Billie glances at her phone.

"Hope can't come. She's busy with some show tonight," Billie says, throwing herself between the twins to sit.

"I didn't even invite her," I grit out, irritated that this turned into a far bigger deal than I'd intended it to be. "And why are you two here? Didn't I let you have tonight off?" I ask Hawke and Ford.

Ford seems too preoccupied with his phone to answer. He's been doing that a lot lately. Hawke shrugs, then answers, "Where else would we want to be when the boss officially introduces his fiancée to the family? Besides, we missed you since you seem to be having date nights and killing sprees together. We're basically chopped liver now."

"You went on a killing spree together?" Billie demands, cheeks going pale. "Please tell me she's not as crazy as Anya."

"Hey, that's our mother you're speaking about," Hawke scolds.

"Yeah, and you're just as crazy," she bites back.

He doesn't disagree with her.

My jaw tics in irritation. I'm often frustrated when this group gets together. I down a mouthful of whiskey as we wait in the living area of my parents' mansion. I'd offered to host it at my place, but my mother was hell-bent on having it here. Now I know why—because she decided to invite fucking everyone.

"To answer your question," Dutton says to his sister, "she's definitely on the spectrum of crazy."

"Watch your mouth when you're talking about my fiancée," I growl. Everyone falls silent, and Dutton raises an eyebrow.

"I thought she was just a means to an end, that you're using her to get everything you want. Isn't that what you told me?" he says quietly so only those of us in the room can hear.

I ignore him. Dutton has already taken over his father's business completely. He doesn't know what it's like to have his future hinging on something as stupid as a marriage requirement. Ever since I was eighteen, I've had to fight for my role and for every new responsibility. I did tell him that Jewel serves a purpose, but I won't let him speak ill of her.

I haven't spoken to my father since the engagement, and when he walks in with my uncle Dawson after finishing work, I stand to pour them both a glass of whiskey.

"I hear congratulations are in order," Father says. He pulls me in for a one-armed hug and pats my back. "Proud of you, son. The best thing I ever did was force your mother to marry me." He chuckles. I hand him and Dutton each a glass.

"It was my choice to marry you; I want that made very clear," my mother says as she enters the room with Aunt Honey. He goes to her, immediately pulling her in for a kiss. He is, in every sense of the word, obsessed with my mother. Although I grew up watching them unable to keep their hands off each other, I can't imagine myself having the same experience in my own marriage. I just remind myself that Jewel serves a business purpose only. But the fucking is most definitely a perk.

Dawson gravitates to Honey, and she raises on her tiptoes to press a kiss to his cheek.

"So where is she?" my father asks, looking around the room.

I'm not entirely thrilled that she's late to what's supposed to be her introduction to my parents. She had a shift tonight, and although we didn't part on the best of terms last night, I had her swear she'd be here. Then again, when has that woman done anything I've told her to do?

"She was probably scared off after her future

mother-in-law surprised her at her own home," Hawke says. Everyone's eyes grow wide, and realization dawns on him. "Oh shit, that wasn't common knowledge?"

"Rya! You didn't, did you?" Honey yells at her sister. "Oh my gosh, the poor girl."

My mother waves it off, saying, "What? I just had to confirm my suspicions, and I wanted to see what type of woman she is."

I look at my phone. Still no update from her.

Where the fuck is she?

"I'm starving," Hawke complains.

"We'll wait for her. The table is already set, so you can be patient," Mother tells him.

"Besides, you're always hungry." Billie checks her pockets and fishes out a lollipop.

"You're a fucking angel." Hawke grins as he steals the sucker from her hand.

Dutton looks up from the book he's reading and pins Hawke with a glare. Then sends one Ford's way when she hands him one. Ford isn't as big of an eater as his gym junkie brother, but I've never seen him turn down a sweet.

"No, we can start dinner now. Her shift must be going over. I'll try to call her one more time," I say.

"Oh, a shift worker?" I hear Honey ask curiously.

No one knows she's technically a hitwoman, and I have every intent to keep it that way.

I call, but there's no answer. This time, though, she does text back. I grin at the updated contact name I gave her since Stalker didn't seem to fit anymore.

Wifey: I'm running late. Eat without me.

I frown at the short text and lack of apology. But it's likely she's had to stay at work later than she expected. I don't even know why she keeps that job. I understand having a cover, but as my wife, she won't have to hide behind something so trivial. If she were my real wife, that is.

When I enter the dining room, I see it's beautifully set up. My mother stands behind my father at the head of the table with a smile, proud of the outcome. She then looks up at me expectantly.

"She'll be a bit longer yet. But she said to start without her."

I sit beside my mother, leaving the other side free for when Jewel arrives. A private chef brings out entrées, setting a plate in front of each of us. My mother uses this time to ask Dutton about Jewel, and he tells her she will most likely challenge me in every way and that she's flawlessly stubborn. I don't think that's what my mother wants to hear.

By the time we've finished the main course and she hasn't replied or shown up, I can see my father getting irritated. He doesn't have much in the way of patience; I guess that's where I get it from.

"It will be nice to have another woman my age in the family," Billie says after I briefly describe Jewel to them. Billie's only a year younger than Dutton, but he treats her as if she's still a sweet little girl.

"Wait till you meet her," Dutton mumbles under his breath. Thankfully, at the same time, Honey and Dawson are in conversation with my parents.

I glare at him across the table, and his sister shifts uncomfortably. "Don't be bitter because you can't find anyone who won't put up with your shit," she says to her brother.

He raises his eyebrow. "I'll have you know; I don't intend to have a relationship. This family keeps me busy enough as it is."

Hawke snorts. "More like no one wants you because of how fucking intense you are."

Billie then defends her brother. "Hey, like you're one to talk, Mr. Manwhore. You can't even remember the girls' names you sleep with."

"I'll have you know that I do remember them, but if

there's more than one in one night, it becomes tricky," he says defensively, then scarfs down a forkful of food.

"You're such a pig," she snaps back. "The only one who actually has any decency here is Ford. At least he knows how to treat a woman."

Ford looks up from his phone this time.

"Please, Ford hasn't been with a woman since..." Hawke stops to ponder that for a moment. "I don't know when."

An exchange seems to happen between Ford and Billie, and she's quick to say, "It doesn't matter. He still knows how to be at least reasonable. The rest of you are all too macho. Gah! I so want another woman in this family."

I excuse myself from the table as Hawke and Billie squabble amongst themselves about the treatment of women. I swear, Hawke intentionally riles her up just to get a reaction. He's been doing it since the day they first met.

I step out into the living room and call Jewel. She lets it ring out *again*, which makes me angry.

"Is she not coming?" my mother asks as she joins me. Sliding my phone into my pocket, I feel the muscles in my jaw twitch. She stood me up. Maybe for payback, I'll destroy one of her precious guns.

One of my parents' security guards steps into the

living room to announce a new guest, but Jewel bursts in, introducing herself. "Sorry, I'm late. Work wouldn't let me leave." She's still wearing her work attire of black heels and a little black dress.

I stalk across the room and loom over her. She pins me with that challenging stare as I grab her by the hip and pull her to me, crushing my lips to hers. She seems startled and unsure what to do with her hands, but I inhale her, take out my fury on her as I devour her. I drag out her lip and growl, "You're late." I'm fucking furious with her.

Goose bumps erupt along her skin, which pleases me to no end. She pulls away from me and holds her hand out to my mother, who is studying us intently. This isn't going to be easy.

"Nice to see you again, Mrs. Monti. Apologies for being late. I didn't want this to be everyone else's first impression ."

My mother accepts Jewel's hand, looking between the two of us, and I know nothing goes unnoticed by her, so I put my hand on Jewel's hip possessively and tug her back into me. I don't know what the fuck a happy couple looks like, but I'm going to kill my little Kitten with touch and kindness. The very things she fucking hates. This will serve as her punishment for being so late. I had a feeling she was going to be a little late, but I didn't expect her to only come for dessert.

"Of course, dear, but you missed an amazing meal. Come, let me introduce you to everyone." My mother eases her away from me and leads her into the dining room.

Jewel glances over her shoulder quickly and flips me off. The corner of my mouth twitches. I'm irritated that she can make me so fucking angry one minute, then have me smiling the next.

My father makes a point to stand and offer his hand in greeting. To her credit, she doesn't seem intimidated by him. And he is a very intimidating man.

She and Dutton acknowledge one another with an insincere, "Good to see you." She walks around the table and shakes everyone's hand as my mother introduces them.

It's not until she makes it back around to my side that I notice she's not wearing her engagement ring. But when I left her yesterday, she was definitely wearing it.

My mother seems to notice the lack of a ring at the same time. Her eyes narrow almost imperceptibly, and I can tell she senses something is off between Jewel and me. She's one of the top lawyers in the country, if not the best, for fuck's sake; sniffing out lies is her damn job.

"You still don't have a ring?" my mother asks. I wrap my arm around Jewel's shoulders, and she tenses as she lifts her hand.

"Oh, I do. It's beautiful, but I can't wear it to work. It's way too expensive," she replies, as if that's answer enough.

"You should wear your ring," I growl. She eyes me and smiles. It's forced, and I can tell behind that smile, there are sharp teeth wanting to bite.

I drop my arm and pull out the seat, indicating for her to take it. When she does, I sit next to her, and the interrogation begins.

THIRTY-ONE
JEWEL

For such a powerful and dangerous family, they make me feel oddly welcome. And I should be the last person they lower their guard around. And that saddens me ever so slightly. I wish I could buy into the same lie that they all seem to be swallowing.

Don't get me wrong; they have their suspicions, which is obvious with the questions they throw at me. Some I don't have the answers for, no matter how much Eli and I "practiced."

I don't think Eli realizes how lucky he is to have a family that cares so much. Billie is like a pocket full of sunshine. She kind of reminds me of her mother, and Dutton reminds me of their father. But Dawson seems to be more talkative, whereas Dutton is quiet and reserved. Or maybe that's because Dutton outright doesn't seem to like me and has no issues with making that known. I don't blame him. If anything, I respect him since he's one of only a few who knows and understands me as the threat I am.

Crue, who I was most nervous to meet, has been silently watching his son's and my interactions for the entire night. Eli and I might have charming words for one another, but I'm sure you cannot fake chemistry. And I'm not entirely sure if we've convinced him.

I fight my natural instinct to push Eli's hand away every time he reaches out to grab me or whenever his lips are on my neck or hand. It feels like the man's in overdrive tonight because he's either trying to showcase how "in love" we are, or he's doing it to get under my fucking skin because he knows he wouldn't usually get away with it.

Faking that I like being practically manhandled by him is hard to do when I'm so used to not being touched. It's not that I hate human touch. It's just that it's foreign to me. I never had a mother who hugged or cuddled me, and my father's love language was spending quality time with me. And by "quality time," I mean he was teaching me how to shoot. And after he passed away, all I had was Craig. My mother and father had no other family that I know of, and I was old enough to decide where I wanted to live.

And Craig has been my surrogate uncle for as long as I can remember. He never had any kids, and he never married. His life was work until it wasn't. I always thought I was a bit like him, happy to be by myself with my guns. But as I sit around this table and witness their love for one another, I'm a little envious.

I wonder if, in another life, I could lean into something like this. It's beautifully dysfunctional, but I imagine all of them literally have one another's back until death.

Hawke and Billie argue over something, and Ford shakes his head at them. And I have to remind myself not to get swept up in it all. I'm basically a loner. Always have been. And I've come to terms with the fact that I'll go through life solo.

A phantom.

A killer.

Staying in my lane.

I catch Eli looking at my bare ring finger again. I'd forgotten to put it back on, which made him angry. So there's no way in hell I'm going to tell him I was late to this dinner because I had to meet with one of my client's henchmen after work. He'd go ballistic if he knew.

"Do we have a wedding date set?" Honey asks.

All eyes turn to us, and I look up at Eli as he squeezes my hand.

"Well, we were thinking of eloping," he answers. I can tell from his parents' expressions that that is not an option. "Jewel doesn't like crowds," he adds, and I'm certain he's purposefully antagonizing them.

"We could make it small and intimate, just us and your family," Rya suggests. Eli is stroking his thumb over my hand as I take a mouthful of champagne.

"I don't have any family," I reply, and everyone falls silent.

"Oh, apologies." I can see the sadness enter Rya's gaze. I don't want anyone to feel sad for me. I've had a great life, and apart from this little hiccup of marrying a mafia boss's son, I will continue to have a great life. Once I have my guns, that is.

Surprisingly, Dawson interrupts. "That's okay. Neither did I. It's a joy being able to make your own family." He presses a kiss to Honey's knuckles and looks at his children. A somber mood takes over the table.

"With that said, we've decided to marry within the month," Eli announces.

My throat constricts as I inhale sharply, immediately feeling suffocated. His mother's eyes widen in excitement. He said everything would happen quickly, but it still doesn't prepare me for the intense feeling of being sent to the gallows.

"That's so soon! We have to start planning immediately." Rya and Honey start discussing catering. I want a hole to open in the floor and swallow me down so I never have to be in this situation again.

Eli shifts my hand to his cock beneath the table, and I immediately whip my head in his direction, stunned.

The others begin to talk amongst themselves as he smirks and leans toward me. "Breathe," he says quietly. "You look like you're about to kill someone."

"I am. Specifically you," I whisper-shout back.

"This isn't like a shotgun wedding, is it?" Billie asks excitedly.

"What?" My head snaps in her direction.

"No, Jewel is not pregnant. But not from lack of trying," Eli clarifies. I hit him in the shoulder, and he chuckles.

"That's so soon," Crue pipes in, and it draws everyone's attention to the head of the table.

Eli levels his father with a stare. "Well, Jewel knows how important our family business is. And I know without any doubt in my mind that Jewel is the perfect fit for my empire. It doesn't make sense to wait."

I feel the noose slowly tighten around my neck again. I notice the way Ford and Dutton look elsewhere. Hawke gives us two thumbs up. Those three are the only ones at this table who are aware of our lies, and I'm certain that after the wedding and Eli gets everything that he wants, it'll cause a rift between his family. Whether he wants to acknowledge it or not. Won't they feel betrayed when they discover this is all fake? Or is this simply how things are done in the mafia world? Marry, discard, and move on to the next.

A month doesn't give me long to get out of this situation and find my guns.

Fuck. Am I really trapped?

What happens when the order to finally take out Eli comes? I glance around the table as they offer congratulations, wondering what will happen when they find out I killed their son after they welcomed me into their home.

I can't breathe.

Fuck.

Crue stands with his whiskey in hand. Everyone falls quiet as he holds his glass up to make make a toast.

"You've been the bane of my existence since the moment you were born," Crue starts.

"Crue!" Rya reprimands. Oh, is this his father making a joke? It seems everyone else is just as unsure about his humor as well. Now I know who Eli gets it from.

Crue continues. "But you've proved your ambition and ability to take over the business time and time again. I couldn't be any prouder. So I guess congratulations are in order for you both. And I'm looking forward to my retirement."

I shouldn't be a part of this.

I have no right to be sitting by his side, nor do I want to be. This is a place for a *real* doting fiancée. Not one who has every intention of stabbing him in the back once I get the all-clear to do so.

Eli squeezes my hand, pulling me back to him as if aware of where my thoughts have flooded.

Everyone focuses on Eli as he stands, perfectly dressed and poised, and I wonder, truly wonder, why he hasn't already found a wife. Why has he dragged me into his games? These might not necessarily be good people. The majority of them are killers, not that I can talk. But even I can tell this family is special.

If he wanted to sleep around, I'm sure Michelle would have let him, as long as it meant she got to become Mrs. Eli Monti. He could have any obedient wife, so was he truly opposed to being weighed down in commitment like me? Is that why he thinks I'm the perfect fit? Because we're both so disposable to one another?

He nods his head, and everyone claps. Eli smiles at his father, and I'm hesitant to let him bring my hand to his lips as he looks down at me adoringly. I know that look has to be fake. His light eyes emit something into me that I choose to accept as bravery as I stand on weak legs to join him.

I shouldn't be here.

This isn't my place to stay.

After sticking to the shadows for so long, it feels strange to be in the spotlight.

Especially beside a man like Eli Monti.

"We'll make you all proud. I look forward to owning New York." He salutes his father, and his mother looks extremely proud. I notice Dutton take a large gulp of his drink as if swallowing his revulsion, and it's then that I truly agree he might be the only smart one at the table.

Then Eli's gaze shifts to me. "To a happy marriage." He salutes again, and I offer a tight smile, wishing for the world to swallow me whole.

"To a happy marriage," I repeat, and the sinister smile on his perfect fucking lips widens.

I have a feeling I may not make it out of this alive.

THIRTY-TWO
ELI

"Where's your ring?" I ask furiously as we leave my parents' home.

"Can we just focus on the fact that you've just told your entire family we're marrying within a month, and how fucking crazy that is?" she hisses in reply.

I encroach into her space, pushing her back against the car.

"I'm the one running the show here, and you better learn to fall in line," I growl. "Why were you late tonight?" I demand because that's what pissed me off the most.

She looks away. "I'm not some dog that jumps just because you said so."

"Oh, but you'll happily let me fuck you like a dog."

Her scornful gaze meets mine. "You're such a fucking asshole."

I smile at her now, the urge to snap her neck strong. "You humiliated me in there. You were not only late, but then you walked in to meet my parents without wearing your engagement ring?"

She tries to shove me, but I crowd her even more now that we're out of sight of any onlookers. "I never asked for any of this!" she shouts.

"We have an agreement, and if you want to see your father's fucking guns again, you'll do as you're *told.*"

I'm livid because I know she's hiding things from me, even though I accepted that fact when I chose to blackmail her into this situation. Despite that, I still can't help but want to break her into submission.

"Your such an ass," she says defiantly. And that's when I see it, the glisten in her eyes. My heart falls to my stomach, and my brow furrows in confusion because I can't even understand it myself.

I go to touch her cheek, but she slaps my hand away. "Don't fucking touch me."

My rage morphs into something else. It turns itself on me. For as fierce as this woman is, there's still something precious inside her to break.

I take a step back, confused by my swirling

emotions. "Get in the car," I say quietly as I open the door. She shoves past me, and I slam the door behind her.

I'm so angry.

At her.

At myself.

At these raw emotions clawing at my chest that I don't entirely understand. And for some reason, they're only rearing their ugly head because of this woman.

My family is everything to me. And the reminder that she could hurt them or disappoint them in any way butts heads with the idea of simply using her. Tonight, only momentarily, I wondered what it might be like if my family accepted Jewel as my real wife.

It wouldn't be difficult for her to fit in. As quickly as it entered my mind, I closed that thought down, knowing it's not reality.

Perhaps it's the guilt for tricking my family with this ruse because I know it'll certainly break my mother if she ever finds out this is a lie. Four months from now, when I either kill Jewel or pay her so much money so she can flee and never see my family again, how will it impact them? Perhaps it's best I only have them around her for necessary events so they don't become too attached.

I never really considered how other people might

feel after this marriage. I've been focused on my empire, which is now within reach. *No,* I insist to myself. I'm not burdened by that. This is a means to an end to take over the family business. No more, no less.

I open the driver's side door and slide inside.

I grip the steering wheel tightly to keep from placing my hand on her knee. I become strangely addicted to the idea of being able to touch her whenever and wherever I want.

We sit in silence for the entire drive to her place, the tension palpable. She's removing her seat belt before I even pull over.

"Wait, Jewel." But she's already out of the car and slams the door in my face.

A tic flares in my jaw as I wind down the window and call out to her. "I'll pick you up tomorrow. You'll be shopping for a wedding dress!"

She flips me off without looking back, and I curse under my breath.

This fucking woman is driving me insane.

"Fuck!" I slam my hand down on my steering wheel, for some reason considering how much of an asshole I might actually be. I've never questioned how that might be a bad thing until now.

But seeing her eyes glisten with the hint of tears,

knowing she would never cry, made me realize I pushed her too far tonight. And I'm already trying to figure out how to make it up to her.

The next question is, why am I even trying to make it up to the woman who's supposed to kill me?

THIRTY-THREE
JEWEL

I'm an idiot. I don't know why, for even one second, I considered crossing paths with Eli Monti. When I had to meet with one of my client's men tonight in a sketchy alleyway, I was prepared for the worst. I'd agonized all day as to what I should provide in the way of intel. I needed to give them enough information that I appeared to still be in the game but not enough to jeopardize the current balancing act I was doing.

I wanted my guns first and foremost. I didn't give a shit about my reputation compared to that. But even that's a lie; I fucking love my job and don't want it threatened because of this asshole. My saving grace is that I've saved a lifetime's worth of money. If I truly wanted to, I could retire.

I angrily scoop into my caramel swirl ice cream as I sit in my bed, fucking fuming.

It might be easy for Eli to lie to his family about us, but it's not my thing. I don't get close to people. The reality of our wedding now happening within the month has me freaking out. I know it's not real. I know not to take it personally and that it's a business transaction at best. But I still have no idea how I'm going to pull this off. I scoop another spoonful of ice cream into my mouth and internally curse as a brain freeze takes over.

Stop being stupid, Jewel. Really think about this.

I purposefully removed my engagement ring tonight before meeting with my client's man. I don't know how closely they're following me, but I didn't want them discovering my engagement to the man they hired me to kill. For all I know, they might already know, and perhaps that's why they're asking for intel.

I couldn't see the man's face because he was wearing a mask. I tap the back of the spoon against my lip, thinking. If I can figure out who that man is, maybe it will give me a lead about the identity of the person who wanted Eli targeted in the first place.

Not that I care if they're targeting the Monti family. Okay, maybe I like Eli's mom a little, but her son most definitely should have a hit on him just for being the biggest asshole in the history of the world. But I need to understand who I'm working for now that I'm caught in the crossfire.

I grab my phone and call Rory. They answer on the second ring.

"I bought a yacht with the money you've been sending me lately," they say instead of a greeting. I smile.

"Maybe you should offer me to join you sometime," I reply, making them snort. Then, I get down to the reason for my call. "Can you look into any gangs or organizations known for wearing masks?"

"Any particular type of mask?" they ask.

"No, just a plain black mask."

"On it." Rory hangs up, and I'm hit with an intense abdominal cramp.

Wait a second...

I go to the bathroom and realize my period has started.

"Are you fucking kidding me?!" I say, groaning. I'd been so preoccupied with everything going on I must have lost track of my cycle. "Could it get any worse right now?" I sulk, leaning my head against the wall.

On the upside, at least I still have half a tub of ice cream. On the downside, when I reach the bottom of the tub, it most likely won't have all the answers I need.

I'm furious all over again as if it's the stress caused by Eli Monti that caused my period to start without my knowledge.

Fuck this guy and his broodiness. He sent me a message earlier, explaining that he'd like to make it up to me for being an ass, which is surprising for a man like him. He wants to take me for breakfast before we go wedding dress shopping.

That's a hard no on both counts.

It would appear that this asshole needs to be reminded of who he's dealing with. And I need to actually start looking for my guns.

So I grin to myself as I reply.

Me: Breakfast with an asshole.
Delightful. Don't be late. 💋

THIRTY-FOUR
ELI

I'm sitting in my car outside her apartment building. I texted her to warn her I was on the way, and she told me not to come up and that she'll meet me down here.

I've been waiting for over thirty minutes.

No sign of her.

I try calling.

No answer.

I message.

No answer.

I huff in frustration. I have tried to do the "patient and chivalrous" thing, which is so uncomfortable and out of character for me, and I'm now pissed for even trying, especially when I'm rewarded with her silence.

Pocketing my phone, I leave my car and am heading inside the building, when I receive a notification that someone has entered my apartment. Pausing outside Jewel's door, I open the app for the cameras I had set up and see someone wearing all black, walking around my private space. I watch as they go to my fridge, pull out a piece of cheese, and eat it as they open every door, then close them, leaving everything the exact same way. That's when the intruder turns, amber eyes staring directly at the camera I had installed just because of her. She has the fucking audacity to wave before she continues her search.

She's trying to find her guns.

Good luck to you, tigress; that's not going to happen anytime soon.

This little vixen actually has the balls to not only lie to me about her whereabouts and pretend she's taking her time to meet me but to break into my apartment *again.* I'm just now realizing that perhaps my approach of having minimal security personnel besides Ford and Hawke, might have been a miscalculation, especially when it comes to this sneaky woman.

My other camera indicates motion detected as she walks into my bedroom. She spins dramatically and then throws herself backward onto the bed with a smile, her knee-high-boot-clad feet kicking into the air before they land on my bed.

"Jewel," I say into the microphone. She offers me a small wave as she lounges on my bed. "Get your shoes off my bed." She laughs but doesn't do as she's told. Of course she doesn't. I would expect nothing less from her.

Flipping onto her stomach, she gives me a perfect view of her ass in those leather pants as she crawls to my bedside table. She proceeds to pull open the drawer and then wreaks havoc on the contents. My jaw tics. She's purposefully fucking with me because she knows I like things in a particular way.

She finds something and lifts it toward the camera, showing me what she has.

A condom.

"Guess you won't be needing this," she says, opening it and throwing it to the floor so it can't be used again. Not that I ever bring women to my apartment. That condom has probably been sitting in there for years.

She rolls over with an exhausted sigh. "Where are my guns?" she asks, getting to her knees and eyeing the camera.

"Meet me at the dress shop, and I may give you one," I tell her. She rolls her eyes, and I can't help the smile that teases my lips.

Her apartment door opens, drawing me back to

where I am, and her roommate is startled when she almost runs into me.

I drop my phone into my jacket pocket, aware of where I have to go next.

"Oh, she isn't here," she tells me before I can say a word.

"I know."

"Okay, then." She steps into the hallway, locks the door, double-checks that it's locked, then walks around me.

She's a strange one.

I pull my phone back out and check the cameras again. Jewel is lazily curled up on my bed, playing with the remote and trying to get the TV working.

"Jewel Diamond, we have an appointment today," I remind her.

"I don't give a fuck. I have my period. I hurt. And I still don't like you, asshole." She flips me off.

I crack my neck from side to side. It's about time I teach her a lesson... in obedience.

WHEN I ARRIVE at my apartment, I find her right where I saw her last—on my bed. I go to speak, then notice she's fallen asleep. I drop the plastic bag of chocolate, pads, tampons, and something called period undies, which I don't entirely understand the need for, onto the dresser. As much as I want to punish her for being a brat, I still feel a pang of guilt—*not* something I've ever felt before—for how I spoke to her last night.

A soft snore leaves her.

Fucking hell.

I pull off one of her boots, and when I get to the second, she startles awake, kicks me in the chest, and basically crawls up the bed, ready for a fight.

"What the actual fuck?" I shout, rubbing my chest.

She lays her hand over her heart and starts breathing heavily. "You scared me."

"Yeah, well, you broke into my house and fell asleep in my bed. What are you, Goldilocks or something?"

She slides back down the bed with a yawn. "I was tired. I didn't sleep well, and your bed is comfy."

My smile doesn't meet my eyes as I continue to attempt to be... nice.

"Next time, take your fucking boots off," I grumble. I pick up the plastic bag and dump it in front of her. I begin undoing the buttons of my shirt. There's no mark from when she kicked me, but it doesn't feel entirely clean now.

"What's this?" she asks curiously.

I peel off my shirt as I say, "You said you had your period and you were tired, so I brought some snacks."

"And tampons and pads and... are those period undies?" She looks up at me in shock. Her mouth falls open as her gaze scans over my body. I flex my muscles for her, and she looks away as if uninterested.

Smirking, I comment, "Well, I assumed by your pissy mood it must be bad."

A ruthless smile appears on her face. "You're just saying that to really piss me off, aren't you?"

Yes.

I witnessed my father once mention my mother's mood swings during that time of the month, and I learned very quickly it was not the right thing to say.

"Besides, I'd much rather you eat this than steal slices of cheese from my fridge like some kind of rodent."

"Could be worse; I could leave another dead one in your drawer."

"That was absolutely despicable," I reprimand as I step out of my closet and button the clean shirt.

"You're telling me. I saw that thing dead in an alleyway and used a plastic bag to scoop it up. I wasn't touching that. By the way, I noticed you threw the entire dresser out."

She smiles as she breaks off a piece of chocolate and pops it into her mouth.

"Why are you here? If you want a key, I can give you one."

Her knees curl up to her chest, and I hate how... vulnerable it makes her look. I sit at the end of the bed.

"You're a dumbass for trusting me." She huffs out a breath. "Don't you feel even the slightest bit bad for lying to your family about us?"

It dawns on me then; perhaps that's why she was so off last night. Does my little Kitten have a conscience? That makes one of us.

"No. I was backed into a corner by my parents, and this was my way of charging through it. So whether you like it or not, we're going through this together."

"I want my guns," is the only response I get. Glancing at the floor, I find the condom she tore open.

"Why? Has the order to finally kill me been made, and you're worried you won't get your guns before I die?" I antagonize.

Her mouth opens and then closes. She curls further into herself. "This isn't a joke."

"I never thought it was. But I live by the saying, 'Keep your friends close and enemies closer.' And it would appear I don't have many friends."

"With a personality like yours, I can see why someone would want to kill you."

I chuckle at that, then pull her feet toward me. She seems perplexed as I begin to massage her feet and legs. I don't like seeing her shrinking herself into a ball, making herself smaller than she is.

This client of hers has been on my mind for some time now. No matter how hefty a price I pay Will, he can't track them down. It's also strange that the person hasn't yet authorized the actual hit. Part of me has started wondering if perhaps it's not about the hit at all but that someone's using her to get my attention. A gamble considering she could've ended up dead.

I even considered she's working for someone on personal matters, but everything Will has provided me about Jewel indicates her being a lone wolf. The only person she is in touch with is a man named Craig, and he's had nothing to do with my family.

I grow more impatient the longer this is drawn out. I thought her client would've made some move by now. Shown some kind of play.

Jewel slowly relaxes with each press of my fingertips into her tense muscles.

My gaze lands on her engagement ring. "You're wearing your ring again."

She rolls her eyes, but I notice how her body eases

back against the headboard. "I thought it was mandatory since we're dress shopping today."

"Oh, so now you'll willingly come."

She crosses her arms over her chest. "I just want to get this over and done with so you'll return my guns."

"What about the money?" I ask.

She shrugs. "I have more money than I know what to do with. And I'll have even more after taking you out."

Curious, I ask, "How much is my head worth?"

What lengths would someone go to take me out?

"Too much for the prize, but not enough for the hassle," she quickly replies as she slips her feet out of my grasp. "Which is why when you pay me alongside giving me my guns back, it might make it barely acceptable."

"You may be uncomfortable in that when going to try on dresses." I wave my hand at her tight leather pants that she knows I can't look away from. She strides over to the small bag in the corner she must've brought with her.

"The only one who is uncomfortable with me wearing these pants is *you*," she taunts. To make a point, she undoes her leather pants, her gaze on me as she shimmies them down her legs until she kicks them off.

Once she's free of them, she unbuttons her shirt, showcasing her gorgeous tits in a black bra. Discarding it to the side, she stands in front of me in nothing but a G-string, the bra, and a smile.

"You don't really think you'll get away with taunting me like that, do you?" I ask, stepping closer.

"My guns?" she purrs.

"After we're married," I tell her for what feels like the hundredth time. "Momentary truce?" I suggest, my cock already swelling. I grab her by the hip, my thumb brushing over the aggressive neon bear with sharp claws and teeth. The sight of the tattoo causes the corner of my lips to twitch.

With a small smile, she flicks her hair over her shoulder and then turns to a small backpack she left by the door. She bends over, showing me her ass, and my cock painfully strains against my pants. Reaching into the bag, she pulls out a dress and then slips it on.

"Ready." She smiles, but it doesn't reach her eyes. And I know she's trying to work out a way to get out of this marriage and just take her guns.

Lucky for her, I like to play games.

And I always win.

THIRTY-FIVE
JEWEL

I left my clothes scattered on his floor, and he didn't pick them up, which I find funny because he immediately changed his shirt after I kicked him, even though there wasn't a smudge on it. Or maybe he was doing it to show me his body. However, I have a feeling he doesn't need validation from me. I'm sure Eli Monti gets that wherever he goes.

He takes a few phone calls on the drive to the bridal store. I listen keenly to see if anything might be of use to me or my client, not that I gave them any earth-shattering information last time. Despite keeping me close, Eli doesn't seem to be entirely stupid, which is contrary to my previous beliefs.

He has a conversation with Ford and then one with Hawke, who stole Ford's phone. They both complain about not being by Eli's side as much lately. I agree with them somewhat. If they're his seconds and mostly in charge of his security, shouldn't he be more wary about being alone with me? Especially when I could turn on him at any moment. But he doesn't seem particularly worried about that.

He discusses business with one of his father's men, but it's nothing I can use against him. And then he's silent for the rest of the drive. I notice the way he keeps glancing at the ring on my finger. It is a beautiful ring, not something I would've chosen for myself, but it's part of the act, I suppose.

When he pulls up at the bridal store, he stops me from undoing the seat belt. He seems... nervous isn't the right word. Eli is someone who could never be nervous.

"You don't like the ring, do you?" he asks.

My gaze narrows on him. "I don't hate it or love it. I'd rather not have to wear it."

His jaw works back and forth as he pulls out a small box.

"You collecting rings now?" I ask sarcastically.

"No, this is my mother's. She asked me if she could give it to you. When you didn't wear your ring to the dinner party, she assumed it was because you were too nice to say you didn't like it."

"Wait. Why do you even care if I like the ring?" I ask, confused. It's a fake engagement and a fake wedding.

"Because it would look bad on me if I weren't pleasing my wife," he says, opening the box. The smart-ass remark remains on my tongue as the sight of the ring takes my breath away.

It's simple and elegant. I like it more than the showy one he gave me. It's not so big that it's going to scratch and bang into everything.

He takes my hand and slowly removes the first ring. Then, with ease, he slips the new ring on. It's a better fit. Not that I'd admit it to him and not that I should feel a certain way about the replacement.

"You're not pulling it off. I assume you like it better?"

"Why did your mother give me this?" I ask, studying it closer. It's a pink square-cut diamond with a few smaller diamonds embedded around the band.

"It's not her engagement ring or anything," Eli explains, placing the much larger ring in the box. "But it has sentimental meaning to her. I suggested I buy you another ring, but she was adamant you have this one, which might be more to your liking."

"If it means something to your mother, you

shouldn't be giving it to me, Eli." I go to remove it, but he places his hand on top of mine to stop me.

"Trust me when I say there are very few things I can deny my mother. If I didn't give this to you, it'd raise suspicions about the seriousness of our relationship."

The *fake* relationship, I want to remind him. But I can't stop staring at the ring, nor can I ignore the fact that I do like it so much more. This façade is consuming me as much as it is confusing me.

"How sentimental are we talking?" I question, not sure I want to know the answer. Besides, once this is all over, I'll make sure she gets it back. Then again, she might not appreciate possessing a ring her son's killer wore.

My head starts hurting.

"My father bought her this ring when she had a miscarriage a few years after me." When my expression turns sad, he chuckles. "It wasn't because of the loss that he bought it but because, despite the challenges they might face, there would always be love and support within our family.

"I'd forgotten about it until she brought it out, and I agree it's better suited for you than the other one. Might not interfere with your gun-holding and waitressing shenanigans."

I laugh. "Did you just say 'shenanigans'?"

He seems shy and a bit vulnerable right now. I go to remove the ring. "Eli, this is way too personal for me to have." He once again stops me.

"It was always going to be mine, but she wasn't going to give it to me. She wanted my future wife to have it. I didn't know that until after we had dinner with my family."

This is too heavy in sentiment, and it feels as if we're getting deeper and deeper into twisted lies. I'm starting to feel shameful about my part in it. His family's involvement now really adds gravity to the situation. I've never had a family welcome me with open arms like his has. I've only had Craig since my dad died, and I remind myself I should be grateful for him.

But it makes me feel small. It shows me what other people have that I've deliberately stayed away from because I'm scared I'll like it.

Shut up, Jewel. You're just feeling sad and miserable because your body is aching from your period.

"Shouldn't you save this for your *real* wife?"

"You're my wife now. That's the only thing I need to focus on."

"But I'm not." I expel a heavy sigh, trying to break the tension. "I still haven't walked down the aisle."

"And you won't until we find you a dress." He

flashes me an arrogant grin as he hands me the box with the other ring. "Sell this or do whatever you want with it."

I gape at him. "I can't sell this Eli. I—" He closes his car door, cutting me off, and I wring my hands in the air. *That asshole.* He opens my door and offers me his hand.

I set the box on the floor in the car, wondering if it is okay to just leave a ring that's probably worth the amount of some of my top-end jobs, out where anyone could see it and take it.

"Ready to play at being the perfect fiancée?" he asks, and my throat constricts as the reality of walking into a bridal store hits me. I want to run the other way, and I'm certain that's why Eli takes my hand as if it's the most natural thing in the world. I want to pull away, but even I know my limits. Happy wife, happy life, as they say.

A woman opens the door for us excitedly. "Mr. Monti, we're so happy to see you. And this must be the lucky woman."

I smile as I inwardly laugh at the suggestion of being lucky. I'm anything but.

"Your mother is already here waiting," she tells us.

"Your mother?" I ask, trying to keep my tone neutral.

"Yes, my mother," he replies. Before I can pull him to the side, he quietly adds, "When she found out your mother wasn't involved, she wanted to be here."

I take a sharp breath, trying to ease my anxiety. It never crossed my mind to ask if my mother wanted to be involved. Not that I would have for a fake wedding, but the reality is, I wouldn't even invite her to my real wedding. She has no right to be in my life. But Eli's mother... *wanted* to be here?

I want to tell myself it's because she's worried about who her son is marrying and that I should gear myself up to be interrogated or even persuaded to leave him. But unless Rya Monti is a phenomenal actress, she never gave me that impression at all. And that's what makes this situation harder.

She gave me her ring.

I'm in way too deep with his family already, and, for some reason, I seem to be the only one conscious of this. It makes me feel guilty. How the fuck is that even possible since I haven't had a conscience since... ever.

"How long has she been waiting?" I ask nervously. I didn't know we had someone waiting for us. If I had, perhaps I wouldn't have been so eager to piss him off by breaking into his apartment.

"My mother is always punctual. In fact, she usually

arrives in advance." He tries to hide the smile as the blood drains from my face.

"It's not funny," I hiss under my breath. "You could've given me a heads-up."

The older woman guides us through the large space where multiple gorgeous dresses are on display. There's no one else here except for a receptionist who smiles at us. When we're taken into the second room, which is smaller but far more grandly decorated, I spot Rya. She's sitting on a pink sofa, holding a glass of champagne while she rapidly types on her phone one-handed. A bottle of bubbly sits on the side table next to her very expensive handbag.

She looks up and smiles as we enter. "You made it." She stands and says, "Eli called and said you felt sick. Do you feel better now?" She places her hand against my forehead, and I instinctively step back at the touch before realizing I'm doing it.

"S-sorry," I stutter.

"Don't be." She gives me an understanding look. I don't think I've ever had someone actually try to take my temperature, and it's unnerving how obvious I just made it. I don't care what people think about me, but it's becoming more apparent that I've been cast in a role I'm sadly unequipped for.

"I hope you weren't waiting too long," I finally say.

"Not at all. It gave me time to reply to some emails. Lord forbid a law firm run on its own. There would be no fun in that." She chuckles.

"Don't let Pops hear you say that," Eli jokes. She smiles as she presses a kiss to his cheek.

"Please. Your father still comes in with bloody cuffs and thinks I don't notice."

The woman beside us shifts uncomfortably at that comment, and I try my hardest not to laugh at the absurdity of the situation. I must truly be out of my mind, marrying into a mafia family.

"Now, shoo. You shouldn't be here. It should just be us girls," Rya says to Eli, hands on her hips.

I reach out frantically and grab his wrist. His eyebrows shoot up in surprise. "No, I want him here," I'm quick to say. For some reason, being alone with Rya Monti terrifies me. Not because I'm intimidated by her. Okay, maybe I am a little. But because I feel too guilty for lying to her, she's showing me what having an actual mother might be like. I find it strange that had she been my mother growing up she wouldn't have thought twice about my fixation on guns or my killer instinct. It might've been embraced, instead of scorned, and maybe I wouldn't have been abandoned by my own mother.

Eli smirks and slides his hand around my waist. Okay, now the fucker is pushing his boundaries.

"You don't want it to be a surprise?" he asks.

"No. I want to wear what you like. It's your special day, too," I reply, careful not to glare him to death or push his hand away from me. Each time he touches me now, I hate that I like it more and more. I inwardly remind myself that I hate this man. "So yes, I'd like it if you stayed."

"I'll stay, then." He leans, in brushing his lips over my neck. I know we're being watched, so I close my eyes briefly to make it believable.

Rya seems pleased with the exchange, and I realize that Eli probably never had intentions of leaving. After all, he is not a man of tradition, even if his family has some whack old-school rules.

"Would you like a glass of champagne?" Rya offers. "Might help with the nerves."

"Yes." I all but scoop the glass out of her hand and down half of it. I'm not a big drinker, but I need some liquid courage to get through today.

The sales associate seems affronted by my desperate need for booze but walks me to the dressing room and asks, "Do you have any idea of what style you might like?"

"None whatsoever," I deadpan.

"Perfect. Then I'll bring a variety of choices out."

Fan-fucking-tastic.

THIRTY-SIX
JEWEL

I'm two drinks in and rocking a nice buzz. All the dresses are tight. Some are poofy, and others look like layers of tablecloths were draped on top of me.

They look great, sure. But every time I put another one on, I'm sucked deeper into a well of anxiety. I don't get anxious, dammit. But trying on wedding dresses is freaking me the fuck out.

I've listened in on some of the casual conversation between Eli and Rya. They're talking about the wedding planning. I'm grateful to be as far away from that bullshit as possible. Eli is more intelligent than to ask my opinion on cutlery for a wedding I don't want any part in.

I step out of the changing room, now wearing the fourth dress. Eli looks up at me through his eyelashes with an expression of wanting to fuck me in every dress I walk out in. When I spin to look at myself in the mirror, I feel like I can't breathe. Maybe she tightened this one too much?

I close my eyes momentarily, reminding myself just to get this over and done with so we can get married, and I can get my fucking guns back and then run away from whatever bullshit this is stirring within me.

"I think that's a perfect fit," the sales associate says as she tightens the corset on my back even more. I almost keel forward from how suffocatingly tight it is.

The alcohol was meant to help, but right now, I feel like everything is spinning.

"Do you love it? It fits you like a glove. Stunning, really," Rya gushes as she stands and approaches me with a third glass of champagne, holding it out to me. Without a word, I grab the glass, throw it back in one go, and then hand it back to her. Fuck etiquette right now. I'm trying my hardest not to freak the fuck out.

I never wanted marriage. I wasn't made for it. And although I know all of this is fake, my heartbeat is trying to kick through my ribcage.

"Jewel, are you okay?" Rya asks, carefully placing a hand on my shoulder.

I offer a tight smile and nod my head.

"Happy with this one?" I ask Eli through gritted teeth.

He stands and prowls toward me, his gaze taking in every detail before he stops in front of me.

"I think any dress you put on would be perfect," he says matter-of-factly, but then his hand runs up the outside of the dress, bunching it as his fingers trail up my skin. "But you also have amazing legs. What about a slit up the skirt to show them off?" He smirks, and the heat from my anxiety mixes with something else—desire. I need to be grounded again because I feel like I'm spiraling right now, and I keep my gaze locked with his, as if it's the only thing keeping me here.

"I'd like to be left alone with my fiancée for a moment," he announces. Rya and the sales associate share a brief glance and then leave us alone in the room. The moment they're gone, I storm around him, grab the bottle of champagne, and start chugging.

He snatches it from me. "Hey!" I demand. He steps into my space and turns me so I face the full-length mirror. His hands come around to my front as he stands behind me. "What are you doing?"

"Look at yourself," he calmly instructs.

I don't want to. I don't want to see myself in this dress. I've struggled with looking directly at myself this whole time. He grabs under my jaw and tilts my head up. I want to look away but can't because he holds me in place.

"Do you want to know what I see?" he asks as his hands bunch the front of my dress. He then begins trailing his fingers over the exact same spot he suggested I get the split.

"A ticket to your family's business," I snark back.

"A powerful woman," he insists. "A woman who doesn't run from a challenge and hits her fears head-on."

"And what do you think my fear is, Mr. Monti?" I breathe out, unable to ignore his fingers caressing my skin. Unable to look away from the view of us in the mirror.

"Marrying me... or anyone else. Commitment. Having a family."

My eye twitches at the last comment. It was dead on and too close to my truths and vulnerabilities, as they've started surfacing these previous few weeks. I smile with twisted hatred at his insight. I adjust my foot slightly and bring the heel of my shoe down hard on his foot.

He grins as I press down harder. His hands continue to trail upward, then tuck under the dress and into my panties.

"You're out of your mind if you think I'm going to

let you fuck me in this wedding dress. Besides, I'm on my period, motherfucker." I lean back into him, purposefully pressing all my weight onto the heel, digging into his foot. It must hurt, but it doesn't show in his expression.

His other hand wraps around my throat, and he smiles as he holds me against him. "You forget red is my favorite color."

"This is a $100,000 dress."

"The worth of the dress means fuck all when it's the woman beneath it I want to unravel."

I try to move away, but he tightens his grip. "You might not think this dress, this ring, or this wedding is for you. But you are my gift to unwrap until our agreement comes to an end. You think this dress is for everyone else? I couldn't give a fuck what they think. It's about my wife dressing for *me*. It's about my wife tempting me even before she meets me at the end of the aisle. You look delectable in every dress you've tried on. It's not the dress that's the problem. It's time you submit to this agreement entirely."

His thumb circles my sensitive clit, and I want to wring his neck as much as I want him to continue. "So why don't we have a momentary truce?" he suggests.

"Your mother is standing outside this room," I whisper-shout.

"I'm not thinking about my mother, Kitten." He presses himself more firmly against me. Through all the material, I can barely feel him, but I know he's hard. His hand slips lower, and his fingers feather against my folds.

"This is sick," I say, conscious of how heavy my flow is right now.

"You didn't really think you were marrying a sane man, did you?" He chuckles as he gently tugs the string of my tampon. "As I've told you before, red is my favorite color."

The moment the tampon is free from my body, he drops it to the floor. I gape in embarrassment at our reflections in the mirror, but he hisses as he inserts a finger into me, and my expression changes to a mixture of mortified and mesmerized.

"Admit it, it feels good," he whispers into my ear. "Momentary truce?"

I don't want to admit it. I want to tell him to stop. To tell him this is wrong. But my mouth is dry. And his fingers feel so good.

Maybe it's the buzz of the champagne that's locked up my words, leaving me only able to stare into his eyes, as if right now they're the one thing keeping me from floating away. I eventually nod in answer to his question. Momentary truce or whatever the fuck it is we're doing.

"Remove your panties," he instructs as he steps back.

I gulp as I do as he says and then turn to face him. He watches as they slip down my legs to my ankles, and I step out of them. His nostrils flare as he undoes his pants, his cock springing free as he says, "On your knees."

That's when I notice the glisten of red on his fingers and want to shy away. "There is nothing about you that disgusts me, *amore mio*." My heart squeezes at the endearment, but then I realize the type of sick monster he is when he brings his fingers to his lips. He licks them, and I fall to my knees. I'm unsure if I do it out of shock or because I can't not do what he says in this moment. He's so otherworldly in his sexual and primal demand, pushing me in ways I never thought possible. And it doesn't repulse me. No, it calls to something in me I didn't know was there.

"That's a good girl," he praises as he looks at me expectantly. I stare at his massive, veiny cock and lick my lips. The white dress pools around me, and despite the expensive garment I wear, he looks at me as if I'm a whore. My core floods with heat, and I lean forward for a taste. I lick a drop of pre-cum, the salty taste far more inviting than the bubbles of champagne that have clearly gone to my head.

I slide my mouth over his cock, my lips stretching to accommodate him. I fist him at the same time, unable to fit the length of him in my mouth. He brushes my cheek with the backs of his fingers, and I make a point not to look away as I try my best to take all of him. "So fucking beautiful on your knees for me, Kitten. Now, dig your claws in and make me come."

He slips his hand to his back beneath his suit jacket, and a moment later, he pulls out a knife. "If you bleed, so do I."

I pull back as he brings the tip of the knife to my chest. My breath hitches before I realize he's cutting down the front of the dress.

"What are you doing?" I whisper frantically, freaking out that he's so casually destroying a six-figure dress.

"We agreed on a slit, didn't we?" He smirks. "Besides, your breathing is too shallow in this dress, and I want you to accommodate all of me."

Suddenly, I can breathe properly, and he smirks as he hands me the knife. "Carve your initials into a place my mother won't see."

And my mind goes completely blank as he threads

his fingers through my hair and brings my lips to his cock again.

THIRTY-SEVEN
ELI

The moment her lips are around my cock, I'm ready to blow all over that beautiful face of hers. I can tell I'm pushing her to her limits, but she's the first woman I think can actually keep up with my depravity.

Her teeth graze down my cock, and I hiss in pleasure.

This fucking mouth of hers.

She's on her knees, in a wedding dress I can't wait to paint red. She's a fucking goddess. As she edges the blade toward me, I pray that somehow I'll be able to blackmail this woman to stay by my side even after our arrangement is over because she's made so perfectly for me.

She keeps the leisurely pace on my cock as tears streak down her face. She tips the blade to my left leg, right above the pretty little scar she gave me when she stabbed me.

"Do it," I tell her. "Carve your fucking initials into my leg."

I never want to forget this moment.

I never want to forget *her*.

There's a mix of pleasure and burning pain that has my cock twitching with excitement as she carves J.D. into my left leg. Every fine line and curve that slices into my flesh has me so close to coming in her mouth that I'm not sure I'll make it all the way through.

The moment she's finished with the letters, I yank her back from my cock by her hair and bring her to standing. My lips are on hers within seconds as I shove her back until we find a flat surface. She smashes against the mirror, cracking it. When I consider it might hurt her, I pick her up and step back.

She moans into my mouth desperately, her wild beast calling mine. I sink her onto my cock, and grunt as she leans back, her arms around my neck. The white dress is torn in places, spots of blood marring the pristine color.

But it's not enough.

I want more blood.

More of her.

All of her.

She bounces on my cock like a good girl, and my balls tighten at her desperate neediness. She's built so fucking perfectly for me.

"Such a perfect fiancée," I croon, and one of her hands wraps around my throat delicately, but her nails dig into my skin in warning. I smile as I kiss her, letting her take and take from me.

"You want to be fucked like an animal? I'll fuck you exactly like that, Kitten." I bite her bottom lip and pull. She moans in pleasure, but her eyelids burst open as I set her down.

"What are you—" I spin her around and place her hands on the end of the couch.

"I want you to watch me as I fuck you in this wedding dress," I tell her. Her breath hitches, and I smile as I glance down and see the blood on my cock and her inner thighs. So fucking wet and perfect for me.

I focus on our reflection in the broken mirror as I grab her hips and slam into her. She bucks forward, those beautiful legs spread just for me. So fucking beautiful.

I slam into her again and again, mesmerized as I fuck her into oblivion. Her tits bounce out of the ruined dress as I fuck her like a madman.

Her legs begin to tremble as she takes me, and I see

her face contort in pleasure as she meets my gaze in the mirror. "This is how you'll be rewarded the night you walk down the aisle to me," I tell her as I pound into her.

"Only if we have a truce," she gasps out.

I thread my fingers through her hair and arch her back.

"Oh, we'll have a truce on our wedding night." I slap her ass and she moans. I slap again, a red flush beginning to blemish her skin. On the third slap, she comes undone, and the moment I grab her limp body to hold her up, I jerk inside her.

"Fuck," I grit out, surprised by the force as I feed her my cum. I rock into her a few more times, pushing my cum and her blood back inside so no drop goes to waste.

As she trembles, she begins to laugh, and I can't help but be amused as well, even though I don't know what she finds so funny. I lean over and kiss her shoulder.

"Penny for your thoughts?" I say as I continue rolling my hips against her, not yet wanting to leave her warm and messy pussy.

"We're actually going to hell," she says in disbelief.

I chuckle. "We're going to hell together. That should at least keep it entertaining."

"Not when you try to take over the devil's job," she says, pushing away from me.

The room's a fucking mess and the dress she's wearing looks like it was massacred. A faint red blush paints her cheeks when she looks at herself in the mirror. I step toward her and brush my thumb against her flushed skin.

"Let's agree that dress number four isn't the right choice," I say, and she lets out a shaky breath. "Go clean up in the bathroom. I'll take care of the mess out here."

She arches an eyebrow in surprise. "I don't think you've cleaned a day in your life."

"Usually only dead bodies. So blood, glass, and a few items on the floor are nothing."

She glances around again and then back at me, raising a brow. "You know you're not normal, right?"

I smirk. "Depends on whose definition you're using."

She shakes her head in disbelief as she walks away on shaky legs, and before I tuck my cock away, I take in her initials on my leg, a smirk touching my lips.

I don't care what dress she steps out in next because I already got what I wanted from today.

THIRTY-EIGHT
ELI

She's drunk. And I think my mother likes her. I basically carry my soon-to-be wife to the car and close the door behind her once I've deposited her in the passenger seat.

My mother is waving at Jewel, who gives her a thumbs up, and she can't help but laugh. "She's really nervous about this wedding, isn't she?"

I freeze at my mother's insight. I hope she thinks it's only premarital jitters and has nothing to do with the level of intensity that it actually is.

"Marrying into a powerful family has its challenges," she elaborates. "But I see the way you two look at each other. The way she challenges you? I've never seen someone keep you on your toes like that before. Having a family welcome her in might be overwhelming for her, though, so make sure you support her every step of the way. Be *nice*."

"I'm always nice," I say defensively, and she gives me a *yeah, sure* look.

"You only get one chance at this."

"You had two chances," I remind her.

She smiles in memory at that. "I literally shot your father in the leg right in front of his mother and then ran from the chapel. Let's just say the second time, when we officially married, she wasn't so keen on me. But she respected me."

"Are you giving Jewel permission to shoot me in the leg?"

"No, but at the very least, I hope she gives you hell to keep you in line." She smirks. "I really like her. She's lovely, but she isn't used to this. You'll be the only family she has. Don't take that honor for granted."

I already knew that. I know when she gets over-whelmed. I see her nervous habits, for example, when she bites at the skin around her nails.

I look over at Jewel, who's scrolling through her phone. Her feet are on my dashboard, and I feel my left eye twitch. I know all of these things, but I didn't care about them before. Now, there's a sliver of guilt because she's becoming a multifaceted person to me. Not just a pawn. Not just a toy.

My phone starts ringing in my pocket, and I know who it is without looking. It's Michelle, angry I canceled our regular meetups. She's been calling every day. And every day, I don't answer.

My mother taps on the window, and Jewel lowers it. "Make sure my son gets you some dinner on the way home."

Jewel hiccups with a smile and somberly says, "You're a good mom. I wish I had you as a mom."

My mother cups her cheek. "You're already a part of the family, dear." Then she turns to me. "Put her to bed and make sure she drinks plenty of water." With that last piece of advice, she heads toward her own car. I wait until she's gone before I get into mine.

"You. You are a piece of fucking shit," Jewel says with her eyes closed, head leaning back against the headrest.

"Tell me what you really think," I tease, and her eyelids pop open. She swings her head to the side to face me.

"I did, or are you stupid as well?" I can't help the smirk that fights to break out on my lips as I start the car. "I had too much to drink. I hate marriage, and I hate you."

"I know, Kitten. I know," I soothe as I wrap my hand over her knee. She grumbles in complaint as two of her fingers hook around one of mine. When I look over at her again, her eyes are closed, and she appears to be sleeping. She really didn't get any sleep last night, but it is most likely up to God knows what.

She sleeps the entire drive back to her apartment. It's not until I pull over that her eyes open in surprise, and her hand leaves mine.

Turning off the car, I get out and make my way around the car to her door. Opening it, she attempts to unclip her seat belt but fails and throws her hands in the air. "Now you're trying to trap me in this car too."

Leaning over her, I unbuckle the seat belt, and as I do, I can feel her death glare on the side of my head. Having a woman stare at me with such hatred is not something I can say I'm used to. And it actually makes me want to laugh.

"You're free," I say, sweeping my hand toward her apartment building. She huffs before she gets out and walks straight past me to the entrance. I shut the car door and follow her as she stumbles her way inside. I carry the half-finished burger and fries I stopped to buy her. I try not to laugh as she struggles to unlock her door. Growling, she throws the key at the door and rests her head against the wall. "Need a hand?" I offer, my amusement clear in my voice. She scowls at me.

Here she is, a woman with precise aim—probably

better than any of my men—and she's angry she can't get a key in a lock.

It's comical, really.

She flips me off but doesn't reject my offer. She stands to the side and takes the bag of food from me as I bend down to pick up her keys and unlock the door. When I open it, she's elbow-deep in the bag again, pulling out fries.

She steps past me and tries her hardest to walk in a straight line to her room.

Her roommate doesn't seem to be home. I close the apartment door and go to the kitchen to grab her a glass of water. When I reach her room, I can hear her swearing under her breath. Somehow, she's gotten tangled in her dress. I can't take my eyes off drunk Jewel for a second. I chuckle as I put the water on the bedside table and then drop to my knees as she sits on the bed, now trying to undo her boots.

"Let me help," I say. I move her hand from her boot, unzipping and removing them both. She slides up the bed, dragging the fries with her and eating some more. "Drink the water," I tell her.

"Fuck you," she says but does as she's told. I chuckle.

"I'm not opposed to it." I look up and wink at her. She finishes the glass of water and then splays out on the bed. It's not long before a soft snore leaves her.

Clearly, she cannot handle her alcohol.

Standing up, I pick her up and put her comfortably on the bed so she doesn't complain about a sore back or neck the next day. My cock swells as my gaze roams down her figure. She's only wearing her bra and underwear. I feel bad for the mess I left behind on her, so I go to her bathroom and wet a towel.

I clean up the mixture of blood and cum from her skin.

I don't feel bad lying to my parents, but I am starting to notice how perfectly this little she-devil might fit into my life. That thought becomes uncomfortable because just as I feel like I'm getting my fill of this woman, I'm yearning for more. I can't get her out of my head or my bloodstream, which might be turning into a weakness.

She turns over in her sleep, reaching for her pillow and hugging it tight.

She is beautiful. Stunning, really.

And then she starts to snore again.

THIRTY-NINE
JEWEL

My head is sore. Correction—it's fucking pounding. Drinking yesterday was a bad idea. I've never been a heavy drinker. I've had a few drinks here and there, but my father wasn't a drinker, and Craig hardly ever drank around me, so I never had any interest in it. Besides, I never liked the idea of being out of control. But yesterday, I clung to it like a crutch as I freaked the fuck out over seeing myself wearing a wedding dress.

A real fucking wedding dress.

Me.

In a wedding dress.

Heat floods my core as I think about the many sinful things I did in said wedding dress.

I groan as my phone starts ringing. I reach for it a few times, but then I give up. I brush my fingers through my hair with one eye open, and my hand snags on something.

Is my hair in a fucking braid?

My phone rings again, and I grumble as I sit up, the room spinning. I find a glass of water next, plus a couple of headache tablets on my bedside table. How did they get there?

My boots are sitting neatly on the floor at the side of the bed, and my phone won't stop ringing.

I answer it.

"Hello," I mumble, willing my blinds to close themselves to prevent the bright light from seeping in.

"Good morning. Either let me in, or I'll break the door down."

I sigh at Eli's demanding voice.

"Fine," I say as I stand, the room swirling around me. Definitely never drinking again.

Managing to make it to the door, I fling it open to find him standing on the other side, nicely dressed in a suit. That's when I look down at myself and realize I'm half-naked. I grumble because it's all I can manage to do before I turn and head straight back to my room. He closes the front door and follows me.

Crawling straight back into bed, I pull the bed covers over my face and hope he'll just go away. The bed dips under his weight, but he doesn't say anything.

He just shifts my head onto his lap and brushes his fingers through my hair. I want to fight him, but I just don't have the energy, and the head stroking is nice.

I must fall back asleep, and when I wake up again, I peek out from underneath the blanket.

"Did you braid my hair last night?" I ask with a dry mouth.

"I don't know what you're talking about," he replies, staring down at me with a smug expression.

"That's creepy."

"Says the girl, peeking out from her blankets."

Touché.

If someone asked me to describe Eli Monti when I first met him, patient would not be the first word to come to mind. But little by little, as I'm forced to understand him, I wonder if perhaps he's only like this with me. I inwardly frown at that.

"Why are you here?" I ask. Most likely to torture me to death with the embarrassment of yesterday. I don't even remember that much after leaving the shop. Did I give Rya Monti the thumbs up?

"One gun," he says, and it's enough to have me sitting up in a rush. He opens his jacket and reveals one of my handguns. My father bought it for me when I was thirteen. I love that one. "I wish your eyes lit up the same way when I reveal other things to you."

"You better not be referring to your cock."

He leans in with a smile. "What else would I be referring to?"

"If you want me to bounce on your cock in exchange for giving my guns back, no problem. Temporary truce now."

He chuckles. "Not quite, Kitten. Though I appreciate the enthusiasm."

"Then what do you want?" This asshole has had me jumping through hoops this whole time, but for him to actually offer up something important to me means he wants something he knows I'll put up a fight against.

"Move in with me," he says. All the excitement bleeds out of me, and I shuffle back under the covers and turn my back to him.

Is he fucking crazy? I'm not moving in with him. I don't even like him. I'm still grappling with the notion that I have to marry him. Living with him was not part of the deal. Yes, I could buy other guns. And I could finish my job and just fucking end him, but that means I would never find my guns.

And I really, really want my guns back.

"Agree, and you can have the gun. It's as easy as that. Besides, you already said my bed is comfy, and you've broken into my homes on more than one occasion. You might as well have a fucking key."

My gaze narrows as I turn to face him. "Give me two guns."

"One," he growls, and I know that's his final offer. I sigh.

"Is it the apartment or mansion?" I ask.

"Which do you prefer?"

"The one that'll go up in smoke easiest when I burn it to the ground."

The corner of his mouth twitches. "The apartment complex should do nicely, then. You can get the other guns back when the deal is done, and we sign the divorce papers."

Divorce papers. I try not to scoff as if this is going to end so smoothly. It'll most likely end with one of us dead, and we both know it.

"Are you doing a prenup?" I inquire sweetly.

"Of course I am. My mother is a lawyer," he says as if it should have been obvious.

"So you'll add in there about the money you owe me and that I'll definitely get my guns back?"

I wait for his response.

"No, because then she'll know this is all fake."

I cross my arms over my chest.

"That doesn't work for me. You could kill me by

the end or just divorce me and leave me with nothing I was promised."

"I'll pay you half right now." He reaches for his phone and pulls it out.

"You don't have my bank details," I remind him. He keeps on typing, and when he's finished, my phone dings. Checking it, I see he sent me money. "How did you get my account information?"

"I can get anything. The only thing I can't have is sitting across from me, smelling like she's two days past needing a good scrubbing. Now, how about you shower? We have somewhere to be."

He stands, places my gun on the side table, then turns to walk out. As he gets to the door, he looks back at me. "Unless you need help in the shower?"

"Fuck off."

"I'd like to fuck *you*," he says before answering an incoming call.

When he clicks the door shut behind him, I immediately pick up the gun. I sigh at its weight and the comfort of holding it in my hand. The memories with my father and a flood of relief wash over me having it back.

Clinging to these weapons might seem foolish to some, but they're all I have. It's as if they're permanently taken from me, I won't have anything grounding me in this world anymore. I really will be a phantom.

This whole situation with Eli is a shit show, mainly because it's the first time I've been truly seen. This gun placed in my hand is a reminder that that was never my intention.

I'm meant to remain a woman on my own path, dealing out death from the shadows. And somewhere, somehow, that part of me has started slipping. More specifically, started becoming overshadowed by another monster.

FORTY
JEWEL

"Act like you like me," he says as he drives us to fuck knows where. Sometimes, I think he keeps our destinations a surprise because if I had the knowledge of the location, I might be tempted to find the fastest exit route.

I showered and really took my time, intentionally pissing him off. But I eventually joined, him considering my bank account looks really nice right about now, and it's the least I can do as the fiancée of a future mafia boss. Vomit.

I just wanted him to leave my apartment, and I knew that wasn't going to happen unless I did as well.

"Why?" I ask as the car comes to a stop.

"Because it's our engagement party." He gets out of the car without another word.

I'm frozen in my seat. *What the actual fuck?*

This motherfucker.

No wonder he was rewarding me before he got me in the car.

He fucking set me up because he knew the family dinner was the most I could do.

But an engagement party? Get fucked.

I'm dressed way too casually for this while he's wearing a black suit. I mean, I'm used to him dressing above and beyond—no one is denying this man has style—but I have fucking jeans on, for fuck's sake.

"I'm not going," I state, looking at the fancy hotel he has every intention of dragging me through like some broodmare. I know it's fancy because it has a fucking doorman.

"Why not?" he asks.

"I'm wearing jeans," I snap, aggravated. "Why the fuck wouldn't you tell me we were coming to this?"

"You don't really care that you're wearing jeans, though. You don't give a fuck what anyone else thinks." He smiles arrogantly. "Besides, Kitten, do you really think I came unprepared? As you once said, you're just along for the ride, right? So, do as you're told."

I'm in absolute shock. Sometimes I think this asshole might have at least one nice bone in his body, and then it's like he resets to default within the span of seconds.

"You're just saying that so I get out of the car," I grumble, already in a foul mood from being hungover. He walks around to the back of the car and opens the trunk.

A valet waits for Eli to hand him the keys, and I pout in the front seat like a fucking child. I am not getting out of this car looking like this. It's true I don't give a fuck what anyone thinks about me, but I need mental preparation for this fiancée bullshit. And besides, I don't like being in the spotlight. I don't want all the questions about how we met and why we love each other because, truth be told, they'd wish they never asked.

Eli comes back to stand in front of my door and unzips a black garment bag, revealing a dress, as well as a shoebox.

"Will this do?" he asks triumphantly. I stare at the green dress and expensive pair of heels with red bottoms, willing them to burst into flames.

"You just store women's outfits in your trunk now?"

"No, I asked the lady who fitted you yesterday for a dress for tonight because, by the time you were on your second glass of champagne, I knew you wouldn't remember about today. You were actually the one who said you were a fan of green."

I vaguely remember that discussion. Fuck.

"And what, you didn't think to let me put this on in my apartment like a normal fucking person?"

"You are anything but normal, Kitten. If I had, you would've climbed outside your bedroom window and run. I would've spent the majority of the afternoon searching for you. But now you're right where you need to be."

"Fucking asshole," I hiss as I reach for the dress through the window. He seems rather smug, which pisses me off even more. I climb into the back seat and peel off my shirt. I pull the dress on, and when it's covering my top half, I shimmy my jeans down and then kick my shoes off. With a heavy sigh, I hold out my hand for the shoes. He opens the back door and hands me the heels so I can slide them on. I ignore his outstretched hand, exiting the car on my own, and stand beside him, studying myself through the side mirror. I touch up my hair, removing the braids he put in last night. My hair falls into waves, and I comb through it with my fingers, making myself as presentable as possible.

"Shouldn't you be paying some fancy makeup

artist to do my hair and makeup?" I grudgingly say under my breath.

"I suggested that yesterday, too, and you told me to mind my own fucking business." His upbeat tone grates on my nerves.

Sounds like something I'd say.

Once I've finished checking myself out, I snap on him. "What?" I ask, running my hands down my dress.

"Nothing." He grins, then adds, "But I have one more gift for you." He pulls out a black box and opens it. My eyes go wide, and I snatch it greedily from his hands. It's beautiful.

It's a small blade with diamonds scattered throughout the hilt and a thin leather garter to hold it in place on my thigh.

"I figured your outfit wouldn't be complete without a hidden weapon. And, selfishly, I think it's sexy when you have a knife on you."

I smile as I prop my heel on the car's bumper and strap on the blade under my dress. It fits perfectly. Unfortunately, this dress doesn't have a slit, so it's not as easily accessible, but having it there makes me feel secure and powerful.

"Do you like it?" he asks as I adjust my dress.

I smirk at him over my shoulder. "How do you know I won't use it on you tonight?"

"I'm hoping you do." He winks, and a barrage of memories flood me, thinking of him fucking me like a crazed animal while I carved lines down his back. I feel the heat rise to my cheeks as he chuckles and steps into my space. "Let me know if you want a momentary truce in a nearby closet."

I bite my bottom lip, wishing we could forget about all of this and I could just straddle him in the back seat of his car right now.

His hand comes to my lower back, and this time I don't flinch. I blame the hangover. He passes the keys to the valet, who is watching us with amusement before we walk inside. We go straight to the top floor, the elevator opening onto a rooftop. I recognize a few faces, but with others I'm not so familiar. I grit my teeth, preparing myself for the onslaught of attention and questions.

He moves his hand from my lower back to grip mine, where it is clenched at my side. He grips it tighter before I can pull away as if he knows my moves already.

How I wish that weren't true.

I turn to look at him. I've seen him kill people with these hands. Hell, he's almost choked me out plenty of times with their strength. And yet, here he is, displaying unity when these hands have only ever known murder.

"Michelle." I turn at the sound of her name and see the woman he used to fuck staring at me from across the roof. And if looks could kill, she might have a fair shot of putting me six feet deep, like she so obviously wants to.

Well, this night just got more interesting. But what would be more interesting? My bed. When I'm sleeping.

FORTY-ONE
ELI

Jewel pulls away, but I don't let her. Instead, I tug her even closer and wrap my arm around her waist.

Michelle smiles—it's utterly fake—as she approaches us, but Jewel doesn't smile back. I lean toward her, my intention to whisper in her ear to calm down, but she leans into me at the same time, and I take that offering, as a starved man would, and kiss her neck. I feel her body tighten, and her hand grips my trousers as if she is giving me a warning. But warnings are my favorite type of foreplay when it comes to this beautiful vixen. It means I'm getting under her skin. And I like it.

I like making her uncomfortable.

I like *her*.

Darting my tongue out, I slide it up her earlobe and take it into my mouth.

"Eli," she hisses in warning. "We have guests."

"Hmmm..." I hum, not stopping. She squeezes my leg, purposefully gripping the still-healing spot where she carved her initials. I still don't stop, though. It's impossible to stop when I want something so badly, audience be damned. I've always gotten what I wanted in this life, even if it takes a little longer than I initially hoped for. I haven't wanted to crawl between someone else's legs as much as I want to crawl between hers.

"I came to congratulate you, and you put on a performance like this? Rather poor behavior, wouldn't you say?" Michelle says, and Jewel now purposefully pushes me away, but I keep a hand on her hip.

"It's lovely to see you, Michelle," I reply, leaning in and air-kissing her cheek because the thought of touching any woman other than Jewel now repulses me. She places a kiss on my cheek, and she whispers something I don't quite hear. I pull back and see Jewel glaring daggers at her.

"What's wrong?" Michelle asks sweetly, but it's filled with a venomous undertone.

"Tell her to leave," Jewel demands, turning to me.

Michelle's smile remains. "I'm a guest. I'm not

leaving. I don't know if you're familiar with who my father is and the relationship our families have, but—"

"Leave," I say to Michelle as I scan the room. "If my fiancée doesn't want you here, then you won't be here."

Michelle's jaw drops open. "You can't just ask me to leave."

"I didn't ask." I raise a brow at her. "Our families' relationship has nothing to do with me. My priority is my fiancée." I say nothing more as I slip my hand into Jewel's, and we walk away.

Michelle looks as if she's going to explode when one of her friends ushers her away. I didn't know she was coming, but I didn't really think much about the guest list. If Jewel wants to kill her, so be it. I don't care.

I'm not going to do anything to make my future wife upset with me.

Even if this is a hoax, and I have to remind myself it isn't real.

It's somehow starting to feel real, though.

When we're a distance away from Michelle, who is loudly being removed from the party, Jewel leans in with a sickly sweet smile that is as fake as can be. "Kiss me like that again tonight, and I will tear your cock from your body."

"Shouldn't I be rewarded for doing as you said and

kicking Michelle out? And besides, I may like your hands on my cock. How about a truce tonight, Kitten?"

"Not even if your life depends on it." She keeps the smile intact as the twins approach us.

"Boss," Hawke says this to Jewel and not me. Her smile turns more genuine at that, and I want to pummel his ass for making her think he's funny in any way.

"Shouldn't you be irritating Billie somewhere?" I grit between my teeth.

"Nah, man, not in front of Dutton; he'll kill me," Hawke says airily.

"What makes you think *you* can't kill *him*?" Jewel asks innocently.

"That man's a crazy motherfucker," Hawke replies with a smile, slipping his hands into his pockets.

"You say that like you're not," Ford deadpans, then turns to Jewel. "We heard you met our parents at one of the auctions. How did you like the establishment?"

"Your mom's kind of crazy, and I'm into it," she confesses, and Hawke offers her a cheesy grin that I want to rip off his smug little face.

"Jewel. Eli," Dutton says, drawing my attention away from her. She inches away from me, most likely being considerate so I can talk to my cousin, who clearly doesn't like her. It takes everything in me not to pull her back. Dutton notices, and I hope he's the only one who does.

Billie and Hope join Jewel and the twins, who all head over to the food table. Dutton seems to be studying me, but I don't give a fuck. I want to make sure she's comfortable. Watching her freak out as she tried on the wedding dresses tugged at a part of me I never want to feel again. I don't want her to spiral because of me, not in that way.

My mother joins the group and pulls Jewel in for a hug. Jewel is awkward, but I really expected no less from her. My mother can read people very easily, so when I'm around Jewel, I'm careful to show that I want her. Which, let's make no mistake, I do. So that part isn't hard, and it works well that my mother understands that Jewel is not an affectionate person.

So, our game of push and pull is working.

For now.

"You're really doing this?" Dutton asks incredulously.

"Yep," I answer, not taking my eyes off my fiancée as my mother parades her around, introducing her to people. I watch as my mother grips Jewel's hand as if she knows she might try to escape.

"I'm sure your father would have given you the

business even if you didn't marry," Dutton says. Even though he thinks he knows my father, he doesn't.

Crue Monti loves to say how his wife made him a better man, which also includes being a better businessman. And while I don't want to believe him, I know my mother made him a better person. She once went away to Italy for a week without him, and he looked lost without her. Two days later, he was on his private jet on the way to Italy to "surprise her."

"Are you still going to kill her after all of this?" Dutton asks, bringing his glass to his lips. I pin him with a glare, and he shrugs. "Oh, right. Divorce was the agreed-upon plan. Word of advice, cousin. You're not looking at that woman like you want to kill *or* divorce her."

"That's none of your fucking business. Just learn to keep your mouth shut," I hiss as I look over his shoulder and see my father discussing business with a few of his men.

Dutton chuckles in disbelief. "I'll offer a great speech at your funeral."

"Whose funeral?" Billie asks, walking up behind me. "Stop giving Eli such a hard time for his puppy-love gaze."

"It's not a puppy-love gaze," I grit out at my youngest cousin, who just grins back at me.

"I like her." She salutes with her champagne glass. "She's kind of a little mysterious too, you know. We had no idea you were seeing someone, and now we have to tell all of Hope's cutesy artist friends that you're off the market."

"Don't bring them around." Dutton pins her with a stare. "Their type isn't made for this world."

Billie rolls her eyes. "The thousandth reason why you remain single." She pokes her tongue out at him. "Aunt Rya really likes her too. I didn't think your parents would like any woman you brought around, but I guess anyone is an improvement from Michelle. She was a bitch."

"You need to learn not to speak so loudly at events like this," Dutton chastises, but as he looks at his sister, it's with love. She couldn't do anything wrong in his eyes.

I watch as my mother continues to guide Jewel around and introduce her to everyone. Billie spots Hope again and goes to join her.

"Your mother is going to be pissed when you separate," Dutton says under his breath. I resist the urge to hit him. "And are you entirely certain your dad is a fan of her?"

I glance over at my father, who looks miserable to

be here. Most likely because he's watching after my mother, who isn't currently giving him attention.

"If you still want an invitation to the wedding, you'll keep your mouth shut. I told you I have this under control." Dutton smirks and holds his hands up defensively.

I walk away, the only thing I can do to ensure I don't kick my cousin's ass in front of everyone. I ignore the few who try to congratulate me and shake my hand. This party is a formality only. I don't give a fuck who's here. The only person I want to speak to, the only one who matters in this room, is Jewel.

My mother notices me first and drops her hand from Jewel's back, and I replace it with my own. The moment I touch her, Jewel's body goes rigid, immediately sensing it's me standing behind her.

She's gotten used to my touch now, but her body reacts for an entirely different reason. I notice the pink flush heating up her neck, something that often happens to her when she's thinking of promiscuous things.

I smirk and lean in, whispering so only she can hear, "You have a choice. Temporary truce, or we stay here for another four hours and mingle."

Her jaw tenses, and I try not to chuckle. Because the one thing I know about my little tigress is she doesn't like people, let alone being the center of attention. Which is exactly why I threw her to the wolves for thirty minutes, leaving her with only one option for an early exit: my cock.

Someone else tries to engage us in conversation, and we both politely smile and accept the congratulations. That's when she looks up and is quick to say, "Fine. Temporary truce."

I smirk as I grab her hand and sneak out of our engagement party.

FORTY-TWO
JEWEL

The asshole knows how to play me, but I would take fucking this lethal man over socializing at a party any day. Especially a party that revolves around our fake-ass relationship that, as of late, feels more real than it should. It's confusing. I've had these walls around me for as long as I can remember—most likely ever since my mother first looked at me in disgust and then walked away for good—and now I can't help but wonder what a life not being on my own might look like.

I've now had a taste of what many women want, something I once saw as a sure sign of weakness, and now I'm intrigued by it. Or maybe it's because Eli Monti is so good at pretending like I'm the center of his world. And right now, it's not for show because it's only him and me as his hands skate up my dress and he pushes my back against the wall in the elevator.

There is a big part of me screaming to tell him to stop this. But I also really like the warmth of his hands on my skin and the fire it creates in every one of my atoms. It's been a long time since a man has touched me with such need, and I've felt that desire tenfold in return.

When the elevator stops on the bottom level, he continues his sensual assault on my body. His lips graze along my collarbone, and I'm gripping the front of his shirt, trying to find some kind of hold on reality.

I shouldn't want this man. But the more time we spend together, the more I find I'm falling deeper into an abyss I can't get out of. I need to keep reminding myself that the moment our four months are up, he'll most likely try to kill me. And now, settling on a divorce to end a marriage I don't even want makes me feel equally uncomfortable. Because right now, he makes me feel anything but discardable.

I try to focus solely on the carnal attraction we clearly have for each other because that's all I can allow myself to take from this man until I take his life.

Because my client will eventually order me to do exactly that and is throwing out my career for this man worth it? When he'll leave me high and dry once everything is done?

He leads me out of the elevator and then presses me against the wall just outside the lobby and reception desk.

His tongue licks up my neck, over my chin, then teases my lips. I can't stop him, no matter how hard that part of me is telling me to. He cups my bare ass and squeezes it before he lifts me up, and I wrap my legs around his waist. My arms circle his neck, and I'm basically grinding against him in the hallway of this hotel like an animal in heat. I've never experienced a sexual need like this.

His lips assault mine, and I hate to admit it, but I love how it feels and the way he tastes. My hands slide up from his neck and run through his hair as I kiss him back with as much passion as he gives me.

"This isn't a room," someone interrupts and clears their throat. I pant through broken kisses, trying to draw myself back to reality because if I don't do it myself, I might stay high on this kind of lust.

Eli doesn't automatically pull back, but my mouth pauses on his, and my hips stop grinding against him. I'm slightly embarrassed, but when Eli shoots me a boyish grin, I can't help but respond with a mischievous grin of my own.

"I own this hotel, so I suggest you move on," is all he says as I force him to slowly lower me back to my feet. "And you... Don't even think you can get out of this." He pushes his body back against mine, grabbing my hands and pinning them to the wall beside my body.

"I think it's time you take me home," I tell him with a seductive smile.

"To *our* home," he corrects, and my smile falters. His words sap all the energy out of me, reality crashing back in.

"I don't want to move in with you," I whisper. He brushes his nose against mine as if to gesture for me to hold my head high and looks into my eyes.

"Your things are already being moved into my apartment as we speak. You took advantage of breaking into my home yesterday while I was distracted. So I returned the favor today." My jaw drops. I can feel the heat rising up my neck, which often happens when he pisses me off.

The thought of someone else going through my things right now makes my blood boil. But it's also tit for tat, which is infuriating. Every little thing I do against this man, he either throws it back in my face or one-ups me.

"You might be used to strangers touching your

things, but I'm not, and I don't like it." I wiggle free of his hold and manage to step a few feet away.

He chuckles behind me. "We've had this discussion already; I just moved the process along faster for both of us. Why must you fight against me at every turn?"

I lift my hand to my mouth, the habit happening subconsciously, and he lowers it back down to my side.

"Stop biting your skin. If it makes you feel better, I can tell them not to unpack your stuff so you can do it yourself."

"It would make me feel better if you hadn't packed all my shit up in the first place." I walk ahead of him toward the car.

He steps in front of me. "Why must you fight me on everything even after you agree?" he demands.

"Because you're just doing this all at your own pace. And you're blackmailing me in order to get what you want."

He scoffs and looks down at me condescendingly. "You were hired to kill me. Wouldn't you rather me blackmail you and keep you safe by my side than have had me kill you the moment I found out about you?"

"*Protect me*?" I ask in shock. "Is that what you think you're doing?" I can look after myself. Protect myself. But right now, I'm starting to think this might be the one man I can't run away from so easily. "You're like a fucking barnacle."

"Excuse me?" He frowns.

"Let's not get this twisted, that this is anything more than a fake arrangement," I say for both of our sakes, but mostly mine.

He steps closer to me, motioning me to be quieter as he scans the parking lot. When he looks back at me, I can tell he's furious. But it's not like how he used to be when he'd try to break my spirit or force me into submission.

Instead, he says very quietly, "Is it so bad if I wanted to figure out a way for us both to get what we want out of this in the end?"

"And what do you want?" I ask. As I search his gaze, it lights up with something I'm not entirely able to read. And even he might not be sure what it is. He licks his lips as if he wants to speak but can't. I want to laugh, amused by Eli being speechless for the first time.

"You can't control me, Eli. And you may be used to always being in control, but I'm not the perfect wife for the life you're imagining. This is a business transaction. One that you set. I'll deal with my shit after all of this, even if you come after me. Because I'll sure as hell come for you." I barge past him and go to open the car door, but he scoops me up from behind, his hard cock pressing into my back, and it takes all my inner power not to sink into him.

This guy is fucking crazy being turned on by this.

"Got it. Touch something of yours, and you kill me." I can tell he's smirking as he opens the door for me.

He releases me, and I sink into the car that I've gotten all too used to. I've fallen into a steady rhythm with this man, but the thought of living with him terrifies me. Because I just don't know for how much longer I can bury the glaring reality that's right in front of my face.

I'm falling for Eli Monti; his trap is the last one I should ensnare myself in.

When Eli slides into the car, he makes an obvious adjustment at his crotch as he puts his dark shades on. With an arrogant smile, he looks at me and asks, "Can we still fuck when we get back?"

My lips twitch, and I don't know if I want to strangle him or laugh. I think it's both.

This man is insufferable, and so I make an effort to ignore him.

We most definitely will *not* be fucking.

FORTY-THREE
JEWEL

The moment we step into his apartment, and I see my things, he's smart enough to head straight into the kitchen, pour a glass of champagne, and quickly bring it out to me.

"I told them to let you unpack," he says, offering me the glass.

I take the glass and glare at him as I sip it, careful not to drink it all in one go because somehow I end up in situations that I don't particularly care for when I drink too much.

"I would ask if you already know where my room is, but we both know you do. And since you think the bed is so comfy already, we shouldn't run into any issues. I've cleared out a few drawers, and one side of the closet is yours," he tells me as he heads toward his bedroom. "I'm going for a shower; feel free to join me."

Join him? I snort at the arrogance after we were literally fighting only an hour ago. I sober at the thought. Why am I even bickering with him? I can't even grasp onto what's real anymore. If Eli is into something dangerous, I'm certain it's mental fuckery. And he's good at it.

I stare at the stack of boxes, one of them containing his expensive watches. I smirk at that. But in total, there are only six boxes. It's a depressing thought to know I own so little. I could literally buy a house or maybe even a private island, yet I'm always ready to pack and move at the drop of a hat to the next place. For the next thrill and hit. But for how long?

I take a sip of the champagne, still not enjoying its taste.

Where would I move to after this? After New York?

A very dark notion of loneliness sinks in, and I try to clear my throat as if that's what's lodging the heavy weight in my heart.

Loneliness. What an interesting concept. I've worn it as a badge of honor up until this point. If I make it out alive after this situation with Eli, how will I move on?

I close my eyes, realizing my error. I've already let this asshole get under my skin. But I'm not foolish enough to let myself cling to a notion of hope. Hope for what? A happy family? Of killing joyfully together? Of family dinners with his family and having a place to call home? I'd given up on all of those things the moment my father died, and I took my first shot blowing out someone's brains. I don't deserve any of that. I made sure of it.

But never in my life did I think I'd want those things.

Never have I allowed myself to selfishly live amidst the real world instead of remaining a phantom on a lonely path.

I mean, I thought I'd been living. But I hadn't even been drunk until the other day. I don't have friends with whom to celebrate achievements. Well, maybe Sage, but I still keep her at arm's length, so it's easy for me to get up and leave at any given moment. Is that really living?

I can't remember the last time my brain just shut off, and I enjoyed myself. It was definitely before *him*. I want to argue that I still hate the man, but deep down, I know the truth. The question is whether I'm willing to die for it.

And yet, I finish the glass of champagne and start

to undress, leaving only my heels on as I head toward the shower.

The water is already running, and when I step into the bedroom, I'm not surprised to see the bathroom door open, the invitation obvious.

Presumptuous asshole.

I walk in, slipping out of my heels as he opens the shower door expectantly. He flashes that arrogant smirk that I want to slap off his face as much as I want to kiss it. His cock is hard, and his callused hand wraps around my wrist and pulls me under the water with him.

I'm still on my period, but Eli doesn't care about that. In fact, he fucking loves it.

I slide my fingers over his chest, admiring his muscles. Eli's body is exquisite, like a sculpture made by a master artist. The ridges that run down his stomach are perfectly defined all the way to his very hard cock. I smirk at the scar from the knife wound I gave him when we first met and my initials carved into his leg that are scabbed over.

I don't know why, but it fills me with a small amount of smugness. That no matter how this ends—most certainly up in flames—there will always be a small part of me etched into him.

Shouldn't I be at least satisfied by that?

"Jewel?" he says my name, tilting my chin up to study my face. Those beautiful, ethereal eyes that are so breathtaking look into me like he can see all of me. But there are parts of me he doesn't see at all. Parts I've hidden from even myself up until now. And I'd rather keep it that way.

"This doesn't mean anything. It's just two adults enjoying each other's bodies in a temporary truce," I tell him.

His hands run down my collarbone, breasts, and stomach until they land possessively on my hips.

"If you say so," he replies with a grin before pulling me close. He fists my hair possessively, and before I can say another word, his mouth finds mine. He tastes like a mixture of water and greedy lust.

I hate to admit that I like the way he kisses me—with such ferocity that it's like he can't get enough of me. I kiss him more softly as if I want to worship the moment. Because I do. Having a powerful man want me like he does is intoxicating, to say the least. But I can tell I'm savoring it for other reasons. It isn't my place to be by his side as much as I want it to be.

We break the kiss, and I pull back to look up at him.

"I don't want to share a bed with you," I tell him, purposefully antagonizing him.

"You'll be sharing *our* bed," he states, then proceeds to kiss me again.

I shove him back against the tiles, and he smirks at the move. "You do not have free access to me. I am not yours."

His hand glides over my stomach, then slips lower, sliding along my folds, before he inserts one finger into me and hooks into the sweet spot.

"No access. Got it." His thumb rubs over my clit, and he tries to kiss me again, but I push him back. I'm trying to make this thing between us only physical.

"Stop being so..." I wave a hand at him, and he tries to hide his smile but fails miserably.

"You need to let me release some of this tension," he states, and before I can say another word, he's fisting my hair tighter and turning me so my back is to him, ass brushing against his cock. "Let me assist in your release."

"You sound like a dickhead," I inform him as I spread my legs a little wider, allowing his cock to tease my entrance. He slaps my ass hard before lifting his hand to my breast and twisting my nipple.

"Sorry, I couldn't hear you. Did you say you want

this cock"? He pushes inside me, but just the tip, before he pulls back out and gives my ass another slap.

"Eli," I growl, infuriated at his teasing.

"No, you can call me husband from now on."

This time, when he starts to push inside, I push back, and he makes a weird grunting sound as he enters me. The minute he's inside me, we pause, a sigh of relief escaping us both. It feels so good... so full. His labored breathing matches mine. "You shouldn't have done that," he says in a gravelly voice that's dropped a few octaves. He sounds unhinged, as he always does before he turns into a feral animal. I move my hips forward and then push back again, fucking myself on his cock. He remains still for a moment, appreciating the view as water washes over our sins.

Fuck, he feels good. His hands are still as if he can't function. That is until he pulls out of me completely, lets go of my hair, turns me around to face him, and slams me against the tiled wall, one hand going to my throat. I wrap a leg around his hip, and he snarls at me.

"Stop it," he growls.

"Stop what?" I tease

"Trying to be in control."

"I've seen you fuck, or have you forgotten? Shut up and fuck me." I try to rub against him, but he shakes his head, trying to keep a bit of distance between us, as if he knows if he gets too close, I'll have him.

"You have my ring on your finger; you will call me your husband as we fuck."

"You aren't my husband yet."

He smiles evilly, then lifts my hand to his lips, sucking my ring finger into his mouth while maintaining eye contact with me. Something happens between my legs as his tongue circles around my finger before he pulls it free. And then he drops to his knees.

His fucking knees.

"Eli, I—"

"I'm going to ravish you," he warns, looking up at me through wet lashes.

I swallow hard. A small part of me should be mortified, but I've become so used to his wild demands and tastes that I just nod, letting him have me any way he wants—period or not.

He lifts my leg gently and places it over his shoulder, then he leans forward, his mouth finding my clit. He takes one long lick before he sucks it into his mouth.

Oh my fucking God.

My legs start shaking, and my hands grope along the tiled wall, trying to find something to grip onto, but there's nothing. He continues licking and sucking, the pleasure washing through me.

It's like heaven. I've had a man go down on me before, but never like this. Usually, it's a few licks, and they're done.

But not Eli. He keeps on going, even when my knee starts to buckle, and I know I can't keep it up much longer.

"Eli," I beg.

"No." He pauses his assault on my clit to answer.

I know what he wants to hear, but I'm not willing to give it to him, even if he can make me see stars. I could make him see stars, too... with my guns if I shot him. But that would put a stop to the orgasm that is literally about to take hold of me.

And that would really be unfair.

"Holy shit," I gasp, and I grab my tits and squeeze. He stands then, leaning in and kissing me on my lips.

"Next time you come, you will scream 'husband.'" Then he lifts me up like a rag doll, holds me to him, and lowers me gently until he is fully inside me. And then he starts moving. I wrap my arms around his neck as we continue to kiss, and I can taste myself on his tongue.

Fuck, I'm in over my head with this man.

Eli Monti is gorgeous in the most perfect bad boy way.

I'm letting him fuck me, and he wants me to call him my husband.

A small part of me, no matter how hard I try to deny it, wants there to be truth in this claim.

And it's the most terrifying thing I've experienced.

What have I gotten myself into?

FORTY-FOUR
ELI

When she screams, it's like music to my ears.

I want her to call me husband. Fuck, I never knew I wanted it so badly until I had her. But I do.

I fucking need it.

She goes limp in my arms, still wrapped around me, as my cum leaks out of her, mixed with her blood. I don't know why, but lately, I've become more desperate to keep her by my side, as if she's going to vanish any moment now. And that's unnerving as fuck.

I like fucking her. Correction: I fucking *love* fucking her. I could eat that sweet pussy for days on end.

And I think she'd let me.

"You can put me down now," she says weakly, not making any attempt at moving herself.

"I quite like where you are."

"Oh my God, are you getting hard again?"

"Possibly." I laugh as she pushes back, and I lift her up and place her down on her feet. She leans against the shower wall, looking me in the eyes.

"Our temporary truce is over," she says with a smug expression as she runs her hands over her wet hair.

"Even though my cum is currently dripping out of your pussy? I can clean it up if you like."

"I need to get myself checked now," she says, shaking her head with a laugh. But it's not fluttering like it usually is. I want to tug her back into me. It's the same push and pull but different. She's different right now, and I don't know why.

"Now, if you'll excuse me, I have some expensive watches to unpack and potentially *accidentally* smash." She opens the shower door and steps out.

I smirk. "Do you want help unpacking your things?" I call out over the running water.

"No, fuck you."

"You did that already," I say loudly as I step back under the water. Through the frosted glass of the shower door, I can see her wrap a towel around herself before she exits into the bedroom.

My cock is already semi-hard thinking about her fine-ass fucking body.

"Um, Eli," she calls out.

"I told you to call me husband," I remind her.

"Eli!" she calls again, but this time her voice sounds off.

I shut off the water and step onto the bath mat. Not bothering with a towel, I hurry into the bedroom, dripping water as I go. I find her standing near the walk-in closet... and my father sitting on the bed.

"I heard rumors, son," he says, staring at me unapologetically as he avoids looking at Jewel, who thankfully still has a towel wrapped around her.

"Go into the bathroom," I growl to her, infuriated by my father's intrusion. She nods and shuts the door behind her, but I can sense her standing on the other side of the door, listening in.

"I would never ever look at her," my father says, disgusted by the idea. And I know that, but I also have a feeling I know why he's here. The door opens again, and Jewel offers me a towel. I take it and wrap it around myself.

"Since when do you listen to rumors?" I grit out.

"When they involve my son and the woman he's marrying." He raises a brow at me. "There were some unsavory masked men on our turf lately. I handled matters, but what I wasn't expecting was for the final member of the four to come clean after watching us torture his friends. He said there's a target on your back and that it has something to do with the fiancée you've taken up."

"Why didn't you come to me about people snooping around our territory? I thought you were letting me handle things now," I growl, irritated. Athough my father is slowly loosening his hold on the reins of the family business, he still steps over boundaries that were established for his early retirement. I can't effectively take over and do my job if he's hiding things from me. However, I understand the irony since I do the same thing.

"I'm telling you about it now." He gives me a stern look. "You are my son, but if you lie to me to get this business or are keeping anything from me that jeopardizes this family because of or for your fiancée, I'll kill her myself," he warns as he stands. Then he adds, "I could never hurt you or replace you. But her, I could."

"What the fuck did you just say?" I square up to my father, and although I'm taller than him, he looks down his nose at me in the arrogant, cold way he looks at his subordinates.

"I am not one of your friends or cronies; you will speak to me with respect. I protect this family, and that's your role as well. So it's on good merit that I should think you're handling whatever situation they might be talking about."

"You never thought they were lying to you to disrupt our family affairs?"

He smirks then. "I consider all factors, which is why I've come directly to you." He pushes past me, and it takes all my self-restraint not to pull him back and start beating my own father.

"Eli," Jewel calls my name from the partially open door, and I see her shaking her head no.

My father doesn't look back as he lets himself out, and I have nowhere to release this anger. Hearing *anyone* threaten Jewel is a sure way for them to find their way into a shallow grave.

"Your father wants me dead," she says, stepping out in only the towel. "And if your father wants me dead..."

"It won't happen," I say definitely.

"Why?" she asks worriedly. It's the first time I've seen doubt in her eyes. "Eli, he's not wrong."

I grab the back of her neck, pinning her in place and forcing her to look up at me. "If my father tries, I will stop him, even if I have to remove a few of his appendages in the process."

She gasps. "Eli. We need to stop this before we get

in too deep. You and I both know how this will end. Your family is trying to protect you, and you should be protecting *them* from people like *me*."

"You're not going anywhere. You're going to be by my side."

I love my father. But I can love him just as easily if he's in the ground.

She looks agonized. "Eli, this is *fake*."

My jaw tics. "But does it have to be?"

Her mouth opens and then closes.

I'm still furious, barely keeping it together. But one thing I'm certain of is I want this woman to be mine.

Not figuratively or temporarily.

Literally and permanently.

I want her engraved on my heart as much as she is on my skin.

"We're not having this discussion." She tries to push me away, but I grab her.

"So we figure out who your client is and take them out. It's easy," I say, and she looks at me like I'm a madman. "Tell me I'm not the only one who feels this way," I insist.

She's silent for a moment before she quietly says, "I will not be owned, and this has always been about business. Nothing personal."

Liar.

I release my grip on her. "Sure."

I storm past her, and she calls out, "Eli, where are you going?"

"Out." I grab the first pair of pants and shirt I see. Once I'm dressed, I send out a group text. There are only three people who know about my arrangement with Jewel, and if one of them told my father, they're going to pay in blood.

FORTY-FIVE
ELI

I see Ford and Hawke's car first. Then, Dutton's motorcycle. I'd texted them to meet me at one of our regular docks. Ford is leaning against his car, waiting patiently, and Dutton is on a phone call. Hawke seems to be practicing some boxing swings.

I slam my car door shut, furious that Jewel could so easily shut me down.

I'm not a man to be rejected.

But mostly, I'm not the type to be betrayed.

When I asked her if things could be different for us, the words were out before I could stop them. I didn't even know what I was asking until it was already too late. But if she doesn't agree, I can't protect her unless I lock her up in a room and never let her see the light of day, which is starting to look like a good option.

"Dude, I'm too drunk to be here for work right now. I've been drinking all afternoon at your engagement party. Where did you and Jewel go?" Hawke whistles. It's not until I'm closer that his eyebrows dip.

"Everything all right?" Ford asks, stepping toward me.

"We'll speak soon," Dutton says to the person on the phone, ending his call. He goes to speak, but I power toward him and throw my right fist into his face.

"What the fuck?!" Dutton exclaims. He stumbles back half a step before he's steady again and coming at me.

"Did you fucking tell my father about Jewel?!" I demand, swinging again and again. He sidesteps one and then counters the next. My mouth explodes with blood, and I savor it. All my rage and pent-up energy finally have somewhere to release.

"I didn't say shit!" he yells back, aiming his fist at my face. His square ring cuts my cheekbone, and I grab him by the shirt.

"You fucking liar!" I go to punch him again, but someone catches my arm. "What the fuck?!"

Hawke grabs me from behind and flings me away. I laugh like a madman as Dutton wipes blood from his nose and then readjusts his shirt. Ford stands between us like a referee.

"Are you fucking kidding me? After all I've done for you!" Dutton points his finger at me. "I didn't say shit. You're out of your fucking mind! And for what? A pretty little pussy?"

"Don't you dare speak about her in that way!" I yell, my mouth and cheek throbbing. I struggle against Hawke's hold, trying to get free.

"Have you completely forgotten that she is your *enemy*? I never thought you'd fucking fall for it." Dutton's eyes grow wide. "Oh my God. You've actually fallen for her."

A tic jumps in my jaw. "I just needed a wife," I say out loud, trying to remind myself of that much.

"You could've had anyone," Dutton says and then starts laughing. "I didn't tell your fucking dad, but I sure as shit should have."

I wriggle my arm free and then yank the gun out from under my suit jacket. Dutton looks at me in disbelief.

Ford steps directly in front of the gun, his chest pressed to the end of the barrel. "Boss," he says calmly.

"What the fuck are you doing?" Hawke demands.

"I don't answer to any of you," I remind them. "You work for me."

"We do," Ford agrees evenly. "But this is not the way."

"Step aside," I order.

"No." His almost black eyes are unwavering. I lick my lips. "None of us told him. We are all here. *For you.* You know, the moment you shoot Dutton, Hawke will try to intervene. And I can't let you shoot my brother. And I won't let you shoot your cousin. We're family."

"He's not my fucking family," Dutton shouts from behind him. "If you want to go down this path, then you're on your fucking own."

He puts on his helmet and flings a leg over his bike. "You're out of your fucking mind if you think she loves you and that you can protect her!" He's gone before I can make the decision whether I want to kill my cousin today or not.

My knuckles are turning white as I pocket the gun and turn my back on the twins.

"Boss?" Ford calls after me, but I ignore them. I have one more stop to make.

I don't understand all of the roiling emotions trying to break free. What I do know is that it's my job to protect her. Even if she doesn't want me the way I want her. I won't give her a fucking choice when I'm the last one standing.

FORTY-SIX
JEWEL

I feel the blood drain from my face the moment the text comes through from my employer.

> Anonymous Number: In a week's time, I will send you a location to bring me proof of Eli Monti's death.

No. No. No.

One week. Seven days.

I look around frantically, cursing under my breath. Of all the times for this message to come through, right now is the worst. Eli has been gone for over an hour, and I've only removed two shirts from my box. Am I actually doing this? Moving in? With my target?

Fuck.

I stand up and start pacing. Dread begins to fill my

stomach at the thought of finally pulling the trigger on Eli. It would be easy. I could do it the moment he steps into his apartment, and then I could vanish in the dead of night.

I start biting the skin around my nails, considering the things he said tonight. *"Tell me I'm not the only one who feels this way."* I scoff but want to cry at the same time. I don't deserve some fairytale romance. I don't want it. But neither did I ever think I'd willingly give up on a hit.

Dammit.

I jolt as the front door opens. I rush out of the bedroom to find Eli with a bloody face.

"Why is your lip busted?" I demand, closing the distance between us to assess his injuries. He averts his gaze as I grab his chin. Whoever did this did a good fucking job.

He vanished, and now he's back, obviously having been in a fight, and whatever rampage he was on doesn't seem over yet. He looks wild.

"You're coming with me. I have something to show you." He grabs my hand.

"Eli, you're bleeding. Are you going to explain this to me?" I demand, taking back my hand. My heart is beating rapidly as he stares at me with eyes that are shades darker than usual. He's not himself. Or maybe this is the crazed version of him that those who see it don't often live to regret the experience.

"Trust me, okay?"

If only he knew the irony of the text message I'd received. *"Trust me."* Isn't that a joke now? How can I trust him when he shouldn't trust me?

I sink into myself, perplexed by what to do.

It's just one hit.

One man.

One job.

I look at him again.

No, it's not just any man; it's Eli Monti.

Fuck. Guilt twists in my stomach.

"What's wrong?" I ask, tempted to put my hand on his cheek to pull him back into the bedroom because this unhinged version of him is surely looking for an escape. I can tell by the way his knuckles are white, and he's grinding his jaw. He needs a release, and I'm certain not even the sexual kind will put his beast at ease. He needs blood.

I want to bring him back to the now instead of leaving him to drown in whatever rioting thoughts he's having. I don't have that right, but what's another few hours of playing house? Maybe even a few more days? Can't I give myself that much time to decide?

I want to slap myself. What is there to decide on?

I've never failed on a hit, let alone run away from one.

"We need to talk about your father and what he said," I say, ripping the Band-Aid off. His family is protecting him, and rightly so. But this idiot isn't thinking clearly. Neither am I. I shouldn't be convincing him to turn against me, but I don't want to be the cause of him creating rifts with those who care for him.

Fuck, Jewel, when did you start growing a conscience?

"We'll talk about that later." He doesn't listen to me; just waits at the door. "And bring your gun."

"My gun?" I ask incredulously. But I understand the need for primal release through the barrel of a gun. Or maybe he's finally taking me out to meet my maker. Though in my heart, I very much doubt that's the case.

I throw my hands in the air because arguing with this man when he's determined about something is like hitting my head against a wall. "Fine. But I'm not wearing the leather pants you like so much."

He's smirking as he holds open the door. "Do you really think sweatpants deter me from wanting to devour you, Jewel Diamond?"

"I think my gun might act as a deterrent enough," I snap as I pocket said gun inside my jacket. The buzz begins the moment I feel its weight. It feels right and puts me at ease despite the text message I received. A subtle excitement fills me at the thought of where we might be going because I like adventures where my guns are required. But I don't like this energy around Eli. I don't understand it, and I'm not sure if I can tame it.

I follow him to the car, already feeling exhausted from the day. What a wild weekend. From wedding dress shopping to an engagement party I didn't want, and now to a surprise destination that requires a gun. And knowing Eli Monti, the latter is probably going to be some kind of blood bath.

But the part that torments me the most isn't even all this fake wedding shit. It's the text message that now feels like it's burning a hole in my pocket.

Seven days to kill the man who has made my life hell and made me feel alive in equal measure. Who has held captive the only possessions that have meaning to me. And the only man who has seen me for the carnal, reckless woman I am, and instead of shunning it, he encourages it.

I have a feeling tonight is going to be one of those nights.

FORTY-SEVEN
JEWEL

He's silent on the drive, not providing me with any explanation. I note that it's not just his lip that's been split but his cheek as well. His shirt is torn at the shoulder, and the unapproachable energy that crackles around him is palpable.

I don't want to push any further because part of me wonders if it's because of my rejection of him. Earlier tonight, he asked if this thing between us could be real. But I'm too scared of the prospect of rejection, to be laughed at for falling for his mind games, to genuinely believe it could be. This is probably because Eli feels like his father is too close to discovering the truth. If they know our marriage is a sham, who knows how they'll react. It's best for both of us if I squash the delusional thought of us being together. Eli's simply covering his tracks, and I'm over here fooling myself that this man might actually care for me.

I can't tell Eli about the text message. The moment I do, I make myself vulnerable. He might kill me right on the spot.

I try not to laugh at him, mentioning that he was trying to protect me.

Don't fall for it, Jewel.

The second he realizes I might really kill him, he'll get rid of me.

I either use the element of surprise to my advantage or I... Or I what? Don't make the hit?

My thoughts get away from me as I consider what my future might look like, and I immediately shut it down. I can't fantasize about these types of things. It's too cruel. I'm expected to look through a scope and shoot him in a matter of days. No, I don't even have my favorite sniper rifle. I'll have to do it close-up with my handgun so he'll know exactly who his Grim Reaper is.

An uneasy feeling runs through me, and I try to shove it away.

An hour later, we're on the outskirts of the city in a neighborhood I'm not familiar with. We stand in front of an abandoned club. There are a few people on the streets, and I don't feel all that out of place wearing a simple outfit of tracksuit pants and a baggy sweatshirt.

And my gun.

Gosh, how I have missed my gun.

I still don't say anything as Eli stares at the vacant building. I wait for him to... I'm not entirely sure yet.

"I want this to be the next hot spot," he says with determination.

"What do you mean?" I ask, glancing around. This isn't a popular area; in actuality, it's considered a relatively bad area.

"I bought this building two years ago, and it's just been sitting here. I want to change this neighborhood. I want to make it mine."

"But your father already basically owns half the city," I say. Crue Monti doesn't physically own the businesses or property; he owns those who own the businesses and property, which is a much better position to be in.

"I don't want to be compared to my father. I want to own everything. To prove to everyone that I am more than capable of adding to my family's success."

"That's very ambitious of you," I reply cautiously, still unsure as to why he brought us out here.

"I wanted to show you so you understand how important it is that I have a wife by my side who can handle the position and the risks involved."

I angle my head toward him, trying my hardest not

to roll my eyes. He's laying it on thick tonight. But what he's envisioning isn't something that can happen. I've literally received the go-ahead for the hit, and it's scheduled for two weeks before our wedding day. Which is so absurd.

"Eli, you were the one who made this a temporary agreement. Perhaps you should've chosen a *real* wife."

"And an agreement can always be renegotiated. I won't stand for my father threatening you. You have proved yourself in so many ways that you're the perfect candidate for me."

I scoff. "Why? Because I can fit your cock in my mouth?" I try to derail his intensity because I know there's something off about him tonight, and I'm still not sure why he's brought me here. I want him to come back to me like the Eli I know. He's easier to keep at a distance that way.

But these things he's saying, the way he's talking about us having a *real* future, hurt too much to consider it as a possibility. I've denied myself that fantasy because it's been the one thing that's kept me alive all these years.

I want to believe him, but I can't risk exposing myself and being discarded once again. I can't take the risk of being humiliated by admitting what I'm feeling inside.

Love is not unconditional.

Nor is it nurturing or kind.

Love has only ever hurt me. My parents proved that to me. One left of their own free will, and the other died. It's the only kind of love I know, and I refuse to think that someone like me will receive any other form of it.

Eli smirks expectantly as a car pulls up in front of us. "Took them long enough." It's an older car, and at first, I think nothing of it. That is until four huge men get out and walk directly toward us.

"Jewel?" Eli says charmingly.

"Hmmm?" I reply, not taking my eyes off the men.

"Look at me." I do as he says and find him watching me, not them. "Feel free to kill anyone who touches you."

Motherfucker set me up again for some *Mr. and Mrs. Smith* bullshit.

"Don't you have men for this shit?" I ask with an insincere smile.

"We're not on speaking terms at the moment, and killing with you is the most fun."

I side-eye him, not entirely sure I should be flattered by that, considering how many times he's now endangered my life, but I can't ignore the spark of adrenaline it fills me with. It's like he knows I can't resist my impulsive, curious side that will most likely one day get me killed. In fact, I don't know how it hasn't already.

"Mr. Monti," one says, his hand going to his jeans as he looks my way. "And who is this?" My smile slips as I look in his direction now. His front teeth are chipped and look like they could do with a good brushing, and he's wearing a black shirt that has seen better days. The men who stand behind him are eyeing Eli as if he's their favorite snack.

"Should I know you?" Eli asks, sounding bored.

The man chokes on a laugh. "I'd heard the little Monti had fangs, but you made the mistake of taking our business. And then you left it vacant for two years. Did you really think we'd let you get away with that? We've been waiting for the moment you'd step back in these parts so we could teach you a lesson."

Eli shrugs as if it's not his problem.

"You've been warned several times, Anthony. This is no longer yours," Eli says with a false sense of casualness. And I realize with startling clarity that even in his deranged, ecstatic state, Eli brought me to not only make a point of the empire he envisions to continue to build but to execute this pent-up wild energy that hasn't entirely left him since his father threatened me.

Eli came here to kill, and he simply waited for someone to come for his head.

"This is my fucking area!" Anthony screams, spit flying. His men take a wary step closer. Then, their boss's gaze lands on me again, and a cruel, twisted smile appears on his lips. "Maybe I'll take what's yours once I kill you. It's very rare and very stupid for you to go out at night without backup."

"Who said I don't have backup?" Eli replies.

I slowly and stealthily move my hand to my hip, but I make a point not to show my gun because I always appreciate the element of surprise. I've been using this gun for so long it feels like an extension of myself.

When the men take me in, thinking they've sized me up, they throw back their heads and laugh. That pisses me off. Not because their response is unexpected but because of the opposite. It's always the same. They always underestimate me simply because I'm a woman, which is why they end up dead.

"You made a mistake coming back here without your men, boy. And we'll send you and your little gal pal back to your father chopped up into little pieces to send him a message."

I try not to laugh at the "gal pal" comment, and I can also see the corner of Eli's mouth twitch. It's an unfortunate thing that Eli knows my weaknesses. I'm a moth to a flame when it comes to being reckless, and having an enabler by my side might be the most dangerous thing for me... and him.

I find it hilarious that they think they can hurt me; I could kill at least two of them before they reached me.

Two of the men behind Anthony start toward Eli. He doesn't seem concerned about their approach. If anything, it appears he's willingly letting them get close. Is he testing me or something? He even lets them slowly take hold of his arms, one on each side. What the fuck is he thinking?

"I should make it known I don't like being touched," Eli says but still makes no attempt to get away from them. I don't know how to read this version of Eli. Is he ensnaring them to make the kill more exciting?

"But you seem smart enough to understand your situation," Anthony chirps with pleasure.

"Oh, it's not me you should be worried about," Eli sing-songs as they start to drag him toward the car. I stand there, shocked, wondering why he isn't fighting back when I notice the fourth man heading in my direction. For every step he takes toward me, I take one back.

What the fuck are you doing, Eli?

"It's okay, darling, we won't bite..." The man smiles, and I see he needs a toothbrush as well. "Much." He laughs.

I'm shocked when Eli lets them punch him in the stomach, and then he laughs like a loon. They hit him again, and he laughs harder. Oh my fucking God, he's actually lost it. He's lost his fucking mind. They warily glance at one another, confused. That makes three of us.

"You think this is funny?" Anthony barks, finally walking over himself and kneeing Eli in the stomach, which forces him to double over. Eli goes quiet, most likely because it's knocked the wind out of him.

I still have no idea what's happening. I'm waiting for a sign something from Eli to indicate what I'm supposed to do. I'm not sure what he's wanting out of tonight. I thought it was blood, but is it something else that I'm not clearly understanding?

"It is," Eli says, still amused, as he stands to his full height, towering over all of them. "Because it's not me you have to worry about." He licks his bloody lip, and his lethal gaze finally lands on me. "It's my future wife."

I guess that's my sign. Now's my time.

This fucking psycho.

"Leaving it a bit close, aren't you?" I growl at him.

As the first man turns to face me, my gun is already out. His eyes go wide as he goes to pull out his own weapon, but it's already too late. I shoot him between the eyes, stepping back to avoid the body falling. Then I take aim at the one on Eli's left, shooting him in the chest, and then the one on his right, putting a bullet in his forehead. It all happened so quickly that they didn't have time to grab their own guns. Eli basically baited them into thinking they were in control. He was playing with them the whole time.

Eli shoves them to the side as their bodies fall. Anthony pulls out a gun, but I've already shot it out of his hand before he can raise it. He screams at the sight of his bloodied hand, and I shoot his kneecap just for fun.

Anthony continues screaming as blood begins to pool on the ground. Eli dusts off his shoulders as if disgusted that they placed their hands on him.

"You piece of shit!" Anthony curses.

Eli smirks as he turns to me, and my mouth goes dry as I watch him come toward me like a lethal God. He clears his throat and readjusts his cock. Is this motherfucker hard from watching me kill while he played damsel in distress?

I'm startled when he cups my face and pulls me in

for a passionate kiss. I'm too shocked to do anything but stand there and let it happen. His lips are gone just as quickly as they were pressed to mine.

"Fuck, you turn me on. I would marry you tomorrow for that." He pulls back, and as he does, I realize he's taking my father's gun out of my hands. It slips from my grasp, and I'm conflicted at the loss but still too stunned about Eli's turn-ons. Is this asshole actually a masochist?

Anthony tries to crawl toward the closest gun, but Eli points my gun without even looking in his direction. He pulls the trigger, and the man's body goes limp.

Did he seriously drag me out here to show me the future he wanted to build and, at the same time, purposefully look for a fight to simmer down and get hard in the meantime? That wild energy beneath his skin shifting from one vice to another.

"I like this look on you." He touches my cheek, and I realize he's wiping blood off of it. He slips the gun back into my hand while I stand there, stunned by the gentle touch of the killer in front of me. His eyes have cleared if only slightly, as if murdering a man swept away his agitation and left an easy calmness behind. "Did you think I was taking the gun back?"

I curl my fingers around the weapon, my heart

racing for an entirely different reason now. Much like his own nature, the buzzing adrenaline within me needs to go somewhere, and I'm transfixed by him. I'd never thought of fucking someone after a kill until meeting him, and now I realize it's the most incredible high I've ever had. Or maybe that's only because of this man.

"I had my doubts," I whisper.

"I'm ready for dessert now," he says and cups my pussy. I stifle a laugh as he reaches into his pocket and pulls out his phone.

On the second ring, someone answers, but I don't recognize their voice. "I'll pin you the address for a cleanup." His gaze never leaves mine, and I feel like I'm hanging on his every word and breath.

"Let's go so I can bury myself in that sweet pussy. That should be my reward, shouldn't it?" He removes his hand from between my legs, and I can feel myself gushing.

"For setting me up?" I breathe restlessly as my feet naturally follow behind him.

"For showing you our future," he corrects with a devilish smile as he glances over his shoulder at me.

Am I about to fuck him again?

Surely not.

Right?

FORTY-EIGHT
ELI

I already knew she was a badass, but watching her effortlessly kill on my behalf has my cock twitching to life. I've never seen anything more beautiful. I didn't actually think I would be attracted to someone who could so easily kill me. But it turns out it really does it for me. Who knew? It was all meant to be a business deal. But as the date of our wedding approaches, I feel like it's more likely she's going to run, and I'm more desperate to keep her.

I'm not sure how or when it happened, but it definitely did. I've fallen for my fake fiancée. Maybe it's because of the way she whimpers with need when I'm inside her. Fuck, I'm getting hard just thinking about it.

She yawns in the seat next to me, her baggy clothes now covered in blood. She turns slightly, and I watch as her eyes grow heavy, and she falls asleep. I don't want to wake her, so I just keep driving. I'd gotten my fill the moment we got in the car, and she straddled me, riding the wave of sweet adrenaline and pleasure.

Now she's wiped. There's only one more stop I have to make, and that's to prove my father wrong.

When I arrive at my parents' mansion, she's still passed out. I graze my knuckle along her cheek. I'd lost it tonight. Absolutely fucking lost it. And I know the reason why. It has everything to do with this woman sleeping so peacefully in my passenger seat. This woman who, without realizing it, settles my spiraling beast. When I see red, it's very rare I'll come out of it quickly or easily.

I leave the engine running so Jewel doesn't get cold, and then I exit the car and walk up the stairs to my parent's home. Before I knock, one of the security guards opens the door.

"Mr. Monti," he says respectfully. "What brings you here so late in the evening?"

"Eli, is everything okay?" my mother asks, wrapping her silk robe around herself. It's only midnight, so I know for a fact they're still awake. Even if they weren't, I don't give a shit. "Why are you bleeding?" Her voice is laced with concern. Before she can step forward, my father peeks out from behind her with a gun in his hand.

"Son?" He puts the gun away.

"Where is Jewel?" she questions worriedly, glancing behind me. With the car's tinted windows, she can't see that Jewel is in there sleeping, but she's probably guessed that's where Jewel is because I've left the car running.

I look at my father then, still outraged about how he came into my home and threatened her earlier. "You ever come into my house and threaten me like that again—"

"You what?!" my mother screeches, whipping her head around toward my father. He looks away, cursing under his breath. "You better not have threatened our son," she warns. "So help me God."

"I didn't threaten Eli. I threatened to kill Jewel," he clarifies. My mother smacks his shoulder.

"How dare you?" She turns back to me. "He won't do that again because if he does... I'll leave him."

My father's eyes widen in shock. "You would do no such thing. Don't joke about that."

"Why would you go to their home and threaten her? I like her." Then, to me, she repeats, "I like her." My mother doesn't like many people. She likes to read them and assess them. I guess that's part of being a criminal lawyer.

"I heard there was a hit on our son, and it might involve the woman he's marrying," Father explains.

"There's a hit on you?" she asks worriedly.

"It's been dealt with." I grind my teeth. It's not entirely true, but I have video footage with me right now to at least get my father to think of Jewel as my partner instead of my enemy. If they, for one second, are doubting Jewel's position as my fiancée, I have evidence that should suffice. Not that I have to prove anything to them. But it's a reminder to my dad that the woman I've chosen is equally as lethal as me. And if he targets her, there will be hell to pay.

I've fallen for my own lies and plan. It's all gone to shit as I realize I'll do everything in my power to make my temporary fiancée my permanent wife.

"Are you marrying her simply to take over?" my mother asks suspiciously. She speaks of grand love and unity. Months ago, I thought she was a liar. Now, I'm not so sure she was as delusional as I thought. She wants me to find love, and deep down, I'm certain my father wants the same, but it was the pressure of time being against me to take over and find someone quickly that strangled me. That and my aversion to marriage in its entirety. Until I met *her*.

"Even if I were, it shouldn't matter since my father was trying to set me up in arranged marriages anyway."

"I only suggested that with women I thought you might genuinely build a connection with," my father grits out, and it's strange to hear him say something so... emotionally involved? But I wonder if he's just saying that because he's in major shit with my mother now.

"I have something to show you." I go to push past them, but then I hear the car door open behind me.

Jewel lazily rubs her eyes before realizing we're not at my house.

"Why do you both have blood on you?" My mother asks expectantly. "Both of you come in and clean up. Have the bodies been taken care of?" She's immediately in damage control mode, and I try not to laugh at her, the famed criminal lawyer, who immediately assumes her son has gone on a killing spree. But she's not entirely wrong.

I offer my hand to Jewel, and she looks torn as to whether she should close the door, as if she never woke, or whether to silently obey. She chooses the latter. When she's beside me, I clasp her hand with mine and pull her into the house.

"I have something to show you," I announce, leading everyone into the living room. The fireplace is crackling, and both of their laptops are open on the coffee table. I assume they were both working. Semi-retired my ass. They just can't help themselves.

"Hi, sweetie." My mother pulls Jewel in for an awkwardly received hug. "I apologize for my husband and any unruly situation my son got you into tonight."

"Unruly?" I ask, my eyebrows shooting up.

"Yes. Not everyone is used to this lifestyle," she chastises. If only she knew about my fiancée's line of work. Then again, I'm certain she's about to see how much my wife isn't to be trifled with. "Albert, bring out two sweaters for them, please. Both of you at least remove your shirts so we can burn them."

"We were just about to go to bed," my father grumbles in complaint.

I type a few things into my phone and set up the widescreen TV just as Albert brings in the sweaters. I slip my shirt off, used to this treatment; however, Jewel seems hesitant. And I know she has nothing under the loose sweatshirt. I stand in front of her, backing her into a corner so I can block her enough so she can change. She's quick to do so. I'm positive my mother does this mostly because she doesn't want blood on the furniture.

My father is leaning against the wall with a glass of whiskey. Jewel moves to sit on the sofa beside my mother, but I pull her onto my lap, where I sit in an armchair, and hit play on my phone. The footage was recorded from my car's front camera, giving the perfect angle for the business I dealt with.

"You threatened the legitimacy of my fiancée. I've come to show you that no one else is so perfectly matched for me. That, and she's a good shot, so the next time you feel the need to come over and threaten her, I've given her permission to deal with it accordingly," I say to my father.

Jewel's eyes go wide as the footage begins to play. It starts with the casual chatter, and then all hell breaks loose, me laughing as I'm being dragged off by two men.

My mother is worriedly glancing over at me. Most likely because of the way I like to, as my father says, "play games." He's lectured me about this a time or two. I'd become better at refraining from instigating them, but tonight, I needed to torment my prey a little.

I stroke my thumb over Jewel's leg as she stares at the screen, and she looks a shade paler. I wonder if she's ever seen herself in action. The reality of how gruesome it is to take a life. Or to the lengths she would go to protect me. More importantly, how well we work as a team.

Just as I give her the signal, she smiles and then

pulls out her gun. This is who she is, just as much as I am.

A hunter.

A killer.

Beautiful.

"Oh, you are good with guns," Mother says, mesmerized. That's when Jewel looks at my parents. Where she might've thought there would be judgment, all she sees is approval. Not that anyone could ever tell by my father's expression, but there's definitely a hint of respect there.

"Do you think you should threaten the same woman who chooses to use her gun to save me rather than take an easy shot to take me out? Does that disprove your previous thoughts?" I direct the questions to my father.

Jewel tenses up, and I weave my fingers between hers, knowing why because I'm burying us deeper into our lie.

But a fabricated truth is what will get her down the aisle, and from there, I'll figure out a way to make her stay. The last thing I need is my father looking into my affairs and doubting my abilities right before he hands me the last of the business.

"Apologize right now, Crue," my mother demands.

No one can make my father apologize but my mother. And he usually won't unless it's to her.

The hint of a smirk touches his lips. "She's a very good shot. But you're as reckless as ever. What happened to Hawke and Ford following you everywhere?"

"Crue!" My mother jumps to her feet, furious.

He raises his hand, signaling her to let him continue. "I'll apologize for threatening you, Jewel," he says sincerely. "But you, my son, need to stop being so reckless and going into these situations on your own. It only takes one time to have yourself killed."

"I'm not a child," I snap. "How many times have you 'dealt' with things on your own? How many times did you return bleeding and have Mom worried? I don't need this lecture from you! And besides, I wasn't alone; Jewel was with me."

My father's jaw goes tight. "I will always protect this family and our name, but I won't do anything crazy just to make a point."

That's a fucking lie. I've heard stories of how he used to act in the early days after taking over New York. I'm certain he and I probably aren't so different in our way of thinking. But he's pushing me, and I don't fucking like it.

I stand and bring Jewel with me, our hands joined.

"In less than two weeks, you will be signing everything over to me, as we discussed and agreed upon. I'm sorry if you don't like my methods, but they're turning in plenty of profit. Now, if you'll excuse us, we have a wedding to plan."

"Wait, Eli!" my mother calls out after us. She follows us to the door. "I know your father doesn't always express himself well, but he only wants the best for you. For both of you." I can sense Jewel locking up again. "But I agree with him. Just please be a little more careful. No matter how invincible you think you are, it only takes one bullet to finish it. We love you."

A tiny sliver of guilt pricks me, and I take her hand and squeeze it gently. "I know, Mom."

I shove down the guilt because it has no place here or in my plans for the future. I might be lying to them about Jewel's background, but I'm not lying about how I have every intention of making her my wife and taking over the business entirely. That is the complete truth.

When we return to the car, Jewel is biting the skin around her nails. I don't ask her about it because I know exactly why she's uncomfortable. I'm weaving her tighter into my family affairs. As close as I pull her, I still have the sense that she's going to run. And that fucking terrifies me.

FORTY-NINE
JEWEL

I attempt to glare holes into Hawke and Ford, who are sitting at their usual booth. It's been four days since Eli dragged me into his "Shootout so I can rule the world" date. He's been glued to me during the night and fucking me in every hole available ever since. Every time I think about killing him while we fuck, he seems to dominate me even more, as if instinctually sensing the switch within me.

"Is there a reason why they're coming in every day?" Sage asks as we lean against the counter. After the incident at the Chinese restaurant, I owed her an explanation, not some half-twisted cover-up, because after being in that situation, she deserved to know the truth. That, and I realized during that ordeal how much I valued her as... a friend. I was certainly ready to fight to the death to protect her that night.

And in some ways, I'm grateful for Sage. Coming to this restaurant and talking with her makes things feel normal during the day, as it distracts me from the chaos happening in my life.

I sigh, crossing my ankles. "Because my asshole fiancé told them to watch me every waking hour, I'm not at home."

"Oh wow. That's pretty intense. But I guess you are marrying mafia royalty, so it makes sense."

I give her an unimpressed look. It's not that I'm offended that Tweedledee and Tweedledumb are following me; it's more about the fact that they're *not* following Eli. I'm certain something has happened between them, but no one will tell me what. I don't blame them, but it's irritating. And Eli has been more intense lately. It almost makes me wonder if he knows the final order for the hit has been given. He's acting abnormally attentive, making it harder for me to believe every sleepless night that this is a game.

I can't endure the idea of telling him how I feel because I can't even put it into words. The moment I do, I've lost and will most likely be killed. I've imagined that he's finally got me, and when I admit I got the order for the hit, he'll know his time is up, and he'll kill me. Then he'll most likely find another fiancée to replace me and wear the dress, all so he can claim his empire.

Huffing, I walk over to the twins, my hands on my hips.

With the generous tip, they leave every day; my boss doesn't seem to care much when they sit here all day, leering at anyone who speaks to me. I'm almost certain Eli has bought this run-down restaurant only because I work here.

He tried to persuade me to quit altogether, but I refuse to be owned in any capacity. I don't need this job, and at this point, I don't need a cover anymore, either. But I cling to it like it's my only salvation.

"Do you need a refill?" I ask Hawke, regarding his fourth soda of the day. Ford is taking a sip from his coffee and doesn't bother to look up. I quite like Ford; he keeps to himself, orders our selection of sweets every day, and reads. If anything, it looks like he's quite enjoying this change of pace. Hawke, however, is an attention whore, and I think that's mostly because he's bored.

"Remind me why you guys aren't following your boss again?"

"Because he's not talking to us," Hawke replies sulkily. They still haven't told me what happened, but

I'm confident it has something to do with the night Eli vanished and came back with the busted lip. And I haven't seen Dutton since before then, either.

"There you guys are!" Billie yells from the front door. She ignores Sage, who goes to greet them and walks over to us. Behind her are two other women. One is Hope Ivanov, who I officially met at the engagement party, though I knew who she was before that. The other woman I'm not familiar with. She has short blonde hair, blue eyes, and a curvaceous figure.

Hawke looks away as he asks, "Why are you here?"

"Because we haven't gamed in so long, and you're avoiding me!" she exclaims. "Hey, Jewels!" She beams as she pulls me in for a hug. "Oh, you know Hope." She awkwardly waves at her. "And this is Ivy." She points to the blonde-haired woman who looks to be the same age as the others. "Have you met Will and Alina Walker yet? She's their daughter."

"And a pain in the ass," Hawke says under his breath.

My eyebrows shoot up. Will Walker's daughter? I give her a quick once over. I knew the infamous tracker had a daughter, but I didn't know what she looked like or where to find her. Apparently, Will is not only good at finding people but at hiding them too.

"It's lovely to meet you. I've heard so much about

you. Apologies. I was in Puerto Rico with my family during your engagement party. Congratulations."

"Such formal language doesn't sound right coming from your lips," Ford says as he turns to the next page.

"Ha. Ha," she snarks as they cram themselves into the booth.

"What are you doing? No one invited you," Hawke says as he's squished against his brother. I inwardly roll my eyes. How did I end up with the majority of the group here?

"Why aren't Dutton and Eli speaking? Dutton's been sulking all week," Billie presses, and Hawke sighs.

He goes to speak but is dissuaded by Ford, who glares at him over his book. "I don't know. We're just making sure little miss makes it down the aisle."

Billie laughs. "I almost feel sorry for you, Jewel. I've never seen Eli so possessive."

I offer an awkward smile. Because the casual way they speak to me is starting to feel too friendly. Too fun. Like I'm part of their world. They don't know me, and yet they've already started hanging out at my place of work. It's showing me a world and existence that I've never known was possible for me. And it's not right because I don't belong here. I only have a few more days to deliberate over my decision, but the closer the deadline comes, the more I wonder how I could kill Eli, knowing it would impact all of them.

"Jewels, are you okay?" Ford asks me quietly. The rest stop squabbling between themselves and look at me then. What kind of face was I showing just now?

"Yeah. I'll just go grab some more menus for you," I say with a tight smile before I turn and walk straight to the bathroom as an insufferable amount of emotion crashes over me. I feel like I'm going to have a heart attack.

I close the bathroom stall and sit on the closed toilet lid. I don't get anxiety. Well, I've never had anxiety before, but right now, I have a disastrous number of feelings that I don't want to address. That I can't address because admitting them is going to break me.

One man is breaking me from the inside out, and I don't know what I should do.

Three days, and then I have to offer his head to my client.

And I'm supposed to marry him in ten days.

Tonight, I'll lie in bed with him again.

What the fuck am I doing?

I can't breathe.

I fish out my phone, which is almost dead, and call Craig. He answers on the second ring. "Tell me what to do," I demand, shocked by the desperation in my voice and how quietly I'm whispering into the phone, paranoid that anyone could hear.

"What's happened?" Craig asks, and I can tell he's on his feet already.

My bottom lip wobbles, and suddenly, I'm on the verge of tears.

What?

I try to keep my tone neutral as I consider my next words. "I don't think I can complete the hit."

My voice is shaky, and I hate how it sounds. It's the first time I've said it out loud. I detest the tear that slides down my cheek as I realize with utter clarity the force of what I feel for Eli Monti, which is exactly why I have to leave New York.

"Your client will put a hit on *you* if you don't finish the job. You understand that, right? Is he worth it?" Craig effectively summarizes the situation I'm in without further digging. I'm nodding my head, realizing the gravity of my decision.

I only got one gun back from Eli. I'll be leaving everything else behind. I wanted all of my father's guns, but I only have two choices. Put a bullet in Eli's head or flee with only a fragment of my father and all the new memories of Eli.

I have to leave. I refuse to run the risk of telling Eli

about the hit and have him turn on me. I'd rather leave, wondering if what we have between us was ever real, than having him laugh in my face for falling for this orchestrated hoax.

I'll walk on my own terms instead of giving anyone else that power.

Only I can protect myself, and if I foolishly choose to protect him in the only way I know how, then so be it.

"Yes," I reply. "I understand," I admit defeat. I never thought I'd be so weak for a man. Especially one as unhinged as Eli. But it makes me all the more foolish to realize I've fallen for a man who probably still has every intention of discarding me.

"Okay then. You know the contingency plan. I'll take care of the rest. But Jewel, are you sure about this? It'll ruin everything you've built."

I let out a shaky breath in disbelief that I've been careless enough to let myself get caught up in this. I look at the ring on my finger. I don't have a right to it. As much as I love it and the fact that his mother gave it to me, I have no right to this ring or claim to the man.

I fell for our lie, and I can't leave anything else to chance.

I'll leave alone, slipping into the shadows I was so used to before.

At least there, I was safe from these emotions.

I try not to cry as I think about my mother's disgusted face as she realized I was different and then turned her back on us. She had the same expression of contempt at my father's funeral when she learned it was Craig who took me in.

My father always said it'd just be us. And then he left, too.

A tear slides down my cheek as, one more time, I try to steel myself to say goodbye.

No one can love me, but it's okay if I love them...

Just this once.

Only once more.

But I'm not brave enough to face the reality if Eli decides to walk away from me, too, so I'll walk away from him first, even when it will cost me my reputation, career, and safety.

I agree with all of this, and I pray silently that all of this pain just goes away.

With years of feeling no emotion, I don't know how to handle its might.

I close my eyes and clear my throat, pushing it all back down.

I just have to keep moving forward.

I feel the lid seal back over those emotions.

"I understand. I'll leave tonight," I promise.

FIFTY
JEWEL

Hawke and Ford drop me off, as usual. Today was a blur. I feel numb, but I know without a doubt what I have to do. I make sure I do everything to keep my shit together. I have tonight. I can embrace what might have been for one last time.

When I step into the apartment, Eli is fussing in the kitchen, shirtless. I lean against the doorframe, admiring his muscles flexing beneath his tattoos as he cooks. He's been home early most days since I moved in. I know because I used to track his schedule. But now he makes sure only to conduct work while I'm at work or asleep.

When he notices me, I shut down every emotion and do all I can to keep myself together. Because what's more challenging than killing this man is realizing I love him, only to have to run away from him.

He tilts my head up and leans down to kiss me. I savor it, wanting to break apart at the touch. Will this be the last time he'll look at me like this? Like I'm the only one in his world? I'm deluded if I think that's the truth. But I let myself believe the lie so I can tell myself a prettier story. So I don't feel so stupid for everything I'm about to throw away for this man. But even though I know that I won't change my decision.

"Hungry?" he asks. I nod with a tight smile. He returns my smile and then goes back to what he was doing. I place the handbag he bought me a few days ago on the counter and then go into the bedroom to change into one of his shirts—something he's insisted on since I moved in.

I sigh as I undo the bracelet around my wrist, and consider what's next in my plan. When I return to the kitchen, his back is to me, his pants hanging low on his hips. I take a moment to appreciate his tattoos and the marring of his skin from his particular liking of me inflicting pain while we fuck like savages.

"Is there a reason why you're not speaking with Hawke and Ford? They miss you."

He tenses at my question, then shifts over to fill

two glasses with wine. He hands me one as he says, "No. Your safety is my top priority. Sit."

I do as he says, and he goes back to cooking. Even as he said it, I wanted to believe him. But I know it has nothing to do with my safety and everything to do with ensuring I remain in check and watched over the next couple of weeks to make sure the marriage goes off without a hitch. After that, they only need to keep me around for three months until Eli gets everything he's wanted.

We don't speak again while he finishes cooking. I watch him move effortlessly as he puts a plate in front of me and starts to dish up some food.

My mind tumbles over so many thoughts but latches on to nothing at all. I do everything in my power to memorize every inch of his body. The fluidity of his movements. He seems to enjoy cooking and having me watch him while he does it.

He seems impressed by his handiwork, and I lean over to take a peek. "What is it?" I ask.

"Chicken. Sorry, I couldn't find anything vegan." I fight a smile as he puts some creamy pasta with chicken on my plate.

"I guess it will do." He hands me a fork and then fixes a plate for himself before he comes around to sit next to me. We eat in comfortable silence.

"You're awfully quiet tonight," he eventually says. I turn to face him, and when I do, he lifts his hand and wipes the side of my mouth with his thumb. "Are you getting nervous about the wedding again?"

"Do you think I'm the type of person to get nervous?" I ask sarcastically, pushing down all of the thoughts that so desperately want to surface and break me into pieces. *One foot in front of the other.*

The moment I don't make the hit, I'm a dead woman. It was my own fault for not being able to identify my client. Even with Rory trying their hardest to find out. When I met with my client's henchman last time, I advised I wanted to break the contract, but I never received a response. No response means the contract and expectation are still valid. It's time to release what was never mine in the first place.

"I can make you nervous, Kitten," he croons with a smirk as he drags my stool closer.

"Oh? And how do you plan on doing that?" I ask with a small, bittersweet smile. I'd be lying if I said I didn't want to be with him one more time. To say goodbye to this part of my life that has definitely been the most important.

And I hate and curse him for having such an impact on me, even when I hadn't known it myself.

He chuckles, and it vibrates straight through to my core. "Shall we bring ropes into playtime this evening?"

I smile, wrapping my arms around his neck and letting myself get carried away by his antics. "Don't you mean momentary truce?"

His fingers thread through my hair as he slides his other hand under my ass and lifts me to his hips so I can wrap my legs around his waist. Then he carries me to the bedroom.

"Call it whatever the fuck you want," he says against my lips before he kisses me. And I fall into him once more. The only man I'm certain I will love and the one to whom I'll most painfully say goodbye.

FIFTY-ONE
JEWEL

I shove a few belongings into a bag and throw the strap over my shoulder. When I look back at Eli peacefully sleeping in all his naked glory, I can't help but sneak over to him and bend over to press a kiss to the scar on his eyebrow.

He won't be waking up for a few hours yet, after the potent sleeping powder I put in his drink, I hate myself for doing it, but I had no other choice. The moment I leave the apartment, he'd be alerted, no matter where he was. This was the only way.

Shakily, I remove the engagement ring and put it on his bedside table. I stare at him longingly from the door, not able to leave yet. It's the most peaceful I've seen him sleep, and I fight my impulses to naturally gravitate to him and tuck myself within his hold.

But this was never going to end well.

I was always disposable; I just never thought I'd remove myself from the situation for his sake.

A sad smile curves the corners of my lips. But I'm grateful for how, in his own twisted way, he forced me to open my eyes and heart to the reality of a family I never knew was possible. I thought after Dad's passing and my mother's rejection that staying close to the shadows was best for me. And it still is, especially if it keeps the attention off Eli Monti. I have no doubt someone else will put a hit on this asshole, but at least whoever my anonymous client is will focus on tying up loose ends with me first.

Besides, I can't lie to his family and walk down that aisle. That should be reserved for the woman who should rightly be by his side. I curl my fingers into my palms, noticing the absence of the ring I'd hated but have come to love.

I leave my yellow car behind, not taking anything with me that might be traceable. I take a cab to the train station, and when I'm there, I grab the few belongings I have and change into a different outfit, including a hoodie. I keep my father's gun close to me, scared that any moment Eli might appear. I just need to get out of the city and away from this mess.

I switch my phone off, knowing better than to mess

with Eli and his connections to people like Will Walker, who could easily trace me.

I don't like these feelings that he evokes in me; they're unwanted and unnecessary. And really, it's unfair. We know so much about each other, even though most of what we learned was from stalking and research, not actually talking to one another. I know that that's not healthy, but what in my life has ever been healthy? I'm not about to start walking a straight line all of a sudden when I love to jump over the edge. Maybe that was my problem. I saw the risk in him and wanted to jump.

My mind circles with thoughts of Eli, of everything I'm leaving behind, and I hold my bag close to my chest as I wonder if he'll be furious because his plan didn't work. I lay my face on the backpack, exhausted. This was always going to be a disaster. And I still don't know if I'm doing the right thing.

But I know, without a doubt, I can no longer kill Eli. Perhaps I could've once. At the start. But not now. I sigh, exasperated.

It's the early hours of the morning when the train comes to a stop. I've been sitting here for hours, stuck in my own head and trying to work out the best course of action, and I have come up with no resolution whatsoever. Well, nothing past the contingency plan Craig and I have always had if a hit went to shit like this. I just never thought it'd be for these reasons.

I get in the nearest cab and give the address for my destination. It isn't long before we pull up in front of a familiar house. The front door opens, and I step out of the cab, exhausted. I meet Craig's gaze. He has a cigarette hanging from his lips, a can of Pepsi in one hand, as he waits for me expectantly. It's as good as any welcome I've ever gotten from him.

I offer a sad smile. It's been months since I've seen him, and he's technically the only family I have left.

"Jewel." He shakes his head, and the moment my name leaves his lips, tears spill over my cheeks, and I rush into his embrace. "Oh shit. It's that bad, huh?" he asks, tucking my head below his chin. I hate that I'm crying. I hate that I could only hold in the tears until now. I didn't want Craig to see this side of me. The vulnerability and embarrassment of letting someone get into my head and failing at my job.

Maybe I'm not as tough as I thought. I'm a disappointment. I inhale his scent, trying to refamiliarize myself with my old life. But it does nothing to bring me back to that simpler time. When I pull back, he still has the cigarette dangling from his lips.

"So you ran away. I hope that asshole knows what it's cost you." And I know he's not talking about the money. A hitwoman on the run is the worst position to be in. Others will come for me the moment the client knows I took off without completing the job. I can't return the money, and their fear of being blackmailed is strong, so they'll just wipe out the problem entirely.

"It would appear I like the asshole," I say with a sad sob as he leads me into his home. I bite the skin around my nails as I sit down on his couch. I kick my shoes off and tuck my feet under my ass. I know we'll only have a few hours together at most, and the moment I flee the country, the reality is, we won't be able to talk for some time. I might not even see him again. That thought rattles me. *Am I sure Eli Monti is worth all of this?*

"Well, it was bound to happen," Craig says sympathetically.

"What was?" I ask.

He smiles. "You liking someone," he jokes, and I laugh at the stupidity of it. "You can't be lonely like me and your father for the rest of your life. You're young, meant to fall in love. But, unfortunately, with that, sometimes heartbreak happens, and then you kill some fuckheads to make yourself feel better."

I laugh because I still wish I saw it in black and white. "I shouldn't like someone like him. He's reckless, powerful, egotistical, potentially a psychopath, overbearing and dominating, sadistic, and I think a bit of a masochist, and he sure as shit doesn't take no for an answer."

He sighs as he taps his cigarette into an ashtray. "Kiddo, you're describing yourself in male form."

"I'm not his kind of powerful," I reply.

"Bullshit," he says. "I bet you could take him and all his men out from a mile away. What's not powerful about that?" He raises a brow and lights another cigarette. "It doesn't mean that you're weaker than him for falling for him. I wish I could advise you to kill him instead. But I know your mind is already made up."

I shake my head because he's right. Once I've made up my mind, I won't change it. I am a powerful woman. It's not that I doubted myself in that situation; it's just that I knew my entanglement with him would ruin me. Even if I were to marry him, I'd still be disposable. And the thought of falling for any of this, and loving him too deeply, then being discarded so effortlessly the moment our contract is over, would destroy me. Maybe I'm a coward for not letting that come to fruition. I'd rather leave him before having him reject me.

"He made it sound like he was serious about the marriage," I tell him as I tuck myself tighter into a ball.

"Is there a chance he was?" Craig asks. "I know we do things on our own, kiddo, but he is the mafia heir.

I'm sure if anyone can make your problems go away, it's him."

It goes unsaid that Eli Monti is my biggest problem. And the thought of carrying through with the marriage and then being left behind, after tasting what having a real family is like—no matter how whack they are—is heartbreaking.

"I wouldn't write it off as a possibility. You are, as the youngsters would say, a catch."

I chuckle, then say matter-of-factly, "I'm a liability." He grimaces at that, and I lean over to turn the TV on. I have until the evening before I need to leave.

"Let's just enjoy today like old times before I have to go, okay?"

Because no matter how tired I am, I want to memorize my family. What's left of it. Because I'm willing to let it go for another.

Doesn't that make me a truly stupid girl?

FIFTY-TWO
ELI

I'm groggy as my eyes peel open. I feel around the silk sheets, looking for Jewel, but when I realize she's not there, I sit up in bed with a pounding headache. I groan as I search the room. "Jewels?" I call out, but it's deathly quiet. Why the fuck is my head hurting?

My gaze stops on the shiny ring on my bedside table, and my eyes widen. "Jewels?!" I demand, flinging the sheets off. I'm naked, and I can remember being with her last night, but not much past that. I rub my head and grab my favorite Rolex. Five in the morning? What the fuck? "Jewels?!" I shout again. I search every room, dread sinking in.

I lick my dry lips as I grab my phone and call Ford. He answers on the first ring. "Boss, you're finally calling."

"She's gone." I breathe heavily. And the moment I say it out loud, fury, rage, and sadistic determination kick in.

"Wh—"

"Jewel. She's gone. I need everyone in action to find her. The moment you have her location, send it to me. I'll call Will now."

"Eli, wait. Is it possible she was given the green light for the hit on you? Shouldn't we be coming to you to make sure she doesn't follow through?"

My jaw tics. I understand his concern, but right now, I'm anything but rational. "You have your orders," I bark, then I hang up.

There is every possible chance that Jewel might have gotten the final order, and she might kill me, but I'll be fucked if I'm willing to die at the hands of anyone but my soon-to-be wife. I knew it. I knew she'd run. And I have no doubt that's exactly what she's done. But I'm floundering; a part of me is terrorized by the idea I might not reach her in time.

And even if she does make the hit on me, at least it'll put me out of this fucking intense sense of fear I've never before felt in my life.

I've never met a woman so infuriating that I just want to strangle the life out of her and, at the same time, make sure no one could ever hurt her. And I know full well that she can protect herself; she proved that time and time again. I don't think she's had anyone other than herself to protect her in a very long time.

Yes, she has Craig, and I'm not denying he's a special part of her life. He looked after her when she had no one else, but now she has me to depend on, and I don't know how to prove that to her.

So she fucking drugs me and runs away like a coward. I know she sees this as just a contract. And, yes, that's exactly what it started off as. But I kept pushing myself closer and closer to her until all I could breathe was her.

I dial one more number before calling Will.

Dutton doesn't answer, so I call again. On the third try, he answers. "My nose is fine, in case you're wondering."

"She's gone," I say, defeated, and it's the first time I've let the noticeable change in my voice show. As the fog of whatever she drugged me with clears, I'm facing a startling reality that someone else might get to her first. Or maybe I'm deluded in thinking I could really make her stay. To make her mine.

Dutton's quiet for a moment, and I consider maybe I really fucked up. I know I'd acted on impulse, hitting him, but we'd come to that point multiple times in the past. But was this time different? Was I wrong to call him for help?

"Have you already called Hawke and Ford?" he asks, and I can hear he's moving. I take his cue, dressing myself, the sense of urgency crippling me. But it's his voice that steadies me as we begin to place everything into motion.

"Yes, and I'm about to contact Will." I tighten my belt.

"Let me work on my end and see what I can find. We'll find her." He hangs up, and I let out a shaky breath because I hear what he didn't say. We'll find her... dead or alive. But there's the possibility we won't find her at all. Because my woman, if nothing else, is cunning and used to running through the shadows.

And I refuse to believe that I was the only one in the quicksand of whatever this is we've fallen into.

If I die because of that delusion, then so be it.

I grab the engagement ring before I storm out of the apartment, willing to rain hell on New York if only to smoke her out.

FIFTY-THREE
JEWEL

I'm going through the small collection of photos of my father and me. There are a few of my mother and me when I was younger, too, but I ignore them. I've never entirely had the heart to throw them out, but neither do I care for her in any capacity.

I have the last of my items packed and plenty of cash stuffed in my bag. Craig has organized a private jet for me. He hasn't told me the location of where I'm going, which was always the plan if one of us got in trouble. I sling the backpack onto my shoulder and look at myself one more time in the mirror. I'm more determined than ever to flee the country.

My deadline to offer Eli's body is in twelve hours. By then, I'll be out of the country, and no one will be any the wiser to where I am.

I hear Craig rummaging in his gun closet. I frown, stepping out behind him as he holds a rifle and opens the door. "Wh—?" The question dies on my tongue.

Eli is standing there, looking like a deadly god, as he always does. But, for once, his hair seems a mess, and the shadow of scruff on his chin is heavier than usual.

His gaze finds me where I stand frozen in the hallway, then moves back to Craig. Eli offers him his hand, and Craig looks at it, confused.

"I'm Eli."

"I know who you are," Craig says, then goes to slam the door in Eli's face, but Eli wedged his foot between the door and the jamb despite the crushing force Craig used to close it.

"I'm going to try and do this nicely, but I must confess, I'm not in my right mind at the moment," Eli says with a smile that is anything but sane. "I understand you're important to my fiancée, which is why I haven't blown out your brains for keeping her from me. But I don't know how long I can continue to be so patient."

Craig points the rifle at Eli, and I'm shocked by how quickly everything is happening. "I can make this easy on you, kiddo," Craig says to me. "I can take the shot, and you take the body."

Eli smiles insanely as he steps forward and presses his forehead to the muzzle of the rifle. "Yes, Jewels. What will it be?"

"Stop it," I grit.

"Stop what?" He raises a cynical eyebrow with his hands in the air as if he's doing nothing wrong.

"Playing mind games with me. You need to leave."

He laughs. "Me? Playing mind games with *you*?! Want to explain why I woke up drugged with no trace of my fiancée this morning? You can imagine why I'm at my wits' end."

"Just let me go! Find yourself a perfect little wife, and stop tormenting me!" I shoot, pulling out my father's gun and pointing it at Eli.

He angles his head toward me, then approaches me as if hypnotized by the point of my gun. Craig tracks him the entire way, but Eli treats him as if he's irrelevant.

"I'm not letting you leave," Eli states.

I scoff. This arrogant asshole. "I think it's the other way around. All I need to do is put a bullet between your eyes, and it's done."

"So why don't you?" he asks, coming closer. I take two steps back.

"Stay where you are!" I demand, trying to keep my

emotions in check. I made up my mind. I didn't expect him to find me so soon.

"The way I see it, Kitten, you could've easily killed me in my sleep last night. In fact, you've had a lot of time and opportunity to kill me, haven't you? But you haven't."

"Maybe you're not the only one who enjoys playing with their prey," I say, and I hate how my voice wobbles.

His smile stretches despite his eyes being anything but friendly. "Leave us," Eli commands to Craig.

"I beg your fucking pardon?" Craig steps forward. And that's when I realize Craig is definitely about to kill him.

"Wait!" I shout, and it tears at me to see how the two snarl at one another. "We'll go outside."

"I don't want this asshole being in your head for one more second," Craig angrily says.

"Mmm, yes. I much prefer being between her legs," Eli says with an antagonizing grin.

I shove him toward the door as he laughs sinisterly, purposefully pissing Craig off. I slam the door behind us.

"You *left* me." Eli turns on me, imposing on my space. The barrel of my gun is pointed at his chest as he slams both hands against the door above my head.

I'm pressed back against the wood and I'm not okay with being cornered.

"It was never real!" I scream at him, trying to shove him away, but he doesn't budge. The gun is irrelevant to Eli. "Do you really think so little of me when I have a gun pointed at your chest?"

"You're the only one I'd let do it, sweetheart," he says, and the truth in his words hits me in a tender place.

"Stop lying to me." My voice comes out as a squeak, and I hate how small it makes me sound. I feel like a frightened mouse compared to the prowling tiger I usually am. Something flashes in Eli's gaze, but I don't understand it. I don't understand *him*. Or maybe I do, and that's what scares me so much. I see so much of myself in him, and it terrifies me.

It terrifies me that he has so much power over me and that I willingly gave it to him without even realizing it.

"Tell me what's happening in that beautiful mind of yours," Eli begs, his forehead dropping to mine in defeat. Tears well in my eyes, and I hate that he draws this weakness out of me. I hate this vulnerability. The way he's able to split me in two and bring out these emotions I've buried for years. I hate that he ever gave me a ray of hope. I was fine by myself.

I push him back forcefully enough that he staggers, and I aim the gun at him again.

He cocks an arrogant smile as he puts his hands up as if defenseless. "Oh, I get it. You don't like that you like me."

A lump forms in my throat. It's past "like." I'm certain that I… Nope, not going there right now. I hover my finger over the trigger. "I just have to take your body to my client in twelve hours and be done with this."

"So why don't you do it?" he questions. "Or you can have a little more faith in your fiancé, and we can meet this head-on together."

"You're not *real. This isn't real!*" I scream desperately as the emotions flood over me, and my hand begins to shake. He's playing with me, isn't he? In the same way, he likes to torment his prey. His mind fuckery game is strong.

"If it isn't real, then tell me why I'm here, Jewel, begging like a desperate man for you to come back with me. Do you think I've ever begged anyone for anything in my life?!" he says hysterically.

"You just want to marry me for convenience so you can have your stupid empire!" I scream.

He takes a step back as if something just clicked into place. "You and I both know that what's between us is real. Truce be damned. You are mine, Jewel Diamond, and unless you put that bullet in my brain, I will not stop pursuing you."

My hands are shaking, and I feel like I can't breathe. *What if he leaves me? What if it's a lie? What if I'm just convenient and can be thrown to the wayside?* I've never loved anyone other than my father. Don't know how to. I tighten my grip on the gun, wanting so badly to pull the trigger, knowing it'll take all of this pain away with it. Because if I kill Eli Monti, it'll take all of me with him.

"I want you to say yes to me," I speak truthfully. "But I know your ambition will always put me second."

"What are you talking about? It's always been yes! You have been the only woman I've ever gotten on my knees for. I don't know what else I have to do."

I can barely see through my tears, and it happens so quickly that I'm stunned. He swipes the gun out of my hand, but instead of aiming it at me, he puts it to his own temple.

"What the fuck are you doing?" I step forward, but he takes a step back with determination in his gaze.

"Is this really the only way to prove to you?" he asks earnestly.

"This is stupid and manipulative, and I can't do this!" I yell, closing my eyes. It hurts. It hurts all over.

"Of course it hurts, Jewels! Neither of us has ever fallen in love! We don't know what the fuck we're doing!" he says, and my eyelids burst open. He looks sad as he throws the gun to the side. "That's right, Jewel Diamond! I fucking love you more than I thought I was ever capable of loving someone! I know I have my faults. But if you asked me right now to give it all up for you, I would."

I shake my head because imagining Eli without power has never crossed my mind. It's not even an option. "You wouldn't, Eli. Power, blood, and money are all the things you are. Being at the head of your family is your rightful place."

"As is being by your side." He takes a step forward, and I take another step backward, my back meeting the door.

"You wouldn't," I repeat, my bottom lip trembling and tears streaming down my face. How does this man so easily slip under my skin?

He reaches out to me slowly. "Why wouldn't I give it all up when you've already done the same thing for me?"

It hits me with a force I'm not ready for. I choke on the tears that seem to suffocate me. His callused hand lifts to my cheek. "That's why you ran, isn't it? You got the final order for the hit?"

I fall into a million pieces, barely able to hold myself up as I lean into the man I tried to run away from. He cups the back of my neck and rests his chin on my head as I cry hysterically. "I tried," I sob out. If only he had left me alone. If only he didn't follow me here.

"I know. But don't ever do that again. You are a part of my family, Kitten. From the moment you threw that dagger into my leg, I knew you were mine."

I choke on a laugh because it's so absurd with how hysterically I'm crying. I haven't really cried since my father's funeral. The irony is not lost on me; I'm crying over the man I chose to save by leaving him, but he still won't let me walk this path alone.

"Let's meet your client and finish this. We'll kill them and then get married," he says as if it's the most obvious and easiest answer.

"We don't even know who it is, Eli. What if you get killed in the process?" I ask, looking up at him, and he laughs as he wipes away my tears.

"Wasn't that the goal in the first place? And, unfortunately, I'm hellbent on marrying you."

I choke on another laugh. This asshole is absurd and unhinged. But now I'm certain he's mine—if we make it out of this alive.

I let myself fall into the truth and the lack of guarantee that this love won't break me like all the others.

But I only had the strength to walk away from Eli Monti once.

He presses a kiss on my forehead. "And if we die, then so be it. We were always meant to die together, married or not. But, surely, by now, the one faith you have in your husband is that nothing can kill me. And I sure as hell won't let anyone or anything touch you."

I wipe at my tears, happiness, and fear rolling together inside me. "Those are some vengeful lies, Eli Monti because you're nothing but reckless."

"The world is about to discover how devoted I am to my wife, Jewel Monti," he declares as he leans in and kisses me with the fierceness and depravity of a man who has only one reason to live. His hands cling to mine, and I feel the cool touch of the engagement ring slide onto my ring finger. For the last time. Because I'll take it to the grave with me.

I hold on to him, too scared that he's a mirage. Or even worse, that I'm just a phantom destined for a life without him. Luckily, Eli is a ball and chain I'll happily force onto myself.

FIFTY-FOUR
ELI

I have to assume Anthony's gang is involved. Particularly because after Jewel turns her phone back on, she's been sent an address—the same address of the abandoned nightclub I'd shown her only a week ago. Either that or whoever has the hit on me has been tracking our movements.

"It never made sense to me that your client asked you to toy with me instead of taking me out immediately. I think they've been using you all along as bait to flush me out," I muse. I'd been thinking about this for some time now but wanted to figure out who the culprit was first. But even Will couldn't track the mysterious client, which says a lot about the mastermind behind all of this because Will Walker can find *anyone*.

"But that doesn't make any sense either because there was no value for you to try and risk anything for me," Jewel is quick to reply, pragmatic about the situation. "You could've killed me that first night we met."

"But that wouldn't have impacted the client if they had no attachment to you. So whoever it was must've known I'd be intrigued by you, or at the very least, I'd want to sniff out who your client was by using you."

Jewel is quiet for a moment as we drive throughout the neighborhood, then she blurts, "I don't like that it's only us going in. It's too risky when we don't know what's on the other side."

"I'm mostly certain this person wouldn't have gone to all these lengths to simply kill me. Had they not, I would already be dead." I can't help the smirk as I add, "Well, they'd have *tried* to kill me." I grab her hand and stroke my thumb over hers. I can tell she's uneasy about this situation, but if this is the only way I can free her, then I'm willing to get to the bottom of it. No matter the risk. "I think they want to do business with me."

"It's still too risky." She sighs, watching me carefully.

"That's the line of work we're in, Kitten. Don't go soft on me now just because you're willing to admit you have feelings for me."

"Shut up." She smiles and chuckles. "Had I known

it would go to your head, I wouldn't have confessed to it."

"I don't recall giving you an option," I purr, and she rolls her eyes.

I'd already called Hawke, Ford, and Dutton to organize reinforcements. I don't want to leave anything at risk when it comes to Jewel's safety. The other times I'd taken her into potentially dangerous situations, I was certain she'd be able to hold her ground and handle herself by my side. But I can't gauge the risks involved because I still don't know who the enemy is in this case,.

I hate to admit my father was right, but I've become arrogant about not having my men by my side. I need to have more faith in the men who are willing to lay down their lives for me instead of thinking I'm always able to conquer things on my own.

When we pull up at the abandoned building at midnight, three cars are waiting outside. I purposefully had Hawke and Ford take sniper positions. They're not as good as Jewel is, but they're decent enough shots. It was actually her idea to position them this way.

I notice Dutton parked on a side street on his motorcycle, but I doubt Jewel has seen him. He still has his helmet on and is sitting in the dark. I asked him to remain hidden in case this goes badly. Jewel is to be protected no matter what, and he's her ticket to safety if we need it.

I don't like the fact that only two men standing outside the building; it means the rest are inside, and I don't know how many of them are waiting for us. I wait for Hawke and Ford to report back, but they don't have a clear enough view to give us a headcount.

Fuck.

"Stay in the car," I order Jewel, unbuckling my seat belt.

She doesn't reply as she unbuckles her own seat belt and opens the car door. When I step out on my side, I realize she's standing across from me. "I said stay in the car."

"No. We're in this together," she states. "This is my mess to clean up. I'm not letting you walk in there on your own."

She storms toward the entrance, and the two men guarding it, but I grab her wrist. "Jewel, I'm serious. I'm certain whoever it is only wants a meeting with me, and I'm not willing to risk your involvement."

She smiles up at me. "I was involved the moment your name came across my desk, Eli Monti. We're in this together." I lick my lips, wanting to get through to this stubborn, beautiful creature. "You are my fiancée, not my bodyguard." She places her hand on my heart.

"We are equals in this. We're meant to protect each other. Those are the only vows I'll commit to, so you are going to have to take me as I am."

"Please don't make this hard on me," I ask earnestly. I would do anything for her, but that might also be oppressing her stubborn nature sometimes.

She raises onto her tippy-toes and presses a kiss to my lips. "You were the one who said we stay together and we die together. We're in this together, no matter what. You just better be as good at negotiation as you think you are. You dragged me back here so we could handle this head-on, and that's what we're going to do. Okay?"

I want to strangle her, this beautiful woman who so easily reads me and soothes me in ways she's not even aware of.

Before she tries to take off on me again, I grab her hand and walk by her side. I've basically been flaunting her in an attempt to lure her client out sooner. I just didn't think she'd take matters into her own hands and run. I side-eye her. I'm not surprised that this warrior of a woman would be so self-sacrificing, though. She pretends to be selfish, but she'll die for the people she loves. And I hope she's not about to learn that I'm willing to do the same.

Because I meant what I said, Jewel Diamond is my family now.

The two men waiting at the door are wearing masks. I don't like that none of my men have visuals of what's happening inside, but I trust my instincts greatly.

The men stop us from entering. One of them knocks on the door, and someone from the inside pulls it open, the hinges creak to reveal a dusty, broken-down interior. When I bought the place years ago, the main selling point about it was the amount of space. I'm not so much of a fan of it now as I quickly assess the multiple levels that most likely have men hidden in the shadows.

"I believe I requested Eli Monti dead," a man standing in the center of the room says. His voice is mechanically altered, which doesn't put me at ease. Whoever this fucker is, he's really sensitive about his identity being exposed. He could be a wealthy businessman, but his size is giving off fighter vibes. Men in masks stand around him, all of them holding weapons.

When I glance down at Jewel, her nose is tipped high in the air, and I try not to smirk at my tigress, who, even with the odds against her, refuses to be intimidated. But right now, more than ever, I realize she is my weakness, and I want to pull her away from the entrance as quickly as she's trying to push through it.

"Unfortunately, my fiancée and I came to an agreement over caring for one another's health and well-being," I say with a tight smile. "I'm assuming, however, that you used Jewel to grab my attention rather than kill me. So you want to discuss business?"

I'm almost positive that's what this is about. Whoever ordered the hit on me wants to destroy the Monti family businesses and any alliances we currently have in place. Unfortunately, I've pissed so many people off coming into my reign it's hard to narrow down who might be so personally offended. Had I actually ended up being killed, I'm sure this person would've been happy with either result.

The two guards at the door begin to pat us down. "If you want to discuss business, you will do so unarmed," the boss says. My jaw grinds as they fish out my multiple weapons. And it's not just me but Jewel as well. They're even careful to check her boots. Whoever this is, they seem to know all our hidey holes.

I give Jewel a pointed look. I just want her to turn and walk away, but the silent communication makes her seem more determined.

"Sit," the boss orders once we've been thoroughly patted down.

Two chairs are positioned opposite one another. The boss takes one seat and crosses his legs, expectantly waiting for me to join him.

Not for a moment do I consider letting Jewel sit instead of me. At least this way, I'll be partially blocking her. When I take the seat, she stands behind me, regal in the way she scans the upper levels and masked men who surround us.

Whoever the fuck this is has money—lots of it. And not only that, but power. How had I been so blind that I didn't realize someone with this amount of influence was in our city?

I spread my legs and lean against the chair casually. "You have my attention. What do you want?"

"You young ones seem to have a lot of fire in your belly. But what you lack is respect." The voice-altering device irritates me. I want to know exactly who this motherfucker is.

"Says the man who hides behind a mask and men with guns," I counter. But he has given away that he's older. How old, I'm not sure.

He seems to consider that. "Kneel. And I'll consider a discussion. If not, we'll shoot down everyone here, including your two snipers on the rooftops. In fact, they'll be the first two targets."

I clench my jaw with the realization that whoever

this is, is smart enough to have already noted Ford and Hawke's positions. *Who the fuck is this?*

"Is your pride too much?" the man challenges.

Jewel moves in front of me, and I reach to pull her back. "The Montis do not kneel for anyone," she says proudly. "I'll give you your money back times ten, but don't offend my fiancé and his family."

Dammit. If we didn't have a crowd, I'd bend her over my knee right now because of how fucking hot she looks.

The man seems to ponder this. "Unfortunately, money isn't such a rare asset for me that it actually has value. Removing the Monti heir does. Or at least his pride. What will it be, your men and woman or your pride?"

I'm raging inside, but I smile. I am a proud man, but I am nothing without any of the people behind me. I'll kneel for only one person, and that is my fiancée.

I slide from the chair, and she curses under her breath. "What are you doing?"

"Doing what I'm told for once." I wink at her. I know I'm an idiot. I should've, at the very least, told my father about the situation I'd gotten myself into. Instead, I came barreling over here. But I wouldn't have it any other way.

Jewel stands in front of me as if protecting me from

the man watching me fall to my knees. Had she a gun, I imagine she would've pulled it on him already.

"Jewel, get out of the way," I growl.

"No," she replies fiercely. "I know exactly what you're doing, and you're not sacrificing yourself for me or making yourself seem smaller because of the shit I got us into."

The man stands now, studying her. "Mr. Monti was correct about one thing. I was always using you as bait to bring him to me. Dead or alive, I didn't care. That goes for both of you. Although, my bet was on him."

Her knuckles turn white as she curls her hands into fists.

"What I want from Mr. Monti is not something you can provide, so step aside," he says to her. "I plan on tying him to that chair and using him for ransom. His father and I go way back."

I should've known it would be something like this. The show of making me kneel was a power play more against my father. I easily rise and sit back on the chair.

"Stand behind me, *amore mio*," I say to Jewel. "Please. Trust me."

Torture and ransom, I can survive. But I can't survive her being hurt.

"I'll let you tie me up and use me against my father as you please, as long as you let her go."

"No," she hisses defiantly.

"You trust me, right?" I say to her. So much emotion runs through her features, and she bites her lip as she steps to my side obediently.

I sit still while one of his men ties me up as the boss says, "Well, I never said either of you would make it out alive. Sometimes vengeful lies are the best type of motivation compared to ransom."

My heart falters as the man signals to his men to point their guns. I'm trying to tear loose from the restraints, trying my hardest to shield Jewel, but I can't stand up.

It all happens too quickly. Before I can get to my feet, Jewel throws herself against my chest as if to shield me. "What the fuck are you doing?!" I yell, panicked, as gunshots ring through the empty space. "Get behind me!" I scream wildly and furiously as I fight against my bonds.

"I love you!" she whispers into my ear as she curls herself around me. I buck and pull at the ropes, a storm raging within me. Pure panic and dread grip me with the thought that I'll lose the only person who has become the sanctuary for my inner beast.

My heart is pounding, and it's only when I

realize in the now total silence that any type of reality seeps back in. Tears run down Jewel's face as she slowly pulls away from me. She looks around, confused, and then we both look over her shoulder at the man who has signaled for the men to stop shooting.

I frown, only realizing then that the guns were pointed up at the ceiling instead of at us.

"I'll ask for your apology while you're still tied up," the boss says as he removes his mask.

"What the fuck?!" I demand as my father reveals himself.

"Crue Monti?" Jewel exclaims, shocked.

My father brushes off a piece of non-existent dust as he takes his seat again.

"What the fuck are you doing?" I demand, wanting to break from these restraints and snap my father's neck.

"It was a calculated gamble," my father says calmly. I should've known the old fucker was far from done playing games. "You might consider this as a pairing or matchmaking of sorts." He waves his finger from Jewel to me.

"What?" My heart is racing, and the pump of adrenaline is doing nothing to let through any rational thinking. I thought only a moment ago that I was about to lose Jewel. That I'd made a miscalculation ending with my greatest loss.

"You wouldn't take a wife, so I chose one for you. When I was informed that a hitwoman had arrived in New York, I was curious. I met your father once, Jewel, and I hated everything about him. He was righteous, worked legitimately, and by a code. Opposite to everything I'd built my own business on. But he was a hell of a shot," he says, which is high praise coming from my father.

"When I discovered you'd taken a different path with a nature that much mirrored my son's, I considered it was a likely pairing. So I offered you money to toy with Eli. I gathered you'd either intrigue him or he'd kill you. What I didn't expect was my son to take matters into his own hands and use you as a fake fiancée, which I now know is anything but fake."

My mouth is dry, and my mind is whirling. "You set all of this up?"

"Well, of course. What better way to teach my son a lesson about depending on his men and not being so reckless as to head straight into an unknown situation, as well as test my future daughter-in-law to make sure she would give her life in exchange for my son's?"

The man who tied me up approaches and undoes

the rope, but when I go to stand, Jewel puts her hand on my cheek and shakes her head.

I lick my bottom lip, rage still consuming me.

"Had you looked at the folder where I provided you with suggestions of potential brides, you would've seen she was the only one in the folder. Your mother might be upset about this, but I only ever have your best interests at heart."

He adjusts his suit jacket and stands.

Jewel slides off me as I stand, and I'm doing everything within my power to not lose my shit.

So, Dutton never told my father after all. My father was applying pressure to both of us all along and waiting to see how we'd react. This man and his mind fuckery.

"If I'm being entirely honest, it was fun to play one more game before my retirement," he says, coming to stand by my side. "I might've played you both, but what you created together is genuine." He glances around the abandoned warehouse. "I look forward to seeing what you do with the place."

He walks out, and I see the hint of a smile as he does. His men follow behind him.

Motherfucker.

I let out a shaky breath, closing my eyes as I tried to push away all the fears that just devoured me. My father's lesson has been learned because I never want to suffer through something like that again.

"Eli," Jewel says, drawing me back to the here and now with her.

I grab her by her arm and pull her to me. "I thought I was going to lose you. Don't you ever do anything reckless like that again."

"I'm sorry," is all she says as she hugs me, her arms barely able to wrap around my chest. "But when I thought of you being hurt... I just acted before I knew what I was doing."

We remain there silently for what feels like minutes, and I just hold her.

"Your father is just as ruthless as the rumors suggest," she says, a mixture of awe and fear in her tone.

"Does that make you uncomfortable?" I ask, pulling back to look at her. Does she have regrets now? Does she feel differently about us, knowing we were manipulated to be together?

"No," she says earnestly. "No matter how much he tried to twist us indirectly, we made our own decisions. I don't think even he could've planned this so perfectly. Well, actually, maybe he did." She frowns with an uncertain laugh. "To be honest, it's terrifying."

My father is many things. Terrifying is definitely one of them.

"But I also see who you get it from now." She smiles up at me. "Just don't kill him over this, okay?"

A tic jumps in my jaw. "I won't have to. My mother will the moment she hears about this."

She laughs and hugs me again. "Well, yes, your mother is a force to be reckoned with."

I tuck my finger under her chin. "Not as much as you, though."

She beams at me. "We're in this together now, right? No second thoughts?"

"You were mine from the very start, Kitten. You're the only woman who was made to be my side. Even if you do torment me."

She laughs then. "I think you like it, especially when I torment you." She leans up and kisses me. I scoop her into my arms, stepping toward the closest pillar as desperation takes over, and I feel the carnal urge to reclaim her as mine and to dissipate this restless energy from feeling like I almost lost her twice today.

"Only when you include knives," I purr through our kisses, and she throws her head back and laughs.

Jewel Diamond matches my depravity and fires up my wildest fantasies. But most importantly, she feels like home.

FIFTY-FIVE
JEWEL

I can see Eli's temple pulse as Hawke curses at the game that Billie seems to be destroying him at.

Ford, Hope, and Ivy appear to be playing some kind of card game as I sit on Eli's lap in his mansion. It's only two days until the wedding, and I'm still reeling at the thought that only days ago, I thought I'd never be a part of this again. I don't know them well yet but I already know that this is my family and that I belong here.

Eli's thumb strokes up and down my outer leg. He's irritated that I invited them all here. But I've come to discover that there's very little Eli will deny me. The others have seemed to clue in on that as well.

But I wanted to be here, together, before the chaos of the wedding. The thought of marriage no longer grips me like a vise. I'm actually getting excited about it.

The doorbell rings, and Eli makes a move to get up and answer it.

"I'll get it," I tell him because there's one more person I invited who is as equally important to this family. Besides Eli's parents, who will always have his back no matter what—even against me. *Especially* against me.

Eli looks at me skeptically but releases me.

When I open the door, Dutton looks down at me. I inhale and square up to him.

"You have a lot of nerve inviting me over here as if I'm only a guest in this house," he says.

The truth is, I like Dutton. Despite how terrifying he might be, I know the lengths he would go to protect his family. And I respect that.

"This will always be your home more than it will be mine," I say honestly. "But I'd like us to at least tolerate each other for everyone else's sake."

He raises an eyebrow. "You think I barely tolerate you?"

"Clearly," I sass back.

He kicks up a smile then as he pushes past me. "Would you believe, Jewel, that I actually like you? I just don't like how annoying my cousin has become after falling in love with you. It's unbefitting of him."

I'm shocked, my jaw open as I stare at him. "Wait. You *like* me?"

He frowns. "You're not dead, are you?"

"You'd kill me even if Eli would come after you?"

"Even then. Whether my family hates me for it or not, I'll remove anyone and anything that threatens us."

I realized then that, although I'd gotten used to one monster, I don't think I'll ever get used to the other. So I smile and point in the direction where everyone else is. And it's not my place to figure out his monstrous ways. One day that will be some other poor woman's responsibility.

FIFTY-SIX
JEWEL

The wedding day.

Had someone told me months ago I'd fall for my fake fiancé, I would've openly laughed and then shot them in the head. I never imagined this day for myself. In fact, before now, every time I even thought of it, it felt like a noose around my neck.

Although I don't feel like I'm suffocating now, jittery nerves still take hold. The hair and makeup team arrived half an hour ago, around the same time as Rya. I told them all I needed to have a quick shower, and I haven't moved from the bottom of the tub since.

Thoughts still plague me as to whether marriage is right for me. I know I love Eli and that there will be no other man who can handle me like he can. But marriage still scares me. Because, ultimately, I could be signing myself up for the most painful type of love. But also the most rewarding. It was just deciding to take the risk.

I love Eli, but it's still a wild concept to be marrying a mafia heir.

"Jewel?" Rya's voice comes through the bathroom door.

She apologized profusely when she discovered what her husband had been up to. And despite the strange situation, I can't say I'm entirely surprised by Crue's involvement. He's a terrifying man in the same way Eli is, and I definitely think Eli got his scheming brilliance from both his father and mother. They just execute their goals differently.

"I'll be right out!" I say, realizing I've been in here for too long. Yet again, running away. I turn the shower off and reach for a towel to dry myself. When I step out, Rya is waiting patiently. She's a vision in a light blue dress. The makeup artists are nowhere to be seen, and I sigh in relief that she sent them away to give us some privacy.

"Are you okay?"

"Of course," I reply tightly.

"It's okay if you aren't." She takes a seat at the end of the bed and taps the spot beside her. I inhale and sit down.

I've never really had a woman-to-woman conversation. Or a mother-daughter heart-to-heart. Is that what this is? "I was so scared of marrying Crue, I pushed him so far away, he got engaged to my sister," Rya says calmly.

I try to mask my surprise, and she laughs at my shit way of hiding it. "Don't worry, neither of them liked each other. And it all worked out in the end."

"That sounds a little hectic," I whisper.

"Oh, it was." She chuckles. "All I'm saying is, I know this is scary for you, but I raised a good son, who is now a good man. Well, he's good to the people he cares about at least." At least she's aware that her son isn't the definition of "normal" or "good."

"He can be a little ruthless like his dad, and I actually liked that about Crue a lot," she says with a smile. "I've come to terms with the type of people they both are, and I'm elated that Eli has found someone who accepts him just as he is. It makes me feel a little better to know you can also protect him as much as you can threaten to put him in his place." She laughs, and I can't help but find that amusing as well.

"What I mean to say is, this might be a scary day, but it's also a beautiful day. I've never seen my son come to life the way he does when he's around you. And so I thank you for being that beacon for him and joining our family," she says, hugging me. I feel awkward at first until I lean into it. Much like I have with Eli. Perhaps having a mother isn't so bad after all. Perhaps having a husband won't kill me either. "Now, let's get you ready."

She requests that I keep on the towel and come out to start my hair and makeup. When I'm sitting on the seat, feeling overstimulated, she passes me a glass of champagne but warns me I only get one before walking down the aisle. I blush at that, remembering how drunk I'd gotten when trying on the wedding dresses.

Rya tells me stories about Eli growing up and how his favorite word was "asshole." That makes me giggle because that was one of my first words to him. I tell her that, and she absolutely loses her shit, laughing. I like hearing her laugh. I wonder if my mother ever laughed the same way when someone talked about me.

I doubt it.

But despite feeling a loss at that, I'm filled with acceptance from this woman who owes me nothing but is giving me all of her love anyway.

"Eli said you had no one to walk down the aisle, and I did offer that I would do it for you, but he requested something special for you."

I have absolutely no idea what she's talking about. I know when you get married, someone usually walks you down the aisle, but I never dreamed of being married in the first place, so I never even thought about that part of it. By the time my hair and makeup are done, I'm starting to feel the jittery nerves again.

I look in the mirror as Rya zips my dress up in the back. It's a simple but elegant gown with a slit up the side. A tiny smile pulls at my lips as I consider what happened to the first wedding dress we had to buy because we absolutely destroyed it in the bridal shop.

"He really outdid himself when he picked you," she says as she admires me. I turn to her then and hug her. She seems caught off guard as I embrace her.

"Thank you for accepting me into your family," I say, and I feel the gentle caress of her hand on the back of my head.

"We will always be home for you now," she replies, and I can sense her smile.

I'M STUCK in the car, frozen in place. My breathing comes in shallow pants as I reconsider this wedding. I know I want to be with Eli, but it makes this no less terrifying.

Rya left the car ten minutes ago. I'm certain she

knew I wouldn't be able to get out without some sort of encouragement.

I consider running away, as cowardly as it is.

I'm scared.

I'm scared mostly of the unknown, even though Eli is one of the things I've been surest about.

The car door suddenly opens, and I let out a shaky breath as Eli's beautiful face comes into view. I try to turn away from him as if that will keep the dress hidden. We are far from traditional, but I feel like I've wasted the surprise moment.

He gently pushes me across the seat and sits down beside me, closing the door. He pulls my hand from my mouth as I bite the skin around my nails and brings it to his lips. I watch as he does, those silver eyes staring at me expectantly. "You're beautiful. And late."

"I'm not late. I'm just thinking..."

"About running away?" he says knowingly. Rya most likely went inside to get him. I hate how well he understands me. How did he so quickly learn my ins and outs?

"Aren't you supposed to be inside?" I ask. His gaze greedily takes me in.

"I'm wherever you are. Everyone else can wait." He gets comfy in the seat. I nervously laugh as I rest my head on his shoulder.

"What's bothering you?" he asks as we both look out the front windshield.

"I don't know. I'm just scared."

"I'm not. I know without a doubt that you are meant to be my wife, and we will have a permanent truce," he says, cupping my cheek.

"Well, maybe not *permanent*," I tease. "We want to keep it spicey, don't we?"

He looks at me with a smile. "I have a surprise for you when you're ready."

"I think it's redundant when you say that because I will always be surprised by you, Eli Monti," I tell him, feeling the tension leave my body.

"I take that as a compliment, Jewel Diamond."

I stare at our linked fingers, thinking that, after today, I'll have his has last name. This is real. Me moving forward into a world I thought never existed for me. And maybe that's why it feels so terrifying.

A tap on the window startles me, and Eli opens the door. When he does, Craig peers into the car. He's wearing a suit, which is strange considering his usual casual attire.

"Craig?" I straighten.

"Hey, kiddo. This little shit asked me if I'd do the honors of walking you down the aisle since, apparently, this is legit. You're really marrying him, right?" He hooks an accusing thumb in Eli's direction.

Eli turns to me then. "I'm going to wait for you at the end of the aisle. I came here to make sure you aren't overwhelmed. So let's go get married, get drunk, and fuck all night."

Craig looks away, and I can feel a blush spread across my face in embarrassment. Eli presses a kiss to my cheek with a smirk as he slowly but surely pulls my hand farther out of the car and into Craig's waiting hand.

"Come on, kiddo, you've done worse than this," Craig jokes as he leans in. "Unless, of course, you do want to run, and we can fuck off and stick to the previous plan."

I laugh, my nerves feeling as if they're subsiding. It's like the final missing piece has arrived. I would have never been brave enough to ask Craig. He barely leaves the house, and I didn't want to be disappointed if he said no.

Craig idly speaks about the latest episode of his TV show as he walks me to the chapel. It's massive and, apparently, the same chapel where Eli's parents tried to marry before Rya shot Crue in the leg and ran away.

I smirk at the thought. Rya's such a badass. But

why do I feel like she'd laugh if I did the same to her son?

I focus on my breathing as I wait outside the doors. I can hear the commotion on the other side as Craig clears his throat. "I don't like the little arrogant asshole, but if he really makes you happy, this is where I want to be."

I turn to him, and there are so many things I want to say and thank him for. We've never been the kind to share feelings or gratitude, so instead, I hug him. Craig seems surprised, and he awkwardly hugs me back. I still don't enjoy touching people, but I think a small part of Rya is rubbing off on me.

"Thank you for being here today, Craig, and for everything you've done for me. You're my family and are always welcome here."

Craig clears his throat, and I'm pretty sure he looks away to wipe a tear. "Your father would be proud of you. You've turned out to be such a beautiful woman. Though, I don't know how he'd feel about handing you over to Eli Monti."

I laugh and agree with him. But I also consider how he could fault my soon-to-be husband, who would move heaven and earth to get to me.

The wedding planner grabs our attention and

counts us down. I try to clear my throat and roll back my shoulders.

"Why do the moments before pulling a trigger on someone feel easier than this?" I ask nervously to Craig. The wedding planner looks horrified as Craig laughs and puts his hand over mine.

"Make no mistake; you'll give them hell just as much as you do when you shoot."

The doors open, and I can't smile, my gaze dances along the colossal number of people. Most of whom I don't know.

But at the end of the aisle is a man I do know.

The man I love.

The man I hate.

The man who calls to my dark soul and feeds it instead of shuns it.

I take my first step. And that's when I spot the other familiar faces.

His parents. Hawke and Ford. Dutton and Billie. Hope and Ivy. Sage.

Even the rest of the Ivanov family are here.

My heart is pounding, but I use Eli as the anchor he is, allowing my feet to take me home. To take me to *him*.

Eli's gaze devours me, and heat rises up my neck. Suddenly, it feels like it's only us again. Just him and me in that small room the night of the masquerade. Him looking like a monster coming out from the shadows, and me holding a dagger. He was my target. My enemy. And now he's my everything.

Craig slides my hand into Eli's, and all the tension and fear I felt evaporates because I realize this wedding means nothing. Because it's only Eli and me.

His fingers curl around mine as he leans in. "You're so beautiful. It's a crime, really, and I can't wait to rip this dress off you just like I did the last one."

My core throbs as I think about the last time he ripped apart a wedding dress I wore.

"Are you ready for this, Mrs. Monti?" he asks as he leans back. Dutton, Hawke, and Ford are his groomsmen. Sage, Hope, and Ivy stand as my bridesmaids. I'm not that close with these women yet, but have a feeling that I will be soon.

"I was ready for you the day your name came across my desk, Mr. Monti," I say with a smile. And I once again lean into the man that my world was always going to collide with. And now I'm sure as hell going to make his life go up in flames and enjoy every moment of it.

FIFTY-SEVEN
ELI

I didn't think I would ever wait at the end of the aisle to marry for the right reason. But I know I'll enjoy my life with Jewel. I lean in and breathe her in; she smells of so many possibilities, and I really can't wait to see what the future holds. She doesn't know it yet, but her wedding gift when we return home after our honeymoon is her father's guns. The truth is, I always intended to give them to her; I just needed her to fall in love with me first.

The party has already begun, and everyone congratulates us. She awkwardly thanks people she doesn't know, and I hate myself for somehow falling in love with her even more.

She pulls back when everyone heads for the dance floor, and I can see her searching for the only other person in this room she cares about. A part of me is jealous that I'm not the only one.

"His car is still here," I tell her as she searches for Craig, probably afraid he's already left. She nods and grips her dress before she walks off, and I watch as she goes.

"Beautiful wedding," Dutton says as he comes up next to me. "It seems to have worked out in the end, I suppose."

"I'm not going to apologize if that's what you're looking for."

He smirks. "Knowing I left that scar on your cheek is more than satisfying for me."

I turn to him and pull him in for a hug. My cousin and I might have our differences. We might, at times, be tempted to kill each other because of them. But no matter what, we'll always have one another's back.

"But thanks to you, now my parents are asking me when they're due for a wedding and daughter-in-law." He pins me with a glare.

"That sounds like a you problem," I tell him. "But I'm here to tell you it's not all bad."

"Wow, you really are pussy whipped, aren't you." He grins, bringing his glass to his lips. The mischief leaves his eyes as he notices a man looking in the direction of his sister. The twins are with her, Hawke holding her drink above her head where she can't reach it, even when she jumps. Ford is looking at me, shaking his head.

Without so much as another word, Dutton is stalking in their direction, quickly intercepting the guest who had his eye on Billie. I've never had the heart to tell him that perhaps he should be looking closer at his friends than at other men. If anything has happened between Billie and one of the twins, Dutton will definitely kill them first and ask questions later.

"Your mother is finally speaking to me again," my father says as he comes to stand by my side.

"Well, that makes one of us."

I can see his smirk in my periphery. "Don't be mad that I got one up on you for a final time. I'll miss it, you know. The mind games."

I sigh and look at my father. For all his cold calculation, he is the person who taught me almost everything I know about business. Respectfully, I should've known he was scheming something.

He pulls out a folded letter and hands it to me. "I pressured Jewels into handing me information regarding the Monti family as her client. I wanted to know what she'd give away and if she was, in fact, someone I could trust. You can keep it." I take it, and then he pulls me in for a hug. "I'm proud of you, son.

With or without marriage. I only wanted the best for you."

I pat him on the back because my father might be many things, but he's not a liar. When he spots my mother, he gravitates toward her, and I unfold the letter. I chuckle. It might as well be a personalized love letter to me, even when she tried to make it professional.

Eli Monti is an asshole. Currently, I can't see a crack in their organization. Rya Monti makes it difficult as an adversary because she can easily get them out of whatever misdeeds might come out in the public eye. Crue Monti is as lethal as they say but has seemingly taken a step back to allow his son to take over the majority of the business.

However, I am not surprised Eli Monti has a hit on him. Though he is versatile and capable in most environments, he doesn't avoid confrontation, so I would suggest keeping your whereabouts unknown. I would approach cautiously. He should've been killed immediately instead of toyed with because he seems to enjoy such games.

Due to not having direct contact with you, I would like to forfeit my involvement with this project and will pay four times the amount in return, as well as offer my sworn secrecy. I am a hitwoman. Gathering intel is not my specialty, and as such, you can find someone else better suited. Please text me details so I can end this contract on peaceful terms.

If you choose to continue to pursue the Monti family, I thoroughly advise caution. There's a reason why they run the Italian mafia in New York City.

Best,

Jewel Diamond.

I TUCK the letter into my pocket. She had, even back then, tried to step out of the situation, and I don't even know if she realized at that point she was falling for me. Obviously, my father didn't respond to her and applied pressure by not acknowledging her demand to be released from the contract.

Eli Monti is an asshole. My lips twitch.

I search for Jewel again, and when I find her, I watch as she hugs Craig. They look deep in discussion, and she smiles as he goes to leave. Before he does, he searches the crowd before his gaze lands on me. He gives me one nod before he turns and walks out. I already know the meaning of that nod. He pre-warned me when I sent him the suit that if I did anything to hurt her, he would come out of retirement and hunt me down. I do quite enjoy a challenge. But he should know better than anyone that I'm the one who needs to be protected... from *her*.

She gazes after him as he leaves, her shoulders sagging slightly, and then she spots me. She ignores those who try to approach her and comes to a stop in front of me. The minute she's within reaching distance, I pull her into me and begin swaying to the music like we were before. Neither of us enjoys dancing, nor are we traditional. But I like holding her in my arms. I like the way she stares up at me, and we soak in this day that was only ever meant to be a ploy but turned into something far greater than we could've ever imagined.

"I reckon we can escape soon," I whisper into her ear.

"We haven't even eaten yet," she says. "Your mother was telling me all about the food."

"But I like to have dessert first." I wink, then lean down and kiss her lips, my hands finding her hips and holding on to them so she can't escape.

I don't want her to ever escape me.

"I didn't get my dessert last night. Don't you want my cock buried deep in that sweet pussy of yours?" I croon softly. Red streaks across her cheeks. "What about how my tongue plays circles on your clit? Do you like that?"

She swallows hard and nods.

"I believe you still have to carve your new initials into my other leg." She pulls me by the neck so I'm at eye level with her. Her hot breath brushes against my ear.

"I like it when you choke me."

My cock hardens to its full, thick length.

"We have an issue," I tell her.

"What?"

"My cock is hard, and if I pull away right now, everyone will see."

She laughs, literally doubles over, and laughs. But I quickly pull her back up to block my cock. My grand-parents are here, for fuck's sake. That's the last thing they need to see.

"It's not funny," I growl.

"It is," she insists as someone approaches. "I can make it go away... with my mouth." Whoever it is starts to say something as they reach us, but now all I want is her lips around my cock. I pick her up, throw her over my shoulder, and head straight to the restrooms. Shutting and locking the door behind us, I place her back on her heels. She's giggling, and I can't stop my cock from hardening even more.

"You seem keen on the idea," she purrs, hiking up her dress. I watch in fascination as she drops to her knees. Careful not to kneel on her dress, she reaches for my zipper and rubs me through my pants, looking up at me with those amber eyes.

Someone knocks on the door.

"Fuck off!" I tell them, still staring down at her. Her smile never wavers as she unzips my pants and pulls my cock free. She licks it—just the tip—before she takes me into her mouth. All the way as far as my cock will go before sliding back to the head.

I moan, trying my hardest not to mess up her perfect hair.

Instead, I slide my hand under her chin and hold her jaw as she proceeds to fuck me with her mouth. I think she hates me, but then again, I think she fucking loves it when I fuck her, and that's what I plan to do.

Pulling from her mouth, my cock stands tall, and I bend down to help her to her feet. Then I spin her so her back is to me and hike up the dress. That's when I realize she's not wearing any panties.

"Fuck me," I say on a moan.

"I'm wet for you, Mr. Monti."

"Fuck yes, you are." I slip my finger between her folds, and she moans. "Fuck, you were built so perfectly for me, Mrs. Monti." My finger, now wet with her arousal, I plunge it inside her.

Another knock comes at the door.

"Fuck. Off!" This time, it comes from her, and I can't help but be proud.

Her breath hitches as she watches us in the mirror. I slide a knife out of my suit jacket. It's not just any knife; it's the one she assaulted me with when we first met. I've carried it around ever since that night.

"I want you to carve your initials, Mrs. Monti. The bloodier, the better." My cock twitches at the anticipated pain.

She smiles as she nuzzles her pussy against my cock. "But first, you'll service me, husband, and wait your turn."

My lips stretch in a wild grin as I grab the back of her hair. Fuck being polite; it never suited either of us anyway.

"I'm going to break you," I promise her, and she laughs.

"Such vengeful lies. Give it your best shot."

ALSO BY T.L. SMITH

Black (Black #1)

Red (Black #2)

White (Black #3)

Green (Black #4)

Kandiland

Pure Punishment (Standalone)

Antagonize Me (Standalone)

Degrade (Flawed #1)

Twisted (Flawed #2)

Distrust (Smirnov Bratva #1) FREE

Disbelief (Smirnov Bratva #2)

Defiance (Smirnov Bratva #3)

Dismissed (Smirnov Bratva #4)

Lovesick (Standalone)

Lotus (Standalone)

Savage Collision (A Savage Love Duet book 1)

Savage Reckoning (A Savage Love Duet book 2)

Buried in Lies

Distorted Love (Dark Intentions Duet 1)

Sinister Love (Dark Intentions Duet 2)

Cavalier (Crimson Elite #1)

Anguished (Crimson Elite #2)

Conceited (Crimson Elite #3)

Insolent (Crimson Elite #4)

Playette

Love Drunk

Hate Sober

Heartbreak Me (Duet #1)

Heartbreak You (Duet #2)

My Beautiful Poison

My Wicked Heart

My Cruel Lover

Chained Hands

Locked Hearts

Sinful Hands

Shackled Hearts

Reckless Hands

Arranged Hearts

Unlikely Queen

A Villain's Kiss

A Villain's Lies

Moments of Malevolence

Moments of Madness

Moments of Mayhem

When He Read To Me

Connect with T.L Smith by tlsmithauthor.com

ALSO BY KIA CARRINGTON RUSSELL

Insidious Obsession

Fractured Obsession

Mine for the Night, New York Nights Book 1

Us for the Night, New York Nights Book 2

Stranded for the Night, New York Nights Book 3

Token Huntress, Token Huntress Book 1

Token Vampire, Token Huntress Book 2

Token Wolf, Token Huntress Book 3

Token Phantom, Token Huntress Book 4

Token Darkness, Token Huntress Book 5

Token Kingdom, Token Huntress Book 6

The Shadow Minds Journal

T.L. SMITH

USA Today Best Selling Author T.L. Smith loves to write her characters with flaws so beautiful and dark you can't turn away. Her books have been translated into several languages. If you don't catch up with her in her home state of Queensland, Australia you can usually find her travelling the world, either sitting on a beach in Bali or exploring Alcatraz in San Francisco or walking the streets of New York.

Connect with me tlsmithauthor.com

KIA CARRINGTON-RUSSELL

Australian Author, Kia Carrington-Russell is known for her recognizable style of kick a$$ heroines, fast-paced action, enemies to lovers and romance that dances from light to dark in multiple genres including Fantasy, Dark and Contemporary Romance.

Obsessed with all things coffee, food and travel, Kia is always seeking out her next adventure internationally. Now back in her home country of Australia, she takes her Cavoodle, Sia along morning walks on beautiful coastline beaches, building worlds in the sea breezes and contemplating which deliciously haunting story to write next.